The Slaves of the Horned God

THE AP'LYDIN CHRONICLES

The Heirs of Lydin
The Slaves of the Horned God
The Tears of the Divine (2019)

THE TALES OF AELZANDAR

The Grey Mage
The Errant Princess (2018)

The Slaves of the Horned God

Book 2 of the Ap'Lydin Chronicles

AIDAN HENNESSY

Published by Atallas Publishing 2017

Copyright © 2017 Aidan Hennessy

Cover Design by James, GoOnWrite.com

Cartography by Sebastian Breit

ISBN: 0648186423

ISBN-13: 978-0648186427

For Taran and Salman.
Look after each other.

SKURI

Liderial

Harralin

MOUNTAINS
OF
SORROW

Dilmun

Port
Jemesch

TARKEN

Lerid

Port Nikolaus

Teagleberg

LERIDIAN PLAINS

CARUILLIN

GORIENCHIA

Emperor's Palace

Oldharbour

Georgeton

Qar Arrid

Socorific

Gorin

EMPARIA

QARLD

Gorlion

Selvarial

NECROMANCER'S
PEAKS

VALLISTIAN MARCHES

Ralom

Vallanzik

Dracacoilis

N

Nefencoilis

W   E

S

Jagoncoilis

Anacoilis

CARURLONIA

0   60 120 180
· SCALE IN MILES ·

YEAR 234 OF THE THIRD EPOCH

MACRODONIA

Kieocoilis

SOTAR
MOUNTAINS

Aderial

ADERILUND

THE LANDS OF
EMPARIA AND GORIINCHIA

0 25 50 75   SCALE IN MILES

· YEAR 234 OF THE THIRD EPOCH ·

PROLOGUE

Autumn, Year 133 of the Third Epoch

Acrid smoke hung in the air. The horsemen approached the smouldering ruins. The first of the men was finely attired compared to his companions, and his garb spoke of noble standing. He wore a green tunic, emblazoned with the symbol of a rearing lion. He looked at the scene before him with disbelief.

"By the gods, you were right. There is nothing left."

What once was a thriving village was now little more than ashes and the smell of burned corpses assailed the man's nostrils. The town was dead, the night sky punctuated with nothing but the light of flickering embers and a few small fires.

"Sir Talbot, what happened here?" the nobleman asked one of the other horsemen.

The knight brought his horse closer and spoke with a sombre tone. "Goriinchians, my lord. They streamed across the border at nightfall and took the town unprepared."

"No garrison?" said the lord.

Sir Talbot shook his head. "It's not much more than a village. Goriinchian refugees mostly. Fairly isolated."

The lord shook his head. "They've killed everyone. Bloody savages." There was a note of sadness in his voice. "Why would the Goriinchians attack their own?"

There was a piercing scream. Out of the darkness, a terrified woman came towards them, covered in soot and blood. Her clothes were tattered, scorched rags; desperation was etched on her terrified face.

"Help," she cried. As she stumbled towards them, three men rose from the shadows behind her. The crossbowmen next to Sir Talbot and his lord loosed their bolts and the woman's pursuers fell to the ground.

"Thank you, my lord, thank you," the woman cried in relief. As the lord dismounted his horse the woman suddenly swooned, and the lord caught her just in time.

"I am William, Earl of Genio, of House Genio. What happened here? Who were those men?"

The woman looked about. "I don't know. They killed my husband, pursued me. They destroyed the town. Murdered everyone...everyone's dead."

Sir Talbot and the other knights exchanged worried looks. "Goriinchians in the earldom, my lord. This does not bode well."

The woman grasped at the earl's sleeve. "Not just Goriinchians, followers of the Horned God."

"I don't care what bloody god they follow," said the earl. "No one invades my land and murders anyone under my protection. Sir Talbot, take some men, look for other survivors." Earl William turned to the woman sobbing in his arms. "What is your name, my lady?"

"Adela. Adela Ap'Lydin." Her face was stained with tears.

"Adela Ap'Lydin, you are safe with us."

"Thank you, my lord, but it is not my safety that worries me." Her hand moved towards her swollen belly.

The earl regarded her carefully and nodded. "You are with child."

"My husband is dead. My child will be fatherless."

The earl smiled at her. "All will be done for the child, Adela. Do not worry, there is always sanctuary in Hotar Citadel for the innocent."

Adela sobbed with relief.

They were interrupted by shouts and rearing horses in the distance. The earl peered into the darkness, hoping to glimpse Sir Talbot or the other knights, but he saw nothing in the haze. The earl's heart beat rapidly as he called out. "Sir Talbot?"

"My lord!" The knight emerged from the darkness, the rest of his companions following closely behind. They rode with a sense of urgency and with them was a badly burned figure, so scarred from the fire it seemed scarcely believable that he still lived.

Sir Talbot pulled his horse short. "All dead," he said, panting. "Except one, my lord."

The earl looked at the burned figure. Cold eyes stared out from a red and twisted face. The wretch's eyes blinked as he took in his surroundings. The earl stepped back. He felt the hair on the back of his neck stand up and his mouth go dry. "Can you speak? Who are you, stranger? Are you friend or foe?"

The figure pursed his blackened lips. "Friend...friend."

The earl shouted to the others. "Get him some help. Damn it, where is that healer when you need him?"

As Sir Talbot and the others rode off in search of the healer, the earl stared at the pitiful burned form in front of him. He was scarcely able to believe that the wretch was still capable of speech. "What is your name?"

The burned man groaned, and pursed his lips as if trying to say something. He beckoned to the earl with a blackened hand, motioning for him to come closer. The earl did so, until he could feel the wretch's breath on his cheeks.

"Enlim," came the voice, little more than a tortured whisper. "My name is Simon Enlim."

CHAPTER 1

Spring, Year 235 of the Third Epoch

Bellaydin woke, shivering and covered in a cold sweat. *Another nightmare.* They had plagued him since William's death and Bellaydin woke each morning in fright, with little memory of what had scared him so.

"Young master Ap'Lydin," came a voice. It was Carfel, the Steward of Castle Wishapton. The loyal servant, approaching middle-age, was attired in the livery of House Ap'Lydin – the cross of Kytilas. It had been Earl William Ap'Lydin's symbol, now it belonged to the earl's daughter, Maria Ap'Lydin, the new Countess of Genio.

"You are awake, I see," he said, pulling back the curtains and letting the early morning light flow into the room. "That is good. Their Graces the Dukes of Oldharbour and Alariat await you in the Great Hall. I have told them you will not be long."

Bellaydin groaned. The nightmares had prevented him from getting much sleep, and like most mornings since the battle he found himself tired and irritable.

"Just a moment," he grumbled.

"Very good young master," Carfel said, bowing and leaving the bedchamber.

Bellaydin flung back the covers. Rubbing the sleep from his eyes he staggered over to the washbasin and doused his face with cold water. He left his chambers and headed to the Great Hall of Castle Wishapton.

The large airy chamber was dominated by a large set of windows that took up the entire west wall. A great fireplace was situated in the centre of the room and against the north wall was a raised dais, where the lord of the castle would sit and hold court over important events. It was on that dais that Bellaydin had sat with his cousin, William, the two dukes and Sir Geoffrey Keslin as they planned the defence of Wishapton. Walking in here now he sorely felt his cousin's absence, especially with the large Ap'Lydin sigil emblazoned pennant hanging from the rafters.

"Excellent Bellaydin, you have arrived," Haakon de Morcor, Duke of Alariat said as Bellaydin entered. The duke, as always, looked like the kindly old grandfather Bellaydin had never had.

"You are late, Ap'Lydin." The Duke of Oldharbour, Wulfric Highcrown, had the same sneer on his face that Bellaydin had seen countless times. Next to him stood a hulking, green-skinned Ahktarran lizardman – the duke's manservant, Kahlaf el'Lahn, silent and loyal.

In the centre of the dais was an ornate chair, padded with extra cushions to give height to its occupant. Maria Ap'Lydin, the new Countess of Genio and little more than an adolescent, sat there, a tiny figure dwarfed by her surroundings, her face taut with anxiety. Sir Geoffrey Keslin, foremost of the Earl of Genio's sworn swords, stood near her for emotional support.

"The time for mourning is nearing an end, Bellaydin," Wulfric said, his face cold and impassive, "and our attention must now turn to the future of House Ap'Lydin."

"Your cousin, William, was the head of your House, Bellaydin, and everyone would have expected him to be so for many years to come,"

Haakon said. "But with his death, we must throw out all these presumptions and start anew."

"It was William's wish that his daughter succeeds him," Bellaydin said.

"Of course," Haakon said, "and the Duke of Oldharbour and I will use our influence at court to ensure that she is allowed to succeed to the earldom without challenge."

"But the court will never allow Maria to become head of your House," Wulfric said. "Regardless of what title they allow her to bear. That is your duty, as last male of the House Ap'Lydin. But for that to happen you will need to be properly educated for your role."

"Educated? On what? What exactly is it that I need to know?"

"I understand you were taught much during your upbringing in Aderilund," Haakon said. "But there are things an Emparian nobleman must know that elves cannot teach. It is our responsibility to teach you those things."

Wulfric pressed his fingers together. "As William made you a squire, so shall you remain."

"First, you will be accompanying me," Haakon said. "I am returning to the capital, and I believe it is time you were presented at court and properly socialised with the other young noble squires. You will spend the next six months learning etiquette and social protocol."

"Then when you are done, you will join the army of Oldharbour for six months, where you will be taught the arts of war at my side," Wulfric added.

Haakon looked at him with gentle eyes. "I know this is a lot to take in, Bellaydin. Particularly after what you've been through, but it is vital that we move quickly with this. You are already quite old for a squire, especially for one who has not yet been presented to the royal court."

"When is all this happening?" Bellaydin asked.

"We leave Wishapton tomorrow," Wulfric said. "We must present the countess to the queen to have her title confirmed, and you shall travel with her to the capital. The Duke of Alariat and Sir Geoffrey will accompany the countess' entourage. Kahlaf and I will be with you for a portion of the journey, but after that we are headed to Oldharbour, where I have matters of my own to attend to."

"And what happens to Maria and myself after the capital? Are we to return here?" Bellaydin asked. Maria was the only family he had here, and it didn't feel right for them to be separated. In addition, he had grown quite found of Wishapton since he arrived. It now seemed more like home than Aderial ever had.

Haakon folded his hands. "The countess has more important responsibilities to attend to, duties that cannot be carried out here. Carfel will tend to things here while the countess is in the capital. Once she is confirmed in her title, however, it is expected she will spend most of her time in Hotar Citadel, so no doubt the queen will appoint some other noble as castellan of Wishapton."

"And what is to be my future?" Bellaydin asked.

Haakon's eyes fixed on him. "You are now heir to the earldom, Bellaydin, and will remain so until Maria bears a child. Though she is barely in her thirteenth year we cannot tarry too much longer. Have no doubt that ensuring she is well-married will be a priority."

Bellaydin frowned. They were speaking of Maria as if she wasn't present. His eyes moved to the girl. Maria obviously knew better than to say anything out loud, but she couldn't completely hide the expression of disdain on her face. She was William's daughter, after all – it would be difficult to believe that she would not object to having her life decided for her.

"We must also make similar considerations for you, Bellaydin," Haakon continued. "You have reached your eighteenth year. A suitable marriage for yourself is necessary if House Ap'Lydin is to live on."

As Haakon spoke, Geoffrey Keslin frowned. The knight clearly took issue with the duke's words but said nothing out loud. For his part, Bellaydin felt like he was rapidly becoming a spectator in his own life, just as much as Maria. Before he knew it he was voicing his objections openly. "Don't I get a say in any of this?"

Wulfric looked annoyed at the question. "Sometimes pride must be abandoned, and we must do as we are expected."

Maria's lip curled in response, but Bellaydin was the only one to notice.

"Don't worry, my boy," Haakon said. "We will look after you."

Bellaydin smiled, but the expression was not genuine. "Is that all?"

Wulfric nodded. "We will leave at first light tomorrow. I would spend today gathering your possessions and saying your farewells to this place."

Bellaydin nodded, and returned to his room. These simple chambers had been his home since he arrived in Wishapton. Against one wall was the small bed he slept in, next to it a small washbasin. The only other piece of furniture was the simple wooden cabinet that contained everything that Bellaydin possessed in the world. He opened it and took stock of his meagre belongings. The first was the sword he had used in the Battle of Wishapton. In most respects it was unremarkable, and indeed it would hold no significance for Bellaydin had it not been William who had given the sword to him. Since William's death the sword had become part of his memory. The suit of elven mail Bellaydin laid next to the sword, as he had received it from William at the same time. The mail was even more special to Bellaydin, as Alusine Ap'Lydin had owned it – the father Bellaydin had never known.

A few bundles of clothes were next, all of which William had given to him when Bellaydin arrived in Wishapton. When he, Geoffrey and Kahlaf were attempting to escape Goriinchia they had burned the elven fabric Bellaydin wore from Aderilund in an attempt to go undetected. He had long since discarded the rags he had disguised himself in after that. Some of the new clothes were quite fine and emblazoned with the sigil of the House Ap'Lydin. He set those aside, intending to wear them for tomorrow when they left Wishapton. Bellaydin thought he probably should look his best.

Wrapped up in his clothes was a final possession, a book he received from the Goriinchian girl Morgan Culainn. In an attempt to enlighten Bellaydin, Morgan had given him her copy of the holy book of the Horned God. Bellaydin had taken one look at the book, with its scrawled writing and strange unsettling imagery, and resolved not to read it. It had not helped that the book was in Goriinchian, of which Bellaydin could not understand a single word. Still, he looked back on Morgan fondly. She had been kind to him, and saved his life on multiple occasions at her own great risk. He also had to admit to himself that he had found the girl quite striking, particularly when she had stared at him intently with those bright blue eyes. She would be back in Goriinchia now, and Bellaydin wondered if he was in her thoughts as she was in his.

With a smile, he placed the book with the rest of his things. He looked down at the small pile of items in front of him. *Is this it?* He wondered. *Is this all I have to show for the past year? I left so much behind in Aderilund.* The room seemed tiny, claustrophobic. He needed to get some fresh air. Carefully tying his things together in a blanket, he placed them to one side and went for a walk.

Outside the castle, the signs of battle were still evident. There was substantial damage to a lot of the exterior, scorch marks still covered the walls of the castle, and there were piles of rubble everywhere. Workers had disposed of the dead, for which Bellaydin was grateful. It was one thing to see a man freshly dead, and another to see his corpse a week later.

Nearby, a group of Eldara was loading a wagon with the corpses of their fallen comrades. One of them struggled with a body, almost dropping it to the ground. Bellaydin went to the Eldara mercenary's aid, and the pair of them lifted the corpse on to the wagon. As Bellaydin did so he recognised the body. It was Neriaos, leader of the mercenaries who had fought to protect Wishapton.

"Thank you, my friend," said the Eldara, leaning against the wagon to catch his breath. Bellaydin noticed that the Eldara was quite young by his people's standards, most likely less than a century of age, with light brown hair and green eyes. "Our fallen brothers have a long journey ahead of them if we are to return them home. They must be entombed in the land of their birth. It is our way."

Bellaydin nodded. "I remember."

The Eldara looked at him. "Of course, how foolish of me. You are the younger Ap'Lydin. You were raised among us in Aderilund." He extended a hand in greeting. "Talthas li'Lyros."

"Pleased to meet you, Talthas," Bellaydin said, shaking his hand. "Are you a ranger?"

"Hardly," the Eldara smiled. "I'm still training. Neriaos, our leader, he is – sorry he *was* – my uncle."

"Oh," Bellaydin frowned. "I'm sorry for your loss."

Talthas smiled. "He died as he wished, in battle, fighting for a just cause. The bravery of the people here inspired him. Neriaos told me had never seen the like before."

Bellaydin shook his head. "I don't believe that. The comparison flatters us. I've seen Eldara; they are fearless in battle."

"It takes no courage to be fearless when death is never a possibility." Talthas inclined his head. "This is something different. There is something romantic about hopeless causes."

Hopeless, Bellaydin thought. *Was that how Neriaos had seen the defence of Wishapton? Yet he stayed and fought...*

"Are you leaving Emparia?" Bellaydin asked.

11

"Most of the rangers consider their contract fulfilled, and that Neriaos' death frees them of the need to stay here any longer. To be honest, I think most of them feel uncomfortable in this strange land, so far from home."

"Do you feel the same?"

Talthas looked thoughtful. "I must admit this land intrigues me. There is a frisson of excitement in the air that makes Aderilund look staid. Tell me, who commands the forces of Genio now that the earl has passed?"

"His daughter, I suppose. But until she comes of age, it would be Sir Geoffrey."

"Perhaps I should speak to this Sir Geoffrey," Talthas mused. "Thank you for your help, Ap'Lydin. I hope we speak again soon."

As Talthas and the other Eldara continued with their task, Bellaydin moved through the courtyard. All about him peasants went about their tasks. Many were removing rubble, rebuilding broken wooden structures or otherwise cleaning the area. As he went past, some looked his way, sullen and resentful, but most paid him little attention, absorbed in their duties. He strolled out of the keep proper, and towards a hill some distance away.

The remains of a funeral pyre still smouldered atop the hill. As Bellaydin approached, he thought it strange how ordinary it looked, how unremarkable. During William's cremation, the flames had burned high and bright, and the embers had danced in the night air, and just for a moment, Bellaydin had imagined seeing William's spirit depart his mortal frame.

Now there was nothing left but ash and half-burned timber. A glint in the grass caught his eye, so he bent down to pick it up. It was a small silver ring, with the symbol of the House of Ap'Lydin engraved on it. It was quite obviously William's signet ring and had probably fallen off while they had carried him to the pyre. Bellaydin held it to his chest for a moment, and then slipped it inside his clothes. For a while he contemplated leaving it on the pyre, but then reasoned that it ought to remain within the family – with him or the countess. It did not seem right to leave it out here in a field to disappear.

Atop the hill he could see across to the horizon. The sky was clear, with only a few clouds moving lazily overhead. To the south, in the distance, he could see tall, snow-covered mountains reaching into the sky – Goriinchia. Somewhere beyond those peaks were those responsible for William's death, the worshippers of the Horned God, and their despotic Prophet-King Ygarak. Morgan's uncle, the deranged high priest Cathan had tortured William to death, but it was Morgan and her father Aonghus who had shown mercy. Not all of the Horned God's followers were incapable of empathy.

Bellaydin longed for a chance to avenge his cousin, but his life was now seemingly decided for him, and for the next six months he would be learning etiquette and court intrigue in the capital. He had had enough of both of those things when he lived amongst the elves in Aderial.

"Ah, I thought I might find you here."

Geoffrey Keslin strode to the top of the hill, a smile on his face. Though he had mostly recovered from his injuries acquired during the defence of Wishapton, Bellaydin noticed that the knight still walked with a noticeable limp.

"The leg's feeling better," Geoffrey said, noting where Bellaydin's eyes had moved. "But it still hurts every now and again." He looked concerned. "How are you then, Bela?"

Bellaydin was non-committal. "Fine, I guess."

Geoffrey looked over at the pyre. "If it's any consolation, it's hard for me to handle too."

Bellaydin smiled weakly, and nodded.

Geoffrey stared into the distance. "William was not just my liege lord, he was my oldest and closest of friends. When I was a squire, still finding my way in the world, he befriended me, and went out of his way to make me feel I belonged, even though he was already an earl and I was just the unfavoured son of an unknown knight. He was my greatest champion, so I did my best to become the same to him." His eyes shone with tears. "I will miss him."

"He was the last link to my parents, and now he's dead," Bellaydin said.

Geoffrey placed a hand on Bellaydin's shoulder and looked at the younger man with sympathy. "He will never be forgotten, not while either of us draws breath. He was a great man, a skilled warrior, and a good friend. The gods favoured him."

Bellaydin stared ahead. "And yet he suffered a horrible death."

"Focus your rage, Bela," said Geoffrey. "We will hunt down and kill those who did this, I swear to you. The war's not over yet. The Goriinchians have lost one battle, but that's not enough to dissuade them. They're just biding their time, mark my words. Soon enough they'll attack again – but this time we'll be ready for them."

"Are you coming to the capital with me?"

"Of course," Geoffrey said. "But I can't say how long I'll be staying. I'm supposed to attend to the countess once she's had her title confirmed by the queen and the Privy Council. But don't worry, I'll drop back in from time to time to visit."

"I'd appreciate that," said Bellaydin.

Geoffrey put an arm on his shoulder supportively. "You need a drink, my friend. Come with me, and let me see what I can do."

Geoffrey led Bellaydin back down the hill towards the keep, and, taking him inside, led him to the dining hall. "Take a seat," Geoffrey said, motioning towards the long wooden stools. Bellaydin did as asked and Geoffrey placed two goblets on the table. He poured a dark cloudy liquid from a cask into both goblets.

"Don't worry. It's cider. You'll enjoy it," Geoffrey assured Bellaydin. He picked up the goblet. "To William Ap'Lydin, Earl of Genio, and the finest man I've ever met," Geoffrey said.

Bellaydin picked up his goblet. "To William."

They both drank. The liquid was sweet, but also tart, and warmed Bellaydin's throat as it went down. He drank some more, and then drained his goblet. Within minutes he was beginning to feel more relaxed.

"Looks like you want some more, I'd wager," Geoffrey said and filled Bellaydin's goblet again.

"Not too much," Bellaydin said. His head already felt a bit foggy.

"No such thing as too much," Geoffrey murmured as he refilled his own goblet.

Bellaydin became aware of someone else nearby. "I hope I'm not interrupting anything." Maria stood in the doorway, a sad smile on her young face.

Both Bellaydin and Geoffrey rose from their seats. "No, my lady," said Geoffrey said. "Of course not."

"I would like to talk to Bela, if you don't mind," Maria said.

"Of course, my lady," said Geoffrey. "I'll wait outside." He bowed to Maria as he walked past her out of the room.

Once Geoffrey was gone, Maria took a seat. Bellaydin continued to stand. He wasn't sure what the protocol was. He might be the Head of House Ap'Lydin, but Maria was countess.

"Can we talk for a moment?" Maria asked. "About my father?"

"Of course," Bellaydin said. "I hope I can be of some help."

"I saw you up on the hill, Uncle Bela," Maria said quietly. "I think you might be the only other person who can understand how I'm feeling right now."

Bellaydin nodded slowly. He saw tears on Maria's cheeks and, by her red-rimmed eyes, she had been crying for some time. "They tell me that I won't always feel like this," she said, sniffing. "I don't know what's wrong with me. It just keeps hurting. I feel like I've lost everything."

Maria wept. Bellaydin had no words to comfort her with. Instead, he came to her, and wrapped his arms around the girl, holding her tight. "You haven't lost me. And you won't. We'll look out for each other."

She looked at him, blue eyes shining, and wiped her eyes. "Promise?"

"Promise."

"They're going to split us up," Maria said. "You're going to the capital, and I'll be going to Genio."

"I know," Bellaydin said. "But we'll be at the capital together until the queen confirms your title."

"And after that?"

Bellaydin chuckled. "You'll have to come visit me."

Maria smiled and nodded. "As often as I can."

They sat there together for a moment, enjoying each other's company. For Bellaydin, Maria's presence made him think of his sister, Polnygar, who he had not seen for many months. He felt a pang as he remembered how long it had been since they last spoke. Maria looked at Bellaydin and he thought of William, but this time the memory was a comfort, not a burden.

"You have your father's eyes," Bellaydin said to her. "When you look at me, it's like William is still here."

Maria gave him a warm embrace and said, "Thank you so much for saying that."

"My lady, I must apologise," Geoffrey said, cutting in, "but it appears the Duke of Alariat is desirous of your presence. He has been asking after you for the past ten minutes."

Maria nodded. "I'm sorry Uncle Bela, I think I have to go. We will talk again soon, yes?" Bellaydin nodded. "Don't stay up too late," she said with a smile as she left.

Geoffrey waited until the countess departed, and then sat down again. Bellaydin slid the knight's goblet back towards him, a gesture the knight accepted with a nod. "We have to look after her, you know? It's up to us." Geoffrey's face was serious. "Nothing can happen to her. That has to be our promise to William. That is how we will honour his memory. Agreed?"

"Of course. For William," Bellaydin said.

"For William." Geoffrey leant back and took another swig of his cider. "And for Maria. I still can't believe her mother was one of the Zalltors."

Bellaydin blinked. "Who or what are the Zalltors?"

"The family of the current Duke of Georgeton, and one of the richest families in all of Emparia. Margaret was an all-right sort, but she had the airs and graces of a true Zalltor."

"I can't imagine William being with someone like that," Bellaydin said. William had always struck him as a practical, humble man, someone with no taste for the pomp of the aristocracy.

Geoffrey laughed. "Maybe not. But he was, and he loved her deeply. I remember their wedding day. I was still a squire, serving in the household of your father. What about you Bela?"

"What about me?"

Geoffrey smiled. "Have you ever been in love?"

"I don't know." He blushed a deep shade of crimson. "I don't think so."

"I have, once."

"Well, you are married," Bellaydin said. "That stands to reason."

Geoffrey laughed cynically. "Bela, if you think marriage here has anything to do with love you are likely to be disappointed. My father chose my wife for me. He wanted a great match for his son. He had dreams of his grandchildren being nobility."

"So you don't love your wife?"

"We don't bear each other any ill will, but we both know the marriage was never our decision. We did our duty, produced an heir and a spare, and now we leave each other to our separate lives."

"So, the time you were in love, what was that?"

Geoffrey looked wistful for a moment, holding his mug tightly as he ran his fingers around the rim. "I was freshly knighted, not much older than you are now. She was more than a decade older than myself but the most beautiful woman I'd ever seen. We made promises to each other, promises that we knew we could never keep."

"Why not?"

"She was already married, and to a noble lord of great standing. There was an arranged marriage, it had not been her choice to wed. I hoped vainly that something might happen, perhaps he would give her up. But it was not to be."

"What happened?"

Geoffrey was quiet for a moment, and a tear welled in his eye. "She died. She and her husband both. Even in death, she was still his."

"I'm sorry," said Bellaydin.

"It's alright," Geoffrey said, wiping his eyes. "It's alright."

"I know how you feel. I've lost people close to me."

Geoffrey looked at him with fatherly affection, and nodded knowingly, "Your parents… yes. I was in Genio when it happened."

"Do you remember my parents well?"

Geoffrey coughed and looked away for a moment. "Only a little, I was fairly young at the time. I saw them a few times with my father, but most of the rest I only know second hand. Your mother, she was much younger than your father and far more spirited. It was an arranged marriage, at the insistence of King Henry. He and your father had fought together in the Emparian Civil War."

"So, what were my parents like?"

"Alusine was charming," said Geoffrey. "And never wanted for female company. My own mother had hoped to marry him before she met my father. Despite all that, though, he managed to stay a bachelor until well into his fortieth year.

"And my mother?"

Geoffrey rubbed his temple, half-smiling. "Your mother was of the old blood – she was a Tyron. Striking, like most of them, but possessed of an awesome temper. She always felt she had lowered herself marrying an Ap'Lydin. They were new nobility in the same way the Tyrons were old. Of course, there was the fact that your father had also set aside his love to marry your mother, and I think Eleanor always believed her husband still had feelings for Saegralanna." Geoffrey drained his cup. "I wonder if your stepmother knew that."

Bellaydin shook his head. "She never spoke about it, not really." He drank the remainder of his cider, and Geoffrey refilled his goblet before he could ask for another.

"It couldn't have been easy for your stepmother," Geoffrey mused. "She lost her true love twice: first to another woman, then to death. In a way sometimes the unluckiest of us are those left behind." The knight's eyes seemed wet, but it seemed unlikely that it was Saegralanna's heartbreak he was thinking of.

Bellaydin and Geoffrey continued drinking and talking well into the night. At one stage a rather inebriated Geoffrey decided to teach Bellaydin his favourite bawdy drinking songs and loudly belted out a few verses which managed to be both blasphemous and innuendo laden. Eventually, however, as the flickering fire dwindled, both decided to call it a night.

Bellaydin staggered back to his room, feeling light headed but also blessedly free of the low feeling that had gripped him since William's death.

It was with great relief that he collapsed onto his bed and finally went to sleep.

CHAPTER 2

Bellaydin groaned. His head felt like it had been hit with a warhammer, and his blankets were sweaty and smelled of stale alcohol. Bellaydin felt like every last drop of fluid had been leeched from his body overnight. He tried to move, but the throbbing in his head made him reconsider. He resolved to remain as still as possible, until he either died or his head returned to normal, whichever came first.

A bugle blared outside, causing his head to throb again. Bellaydin decided there was nothing for it except to try to stand up. Rolling over proved to be the first obstacle for him to master, but he managed that and planted his feet on the ground. Wobbling unsteadily, he was soon upright. The bugle sounded again, and as if on cue Bellaydin's stomach decided to disagree violently with his current situation. Panicking, he quickly ran to one of the windows, just in time to see his stomach's contents land on the ground below.

Remarkably, after this he felt a little better, at least well enough to take a trip down to the castle kitchens. The castle was alive with activity even this early in the morning, as the servants made preparations for the departure of the Countess and her retinue. Bellaydin moved down the stairs quickly, exchanging a few hurried pleasantries with servants as they passed by. When he reached the ground floor he saw the Dukes of Alariat and

Oldharbour in conversation with each other, and gave both the men a quick greeting. Haakon smiled at Bellaydin, but Wulfric for his part only exchanged a brief nod. Judging that both men were busy, Bellaydin didn't tarry any further and made his way through to the kitchens.

The steward was supervising the kitchen staff as they prepared the first meals of the day. "Good morning Master Ap'Lydin," said Carfel, "If you'd like something to eat, please take a seat and I'll have them fetch you something.

Bellaydin nodded and sat down at the long table. Carfel said some words to one of the servants who nodded, bringing Bellaydin a plate of bread and cheese with a mug of ale to drink. Bellaydin ate readily and drained the cup.

"I hope you have a good journey today," said Carfel. "Be careful in the royal court. It can be dangerous place for the innocent."

Bellaydin wasn't sure whether to take Carfel's description of him as a compliment or not. "I'll be wary. Thank you Carfel."

Carfel gave him an appreciative nod and returned to his duties. After Bellaydin had his fill, he returned to his room to retrieve his possessions for the journey ahead.

It was a short while later that he was in the castle courtyard, waiting as one of the stable-boys prepared his horse. "How did you fare this morning, Bela?" Geoffrey said, slapping the younger man on the back. "I must say those eyes look a little red."

Bellaydin looked at Geoffrey through slitted lids. "How in the name of the Underworld are you so jovial today?"

Geoffrey laughed. "Practice my young friend, practice. That's all it is."

"Sir Geoffrey!" The Eldara ranger Talthas called out from some distance as he hurried towards Geoffrey.

"Here's trouble," Geoffrey said, good-naturedly. "I thought you must've slept in."

"We Eldara do not sleep, friend," Talthas said, straight-faced. "Not in the same way as humans at least."

"We met yesterday," Bellaydin said, shaking the Eldara's hand.

"Yes, so he said," said Geoffrey. "Unlike the other Eldara, Talthas here appears to have enjoyed his time and wants to stay longer. I'm taking him to Genio with me. We'll find a place for him there in the countess' retinue."

"You're liking Emparia?" Bellaydin asked Talthas.

The Eldara smiled. "Everything except the food."

A stable hand brought Geoffrey's horse to him and the knight mounted the animal swiftly, "Come Talthas, I'll find you a place amongst the troops. I'll see you shortly, Bela," Geoffrey said as he urged his horse forward.

The entourage that would accompany Countess Maria to the capital was beginning to take shape, and it would be quite a procession leaving Wishapton. The countess, accompanied by Sir Geoffrey and Bellaydin would ride in the centre, under the cross of House Ap'Lydin. On her left flank would be the Duke of Oldharbour, Wulfric, under the sigil of the twisted pair of snakes that represented House Highcrown, and on the countess' right would be the Duke of Alariat, Haakon, with his standard of a rearing stallion – the sigil of the royal family and House Morcor.

Bellaydin's horse was ready; he quickly mounted the animals and a groom led him to his place in the procession. Maria was being conveyed in a covered wagon, where she sat along with her attendants.

Geoffrey returned. "I guess it will be you and me for the journey, Bela. Hope you're up for it."

Bellaydin smiled. "I guess I can manage."

As they rode together with the rest of the entourage, Bellaydin pressed Geoffrey for details on what he could expect once they reached the capital.

Geoffrey was only too happy to share what he knew.

"Well, Emperor's Palace is one of the largest cities in all Emparia, only Oldharbour is bigger, and the capital is much more opulent. The politics of the royal court are renowned for their cold brutality. If all you've ever experienced is Wishapton, you may be in for a shock. Even Genio seems a provincial town when you compare it with the splendour of the royal city. The centre of it all is Castle Emparia, the greatest palace in the entire kingdom, and built after the style of ancient Davorea.

"You'll no doubt meet the Privy Council, the greatest nobles in the land. There are seven of them, four dukes and three earls, though the earls have little say. It's the dukes who are really in control and each has their own agendas and desires. William was Earl of Genio, and while he may have spurned the game of palace intrigue, other nobles are not so uninterested."

"What do I need to know about them?"

"First of all, there's the Duke of Emperor's Palace, Edmund Tallcastle. He may be old now, and reputably so fat he barely leaves his bedchambers, but he's still one of the finest tactical minds in Emparia. It was Tallcastle who masterminded King Henry's war to seize the throne from the Tyrons, and he was Henry's chief advisor for the old king's entire reign. Henry's first wife was Tallcastle's daughter, but she, and all of the sons she had born Henry, died during the Civil War. Tallcastle still advises Henry's daughter, but I don't think he'll be around for that much longer. He has no living descendants, so House Tallcastle will die with him. At the moment he spends most of his time keeping the other dukes from lynching one another."

"They don't get along very well then?"

Geoffrey gave a quiet chuckle. "It shouldn't be much of a surprise to you, Bela. You know the Dukes of Oldharbour and Alariat. Wulfric and Haakon were very close to each other when they were younger, but they have drifted apart in recent decades. I think the coldness between them started with the death of your father. His murder drove a wedge between them. They both blamed each other for his death. I think each of them believes that if the other had been quicker, then Alusine would still be alive.

"The last duke is a man named Oswin Zalltor," said Geoffrey. "He's the richest noble in the kingdom, with a private wealth that rivals the royal family. The man himself is a bit of an amiable old dullard but his sons – now there's ambition. With three adult children and only one dukedom to inherit, they squabble and jostle for power. I wouldn't be surprised if they each had their eyes on other prizes too.

"The Earl of Warding is Anson Mainstream, and he's an ambitious social climber, a flatterer and a toady of the Zalltors. He has few achievements of his own, but he's always looking to improve the standing of his house." Geoffrey touched his finger as if counting down. "Then there is House Bauer, all the way out there in Tyronsville. Harold was the Earl until recently, but now his son Alfred holds the Earldom. Fond of a drink and a bit of tavern-brawling, they're a straightforward and excitable family, with a penchant for tactlessness. I think that's why everyone was surprised when one of them was made Royal Ambassador. Personally, I think it shows that King Henry had a sense of humour."

"Is there anyone else on the council I should know?"

Geoffrey clicked his tongue. "There is Archbishop Garamond, but I don't think you'll have much to do with him. The great lords have all the power, and queen's ear."

Bellaydin sighed. "So what will any of these great lords have to do with me?"

"It is the tradition that every few years, each House presents a squire for education to the royal court," said Geoffrey. "This time you are to be House Ap'Lydin's candidate. It is expected that the other Houses will also present their own squires at the same time, and all of you will spend the next six months learning and living together."

"Sounds like fun," Bellaydin said drily.

"Well, you're likely to be the oldest of the squires, so maybe you can teach the others a little bit of adult responsibility," Geoffrey said with a grin. "The rest will be anywhere from one to five years younger."

"So are both Haakon and Wulfric sponsoring a squire?"

"Wulfric definitely not. He's never been comfortable at court and spends as little time as possible there. He also has no close relatives left. The only other members of his House are distant and unimportant, and he interacts little with them, if at all. Haakon on the other hand...well, if he had his way he would have probably sponsored you, but I expect he will do right by House Morcor, and probably sponsor one of his distant cousins. Some spoiled brat, no doubt, filled with self-entitlement about being a member of the royal family."

"You almost sound a little jealous there, Geoffrey," said Bellaydin.

"Bah," the knight responded.

They continued to ride for the rest of the day, making good time as they travelled up the northern road. They passed the city of Genio, stopping only briefly to resupply and change horses and by the next dawn's light, had set off again.

The road from Wishapton was busy with travellers. Farmers taking their harvest to town vied with merchants plying the route between the south and the capital. There were others too, refugees heading north, having had their fill of living on the Goriinchian border, the siege of Wishapton evidently being the last straw.

"I don't blame them," Geoffrey said to Bellaydin. "It was a close run thing. If Wulfric hadn't arrived with reinforcements the town would be a smoking ruin, or worse yet, under the control of Ygarak. If I was a peasant I'd be taking my chances in the north as well. At least if you get killed it's by one of your own kind."

Bellaydin didn't think that sounded reassuring.

They passed over the crest of the hill where the procession came to a sudden halt, and Bellaydin heard some of the soldiers begin to mutter amongst themselves.

"What's going on?" Bellaydin asked Geoffrey.

"I'm not sure," the knight said. "Some of the men are saying that the dukes are arguing with each other."

"About what?"

"Let's have a look, shall we?" Geoffrey said, inclining his head. He moved his horse forward, weaving around the throng towards the front. Bellaydin followed closely.

"Let them be, Wulfric," said Haakon, a note of exhaustion in his voice. The Duke of Alariat was facing the Duke of Oldharbour, who loomed over a trio of frightened looking peasants. The peasants kneeled in the dirt, mud staining their shabby black robes.

"They are worshippers of the Horned God, Haakon," Wulfric moved about on his horse, glaring at the scene in front of him. "Here, right under our noses."

"What of it, Wulfric?" Haakon said. "Their faith is permitted by the Queen's law. You know that as well as I do. We were both members of the Ducal Council that decided it."

Bellaydin saw the familiar symbol that hung around each of their necks and felt his blood run cold. His mind flashed back to his travails in Goriinchia, and even earlier in Aderilund, where he had seen the symbol for the first time. It had always been a bad omen for him.

Wulfric shot a disdainful look back towards the cowering peasants. "Treason," he said with a sneer.

"A serious accusation," Haakon said. "You should not make it lightly."

"They are spies, no doubt," Wulfric spat. "Cat's-paws of Ygarak."

"Wulfric," Haakon sighed. "You are reaching. There is no evidence of that. And the law is clear, they can worship in the way they want if it does not undermine the crown."

All eyes turned to Wulfric. The corner of the duke's mouth twitched. "Their very existence undermines the crown!"

"You are not king, Wulfric," said Haakon. "Be careful of pronouncing edicts as if you were."

Wulfric sniffed the air and then turned away. "Fine. Let us be on our way."

After giving a brief apology to the peasants, Haakon turned to Bellaydin and Geoffrey, sighing before he moved off to join Wulfric at the front of the procession.

Bellaydin turned to Geoffrey. "Did I hear correctly? Is worship of the Horned God legal in Emparia?"

Geoffrey rubbed his temples. "Only recently. King Henry banned it after your parents died, but that edict was lifted by Queen Amaryllis just before the Battle of Wishapton."

"Why would she do such a thing?" The religion that had caused his parents' murder existed around him; The thought made him feel sick.

"The Ducal Council advised her to do so."

"You mean Haakon and Wulfric?"

Geoffrey shrugged. "They were split for and against, I believe. It was your cousin who decided in favour of lifting the ban."

"William? William did this?" Bellaydin was shocked. His cousin had been there when his father was found dead. *How could he dishonour my father's memory by allowing his murderers to roam free?*

Bellaydin dwelled on this new information for the next few days of their journey but found himself unable to reconcile it with the memory of his cousin. William had been a stalwart foe of the Goriinchians and all they stood for.

So why did he allow their faith to blossom in his homeland? Confused and frustrated he decided to push the thoughts aside for the moment and focus on what lay ahead. Geoffrey spoke at great length about many topics but Bellaydin focused on little of it, doing nothing more than nodding and smiling where he thought it appropriate.

When it was time for the company to split and go their separate ways. Wulfric Highcrown, made his farewells and peeled off from the main procession. He took his retainers, including Kahlaf, towards the city of Oldharbour, leaving Bellaydin and the others to continue to Emperor's Palace.

"You know, in an odd way I think I might miss that Ahktarran," Geoffrey said, before adding, "But in many others I am glad to see the back of him."

Bellaydin too felt conflicted as he watched Kahlaf depart. Although he found the Ahktarran cold and abrasive, Kahlaf had protected him during the journey through Goriinchia. He had also been the one to find Bellaydin and bring him back to Castle Wishapton in the aftermath of the siege. In a way, the Ahktarran's departure symbolised the end of this stage of Bellaydin's life. What awaited him in the next he could not be sure.

The road past the fork to Oldharbour took on a different character, changing to a harder, paved surface. The passing of years had worn the bricks, and the road was definitely of ancient vintage. Most likely a remnant of Old Davorea, it was another reminder that Emparia had not always been as it was.

For days the procession travelled on this ancient causeway, through periods of rain and bouts of sunshine, until they finally reached a great valley, watered by the River Garns. Rolling fields surrounded them, patch-worked with farms and dotted with small villages. As they passed, curious peasants stopped their labour to gawk before returning to their fields.

"There seem to be so many of these villages. So many people," Bellaydin said. "It's completely different to Aderilund."

Geoffrey looked surprised. "You don't have villages in Aderilund?"

"Not really," Bellaydin said. "The Eldara prefer to live in only a few large settlements. There's not much outside the cities."

"I don't think you've missed much Bela. I grew up in a place like this."

"You come from a village? Is it nearby?"

"No, it's a tiny place to the east of here, near the Goriinchian border. Drakeford."

"Do you miss it? Drakeford, I mean."

"Sometimes," said Geoffrey, "But I had to leave it if I was to ever escape my father."

Bellaydin looked back to Geoffrey. "Why is that?"

"He owned it," Geoffrey said.

"Oh, I see," said Bellaydin.

Geoffrey explained further. "They deeded the land to him shortly after his knighthood. There was no way for me to be my own man if I stayed there. So I took the chance and came to Genio. Of course, that was before I knew my father was perfectly capable of issuing his edicts from hundreds of miles away."

"What sort of edicts did he issue?" Bellaydin asked.

Geoffrey smiled evasively. "That's something for another time. Let's just say I'm not headed home any time soon."

Bellaydin's thoughts drifted to Aderilund, to his sister, Polnygar, and from there to his stepmother, Saegralanna. All were much further away from Bellaydin than Drakeford was from Geoffrey. For years all he'd ever thought about was leaving Aderilund, and returning to Emparia where he was born. But now that he was here the place seemed strange and unfamiliar, and he felt just as much a foreigner as he had in Aderilund.

For a while after that Bellaydin and Geoffrey rode on in silence, with both men absorbed by their own thoughts. Eventually, the group's destination came into view, towering over the horizon – Emperor's Palace, the capital of Emparia. Emparians claimed that the city was ancient, dating back over a thousand years ago when a man named Tyron, the so-called Last Davorean, built a fortress on the Garns River. Claiming to be the rightful heir to the Imperial Davorean crown, Tyron's fortress became known as the Emperor's Palace, and eventually, when a city grew up around it, it took on the same name as well, even after the original structure had long since gone. Tyron's descendants, the House of Tyron, eventually ruled all of Emparia.

Now the Tyrons were long gone and a new family ruled in their stead: the de Morcors. The oldest surviving male dynast of House Morcor was currently leading their large procession towards the city, the black stallion of his House proudly unfurled at his side.

Emperor's Palace's walls were strong and of ancient origin. The mythic king Tyron had built the walls in the traditions of his homeland, and Tyron's successors had continually repaired and reinforced the walls in the centuries since. Great carvings of fantastical beasts covered the walls, a reminder of ancient Davorea.

The royal banner proved to ensure a swift passage through the gates of the city, and within a few short moments, Bellaydin found himself riding down the streets of the city itself. Unlike the rude timber shacks of Wishapton, Emperor's Palace was built chiefly of stone, and the buildings were marvels of architecture, built in the same Davorean style as the rest of the city. The great Cathedral of the Sun dominated the west of the city, and to the east was the great amphitheatre, where monarchs and nobles funded entertainment for the almost hundred thousand people who called the city home.

In the centre, reaching towards the sky was Castle Emparia herself. Home to the queen and her closest advisors, Castle Emparia was not a traditional castle like Castle Wishapton was. Instead, it was a grand and opulent building, with a rounded, smooth aesthetic not at all like the straight lines of traditional Emparian fortresses. The design was also the legacy of the ancient King Tyron and his exotic origins, even if the building itself was completed by King Alarion, one of Tyron's descendants.

As they rode through the streets the townsfolk came from their houses and places of business to welcome them, cheering them on and tossing rose petals into their paths. People cheered and clapped as soon as they saw the royal banner, and Bellaydin was so taken aback by the adulation that he even waved at the crowd a little.

"You'd think we'd already won the war the way they're cheering for us," Geoffrey said.

"Maybe they think we have," Bellaydin said.

They soon arrived at the palace and as they did a veritable army of attendants and stable-boys came out to greet them, quickly taking care of the animals as the travellers dismounted. Geoffrey helped the countess out of her wagon as Bellaydin made sure that his possessions were still in the sack. Satisfied that they were, he tied the sack over his shoulder and went to join the others.

A tall man in his mid-fifties was standing on the castle steps, watching over as the servants did their work. The man seemed drab for a nobleman, yet his clothes were far too fine and expensive for a servant. Grey of hair, he had kind and intelligent eyes, and a face marked with laughter lines. "Your Grace, I am pleased to see that you have arrived. I am Martin,

Steward of Castle Wishapton. I have been expecting your arrival." Martin knelt in front of Haakon and carefully kissed the duke's signet ring.

"Rise, Martin," said Haakon. "And thank you for your welcome. The journey was long, though pleasant enough."

"Of course, Your Grace," Martin said, bowing. "You must all be tired from your journey. Please, my friends, you are to join the queen in the great hall for a feast honouring your arrival. Do not worry, we shall attend to your mounts."

"We have some matters to attend to first," Haakon said and indicated the presence of the countess.

"Ah yes, of course, my Grace. The countess must pay homage for her title. The queen is in the throne room currently. I shall take you there now."

The steward escorted Haakon, Maria, Geoffrey and Bellaydin into the castle and towards a long chamber with a high domed roof. Great fluted columns in the ancient Davorean style lined the walls, and at each pillar stood a soldier, every one of them wearing the livery of the royal house.

At the far end of the room, was a stately throne and behind it the royal banner. Atop the throne sat Amaryllis de Morcor, Queen of Emparia. Bellaydin was shocked to discover that the queen did not appear much older than himself and in fact, she was small and slight, her tiny frame hardly filling the magnificent throne she sat in. Her eyes were a deep brown, and she had pale skin and brown hair which, though straight, had been worked into an elaborate braid. She was pretty, but also rather cold in appearance, and she held herself with a rather superior, haughty expression. Atop her head the queen wore the fabled Crown of Eternity – an ancient and storied circlet dating back to Ancient Davorea.

Next to the queen stood an elderly man, red-faced and overweight to the point of obesity. He was bald except for a few tufts of hair around his ears and he wore ermine robes and a heavy gold chain around his neck. His garb was so opulent that he outshone even his monarch. He carried a rather elaborate gold staff of office. Bellaydin reasoned this could only be the Duke of Emperor's Palace, Edmund Tallcastle, chief advisor to the crown.

A herald in livery announced their arrival. "Your Majesty, might I present Haakon de Morcor, Duke of Alariat, and Maria Ap'Lydin, daughter of the late Earl of Genio."

"We recognise our royal cousin Haakon," the queen said. "We also recognise Maria, daughter of our beloved vassal William, Earl of Genio. Step forward, my lady."

Maria moved towards her monarch with hesitation, blushing as she did.

"Kneel," the queen commanded. Despite the difficulty of doing so in a dress, Maria did as the queen commanded.

The queen stood from her throne and approached Maria, her hand outstretched. Maria took the queen's hand in hers and lightly kissed the royal signet ring. "In the name of the Unconquered Sun, I, Maria Margaret Ap'Lydin, swear allegiance to Amaryllis, the First of her Name, Queen of Emparia, Davorean Empress-Elect and trueborn heir to the royal House of Morcor. I am her bondswoman and true and faithful servant, and swear eternal and everlasting faith and fidelity. May the Triune judge me if I prove false."

The Queen smiled. "Then it does us great pleasure to confirm you fully justified and deserving of the title of Countess of Genio, to be held by you and your heirs for as long as you shall serve us faithfully. Rise, Lady Genio."

Maria rose slowly, head bowed as the Queen resumed her seat and the herald spoke again. "Your Majesty, might I also present to you Squire Bellaydin Ap'Lydin, cousin to the late Earl of Genio and son of the late Alusine and Eleanor Ap'Lydin."

The queen appraised Bellaydin carefully. As she did, the Duke of Emperor's Palace leant down and whispered in the queen's ear. "Of course," she said, nodding. "Squire Ap'Lydin, we are indebted to your cousin for his defence of our kingdom. We owe your family much. We would be honoured if you would join us for the feast in the great hall. You can consider it a personal request."

Bellaydin was lost for words. "Thank you, Your Majesty."

The queen inclined her head in a gesture of acknowledgement. "We shall meet you in the great hall for the evening meal. We must retire before dinner."

The queen arose from her throne and departed from the throne room, accompanied by the Duke of Emperor's Palace and her attendants.

After the queen's departure, Martin the steward led Haakon, Geoffrey, Maria and Bellaydin through the hallways of the castle until they reached the great hall where there was a large table laden with food. The scent of finely cooked meat overwhelmed Bellaydin's senses, making his mouth water. He smelt beef, mutton, venison, as well as a new scent that he would later identify as spatchcock. Though the queen and her entourage were not yet here, the steward and his staff busied themselves by organising seating for the guests. The duke, as cousin to the queen, would sit at her right hand and Countess Maria would sit at her left. The Duke of Emperor's Palace would sit next to the Duke of Alariat, and Geoffrey and Bellaydin were seated next to the countess, as members of her entourage.

As they took their seats the steward filled their goblets with wine and Geoffrey reached for one of the goblets.

"Sir Geoffrey!" the Duke of Alariat scolded the knight. "Try to restrain yourself."

"Your Grace, it was a long journey," Geoffrey said.

"At least wait for Her Majesty. I swear sometimes you have the manners of a pig herder."

Geoffrey shrugged and placed the goblet back on the table, where an obliging servant filled it for him.

Haakon shook his head. "Bellaydin, if you learn nothing else today, please do not take Sir Geoffrey as your role model on how to behave at court. There is a reason he spends most of his time on the frontier."

"There's nothing wrong with the frontier," Geoffrey said, running his fingers over the goblet. "The women have a much more relaxed attitude to life."

Haakon threw his hands up in despair. "Well my lady, I'm sorry to say but this is the man your father chose to be the premier knight of his earldom. And you're stuck with him now."

Maria smiled and laughed merrily. "Do not worry, I like Geoffrey. He amuses me."

"Glad to be of use." He grinned widely and raised his goblet. When Haakon glared at him, he put it down sheepishly.

Two heralds, dressed in the livery of the House Morcor, entered the great hall. They raised their trumpets to their mouths and blared out a series of triumphant notes. "Her Majesty, Amaryllis, First of that Name, of House Morcor. Queen of Emparia." More trumpet blasts. "His Grace, Edmund, of House Tallcastle, Duke of Emperor's Palace, Earl of Garns, and Lord Chancellor."

The Duke of Alariat rose, as did Maria and Geoffrey, so Bellaydin did likewise. The queen entered, followed by the Duke of Emperor's Palace and then by their attendants. The queen took her seat at the head of the table, and the Duke of Emperor's Palace sat in the seat that had been reserved for him. Once they were both seated, the servants sprang into action around the table, cutting and serving the queen's food, as well as tasting portions of it to ensure there was no poison hidden within. Bellaydin's stomach growled as he looked at the food arrayed before him but he knew it was the height of bad manners to eat before the queen had, so he waited. Eventually, after the servants had finished with her plate, the queen could take a bite.

Bellaydin breathed a secret sigh of relief and began to tuck into the feast before him. It was the finest food he had tasted since he left Aderilund, but he didn't know whether to believe that. His memories of Aderilund were slowly receding in his mind, including the delicious meals prepared by his stepmother's cook.

"I wonder what those two dukes are talking about," Bellaydin said to Geoffrey, as the knight chewed noisily on a mutton leg. The Duke of Alariat and the Duke of Emperor's Palace were deep in discussion, their hushed voices and grave faces hinting at something of great importance.

"The war, no doubt," Geoffrey said. "The Privy Council is meeting tomorrow to decide the next action against the Goriinchians. The other nobles will arrive in the city by the night, and they will meet tomorrow."

"Will you be attending?"

"Gods no!" Geoffrey said. "The meetings are always behind closed door, and only the nobles themselves attend."

"So it's all kept a secret?"

"I wouldn't say that, Bela," he said with a wink. "Information has a way of getting out anyway. I know William was always surprised by how much I knew, even after he'd only just come out from a meeting."

"Do you think the Goriinchians will attack Wishapton again?"

"Unlikely," Geoffrey said. "The town itself is of little real importance. I believe they only bothered to lay siege to it last time because they knew there was an earl and a duke hiding within. I suppose they hoped to kill two birds with one stone and cripple our fighting capability by killing two of our most capable leaders."

"What about me? When do I see what is happening to me?"

"Soon. Tomorrow I'd wager, as soon as the other squires arrive. You'll all be pledged together, I expect. You'll be sponsored by your cousin, in her position of countess. Once that has happened, you will join the other squires in being trained right here in the royal palace."

"What about you? Will you be staying?"

"I expect now that she's been confirmed in her position, the countess will return to Genio, and where she goes, I go."

Bellaydin felt a bit deflated, a fact that was not lost on Geoffrey.

"Don't worry, I'll come visit. I'm not so provincial that I can't find diversions in Emperor's Palace."

Before too long the meal was over; the queen departed with her attendants, and servants began to clear the table. The Duke of Alariat and the Countess of Genio likewise excused themselves, servants guiding them to their guest rooms in the palace. Soon only Bellaydin, Geoffrey and the Duke of Emperor's Palace remained. The old duke, leaning on his walking stick, approached Bellaydin.

"Now that formalities are over, I would like to extend my personal greetings to you, Bellaydin Ap'Lydin. Welcome to Emperor's Palace. I hope that the capital has been all that you've expected."

"Thank you, Your Grace, but to be honest I haven't had a chance to see much yet."

"There will plenty of time to become familiar with the city, my friend," he said. "Trust me." The duke coughed violently. "Please excuse me, my health is not what is once was."

Regaining his composure, he continued. "Believe me, I know this city more than most. It has been my pleasure to rule over it for over thirty years. It has not changed much, though I fear I have." He ran his hands over his head, touching his sparse hair.

"You've been duke for a long time," Bellaydin said.

"Indeed I have, young squire. I have served along Queen Amaryllis and her father Henry for the entirety of both their reigns. I was here when your cousin was named Earl of Genio, I was here when your mother was promised in marriage to your father. You may not remember me Bellaydin Ap'Lydin, but I remember you."

He pushed on his walking stick and looked towards the doorway. "Ah, it seems Martin is here to show you to your rooms. With that in mind, I will take my leave. Come and visit me while you are here, Bellaydin. You are a newcomer here, and I would be more than happy to help you navigate the intricacies of the royal court."

Bellaydin nodded gratefully.

"Farewell to you as well, Sir Geoffrey," the duke said. "The countess speaks highly of you. Let's hope you live up to that reputation."

The duke turned to leave as the steward Martin arrived, and as the two men passed each other, Bellaydin saw them exchange a brief smile.

Martin escorted Bellaydin and Geoffrey upstairs from the great hall, and down a few corridors. "Through there if you will, Sir Geoffrey," the steward said. "This way, squire." He guided Bellaydin down another passageway until they reached a door. The door was old, the wood was scratched and slightly warped, and on the door was a strange sigil, resembling a large unblinking eye.

"What is this?" Bellaydin asked.

Martin looked at the sigil. "I believe these rooms were once used by the royal wizard. That is probably some symbol pertaining to his profession."

"There's a royal wizard in Emparia?"

"There *was* a royal wizard. He resigned his post centuries ago and the no one has held the position since." Martin took a large key from a chain on his belt and unlocked the door. "There we are, squire," he said. "I will leave you to make yourself comfortable."

Bellaydin entered the room. It was sparsely furnished, but the pieces within were of obviously fine quality, including a table and a set of chairs, and a bed and a cabinet against one wall. A large window dominated the opposite wall. Peering through the window gave Bellaydin a spectacular view of the city, and on to the horizon. The sheer size of Emperor's Palace became even more noticeable when viewed from above. The city teemed with life.

Bellaydin placed his knapsack upon the bed and unwrapped his possessions. The clothes, including his mail shirt, he hung in his cabinet, and he found a space on the wall to hang his sword. *The Holy Book of the Horned God* he wrapped up in a sheet and bundled it under his bed. It would not be a good idea to leave the book out in the open. With the country embroiled in a war against Goriinchia, he did not want anyone here to get the wrong idea about him. Such misunderstandings could have fatal consequences.

Exhausted from the day he lay down on the bed, and before long he drifted into sleep.

CHAPTER 3

Bellaydin heard William's voice in the darkness.

"Bellaydin...see me," William whispered.

Bellaydin was standing in a desolate landscape. There was no sun in the sky, instead all around him was bathed in twilight. He heard his cousin's voice again. "Bellaydin..."

Bellaydin turned around in the gloom, looking for his cousin, and saw nothing but a shadow. Before his eyes, the shadow coalesced into flesh and Bellaydin saw William, looking just as he had when Bellaydin had last seen him. Alive, but trapped in dying flesh. The wounds of the Battle of Wishapton were still exposed, but his corpse was putrefying, and in some places the flesh had given way to bone. For a while, terror seized Bellaydin. Eventually, he managed to eke out a few words. "William, is that you?"

"Bellaydin, I am alive by the Horned God's grace. He alone has this power...The one lord...the true lord..."

Bellaydin stepped back in horror as William began to scream, his body dissolving into nothingness. In place of William was instead Aonghus Culainn, Warchief of the Goriinchians. He too screamed, before disintegrating in front of Bellaydin's eyes. His screams continued, like the blaring of trumpets...

Bellaydin awoke from his sleep with a start. It was morning. From outside his window, he heard trumpets, just as he had in his nightmare. Rubbing his eyes he looked out to the city below and beheld the sight of a grand military parade marching up the streets of the city. An endless procession of soldiers marched behind huge banners depicting a blue owl on a field of gold. As he took in this sight he heard a voice from behind him. It was Sir Geoffrey.

"Bellaydin, are you awake?"

Bellaydin turned around and rubbed his eyes again. "Only just." He yawned, before looking out the window once again. "The sigil of an owl. Who is that?"

"Oswin Zalltor, Duke of Georgeton." Geoffrey folded his arms as he came up to stand next to Bellaydin. "Do you know why Zalltor has an owl as his sigil?"

Bellaydin thought for a moment. "I suppose an owl represents wisdom..."

"No." Geoffrey shook his head. He grinned. "Zalltor has an owl as his sigil because, like an owl, he's fond of swooping in and covering everyone with shit."

Bellaydin tried to contain himself, but despite his best attempts, he let out a loud laugh. "That's awful," he said.

"Nevertheless, you did laugh." Geoffrey teased. "You'd best get ready. You'll be expected in the great hall with the other squires in a few hours."

As Geoffrey left the room, Bellaydin busied himself getting ready. He washed his face, and changed from his sleeping clothes into the fine outfit he had kept aside for this day. It had the sigil of House Ap'Lydin imprinted on it. Bellaydin was determined to make a good impression, not just for his sake, but for the memory of his cousin.

He washed and combed his hair and then, taking a sharp-edged razor, he carefully scraped the adolescent scruff from his cheeks. William had worn a beard, but Bellaydin did not feel he could pull one off himself, especially when it looked less like a beard and more like some sort of strange patchy moss on his face. Once he had finished, he washed his face again and dried it off with a towel before heading off downstairs to the Great Hall.

By the time he arrived, Geoffrey was waiting for him outside the chamber. "Good, you're here," the knight said. "The Countess is not feeling well, so I've been deputised to speak for her. Are you ready?"

"I suppose so," Bellaydin said.

"We'll go in together." Geoffrey placed a reassuring hand on Bellaydin's shoulder, giving Bellaydin a smile. "Come on."

The great hall looked different to when Bellaydin had last seen it. The tables and chairs were gone, replaced by a single throne for the queen. From the walls hung banners representing the great houses of Emparia; Bellaydin saw the galloping stallion of House Morcor, the twisted snakes of House Highcrown and the blue owl of House Zalltor, alongside the cross of House Ap'Lydin and three others he did not recognise: a grey dog on a black field, a stylised castle on a white background and a white boar on a green background. The queen sat poised, her face serene and showing little emotion. Standing next to the throne was the Duke of Emperor's Palace, his eyes scanning the room.

Bellaydin looked around. To his left, he saw the Duke of Alariat. Haakon was standing next to a blond adolescent male who stood with a superior and smug expression. The duke's hand was on the younger man's shoulder, but it did not appear to be with much warmth. Next to them, a finely-dressed man, his clothes decorated with a white boar of the same design as on the banner, stood with his arm on the shoulder of a rotund adolescent. The boy looked around nervously and was visibly sweating. He looked to be a year or so younger than the blond boy, perhaps fifteen years old.

On Bellaydin's right was another noble, this one with the Zalltor owl on his garments. He was past middle-age and had a proud bearing, but he seemed friendly enough. Most likely this was Oswin Zalltor, the Duke of Georgeton. He was with a boy who looked to be little more than a much younger version of himself. The last noble wore the grey dog as his device, and he too stood with a young man who, though likely not any older than Bellaydin, was tall and muscular, his face hidden with long hair.

"Your Graces, my lords," the Duke of Emperor's Palace began. "You are here today to continue the ancient tradition that we call the Great Fostering. Each of the great houses of the realm has come to the throne to once again pledge their loyalty to the crown, and to offer one boy from their line as a squire to the royal court. These boys will remain here until such a time as they become men, and shall carry their loyalty to the crown in their hearts for as long as they shall live."

"The Duke of Alariat shall approach the throne."

Haakon stepped forward to face the queen. "I, Haakon de Morcor, Duke of Alariat do pledge my loyalty to Amaryllis, First of Her Name, Queen of Emparia. If I should falter in my duty, I will suffer the fate of all who sow treason. Death." He knelt, and kissed the queen's signet ring.

"Who does your house pledge to the Crown?" the Duke of Emperor's Palace asked.

Haakon stood, and gestured towards the young man he had been standing with. "I pledge Squire Edgar Leon de Morcor, grandson of my late uncle. He shall be testament to our House's loyalty to the throne." Edgar de Morcor stepped forward and, like Haakon did, knelt before the queen and kissed her ring before he and Haakon returned to their positions.

"The Duke of Georgeton shall approach the throne," the Duke of

Emperor's Palace said.

The ceremony continued, with the Duke of Georgeton pledging his grandson, Tancred Zalltor, followed by the Earl of Warding, Anson Mainstream, pledging his younger son Otto Mainstream and the Earl of Tyronsville, Alfred Bauer, pledging his younger son, Kurth Bauer. Finally, there was only one house left to pledge.

"Who speaks for the Countess of Genio and House Ap'Lydin?" the Duke of Emperor's Palace asked.

Geoffrey spoke up. "I do. I am Sir Geoffrey Keslin, son of Sir Edric Keslin, and sworn sword of the House Ap'Lydin. I am sanctioned to speak on behalf of my liege lord, the Countess of Genio." The knight stepped forward and repeated the same words as the nobles before he had, and kissed the queen's signet ring.

"Who does House Ap'Lydin pledge to the throne?"

"House Ap'Lydin pledges Bellaydin Tyron Ap'Lydin, cousin to our late and beloved Earl of Genio, William Ap'Lydin. He shall be testament to House Ap'Lydin's loyalty to the throne."

Geoffrey looked at Bellaydin expectantly and Bellaydin did as the four other squires had done before him, approaching the throne and kneeling in front of the queen. When she held out her hand he kissed the signet ring. Bellaydin then stood up and went back to join the others.

"The Great Houses have renewed their pledges of allegiance to the crown," the Duke of Emperor's Palace said. "And let none here forget their oaths." He banged the staff of office on the floor three times. "There will be a short recess before the Privy Council meets. Go about your business."

***

"Well that was relatively painless," Geoffrey said to Bellaydin a short while later as they stood outside the great hall. "I have to go see if the countess is feeling up to this meeting of the Privy Council, I'll leave you to mingle with these other new squires of the court. Have a fun time, or at least try to."

Bellaydin nodded, and Geoffrey disappeared up the stairs.

The other squires stared at Bellaydin. One of them, the blond boy that Bellaydin identified as Edgar de Morcor, looked him up and down. "I didn't think there were any more male Ap'Lydins around," the boy said. "Where did they dig you up?"

"Aderilund," Bellaydin said.

"Wow, have you met elves?" the fat boy, Otto Mainstream, said with excitement.

Bellaydin nodded.

"Quiet, Piggy," Edgar said. "Don't you see that I'm talking?"

Another boy, the Zalltor squire, was standing next to Edgar and tried to be a voice of peace. "Edgar, I think he was just excited."

"Don't be a fool, Tancred," Edgar said. "Otto needs to learn to not soil himself like an overexcited puppy when he meets someone new."

Bellaydin decided to respond. "So who are you then, to be telling others what they need to learn or not learn?"

Tancred spoke up, "He is Edgar de Morcor, fourth in line to the throne of Emparia. A prince in all but name."

Edgar waved a hand, "As my friend Tancred says, I am of the Royal House, but I am not asking you to bow – not yet, of course. But I want you to very carefully consider how you conduct yourself, Bellaydin Ap'Lydin. There are some of us, from families with power and wealth – like myself and Tancred – who it would be wise to have good relations with. There are others," he looked towards Otto and the other boy, Kurth Bauer, "with whom you needn't bother."

Otto burst into tears, but the other boy, Kurth, barely reacted, merely cracking a small smile and shaking his head.

"Something funny, Bauer?" Edgar said.

Kurth said nothing but just stared at Edgar. Eventually, the lordling gave up and turned back to Bellaydin.

"Think about your House and its standing, Bellaydin," Edgar said. "You only still hold the earldom thanks to the queen's grace. If it had been me, I would have stripped you of it the moment William Ap'Lydin died, but it seems your family's plight touched the queen. A woman's heart is a fickle thing, though, Bellaydin. I wouldn't rely on it."

"Well, thank you for your advice, but I think I can work things out on my own."

"It seems your advanced age has not given you wisdom, Ap'Lydin," Edgar said. "So I will not waste any more time with you. Come, Tancred, we have better things to do than spend any more time with these lowborn dunces."

Edgar de Morcor disappeared around a hallway in a huff, followed quickly after by Tancred, who threw a few embarrassed glances over his shoulder before leaving.

"What a charming young man," Bellaydin remarked to no one in particular.

Otto looked at him, wiping tears away.

"Don't worry about him," Bellaydin said. "I'm Bellaydin Ap'Lydin by the way."

Otto gave him a rather limp handshake. "Otto Mainstream," he said. "Third son of the Earl of Warding."

"Pleasure to meet you, Otto," said Bellaydin.

"We all just call him Piggy," said the Bauer squire.

Bellaydin turned to the other boy, extending his hand. "And you must be the squire from Tyronsville."

The squire just stared at him.

"It's a hand. You shake it," Bellaydin said.

The squire smirked and shook Bellaydin's hand firmly. "Bauer. Kurth Bauer. Second son of the Earl of Tyronsville."

"Good to meet you."

"I hear you're the oldest of all of us here," Kurth said. "I thought my father was lazy enough, waiting until I was seventeen before he sent me to court. Tancred and Edgar are about six months younger than me and Piggy here isn't yet sixteen."

"I turned eighteen a month or so ago," Bellaydin said.

"Eighteen," said Kurth, "You *are* old. So, why are you still a squire in your eighteenth year? Are you slow-witted?"

Bellaydin felt slightly offended at Kurth's blunt tone. "Not as far as I know. But I only became a squire a short time ago."

"I guess they don't have squires in the lands of elves," Kurth snorted.

"No, they don't," Bellaydin said.

"What do they have in the lands of elves?" Otto asked impatiently.

"A lot of trees, magic and arrogance," Bellaydin said.

"Well if you miss the arrogance, you'll certainly love Emperor's Palace," Kurth said. "It practically oozes from the walls here. Even the servants look down on you for being provincial. And if Piggy and I are provincial, what on earth does that make you?"

Bellaydin's face felt hot. He tried to change the topic of conversation. "What will we spend our days doing while we're here in Emperor's Palace?"

Otto looked surprised by the question, "We'll be learning the same sort of things that we did at home, only here we will be taught by the finest in the land."

"What are we to be learning?"

"Weren't you having lessons in Genio?" Otto asked.

"I've come from Wishapton," Bellaydin admitted. "I haven't been to Genio since I was a child."

"Wishapton?" Kurth exclaimed. "You've been living in a bigger backwater than even I have."

"What sort of lessons should I have been taking?" Bellaydin asked.

Otto held out a hand, "Well, there's swordsmanship-"

"William did give me a few pointers-"

Otto hadn't finished. "Horsemanship, etiquette, history, poetry, dancing, heraldry..."

"Alright, alright, I think I get the picture. I may be a little behind."

"Don't worry," Kurth said, "you'll catch up. In fact, they'll insist on it."

Bellaydin rubbed his head.

Kurth smiled. There was a rueful tone to his voice. "You have plenty of time to learn everything. We're all stuck here for quite a while."

Bellaydin tried to make conversation. "Are you by any chance related to Augustin Bauer?"

Kurth pushed back his fringe. "He's my uncle. Haven't seen him for years though. Why do you ask?"

Bellaydin scratched his chin. "I met him in Aderilund."

"He's an envoy for the queen, or some such nonsense. Or at least he used to be. Father mentioned some scandal, and apparently the queen recalled Augustin."

The information surprised Bellaydin. Was it possible that Augustin would come to Emparia, and Polnygar with him?

Otto, silent until then, threw out a question. "Shouldn't that mean he returns home?"

Kurth threw up his hands. "Don't ask me, I'm not his keeper. He's probably thought it best to stay far away. He and father do not get on. And it's worse when they're both sober."

"I see," said Bellaydin. He wondered if there was some deeper tale to the rift between the brothers of House Bauer.

In the meantime, Kurth decided to steer the topic back to Bellaydin. "So tell me, you grew up with elves. What are they like?"

"Arrogant," Bellaydin said. "I thought I said that."

"What about the women?"

"About the same."

Kurth persisted. "No, I mean, elven women, what are they *like*?"

Bellaydin blinked and shook his head. "I don't know what you're saying."

"Good gods, Ap'Lydin, do I have to draw you a picture? I mean, you've had lovers haven't you?"

Bellaydin went red and stammered. "I...no..."

"Oh," Kurth said. "I just assumed that... Well, don't worry about it Ap'Lydin, it will happen. I have heard stories about the women in the capital, you know." Kurth gave a knowing smile and Bellaydin grimaced in response. Otto gave him a sympathetic look.

Kurth rubbed a finger against his lips. "So you never looked at any of the elf maids and wondered..."

Bellaydin looked down at his feet, hoping no one would notice his flushed cheeks. "Sometimes."

Kurth smiled widely. "Of course you did."

"But it would have never happened," Bellaydin said. "Most elves see humans as foolish, ugly and uncouth."

Kurth winked. "Smarter than they look, aren't they?"

It was not long after that that the Privy Council began their meeting session, and Otto and Kurth went to rejoin their families. Bellaydin was left to wander the castle alone. Compared to the fortress in Wishapton, Castle Emparia was enormous, and Bellaydin wondered if he might get lost if he strayed too far from the Great Hall. However he was hungry, and following his nose, he felt certain he could find his way to the kitchen.

The smells of roasted meats drew him down several corridors towards a covered arcade. From here the castle connected to a smaller annexe, likely to keep the heat and smoke from the kitchens from flooding the living areas around the Great Hall. The annexe's entrance opened up into several large rooms that radiated heat. With a castle this size, the kitchens spanned across several rooms and Bellaydin thought it likely dozens of servants would be working within, labouring night and day to feed the castle's residents.

He entered one of the kitchens, drawn by the aroma of roasting beef. Inside, several servants worked over a stove, preparing and cooking pieces of meat. A large ginger cat eyed him from a wooden table in the corner, before it laid its head down and went to sleep. Most of the workers ignored Bellaydin, going about their tasks as directed by a large woman who kept moving from between the tables and the stove. A girl, buxom and brown-haired, was sweeping the floor. She noticed Bellaydin and called out to the large woman.

"Ma! One of those squires is in here again. I think he wants something to eat."

51

"It's not that fat one again is it?" the large woman yelled in between tasting he broth.

"No, this one's proper skinny," the girl said. "He probably needs a good feed."

The large woman laughed. "Well, you deal with him, Rhiannon. Give him something to eat if that's what he wants, just get him out of my hair. I've got the queen, three dukes, three earls and however many hangers-on who need to be fed tonight."

"Alright, ma," Rhiannon said. She put the broom to one side, and pointed to Bellaydin, "You, to the tables."

Bellaydin did as he was told, and sat down on one of the long wooden benches at the far side of the room. Rhiannon came closer, putting her long brown hair behind her ears as she grabbed one of the serving plates. The girl had a round and freckled face which made her look younger than she was, but looking at her figure, Bellaydin knew that she was likely his age if not a little older.

Giving Bellaydin a quick glance Rhiannon ladled some stew into the plate, along with some cooked vegetables, and brought the meal over to him. She moved the cat aside. "Shoo Malken." With a miaow of protest, it jumped off the bench and Rhiannon put the plate down in front of Bellaydin. "So, skinny squire, what's your name?" she asked.

"Um, Bellaydin."

"Well, Bellaydin – my eyes are up here."

Bellaydin flushed, and looked up, stammering an apology, but the girl's expression was light and it was obvious she was only teasing. She passed him a spoon, and he started to eat eagerly.

Rhiannon sat down opposite him. "So you're the Ap'Lydin are you?" she asked. "Pleased to meet you. I'm Rhiannon, and that there over at the stove barking orders is my ma, Rowena."

"Your mother's accent sounds a bit-"

"Goriinchian? That's because she is. She came here as a young girl. I was born right here in Emperor's Palace, though, inside the castle at that. Don't take us for Horned God cultists either. We're both true faithful of the triune."

She dipped her finger into the broth and sucked it. "What about you then, Bellaydin Ap'Lydin? I hear gossip that you were raised by elves."

"It's not as simple as that," Bellaydin said in between mouthfuls of broth, "I lived in Genio for the first five years of my life, then my parents were...my parents died, and I was raised by my stepmother in Aderilund."

Rhiannon frowned. "Oh, that's very sad," she said. "I can't imagine what it must have been like to grow up so alone."

Bellaydin shrugged. "As I said, I had my stepmother, and my sister."

"Stepmother." Rhiannon furrowed her brow. "So, did your father remarry before he died or something?"

Bellaydin rubbed his temples. "No. It isn't like that. She's my elder half-sister's mother; my father was with Saegralanna before he was married to my mother."

Rhiannon just stared at Bellaydin. He let out a nervous laugh. "Sorry. I think I even confused myself then."

From the kitchen came Rowena's voice. "Rhiannon! I need you to start cutting those turnips."

Rhiannon turned her head towards her mother. "In a minute, ma." She shook her head and turned back to Bellaydin, "How are you getting along with the squires?"

Bellaydin waved his hand in a non-committal manner. Rhiannon laughed. "That well, eh?"

"Some of them are not exactly friendly."

"Well I know you aren't talking about Piggy," Rhiannon said, "Since he's friends with anyone who gives him a pork pie. And I know Kurth is said to be a bit abrasive, but he rarely holds grudges. Let me guess, you are talking about Edgar and Tancred?"

Bellaydin nodded.

Rhiannon sighed. "Tancred has been here for a while. He was cupbearer to the Duke of Emperor's Palace, amongst other things. His parents have great ambitions for him. But in the end, he is just a follower. He just does whatever his more important friends say. But Edgar, well, let's just say when he sees me in the corridor he doesn't like to make eye-contact. He thinks it is beneath his undoubted good breeding and royal blood. Has he told you he's fourth in line to the throne already?"

"Uh, yes."

"It's his favourite conversation starter," Rhiannon said. "You can see why he's such a charmer."

"Rhiannon! The turnips!"

Rhiannon grunted in frustration. "Alright, ma."

Standing up she turned back to Bellaydin, "Bellaydin, feel free to come here whenever you're hungry. Maybe we can put some meat on those skinny arms." She pinched him affectionately. "And maybe we can start our conversation without you staring at my chest."

Bellaydin went red, which seemed to amuse Rhiannon further.

"Goodbye skinny," she said, and returned to her work.

By the time Bellaydin had returned to his room, Geoffrey was waiting there for him.

"There you are," the knight said. "Where in the name of the gods have you been? I'm just here to say goodbye."

"Goodbye? You're leaving?" Bellaydin said.

"The countess is returning to Genio, and I'm leaving with her. I'm sorry, Bellaydin. I thought I had more time, but Haakon believes she must be established as quickly as possible in Hotar Citadel so that her vassals accept her."

"I see," Bellaydin said, trying to hide his disappointment.

"Look, I'll try to visit as often as I can. Whenever I can make the trip to the capital. In the meantime, keep your nose clean, yes? William would've been proud of you."

"Perhaps we should go for a drink?" Bellaydin asked.

Geoffrey's face dropped. "I'd love to, but there's no time. Maybe next time?"

He caught Bellaydin in a bear hug. "I'll see you around, Bela."

CHAPTER 4

Bellaydin woke early, ready for the first of his lessons.

He assembled with the other squires in the great hall. From there, after a morning meal, Martin escorted them to the chapel, where the first of their instructors awaited them. Religion was something Bellaydin had never paid much attention to in Aderilund, and he knew even less about the religious practices of his birth country. The royal chaplain, Father Athelstan, certainly seemed to be aware of that, if his penetrating questions were any guide.

"So if I am correct, then you have received no education in the Faith of the Triune," Father Athelstan said with a tone of condescension. "You have not heard the word of the holy patriarchs of Ralom?"

"No," Bellaydin said.

The old priest looked sorely troubled. "I heard that elves were outside the true faith, but I am shocked to hear the level of ignorance they have left you in. Do not worry, Bellaydin. We shall endeavour to save your soul. You shall know of the Sun King's glory, you will know the grace of the Queen of Light and Life, and you will know the sacrifice the Divine Martyr has suffered for you."

The chaplain stroked his beard, his fingers twisting the ends of it as he spoke. "But perhaps I shouldn't be surprised. Your father never was one for following the teachings of the patriarchs, and rarely does the apple fall very far from the tree. The Church warned him about the consequences for his soul if he continued to fornicate with that elven temptress, but he chose the empty pursuit of personal pleasure over his soul. In the end, it would cost him."

Bellaydin's face felt hot as the chaplain talked about his father. Even more than that was the disparaging reference to his stepmother. Saegralanna may not have been his birth mother, but he loved her as if she was. She had, after all, raised him for most of his life. He wanted to say something cutting in response, but looking around at the other squires, he could see that nobody else thought what the chaplain had said was unreasonable. He decided not to say anything but merely glared at the chaplain, hoping that his silent anger was apparent.

"Take a seat with the other squires," Athelstan said. "And listen carefully. If you wish to enter the Realms of Righteousness, you must learn what is expected of you."

Bellaydin eased himself down on to the bench next to Kurth, shooting a sullen glance at the chaplain. As the class began, it soon became obvious to Bellaydin that he was going to lag behind all the other squires. They had learned at least something about their faith from a young age and knew the basics. Bellaydin could barely even identify the holy symbols of the Triune – the sunburst for the Sun King, the star for the Silver Lady and the cross for the Divine Martyr. Unlike the staunchly monotheistic Goriinchians, the Emparians were henotheists; they certainly did not deny the divinity of other gods outside the Triune, but only considered the three gods of the faith of Ralom worthy of worship.

The other squires could answer questions that were put to them. Edgar rattled off the name of the first five Patriarchs of Ralom without hesitation, Tancred could list the main battles of the Vallistian Crusades, Otto knew the name of the first missionary in Emparia, and even Kurth could say the name of the four holy books of Ralom after some prompting. By contrast, Bellaydin's halting attempts to answer some of the chaplain's questions only evinced laughter from the other squires.

Eventually, the lesson was over, though not soon enough for Bellaydin's tastes, and he beat a hasty retreat back to his room to save himself further embarrassment. As he hurried back, he encountered the Duke of Alariat in one of the corridors.

"Something the matter, Bellaydin?" Haakon asked. His face was kind and reassuring.

"Oh, nothing really, I'm just beginning to think I don't know as much as I thought I did."

"There is always more to learn, my dear boy. That is one of the one few axioms of life."

Bellaydin shrugged. "I'll survive. How are you?"

"Fine, fine," Haakon said, though he rubbed his chest as he spoke. "The Privy Council wants to take the fight to the Goriinchians. Scouts have reported that the forces of the Warchief Aonghus Culainn are regrouping, and have been sighted across the southern border."

"Already?" Bellaydin said. He thought that the loss the Goriinchians had suffered at Wishapton would cause to them to pull back and pause in their war, but it seemed to have barely delayed them.

"So it seems. The nobles are squabbling over who should lead the army. Most of them expect an easy victory, so are looking to take the lion's share of the glory. "

"What about Wulfric?" Bellaydin knew that the Duke of Oldharbour would not have been one to underestimate the Goriinchians.

"The Duke of Oldharbour did not stay long at the gathering. I think he believes that the other nobles are not taking the threat seriously. For their part, the other nobles accused Wulfric of wanting to wage a private war against Goriinchia without the approval of the crown. So, of course, he refused to answer such slander and left."

"So who is going to lead the army then?" Bellaydin asked.

"The queen and the remaining nobles nominated Anson Mainstream, Earl of Warding, for the task. In truth, it was mainly at the Duke of Georgeton's urging – those two are close allies – but the other nobles acquiesced and they convinced the queen."

Bellaydin remembered Geoffrey's less than glowing description of Anson Mainstream. "Is the Earl of Warding the right man to lead the army?"

Haakon looked around and drew closer. "Anson Mainstream has ambition, but little else to recommend him for the position. Nevertheless, the royal army will depart Emperor's Palace tomorrow under the standards of the Morcor stallion and the Mainstream boar. Luckily his sworn sword Sir Bors Thornton does have a grasp of proper strategy. I can only hope he can influence his liege lord."

"Are you allowed to tell me all this?" Bellaydin asked. "Aren't the Privy Council meetings meant to be private?"

"Do not worry yourself, my boy," Haakon said. "I have not told you anything which will not soon be public knowledge anyway." He rubbed his hands together. "I am planning to raise your profile at court, Bellaydin. I believe you could do well with your name better known. Therefore, I am arranging for you to hunt with Her Majesty."

"Me? Hunt with the queen?"

"There will be others there, but I believe I can ensure that you are the one noticed by Her Majesty. Do not worry about it now, I will make the arrangements. Just keep your schedule uncluttered."

"Yes, of course."

"Good. Now, if you'll excuse me, I have some matters of my own to attend to. Good afternoon."

***

The next morning, at the blast of the trumpets, Bellaydin looked out the window and saw the Emparian armies leaving the city to go fight the Goriinchians in the south. At the vanguard of the army marched the flag bearers. One bore the familiar royal standard of House Morcor while the other flag bearer held the standard of House Mainstream. Their armour gleamed and glittered in the sun as rows of knights, men-at-arms and crossbowmen marched in perfect formation. Citizens of the city waved and cheered as the soldiers passed and there was great confidence in the likelihood of an Emparian victory.

Why then did Bellaydin feel as if this would be the last time he would see this army intact? Haakon certainly had his own private reservations of the Earl of Warding's abilities, but did believe that Mainstream's sworn sword, Sir Bors Thornton, was a knight of ability and with a reputation for competence. The other nobles had confidence that the Earl of Warding could lead the Emparian counter-attack, but Haakon had suggested it was politics that had forced the choice.

Bellaydin shook his head. It was not his place to worry about any of that, and besides, he had far more pressing matters on his mind. He had more lessons today, and he hoped to do better than he had in theology. He washed and dressed quickly and, with food on his mind, he made a quick detour to the kitchens. A familiar voice greeted him amongst the smoke and heat.

"Well, look who's here – the skinny squire," Rhiannon said.

Bellaydin sat and within moments Rhiannon had bought him a plate with some dark bread, salted kippers and a mug of ale. "So, skinny, tell me, how are things going?" Rhiannon asked, placing her hand under her chin and looking at him with interest.

"I realised yesterday that I don't know a damn thing about religion," Bellaydin admitted between bites of bread.

"You and me both," Rhiannon said. "The idiots around here keep asking ma and me about the Horned God, even though she left Goriinchia when she was still suckling at her mother's breast. So how in the name of the gods would I know anything about that?"

"Yes, but you at least know something of your own faith, of the Emparian faith, don't you? I can't even claim that."

"Wouldn't think the elves would bother teaching you any of that. I always thought they were godless folk anyway. Or maybe, they just consider themselves gods. Do they worship anything at all, apart from themselves?"

Bellaydin chuckled. For some elves, especially spellweavers such as Lord Ivellios, "worshipping themselves" would certainly be an accurate description of their beliefs. For the most part, however, the elves took their ancient religious practices very seriously.

"It's called the Transcendent Court," Bellaydin said. "They believe the greatest of their ancestors are ascendant in the heavens and watching over the Eldara on the mortal world below."

Rhiannon laughed. "Does the chaplain know you were raised by heathens?"

Bellaydin nodded. "Oh he does. And I'm sure I'll never hear the end of it."

"You poor skinny boy," she said with mock sympathy. "I tell you what I'll do. You can have my holy book of the patriarchs. Maybe you'll learn something..."

Bellaydin was about to say it was not necessary, but Rhiannon was already walking towards the other side of the kitchen where she pulled an old, worn book from the shelf. "You be careful with this," she said. "It's the only book I have. Don't you dare forget to return it either."

"Thanks," Bellaydin said.

Bellaydin finished up and, thanking Rhiannon again, left the kitchen with the book. He returned to his room to place the book on his cabinet before going on to join the other squires at the day's lessons. He saw Kurth and Otto in the corridor and picked up his pace to catch up with the pair.

"Morning Ap'Lydin," said Kurth. "Did you sleep in?"

"Yes. Truth be told I'm only awake now because of the trumpets."

"Piggy's father woke you up too?" Kurth said.

"I'm sorry," mumbled Otto.

"Don't worry Piggy," said Kurth. "You should see the way my father wakes me up. There are no walls thick enough to block out Alfred Bauer's singing."

The first lesson concerned heraldry, where a herald so ancient he might as well be fossilised droned on about the various noble houses of Emparia and their symbols. Bellaydin was already familiar with the symbols of the Ap'Lydins, Morcors, Mainstreams, Zalltors, Highcrowns and Bauers, but the herald now taught Bellaydin the sigils of other houses, including the chimaera of the Ran-Tyrons and the linnorm of the "True Tyrons". After the disastrous class on religious studies, Bellaydin was happy to finally be learning something he found easy, but the price the class extracted in boredom was startlingly high. He looked around at the other squires and noted that they too were finding the class tedious, so Bellaydin reasoned that perhaps he was not the only one finding heraldry a rather uncomplicated subject.

After heraldry came poetry, where another old man tutored the squires, doing nothing but instructing them to copy out poems written by men centuries dead. Bellaydin had no idea how this was supposed to teach him how to craft poetry, but he did it all the same. The lesson ended with them reciting the poems that had been written down, whereupon the other squires mocked Bellaydin for having a peculiar accent. Bellaydin knew he spoke with the inflection of someone who had grown up abroad, but until now he had not thought much of it. Now he was acutely aware of his accent and felt oddly self-conscious and embarrassed of the way he spoke.

During dancing, Bellaydin discovered, much to his horror, that he possessed two left feet and a propensity to trip over his own ankles. While Edgar de Morcor glided serenely across the floor, Bellaydin was left to stumble and topple over every time he tried to execute a manoeuvre. His only consolation was that he was not the worst dancer there. Otto sweated every time he moved and Kurth barely tried at all.

"I thought the elves were supposed to be light on their feet," Edgar had mocked Bellaydin. "Or is that another thing you never learned?"

Only Tancred had laughed at Edgar's weak attempt at an insult. Otto looked confused and Kurth smirked but said nothing.

Finally, towards the end of the day, the squires arrived at their weapons instructor, where they were to be taught the martial arts. The instructor was a Vallistian mercenary named Don Jalagado, a swordsman possessed of an olive complexion, a neat black beard and a flamboyant fighting style.

"I am here today to turn you boys into men. To teach you the manly art of war. Who here knows how to use a sword?"

Most of the squires raised their hand, including Bellaydin.

"Most of you it seems. We shall see. You, skinny dark-haired one. Yes, you. Come over here."

Don Jalagado handed Bellaydin a wooden sword. "You and I are going to test our skills against each other. You say you know how to use this? Let me see."

The instructor held up his sword and waited. Bellaydin looked confused.

"Now?"

"Yes, now," the instructor said impatiently. "Your enemy will not wait for you."

Bellaydin lunged forward, attacking clumsily, and the instructor dodged out the way easily. He let out a chuckle and mocked Bellaydin. "Oh no, that was awful."

Bellaydin swung again and Jalagado once again evaded the blow to titters from the audience of squires. "Surely you can do better."

"Yaaah," Bellaydin screamed and charged towards the instructor. Don Jalagado merely sidestepped Bellaydin's attack, causing Bellaydin to overbalance and collapse to the floor.

"I think that is enough."

Jalagado held out a hand and helped Bellaydin up.

"There is a vast difference between knowing how to hold a sword, and being a true master of the martial arts. Swinging a sword is enough to defeat a peasant soldier, and many you face may well be as such. But to defeat a truly skilled swordsman, you will need to bring some tricks of your own to the table." He patted Bellaydin on the back. "Good. Get back with the others."

Bellaydin returned to the other squires. Edgar de Morcor sneered as Bellaydin walked passed.

"Now squires, I want you to watch me carefully, and copy my stances as you see them."

Bellaydin did his best to emulate Don Jalagado, but found that he felt stiff and sore all over. It was not just his body that was bruised, however. Sword fighting had been the one thing he felt he had already mastered, but this instructor had shown Bellaydin up as an ignorant clod within minutes.

"Now, let us see how you fare against each other. Come up and take a sword." He brought a pile of wooden swords.

"When are we going to fight with real swords?" Kurth complained.

"Ah, another expert," Don Jalagado said. "You will be paired with me, I think."

He paired up the other squires. Tancred would fight with Otto, and Bellaydin found himself put up against Edgar.

"Is this another thing they forgot to teach you in Aderilund?" Edgar laughed.

"Would you shut up?" Bellaydin said irritably, as he raised his wooden practice sword. "I don't see you doing any better."

Edgar raised his practice sword as well, and after he and Bellaydin performed the customary salute, they began their duel.

The first thing Bellaydin realised was that Edgar was far more skilled than he expected. He was quick as well, able to move about with ease. The only thing Bellaydin had working in his favour was Edgar's colossal arrogance, as the squire often neglected his defence, preferring instead to batter his opponent into submission with aggressive moves. Bellaydin exploited this and gave Edgar a few beatings for his trouble. Edgar scowled at each and every one, but pretended to not be hurt, though a few minutes after the duel had ended, Bellaydin was sure he saw Edgar rub a few new bruises when he thought no one was looking.

The martial arts lesson was the last lesson for the day, and after it ended he went to the kitchens for something to eat. Rhiannon was not there, but another member of the serving staff provided him some bread and salted meat to eat which he took to his room. He decided it might be nice to rest and recuperate with some privacy. He finished the food quickly, eating while he looked out the window at the city below. The teeming streets and noise of Emperor's Palace was so unlike what he was used to. For the twelve years he had lived there, Aderial was serene, sedate and utterly boring. This place made him feel alive, though he admitted the smell would take some getting used to.

Bellaydin hoped to start some of his study for the religious class after his meal, but after flipping through a few pages of the holy book he received from Rhiannon, he found his eyelids drooping, and decided instead to relax for a while on the bed. Within moments he was asleep.

Visions of the Battle of Wishapton consumed his sleep. Bellaydin was fighting there again, with his cousin William and with Geoffrey and with Duke Haakon. This time, however, it was not Goriinchians they were fighting, but men of metal – strange automata who were impervious to any blow. The automata were implacable, unstoppable and they were laying waste to Wishapton. Before long the automata surrounded him, and came towards him. Bellaydin became aware of a presence, somewhere above, a pair of eyes in the darkness – strange, feral and alien. He saw the face of the Duke of Oldharbour, Wulfric Highcrown, but within minutes the duke's face disappeared, replaced with that of Ygarak, the Prophet-King of the Goriinchians.

Bellaydin awoke, heart pounding. He lay on the bed for a few minutes to regain his composure before standing and washing his face. There was a knock on the door.

"Squire Ap'Lydin?" came a voice.

"Yes?" Bellaydin said. "Who is it?"

It was the castle steward, Martin. "I am here to extend an invitation from his grace the Duke of Emperor's Palace. He would be honoured to host you in his quarters for a drink if you are not otherwise occupied."

"The honour would be mine, of course," said Bellaydin. "Um, when?"

"As soon as you are able," Martin said.

"Very well," said Bellaydin. "Lead the way."

Martin nodded and took Bellaydin to the west wing of Castle Emparia, where the Duke of Emperor's Palace kept his private rooms. The steward guided Bellaydin to a sitting room and advised him to take a seat. Bellaydin did so, easing into a comfortable looking armchair.

"The duke will be with you shortly," Martin said before departing.

"Thank you," Bellaydin said.

Bellaydin did not have to wait long until Edmund Tallcastle, the Duke of Emperor's Palace emerged, leaning on his walking stick for strength. "Ah, Squire Ap'Lydin," he said. "How good of you to accept my invitation."

Next to the duke stood a tall elegant woman of middle years. Her hair was dark, and she had a slightly exotic cast to her features. "Oh, excuse me, this is Her Majesty Eloise de Morcor, the Dowager Queen." Eloise held out a hand and Bellaydin took it and kissed it respectfully.

The queen looked at Edmund. "Another Ap'Lydin, Your Grace? Is Haakon planning to throw him at my daughter as well?" She spoke with a foreign lilt.

"I wouldn't know, Your Majesty," Edmund said.

"It is a pleasure to meet you, Squire Ap'Lydin," she said.

"Can you not stay for a moment, Your Majesty?" the duke asked.

"No," she said, "I have an appointment with my daughter. I will speak to you later, Your Grace."

As Queen Eloise left, the duke, noticing Bellaydin's expression, explained, "Our lady the queen's mother is from Lerid, and she still speaks as she did when she first arrived here twenty-five years ago."

"What did she mean by 'another Ap'Lydin'?" Bellaydin asked.

"The Duke of Alariat had some idea in the last four years that he would wed Queen Amaryllis to the Earl of Genio."

Bellaydin blinked. He had not heard William mention that. "I had no idea."

"It wasn't exactly public knowledge. And the sad events at Wishapton have ended such plans anyway." The duke smiled and heaved his bulk down into the chair opposite Bellaydin.

"I must thank you for coming today."

"You honour me with the invitation, Your Grace, I could hardly say no," Bellaydin said.

"Maybe not," the duke said. "But I appreciate it all the same."

Bellaydin fidgeted in an attempt to hide his nervousness. The duke noticed this and smiled.

"There is no need to be nervous, my young friend," he said. "This is nothing formal. I wish merely to get to know you. It is very rare that we have a new member of any of the great families appear, and I have been fascinated by your tale ever since I first heard that Earl William Ap'Lydin had brought his cousin back from Aderilund."

"I'm not that fascinating Your Grace, honestly," said Bellaydin.

"Most of us would think that about ourselves, Bellaydin. If only we could see how others viewed us. As for you, young man, it has been a long time since you and I last met. You were but a babe in your mother's arms when you were first presented to King Henry at court."

"Did you know my parents?"

"Alusine and Eleanor? Oh yes, I can say that I did. Alusine and I were of a similar age and moved in the same circles. I was never as close to him as the Dukes of Alariat and Oldharbour, but we were close enough to have called each other by first name. Wulfric, Alusine and Haakon, though – they were closer than brothers. They were knighted together, shed blood together and were inseparable from that day forth. Alusine rode with King

Henry at the Battle of Goriinch Hill, where we defeated the forces of the Tyrons, and Henry claimed the throne. Alusine's brother, Caradoc Ap'Lydin, had been the Earl of Genio but divided loyalties meant that Caradoc died in the same battle. We all expected that Alusine would claim his brother's title for himself, but instead he settled for regent in his infant nephew's name."

The duke looked wistful for a moment. "And now poor William himself has passed on. A pity."

Bellaydin tried not to dwell on his cousin's death again, since he knew doing so would only cause him pain. He pressed the duke for more information on his parents.

"And what of my mother?"

"Ah yes, Eleanor Tyron. A passionate woman, to say the least. Her mother was Harriet de Morcor – King Henry's younger sister, and there were always some rumours that Harriet's marriage to Kalen Tyron was not entirely voluntary. Henry, for his part, certainly believed they had forced his sister and he never forgave the Tyrons."

"King Henry was my great-uncle then?" Bellaydin asked in shock. He had certainly never heard of this royal connection before. He'd been unaware of his mother's prestigious lineage but that should have been no surprise considering how isolated Aderilund was. Little more than his parents' names and a few vague recollections was all he really had to know them by.

"Well," the duke said, "I suppose he was. Harriet was never likely to inherit the throne – Henry had three sons of his own and two younger brothers, but with the losses in the Emparian Civil War, well...."

Martin entered, carrying a bottle of wine and two goblets. He placed the goblets on the table between Bellaydin and the duke and filled them.

Rather suddenly, the duke sneezed twice, in quick succession.

Martin looked concerned. "Your Grace, are you alright?"

The duke waved a hand. "Yes, yes, Martin. I'm fine." He sneezed again and fingered the side of his chair, holding up a few strands of ginger hair. "I think that damn cat from the kitchen has visited my chambers again. I always sneeze after it sheds in here."

Martin frowned. "I'll talk to the kitchen staff. It won't come in again."

"Don't hurt the poor creature. Just keep it out of here." The duke looked back towards Bellaydin, eyes roaming. "Now, where were we? Oh yes, Eleanor. She was the last of four children born to Kalen and Harriet – in fact, Harriet died bringing her daughter into the world. Eleanor was always a wilful child, and grew into quite a determined lady, more so when she became the last surviving Tyron at the end of the civil war. Some advised the king to have her executed, wanting an end to the bloody wars for good. "

Bellaydin felt uneasy. He stared into his goblet of wine. "They considered having my mother killed?"

Edmund shook his head. "Only some did, and it was not for long. Oswin Zalltor was the principal instigator of that idea, but King Henry would never agree to such a thing. Eleanor was his own niece, and she looked too much like her mother for Henry to want any harm to come to her. So I advised him that there was only one way out. She had to be married off, and to someone whose loyalty to the crown was impeccable. Unfortunately, most of us, Henry's companions from the very beginning of the war, were already married and getting on in years. Only Alusine was still a bachelor, and so it was to him that the king gave the command. Alusine was reluctant but eventually agreed to the match. It was only later that I found out why he was so reluctant. In the years before this Alusine had taken a lover – and not just any lover, but the daughter of the elven ambassador to Emparia. The damn thing nearly caused a war. Alusine set his lover aside at his king's command and married the woman his king asked him to, but I don't think he was ever happy, not truly."

Bellaydin felt a bit deflated. Although Geoffrey had told him his parents' marriage was arranged, he had at least hoped to hear that there had been some attraction between them not a messily arranged pairing intended to end a disastrous civil war. At the same time, he felt for his stepmother. She was a good woman and didn't deserve to be separated from her love because of politics.

"They fought relentlessly about many things," Edmund said. "But nothing caused as many arguments as Alusine's bastard. The half-elf girl."

Bellaydin felt a sudden flash of anger at the duke's words. "Polnygar," he said slowly. "My sister's name is Polnygar. And she's no bastard."

Edmund's brow furrowed. "I understand that you might not like hearing that word, Bellaydin. But it is the truth. There could be no legal marriage between Alusine and his elf lover. The church would never recognise it. Eleanor insisted he send the girl away, claiming she was an embarrassment to his household. Alusine felt otherwise, of course, and treated the girl as if she were his legitimate offspring. He even insisted on others addressing her by his surname, which the girl was technically not entitled to hold."

Bellaydin's shoulders slumped. How could his mother have been that cruel to his sister? The warm, wistful memories he had of his parents were dissolving with every word. He looked at Edmund, his eyes pleading. "Is there nothing good you can tell me of them?"

"Do not misunderstand me, Bellaydin," the duke said, "In time your father and mother grew to love each other in their own way, but their relationship was always tempestuous. That was just the way things happened. It was such a shame, for them to have met the fate they did."

Bellaydin nodded. "Simon Enlim is not a name I will ever forget."

"Of course not. And no doubt he is now in the Underworld, experiencing the ultimate fate of all murderers." The duke made a sign against evil. "When I was a boy, my father told me that Enlim was Goriinchian, brought to Genio by Earl William the Stout. When I was older, I realised this was an impossibility, as that Earl had ruled Genio seventy years prior. Either my father was mistaken, or the Enlim that Earl William discovered was an ancestor of the cultist. Perhaps a grand-grandfather or so?" He seemed to consider it for a moment, before continuing. "The cultist was not well known before he joined Alusine's household and for a period, the two were almost inseparable. Enlim was practically Alusine's shadow." The duke sighed. "And then it happened. I remember how shocked we were that such a terrible crime had been committed. The king banned the faith in retribution, and Haakon spent days in seclusion. Worst of all was Wulfric. It changed him, your father's death. The man we knew died, and a stranger took his place."

"What do you mean?"

"It may not seem like it now, but Wulfric was once warm and cheerful, and one of the most amiable fellows you could ever meet. He made friends easily and was a lover of life. But when Enlim murdered Alusine, all Wulfric's dreams and desires drained away to be replaced with single-minded- revenge against the Horned God and all his followers. He even broke it off with his paramour, expelling her from his castle the day after Alusine died."

"The duke had a mistress?" Bellaydin found it hard to rationalise the information with the cold man he had come to know.

Edmund noted Bellaydin's surprise, giving a small chuckle. "Oh yes, and she was only the latest of many over the years. As I said he was once a very different man. But that day, everything changed. It was as if he was possessed by some spirit of vengeance, one that would not rest until it had wiped the cult from the face of the earth."

Bellaydin remembered the incident on the road to the capital. "He certainly hates the Horned God and anyone who worships him."

"You are putting it mildly, squire. Wulfric's obsession has driven him to dark places. He would nail that crime against every half-mad cultist and deluded worshipper of the Horned God, whether they were responsible for it or not. He stirs up and antagonises the Privy Council constantly, meaning I spend my waning years keeping he and the Duke of Georgeton from each other's throats. Wulfric has few real friends left. He is estranged from what remains of his family. Even his friendship with the Duke of Alariat is strained, and when they were young they were practically joined at the hip."

Martin poured more wine into their goblets, and Bellaydin found himself staring intently at the man's face. It was odd but in many ways, Martin and the duke actually looked quite alike. Bellaydin wondered if it was a coincidence.

"Do you have any family, Your Grace?" Bellaydin asked the duke as Martin bowed and left the room.

"I am the last survivor of House Tallcastle, I am afraid. My daughter was King Henry's first queen, and she bore him three sons, all of whom died in the Emparian Civil War with their mother. Henry grieved for many years before he married again and fathered our current queen."

"I'm sorry I brought it up Your Grace. That must have been heartbreaking for you."

"Indeed it was, my young squire, but I grieved and moved on. In serving the crown I still have my uses," the duke said, draining the rest of his cup. "Now, I have enjoyed this, but I must return to my duties. Perhaps another time then?"

"Of course, Your Grace," Bellaydin said.

The duke stood and genuflected to the younger man. "It was a pleasure to meet you, squire."

Bellaydin had barely left the duke's chambers when he nearly collided with someone in the corridor.

"I'm sorry." He looked up, coming face to face with a giant of a man, dressed in mail and wearing a black surcoat with the sigil of a grey skull. He was of florid complexion and black of hair and beard, glaring at Bellaydin in silence.

Bellaydin stood, frozen in place before another voice spoke up.

"Sorry, squire. We didn't see you there," said Oswin Zalltor, the Duke of Georgeton. "This is Sir Dallen Withers, finest of my sworn swords. Unfortunately, an old battle wound to his throat makes speaking difficult."

Sir Dallen narrowed his eyes and nodded.

"Oh, I'm sorry to hear that," Bellaydin said. He could see the faint outline of a scar on the man's throat.

"We must be going. His Grace is expecting us. Come along, Sir Dallen."

Oswin and his sworn sword pushed past Bellaydin and disappeared into the duke's chambers. As they did Bellaydin shuddered. He wasn't sure why, but Sir Dallen's presence unnerved him. Menace radiated from the man's being. Bellaydin wondered if it might be an omen of some sort but then thought better of it, shaking his head at his own foolishness. He returned to his own quarters, and passed his time reading the holy book he had borrowed from Rhiannon, comparing it with the notes he had taken from his theology lesson.

If the basics of the religion were easy to understand, then it was the theology around these gods that was complicated. Each of the Patriarchs of Ralom throughout history had made their own pronouncements throughout the years and had their own understandings of their god's desires, many of which contradicts with edicts issued by earlier Patriarchs. The result was a rather confused mess of internally opposing ideas. Theologians from Ralom to Emparia and everywhere in between argued vociferously with each other over the most esoteric details of their faith, so much so that Bellaydin wondered if it might be simpler for the gods themselves to come down from the heavens to sort things out.

When it was time for the evening meal, Bellaydin headed down to the great hall. It was tradition for the squires of the royal court to eat together for their main meal, and Bellaydin's tutors had impressed on him that they believed it an important ritual.

Bellaydin came down the stairs to see that Otto Mainstream was already there, tucking into a meal of bread and beef. A mug of ale rested in his meaty hand. He waved at Bellaydin.

"Where are the others?" Bellaydin asked, as he eased himself into a chair.

Otto squinted at him in between bites of food. "How should I know?"

Soon enough, however, the other squires arrived – Edgar de Morcor dressed in his finest clothes, with Tancred Zalltor trailing shortly behind him and Kurth Bauer a good distance behind them.

"Oh look, it's the fat one and the skinny one," Edgar said. "Are you sure it's wise sitting next to Piggy like that, Ap'Lydin? You know that he might flip the whole damn bench and throw you gods know where."

Otto stopped eating, and his face dropped. Bellaydin thought that the boy was about to cry, but instead he just stared at Edgar.

"How's your father going against the Goriinchians, Piggy?" Edgar said, as he and Tancred slipped into their usual seats. "Has he pissed himself and run away yet? The dukes are fools for putting him in charge. If they'd recall my uncle Sir Manford they'd win the war in a week, but the dukes are all too jealous of him so he has to cool his heels in Alariat."

"I thought he was 'cooling his heels' in Alariat because he tried to steal your father's mistress," said Kurth.

Edgar turned red. "You're a damned fool, Bauer. I have half a mind to cut out that tongue of yours and throw it in the fire."

"I'd like to see you try," Kurth said.

"Why you –" Edgar reached for his blade, but Tancred stayed his hand.

"Give it a rest, Edgar." Kurth groaned and rubbed his head. "Gods know that this headache is bad enough without hearing your voice."

Edgar scoffed. "You know what my father says about you Bauers? You have all the qualities of dogs – except loyalty."

Edgar and Tancred laughed. Amazingly, Kurth did as well. "Now, now, Edgar," he said. "We both know your father isn't clever enough to have come up with that."

Edgar sniffed. "Your father is a wine-sodden drunk ruling over a near bankrupt earldom. Or am I confusing him with someone else?"

Kurth just shook his head and began digging into the food laid out before him. Edgar smirked, apparently satisfied that he had silenced the squire from Tyronsville and began to pick out choice pieces of food for himself.

"Gods above, Piggy," Edgar complained. "You've eaten most of the beef. Mind yourself, Tancred, there's not much left."

Tancred Zalltor followed Edgar's lead and moved some meat onto his own plate. Bellaydin turned to Otto and quietly told the boy to ignore Edgar's taunts, but he knew it was already too late for that. The damage was done.

Edgar banged his goblet on the table. "Wine, damn it. Where is the wine?"

Kurth looked towards Edgar, "Would you stop that?"

Edgar banged his goblet again for good measure, giving Kurth a glare as he did so. Rhiannon came from the servant's entrance with a bottle of wine ready for serving. As she passed Bellaydin, she gave him a wink.

"At last. Where have you been, *girl*?" Edgar asked. His tone was patronising, ever more so since he and Rhiannon appeared to be about the same age.

"I am sorry, squire," Rhiannon said. "I was otherwise occupied. Let me fill your goblet."

As Rhiannon leant over to pour the wine Edgar leered over her body, his eyes roaming over the girl's bosom. Bellaydin noticed that Rhiannon kept her eyes on the goblet, and tried to ignore Edgar's obvious gaze. After she had finished with Edgar's goblet she filled that of Tancred, who merely nodded and mumbled thanks. As she filled Kurth's goblet he smiled at her and she blushed and smiled in response. She approached Otto and Bellaydin, holding up the wine bottle.

Otto shook his head vigorously, while Bellaydin pushed his goblet towards her.

"Yes, please," he said. She grinned at him and filled his goblet, emptying the bottle she had brought.

"Please call me if you need anything else," Rhiannon said, and disappeared back through the servant's entrance, leaving the squires by themselves.

"Please?" Edgar scoffed. "Is that the sort of grovelling you do around serving girls in Wishapton, Ap'Lydin? No wonder your house is nearly extinct."

"I think he was just being polite," Otto ventured.

"Shut your fat face, Piggy," Edgar said. "What do you say, Tancred, do you agree with me?"

Tancred looked around nervously and then shrugged. "Ah, I guess... I-"

"Can't let him have an opinion of his own, can you?" Kurth said.

"Bauer, you keep speaking but all I hear is *woof, woof, woof,*" Edgar said. He illustrated his point by making barking gestures with his hand.

"You know Edgar," Bellaydin said, raising his voice. "Maybe if you weren't so horrible to everyone you meet, you might have more friends than Tancred."

"Perhaps I should socialise with the serving staff then, as you evidently do." Edgar laughed. "Come, Tancred, I've lost my appetite." Edgar threw down his cutlery and departed, and Tancred rose from his seat as well.

"You know you don't have to follow him," Kurth said between bites of game hen. For a moment Tancred hesitated then, seeing Edgar depart, dashed past the table to join his friend.

Kurth sighed. "I really thought he might have a thought of his own there for a moment. Oh well." He pointed to Edgar's plate. "You know the kitchen staff probably spit in his food, right?"

Bellaydin looked at Kurth, not sure if the squire was being serious.

"Come on," Kurth said. "Don't pretend you'd be surprised."

The three remaining squires ate the rest of their meal in peace, discussing with each other their first day of lessons and the challenges therein. Bellaydin admitted to some anxiety regarding his lack of knowledge and skill in many areas, but Otto and Kurth were quite encouraging.

"Don't worry about it," Otto said. "You're clever. I'm sure you'll pick it up."

Kurth nodded, and then added, "Besides, none of this matters one bit. Before we know it we'll all be at war, and then, who in the name of the gods is going to care how good a dancer we are?"

CHAPTER 5

A sinister man appeared before Bellaydin. His mere presence was enough to unsettle Bellaydin, but when he spoke it was with a voice that came from the Underworld itself.

"Do you know me, Bellaydin Ap'Lydin?"

Bellaydin stood frozen, unable to respond. The shadows around the man grew, bending and twisting.

"Think on the dread you feel. What does that tell you? What name is written in blood?" At the man's feet was a pile of corpses. One of the corpses moved, and Bellaydin recoiled in shock. His father's face stared at him, glassy eyed and limp.

Bellaydin turned back to the shadowy man. "Enlim," he said. "Simon Enlim."

The figure inclined its head in acknowledgement.

"But you're dead," Bellaydin said, but the protest sounded feeble.

"Death is but a doorway, one that I have crossed through many times." The figure pulled down its hood, revealing a scarred and burned face.

Enlim gave a hideous cackle and as he did his features shifted and changed, his form melting into a younger, stronger one with an austere face and eyes like ice.

"Sir Dallen?" Bellaydin said to the new figure standing in front of him.

Sir Dallen drew a sword from his belt, and then without warning, charged forward, his weapon raised. Bellaydin threw up his hands as he awaited the inevitable.

He awoke in his bed, heart beating rapidly. It had been a dream. He went to the basin, washing his face as if to scrub the memory of the dream from his mind. Why had he dreamed of Simon Enlim? Why now? And why did he change into Sir Dallen?

***

That day Bellaydin and the other squires continued their studies into theology and heraldry, dancing and sword fighting, with tutorials in etiquette to the mix. The redoubtable Lady Edith Foxfield instructed them on the correct way to greet other nobles, how to hold their cutlery without embarrassing themselves, and the proper behaviour to observe when in the presence of royalty.

During the class Edgar declared loudly, for any who could hear, that he already knew all there was to know about etiquette, as he was of royal blood, and so it was particularly satisfying when Lady Edith rapped the squire across the knuckles with her cane when he spoke out of turn one too many times. Edgar bloviated and threatened a terrible vengeance on Lady Edith, but Bellaydin knew it was futile. Haakon had once told Bellaydin that Lady Edith was the queen's old nursemaid and Her Majesty was quite attached to the old battleaxe. The queen would never countenance any harm being done to Lady Foxfield.

Before too long the class was mercifully over and they had a short break before their next lesson. Bellaydin decided to visit Rhiannon in the kitchens to see how she was going and, he had to admit to himself, to satisfy the hunger he had endured while being drilled by Lady Edith on the reason to never to address a duke as "my lord".

Malken greeted Bellaydin, rubbing against his legs affectionately. Bellaydin reached down and scratched the cat behind the ears. Malken responded in kind with a loud purr.

Rhiannon came towards Bellaydin with a tray of pastries. "He likes you," she said, looking down at the cat. "You should be flattered, cats can be quite discerning." She placed the tray down on the table. "Here, we made some pies. Try them."

Bellaydin bit into the pastry, tasting rich gravy filled with chunks of venison. "Mmm...not bad." He washed it down with some ale. "I hope Edgar didn't annoy you too much."

Rhiannon smiled and stole some of Bellaydin's food. "Him? I already knew he was an ass. Well, he may not like to look me in the eyes, but he sure doesn't have a problem with looking at other parts of me."

"What's his problem anyway?"

"Isn't it obvious?" she asked. She shook her head, "And I thought you were clever, skinny boy."

"What's obvious?"

"He's threatened by you. He might have Tancred and Piggy cowed, and he thinks Kurth too common to give a damn about, but he doesn't know what do with you."

She lowered her voice to a whisper. "Is it true you're the old king's great nephew?"

"Who told you that?" Bellaydin said.

"Never mind that, is it true?"

"Yes," Bellaydin shrugged. "I mean, that's what I've been told."

83

"There you have it then," she said. "He's been so busy talking himself up because of his so-called royal blood, and then he finds you have just as much as he does. Now he'll have to come up with some achievements of his own and stop living off his family name." She chewed a piece of pastry and opened her eyes wide in mock concern. "The poor boy."

"Rhiannon!" came Rowena's voice.

"Coming mother!" Rhiannon called back. She turned to Bellaydin, "I'd better clean up. Until next time, skinny."

She gave a mock curtsy and then, laughing, took Bellaydin's plates as he left to return to his room. He arrived back just in time to change into his clothes for his next lesson. This time a trainer was to be instructing the squires in horsemanship and for a change Bellaydin felt a little more comfortable with what lay ahead. After all, he had ridden horses before – most recently on the trip from Wishapton to Emperor's Palace – and didn't seem to have much trouble. To be fair he'd never moved particularly fast on any of these horses, but he didn't think that would cause too much of a difference. He'd never been anywhere near a horse in Aderilund, so as far as Bellaydin was concerned, he'd done pretty well with what he had already learned.

The horse master was a brawny young man named Ferdy, as slow and deliberate as the horses he trained. He had with him five horses, one for each squire. The other four squires mounted easily, needing little assistance from Ferdy. Bellaydin was the last. He approached the horse with confidence and reached out to pat its nose, but Ferdy grabbed Bellaydin's hand before the squire could touch the animal.

"Now, now young master," the horse master said. He had a strong accent that marked him as an immigrant to the capital. "It be my job to turn ye into a fine rider that be befitting your noble rank, so please be listenin' to me while I show you what to do."

"I know how to ride a horse," Bellaydin said.

"I'll be the judge of that." Ferdy's voice held a tone of mild chastisement. He helped Bellaydin on to the horse.

"Hold the reins like so. No, no squire, try again. Good. That be better."

Ferdy whistled and Bellaydin discovered fairly quickly that he was wrong about his own proficiency. As the horse took off Bellaydin lurched forward in his seat, grabbing on to the animals neck. He heard the tittering laughter of the other squires but the horse master's voice rose above the rest.

"The reins, squire," Ferdy called out. "Ye need to take control and guide the animal."

It was easier said than done, but after some fumbling he managed to grab a hold of the reins and right himself in time to slow down the horse. He looked over at his fellow squires and felt a twinge of jealousy. The others could show off years of horse-riding learned as the sons of nobleman – though for a while Bellaydin feared that Otto's steed was in danger of breaking under the strain – but Bellaydin found himself tossed off his steed four times in the first fifteen minutes.

Ferdy kept barking instructions to him about the correct way to hold on, but as far as Bellaydin was concerned the horse master might as well have been speaking another language. Eventually, Bellaydin got a firm grip of his steed and the class continued on to more complicated manoeuvres. Again Bellaydin struggled to control his mount, an embarrassment only amplified when a smug and self-satisfied Edgar trotted merrily beside him, a smirk on his face.

When the lesson finally ended, Bellaydin felt bruised both physically and emotionally. He retreated to his room, but barely had any time to rest. After a quick wash at his basin he joined the other squires heading on their way to the first history lesson.

"Let's hope your knowledge of history is better than your riding, Ap'Lydin," Edgar smirked.

"I don't suppose elves would know anything about our history," said Tancred. "So if Ap'Lydin doesn't get confused in the first ten minutes he can consider it a victory."

The room they had their history lessons in was unremarkable, little more than a set of wooden chairs and desks arranged facing a well-worn lectern. Brother Alcuin, their teacher, was an elderly man with a tonsure and dressed in a brown cassock. He introduced himself with a voice that was rich and warm, and wasted no time in beginning the lesson.

"I am sure you are all familiar with the de Morcor Rebellion, which began in the one hundred and ninety-second year of the Third Epoch and ended only seven years ago. But how many of you know how it started?"

"The tyranny of the depraved Ran-Tyrons," Edgar said.

Alcuin shook his head. "There were other factors as well. The poisonous feud between the House of Genio and the House of Morcor was one, and the inability of the throne to calm the situation. Who can name one of the pivotal battles of this period?"

"Goriinch Hill?" said Otto.

"Yes Squire Mainstream, but I had hoped for a different answer. The Battle of Goriinch Hill was where our late King Henry first gained the crown. Everyone knows of it."

Bellaydin squirmed in his seat. *I didn't know.*

Alcuin looked about the room. "Anyone else know of any battles?"

"The Battle of Georgeton," said Kurth.

"And do you know the details of this battle?"

"My grandfather used to tell me it saved Tyronsville," said Kurth. "That the Black Duke would have killed our entire family if the king and the Duke of Oldharbour hadn't raised the siege."

"So it appears this is an important part of your family history, squire," said Alcuin. "No doubt you can tell me the important casualties of this battle."

Kurth hesitated for a moment. "Well I *know* that we killed the Black Duke."

"We?" Edgar laughed. "More likely the king killed him while your father and uncle were fighting over who got first pick of the Black Duke's wine cellar."

"Squire, enough," said Alcuin. He turned back to Kurth. "Yes, Duke Kalen Tyron was killed, along with King Henry's sons, the Duke of Oldharbour's brothers, and thousands of others. It was one of the bloodiest battles ever fought in our land. Can anyone tell me the name of the final battle?"

"Travensburgh?" asked Otto.

"No, later than that. The Black Duke's heirs were killed at Travensburgh, but they were not the last of the Tyron pretenders."

Alcuin looked about, his eyes coming to rest on Bellaydin, who, feeling uncomfortable, tried to move from the teacher's gaze.

"Anyone? No? The answer is the Battle of Silverwater Bay. Gervor Tyron attempted to land with his force of Tarkenese mercenaries. It was an audacious plot, but our King Henry defeated the pretender, and with Gervor's death the Tyron line came to an end."

The squires murmured in assent, but Bellaydin felt most of them were not particularly interested. It was a pity because in Bellaydin's opinion the history class was the first interesting lesson he'd had. He'd always been fascinated by the past. Aderilund was a place steeped in history, and the Eldara were a people who looked to their past. A taste for history was one thing that Bellaydin shared with his adopted homeland. Ever since he was a child he'd wanted to know more about his own past, and naturally that had extended into a wider fascination with the events of history. Regardless of the reasons, Bellaydin found the lesson a welcome respite from the alternating tedium and difficulty of his other studies.

The teacher discussed the early history of the Emparian people – of their murky origins in the mythic lands of Thulia, followed by centuries of slavery in the Shen'Eldara Imperium, a bloody struggle for freedom and their eventual migration to what was now Emparia. Alcuin discussed the settlement of Emparia in a manner that seemed to brush over the fact that there was already a race of humans dwelling in the lands the Emparians took for themselves. The Goriinchians still resented Emparians for the conquest of centuries past, whereas modern Emparians seemed to have almost forgotten that there was a conquest at all.

Alcuin looked about. "I do believe that is where we shall leave it for today, squires. I shall see you at your next session."

The lesson over, Bellaydin and the other squires returned to their chambers, where Bellaydin had an unexpected guest. The Duke of Alariat was standing in front of the door, with a warm smile spreading across his face as soon as saw Bellaydin approach.

"Bellaydin, my dear boy." Haakon greeted him, arms wide. "How have you been?"

Bellaydin smiled weakly, and waved his hand in a non-committal manner, eliciting a small chuckle from Haakon.

"Don't worry, my dear boy," he said. "Things will get easier. I remember my days as a squire of the royal court. Still, consider all of this character-building. You will come out of this a better person, mark my words. Now," he said, taking a seat next to Bellaydin, "I have some good news. Tomorrow the queen and I are going falconing. You, my young friend, are to join us."

"That must've taken quite some clout to organise," Bellaydin said, impressed.

"Indeed it did, and unfortunately as part of the price for doing so the other members of my House asked me to extend the invitation to Squire Edgar de Morcor."

Bellaydin was about to protest, but Haakon raised a hand. "Now, now, Bellaydin," he said. "I understand there is bad blood between you two, and I know that Edgar can be difficult at the best of times, but he is also my cousin's son and a member of my House. You need to show respect. I want you to be on your best behaviour, do you understand?"

Bellaydin frowned. "I will if he will."

Haakon did not look impressed. "Please Bellaydin, I'm asking you to just do this."

"Alright, alright," Bellaydin said.

"Excellent," Haakon said. "We will meet you at the stables in an hour."

The Duke of Alariat left to return to his quarters to prepare himself, allowing Bellaydin to do likewise. He dressed and made his way down to the stables just outside the castle, where the stable-hands were preparing the horses for those who were participating. They had set aside the two finest horses for the queen and the Duke of Alariat. Both were wearing saddlecloths dedicated with the stallion of House Morcor. Two other horses were also being prepared, one with the de Morcor sigil and another with the sigil of House Ap'Lydin. These were obviously intended for Bellaydin and Edgar.

Nearby the falcon keepers were preparing the birds as well, awaiting the arrivals of the noble. These men would travel with the party, but by foot, and stay out of sight when the nobles themselves were with the birds.

Realising he was early, Bellaydin waited for a while, wondering idly where exactly they would be doing this falconry. There was no forest inside the city itself, so most likely they were headed to some place outside the city walls.

Eventually, the others arrived. The Duke of Alariat was deep in discussion with the young queen, and trailing after them, a superior look on his face, was Squire Edgar de Morcor. He was immaculately groomed, with even his hair having been carefully combed and perfumed. Bellaydin felt shabby and ill-dressed by comparison.

Edgar looked at Bellaydin and sniggered. "You're lucky His Grace has an unnatural fascination with you. If it'd been up to me, there's no way you'd be allowed within ten feet of any of us, especially dressed like that."

Bellaydin bristled at Edgar's comments. It was going to be a long ride if the squire kept needling him like that.

The stable workers helped everyone onto their mounts and led the horses from out of the palace grounds to the city proper, with the falcon keepers walking behind. They followed a well-marked cobbled path that took them outside the city walls to a large forested area just outside the city. This was evidently a forest kept aside for the monarch's personal use, as Bellaydin saw little sign that any other humans were within.

"I suppose you must feel at home here, Ap'Lydin," Edgar said. "What with growing up with elves. They live in the forests, don't they? Well, enjoy it, but for gods' sake, don't do anything unnatural with a tree."

"I have no idea what you're talking about, Edgar," Bellaydin said. "But do go on thinking about me and trees doing unnatural things."

Seeing that his insult hadn't stung Bellaydin, Edgar changed tack, "Do you even know the first thing about falconry? Or is that another part of noble life that your peasant upbringing failed to prepare you for?"

Bellaydin ignored the other squire, resulting in Edgar laughing, and pushing his horse forward to join the queen and the duke. Bellaydin did likewise, reasoning that perhaps Edgar would be more reasonable with Haakon and the queen listening to their conversation.

"Ah, there you are Bellaydin," Haakon said. "You know Your Majesty,

The Slaves of the Horned God

Bellaydin's father was quite the falconer in his day. He and I used to hunt together. I never caught anything and half the time my falcon flew away, but Alusine was far better. It was as if he and the bird were in tune with each other. You remember Alusine don't you, Your Majesty?"

The queen looked towards Haakon vacantly and then towards Bellaydin. "I'm afraid not, dear cousin. Did I meet him once?"

Haakon looked a little disappointed, "You would have, but I suppose I shouldn't expect you to remember much. You were about twelve or so when he died. Alusine spent most of his time in the marches. But he was an old friend of your father's from the war."

The queen shook her head. "I'm sorry cousin. I can't picture his face."

Edgar smirked. "Don't worry Your Majesty," he said, "If you can't remember him I'm sure he wasn't worth remembering. He died anyway, probably for the best – his wife was a Tyron, from what I've heard."

Bellaydin tried to ignore Edgar, but if anything, that encouraged the boy to escalate further. He passed by closely, whispering to Bellaydin. "What's the matter, Ap'Lydin? Don't like me talking about your parents? I can understand why. Word is your father was little more than a cuckold and your mother whored herself out to every man from here to Alariat. Everyone's heard the story of how she rode that squire red and raw."

Bellaydin was fed up. His blood boiling, Bellaydin steered his horse towards Edgar and grabbed the other squire around his neck, dragging him off his horse, to the queen and Haakon's shock. He could put up with Edgar jibes when they were just about Bellaydin, but now Edgar was insulting his parents, and trivialising their deaths.

"Let go of me!" Edgar demanded as the two squires wrestled on the ground. Bellaydin was the older of the pair, but Edgar was well-built, and they were fairly evenly matched. They writhed in the dirt, trading blows while their horses, spooked, ran off. Haakon was shouting something, but Bellaydin was too enraged at Edgar to hear. All he cared about was

91

punishing the other squire.

"Get him off me!" Edgar yelled.

Bellaydin forced two fingers into the squire's eye, but Edgar pushed Bellaydin's hand away so Bellaydin had to make do with smashing a fist into Edgar's cheek. Edgar retaliated with a haymaker at Bellaydin and soon both squires were bruised and bleeding.

The noise of their scuffle and Haakon and the queen's shouts soon attracted others, as the attendants who had been following from behind caught up with them. Strong arms grabbed Bellaydin and pulled him away from Edgar. Soldiers of the queen surrounded both of them, and Bellaydin saw that Edgar too had been restrained.

"Keep him away from me," Edgar yelled. "The damn idiot is deranged."

Bellaydin looked Edgar in the eye, making sure the squire felt the full force of his rage. "If you dare say anything about my father or mother ever again, I'll-"

"Squires! Enough," Haakon demanded. "This is disgraceful behaviour, and in front of Her Majesty, no less."

"He started it," Bellaydin said.

Haakon was livid. "I don't care who damn well started it. Enough!" He turned to the queen. "Your Majesty, my apologies are due, I think it is best we have this hunt another time."

The queen nodded. "Whatever you think is right, dear cousin." Her brown eyes fixed on Bellaydin and he couldn't tell whether she was being judgemental of him or not.

They rode back to the castle in silence, with Bellaydin and Edgar separated by Haakon and made to ride on opposite sides of the hunting party. The duke was stony-faced, his expression unreadable to Bellaydin but for someone who was normally smiling and in good cheer, Bellaydin knew that a lack of a frown didn't mean that the duke was not angry.

It was only when they were back in Castle Emparia, alone, that the duke revealed his true feelings. Before the conversation even began Haakon's face was red and his lips pursed. "You have embarrassed me," the duke shouted. "On top of that you have shamed your House and you have made yourself a spectacle in front of the queen. What on earth possessed you to do such a thing?"

Bellaydin's tone was defensive. "I didn't mean...I...Edgar goaded me into it."

Haakon paced about the room. "I don't care what Edgar did or didn't do. I specifically asked you to be on your best behaviour. It took every bit of my influence and court to organise today, and now it is all wasted. Do you understand what you've done?"

"I'm sorry," Bellaydin said. His voice was little more than a whisper.

"Sorry? You're sorry? It's going to take a lot more than sorry to fix this Bellaydin. Think about what you've done." Haakon waved a hand. "Enough. I have to go and see if I can salvage anything from this. You disappointed me today, Bellaydin, in a way your father never would have. The apple has fallen very far from the tree."

CHAPTER 6

Polnygar drank. Her throat was dry and parched. She'd never been so thirsty in her entire life. The relentless sun beat down on her, draining every drop of moisture from her. Her raven hair, usually let loose to well below her shoulders, was tied in a bun, making her elven ears more prominent than normal.

"Don't forget to leave some for the rest of us," said Augustin. His eye patch was damp from sweat; he squinted at her with his good eye from under the cloth he had wrapped about his face for protection.

"Sorry." Polnygar took the flask from her lips, wiped her mouth, and passed it on to Augustin. He caught the flask with one hand, the other hand was missing, the arm little more than a stump. It had been cut off in Ralom, an event that still chilled Polnygar every time she recalled it. She did her best to avoid the memory, pushing it down into the recesses of her mind.

The baron's skin was burned and peeling from the relentless sun. His greying, auburn hair was caked with sweat and grime. Pulling the cloth away from his face, Augustin tipped the flask over his mouth and gulped down water quickly. "Not a lot left," he said. "Do you think we're getting close?"

"We're not far now," said Aelzandar. "I think I can see Selvarial on the horizon."

The archmage had the same determined face he had borne the entire trip. Like Polnygar, his long grey hair was tied in a topknot leaving the points of his ears exposed to the sun. For most of the journey he had been instructing his pupil Polnygar on the mysteries of the Art, but other matters also held his attention. He clearly relished the chance to face Ivellios as much as the others did, but whereas their vengeance burned like fire, Aelzandar's was as cool as ice. He carried the ornate Staff of the Archmage, his badge of office, and at his hip swung *Sakkaru,* the blade known throughout Carurlonia by its sobriquet, "The Flame of Justice".

Hebu, the Royal Scribe of the Macrodonian Pharaoh, was a more reluctant participant on this mission of revenge, and Polnygar was surprised that the Nemoi hadn't taken the opportunity to turn his camel around and return home. The diminutive academic was swathed in robes, having had the sense to protect his bald head from the harsh desert sun shortly after their journey began.

It had been many weeks since they had left Ralom and their Selvara guides had led them across the desert safely. Apart from their encounter with the bandits near Ralom, the trip had been uneventful. It had given her time to reflect on the path she had taken since she had left Aderilund. For years Polnygar had longed to leave her home and explore the world, but now she found herself thinking back fondly on the place she had escaped, and of those she had left behind. Her mother, Saegralanna, was left alone for the first time in twelve years, and her brother, Bellaydin, had been expelled from Aderilund through to the machinations of the spellweaver Ivellios.

Ivellios. The very name turned her stomach. The spellweaver had been the source of so much of the tragedy and misfortune that dogged them. He had broken Polnygar's family, stolen an item of great power from Aelzandar, and put Augustin under an enchantment, a curse that ended with Polnygar being forced to dismember Augustin's hand.

Ivellios is responsible for all of this, she thought. *And he is the one who will pay. If we ever find him.*

They had been pursuing the spellweaver since he fled Macrodonia. They caught up to him in Ralom, but Ivellios escaped, and the hunt had begun again. Soon they would arrive at the Selvara settlement of Selvarial, a trading post known to outsiders as Forestown. Polnygar wondered how it had acquired such a name when it appeared that the most arid of deserts surrounded the place.

As they continued travelling under the midday sun, a vision began to take shape on the horizon, and Polnygar began to see what Aelzandar and the Selvara guides must have noticed before. A blurry, indistinct haze gave way to a forest, an island of green in an ocean of sand. The forest surrounded a shimmering oasis, and in its very centre rose a magnificent, towering tree – the largest Polnygar had ever seen.

"The Tree of Life," Aelzandar said, noticing Polnygar's interest. "Focus of Selvara culture, and our destination."

The desert, so lifeless before, bloomed into a bed of flowers, shrubs and trees. After travelling by themselves for so long, Polnygar was elated that they were beginning to encounter other travellers. Steady streams of people were making their way to Selvarial, just as Polnygar's own group was.

"It is scarcely believable, isn't it?" Augustin said. "I remember the first time I saw it, and I still don't quite trust my eyes. A veritable oasis in the desert, in more ways than one."

The Selvara guide spoke some words to Aelzandar, who nodded in response. "Our guide tells us we must head this way, and enter through the Pilgrim's Gate," Aelzandar said. "There we will find the bazaar, where we can obtain food, water and other supplies from the merchants of the city."

"Let's get going then," Augustin said.

Thanking their guides, Aelzandar watched the Selvara leave, and then waited as Augustin, Polnygar and Hebu came closer to him. "Follow me closely, and don't get lost. Once we are in the city itself, feel free to take some time to rest and recuperate. We have a long journey ahead of us."

The walls of Selvarial were made from living wood, formed from vegetation that had grown together and intertwined to form a barrier as solid as any stone. The Pilgrim's Gate was an archway the height of three men, and more than ten men wide. Crowds of travellers streamed in and out of the gate without end.

They reached the bazaar in good time. The throng of people within amazed Polnygar. Merchants from far and wide and from all races were hawking their wares to the multitude of travellers within. She spotted some Eldara from Aderial, but did not recognise their faces and thought better of approaching them. Macrodonian merchants, both human and Nemoi, also plied their wares. Nearby two tall, muscular green-skinned Lizardmen walked by with self-assured gaits.

"Ahktarra," Augustin said, as he came up next to her. "The slave race of Qarld. Very strong, and with tempers to match."

"I've never seen one before," Polnygar said. "Are we near Qarld then?"

"Very close, my dear," Aelzandar said. "Once we leave Selvarial we shall be in the lands of the Caliphate."

"I think I might browse for a while," Augustin said.

"Not a problem," Aelzandar said. "Perhaps we should arrange to meet here at sunset?"

"Fine by me," Augustin said, and he disappeared into the crowd of people before Polnygar could say anything.

"Don't worry, my dear," Aelzandar said. "He'll be back before you know it."

Polnygar flushed. "I wasn't worried."

"Of course," Aelzandar smiled.

"So," said Polnygar. "Tell me about this place."

Aelzandar raised an eyebrow. "Surely you know of Selvarial?"

"No. A year ago, I barely even knew who the Selvara were, and I'd never met one," Polnygar said

"Selvarial is the greatest and only settlement of the Selvara," said Aelzandar. "They are a nomadic people and have disdain for what they consider to be the soft decadence of settled civilisation. They did, however, come to the belief that they needed some form of place in order for them to be able to maintain a sense of unity, a place for all Selvara to come, even if only for a short time. It was not long after his departure from Liderial that Selvaros came here, and planted the sapling."

"Sapling?"

"The sapling that the Tree of Life was born from. Selvara believe that this sapling was a cutting from an earlier tree of pre-history, a tree that was the centre of Eldara life before they built Liderial and became a settled people. It is a belief of theirs that Lideros and the first spellweavers deliberately sabotaged this original Tree of Life so that they could force other Eldara to conform to their ideology of civilisation."

"And what do you think?" Polnygar asked.

Aelzandar shrugged. "I find the story difficult to believe in its entirety. However, that being said, one often finds that most myths begin with a small kernel of truth."

"You remember the story of Selvaros, do you not?" Aelzandar asked her. "We spoke of him in Macrodonia, and I am sure you have also seen the *Passion of Lideros* performed?"

The Eldara had a rich and established cultural tradition of theatre, a tradition that served both as a means of mass entertainment and as a way to ingrain the younger Eldara with the history and culture of their people. Most plays concerned great heroes of the past, especially those who promoted the idea of Eldara exceptionalism.

The Passion of Lideros was an ancient story and one well-beloved by Eldara. It depicted the life of the legendary Lideros, first king of the Eldara; and the birth of Eldara civilisation nearly six thousand years ago.

Prominent members of Aderilund society usually played the lead roles. The role of Selvaros was typically played for comic effect in the Passion, and the character, though historically male, was usually played by a woman, which tended to make Selvaros seem even smaller and more delicate compared to the other characters. One memorable performance had seen Polnygar's own mother Saegralanna play the part. Polnygar remembered the last time she had seen the play performed; it was many years ago, and she had watched it with her brother Bellaydin.

Remembering Bellaydin, she felt acutely how much she missed him. She tried to change the topic. "There are a lot of humans here."

Aelzandar nodded. "Well, to the Selvara this city may be a sacred spot, and the centrepiece of their culture and faith, but to non-Selvara, it is far more important as the only reliable supply point on the main trading route from Ralom to the Infinite Caliphate. For centuries humans and others have stopped here during their journeys. They know it as Forestown, and it is not hard to see why."

"It is astonishing," Polnygar's said, her voice awestruck. "This forest, it seems so lush, but...how?"

"The Tree of Life is more than just some sacred point for the Selvara, my dear. It is a source of potent magic, and its roots have infused this whole area with the energy of life. So long as the Tree remains, Forestown will always be as it is." Aelzandar smiled wistfully. "You know I have not been here for over a hundred years, yet it still remains exactly as I remember it."

***

Augustin walked about the bazaar, examining the various stalls. Merchants of all kinds tried to interest him in their wares, but he politely waved them away, content to just look for the moment.

"Well, well, well, as I live and breathe, Baron Augustin Bauer."

Augustin turned around at the sound of his name and came face to face with a tall woman, dressed in traveller's clothes, but with a noble bearing.

"Ha. Céline de Lerid," Augustin exclaimed, and embraced the woman in a hug.

"That's Captain Céline de Lerid," the woman corrected with a smile. "Though I know you Emparians don't put much store in titles."

"Sorry, Captain," said Augustin with an exaggerated bow. "What in the name of the gods are you doing in Forestown?"

"I might ask you the same question," Céline said. "I'm merely on my way back to the Empire. I was reinforcing a garrison in the Vallistian Marches but I've been called back to the capital. Unfortunately, snowfall has blocked all the passes in the Necromancer's Peaks, so I've had to take the long route back."

"Are you still with the chevaliers then?" Augustin ventured.

Céline nodded. "The rest of my men are around here somewhere. We're supposed to be leaving tomorrow."

"You're not worried about going through Qarld?" Augustin said.

"There's peace between the Empire and the Caliphate at the moment," Céline said, and when she noticed Augustin looking sceptical, she added, "A shaky peace, I'll grant you, but peace nonetheless. We'll stay away from the major cities, though, and we are not travelling openly."

101

"Still sounds like you're taking an awful risk," Augustin said. "You couldn't wait until the snow had cleared, and take the safer route?"

"Would have liked to, sweetheart," Céline said, "but Emperor Anton's requested our presence urgently. And no is not a word for emperors."

"I suppose not," Augustin said.

"So, Augustin, what is the younger son of the Earl of Tyronsville and Emparia's most reluctant envoy doing here amongst the desert elves?"

"Well, for starters I'm not the younger son of the earl anymore," Augustin said. "My father died three years ago. My brother is earl now."

"Oh, I am sorry. Your father was a good man," Céline said. "And more approachable than most nobles I know." She smiled. "And so Alfred is earl. All the drinking establishments from here to Tyronsville must be toasting their good fortune. He's lucky your father packed you off overseas to give him space."

Augustin laughed. "Yes, indeed. Of course, I'm no longer envoy. They removed me from my post just recently."

"Normally I'd offer my congratulations, Augustin, but from the look on your face you seem somewhat displeased by the situation, which doesn't sound like the Augustin I know…"

"I couldn't give a fetid horse kidney about being an envoy or not, but the circumstances in which I was stripped of the title is what eats at me. And it is what brings me here. We are tracking someone."

"Oh?" Céline said. "Who?"

"An elf. One of those spellweavers."

Céline whistled. "I'd be careful of tangling with elves, sweetheart, especially a spellweaver. They hold grudges and they never forget a face. Odds are they'll outlive you as well, so unless you want your grandchildren to be fighting them off for the rest of their lives as well, I'd steer well clear of them."

"Unfortunately, I don't think that's an option. Have you ever heard of a spellweaver named Ivellios?"

Céline looked confused. "No, should I?"

Augustin gave a wry smile. "Let's find somewhere to have a drink, shall we? I certainly have a tale to tell you…"

***

Polnygar stared at the scar on her hand. It still itched, and every time she touched it, it reminded her of the searing pain she had experienced when she had held the Tears of the Divine.

"Copper for your thoughts my dear?" said Aelzandar. Polnygar and Aelzandar were alone. Hebu was off browsing the marketplace while she and the archmage were enjoying a traditional mint tea.

"One of the cultists who attacked me just before we met," Polnygar said. "He looked at my hands. My palms, as if he was looking for something."

"And?"

"When he saw nothing he seemed disappointed. As if I wasn't the one he was looking for. He expected there to be something here. He expected me to have this scar. Why?"

Aelzandar looked troubled. "Are you sure?"

"Absolutely. They knew I would get this scar, eventually. They knew. How?"

"I'm afraid I have no answer to give you, my dear. But it does suggest a connection between the Tears of the Divine and the Cult of the Horned God."

"Could there be? I mean, you did say you found the Tears in Emparia, not far from the border of Goriinchia, where they worship this Horned God."

"Yes, that is true," Aelzandar scratched his chin.

"What does Ivellios want with the Tears? Do you think he knows anything we don't?"

"Unlikely," said Aelzandar. "And I don't think it would interest him anyway. Ivellios never had much curiosity about the religious traditions of other races. As far as he is concerned anything not of the Eldara is not worth a moment's thought. He probably sees the Tears as a repository of magical power, and nothing more. He would see it as merely a tool for him to use the Art and will destroy the thing trying to unlock its secrets."

"Do you think we'll see any more of those cultists?" Polnygar said. "I hoped we'd see the last of them once we left Macrodonia, but then there were those bandits just outside Ralom."

"The slaves of the Horned God may be numerous, my dear, but they are not everywhere. I think we are safe for the foreseeable future. In fact I —"

Aelzandar stopped mid-sentence and turned his head.

"What is it?" said Polnygar.

Aelzandar turned back to face her. "I could have sworn that I heard..." He turned his head again. "I did hear that. Come, dear, come with me, there is someone I want you to meet."

Aelzandar motioned for Polnygar to follow and they set off to a nearby stall. Seated on a stool, purveying his wares was a fat, tan-skinned merchant, his face turned away from them. He was dressed in finery and drinking from a goblet, but doing so in a way that made it seem like he was trying to do so without anyone watching him.

"Correct me if I am wrong, my friend, but is it not true that the consumption of alcohol is forbidden to those who follow the words of the most holy prophet Sarrius?"

The merchant, taken by surprise, nearly choked, sputtering and coughing, but regained composure and turned around to face them. When he saw Aelzandar, his frown turned into a wide smile. "Do my eyes deceive me? Archmage Aelzandar of Jagoncoilis?"

Aelzandar smiled and extended his hand. "Samir," Aelzandar said, "Salaam to you."

"Oh, effendi," Samir said. "Salaam to you too, and greetings." He kissed Aelzandar's hand and then placed his hand on his chest.

"It has been too long, Samir," Aelzandar said.

"Of course, my friend, of course." Samir looked at Polnygar and his eyes widened. "And who is this vision of beauty I see before me? Your daughter, archmage?"

Aelzandar shook his head.

"Not your wife then?"

"No, no," Aelzandar waved his hand. "This is my pupil, Polnygar."

"Ah," said Samir. He kissed her hand. "Sweet lady, dear lady. My name is Samir bin Adil. I am a purveyor of fine wares, a seeker of truth and a student of philosophy. My humble self is at your service."

"Samir and I have known each other for a long time," Aelzandar said. "I met him many decades ago on one of his trips to Macrodonia. He was of great assistance in locating something of great value to me."

"Flattery, flattery," Samir said, feigning embarrassment. He looked at Polnygar. "Your master exaggerates. Though I am pleased to hear that my own humble part in that tale is still treasured by him." He turned to Aelzandar. "So my friend, what brings you to Forestown? You are not here to sample some of Samir's fine wares, I suppose? No, I would say only a great and troubling quest would bring an archmage to begin a journey such as this, don't you think?"

Polnygar was taken aback by the torrent of words the man directed at them and laughed nervously.

"Ah, such sweet laughter," Samir said, clasping Polnygar's hand. "I am in love! My lady, I hope I am not too forward when I ask you to be my wife? Your beauty has left me spellbound, and I will not be able to live without you."

Polnygar gasped and Aelzandar, sensing her discomfort, gently removed Polnygar's hand from Samir's grip.

"I believe you are already married, Samir," Aelzandar chided

"My dear wife will understand," Samir said. "Oh. I have offended you, my lady. Is it the wine? I tell you, my dear lady, that though I may occasionally let the drink pass through my lips, I never imbibe it, as is the Prophet's wish."

"She's not interested, Samir," Aelzandar said, his tone firmer than before.

"Indeed, she isn't." Polnygar said through clenched teeth. She wanted to maintain civility out of respect for Aelzandar, but she was finding it hard to mask her displeasure at Samir's overtures.

"Oh well," he said, bowing his head. "I shall remain who I am then, a poor merchant with but a single wife to care for me."

Aelzandar patted Samir on the shoulder, "So much the better old friend, so much the better."

"I was thinking that you must have come here with the other elves, Aelzandar," said Samir.

"Other elves? What other elves?" Aelzandar asked.

"See for yourself, effendi," Samir said.

Nearby was a large group of travellers, some mounted and others on foot. One of the most beautiful Eldara women Polnygar had ever seen rode atop a pure white horse. The Eldara's hair was golden as the sun, and she was heavily veiled to protect her skin from the desert heat. Next to her rode a handsome male elf. The two of them had a strong familial resemblance. The male elf was dressed in finely made clothes of white and gold. He evidently noticed the group watching him, and moved his horse towards them.

"Aelzandar li'Geihnos," the male Eldara said. "I did not expect to see you here."

Aelzandar bowed to the newcomer. "Blessed be and honour to your Houses, Prince Caerunos. I did not know if you would recognise me. What brings a Prince of Liderial so far from home?"

"Royal business, Aelzandar," he said. "I am escorting my sister to her wedding in Fudarial. We had hoped to take the eastern route through Valliste, but the mountains there are currently impassable."

"I did not know that Princess Millandriel was betrothed. Please offer her my congratulations."

"I will do so. And what of you, Aelzandar, where are you headed? Are you returning to Liderial, finally? My father has been hoping that you would return for some time."

The archmage chuckled quietly. "I can't imagine many others would be happy to see such a homecoming."

"The king and queen will welcome you, Aelzandar. Tell me that I can expect to greet you there upon my return."

Aelzandar smiled. "I'm afraid any happy returns may have to wait, Your Highness. I am following someone north."

"An old friend, Aelzandar?"

Aelzandar chuckled. "No, I wouldn't exactly say that. It is the spellweaver Ivellios."

Prince Caerunos raised an eyebrow. "I know little of you, Aelzandar, save what my father and mother tell me, but Ivellios I am familiar with. He is a difficult person at the best of times and he has always thought very highly of himself. That hardly engenders trust. You should know that I passed him, on my way here. He was headed through the Caliphate, to the city of Qar Arrid. He planned to stay there for a while. For what reason, I cannot say." One of the prince's companions called out for him. "My escorts are calling me. It is time for me to continue on my way. Good fortune to you, Aelzandar, and whatever your disagreement with Ivellios, I hope to see you again in Liderial someday."

"I would be honoured, Your Highness," said Aelzandar, bowing again.

As the prince and his retinue departed, a sly look came across Samir's face. "I'd wager, effendi, that you did not tell your prince the whole story. So, what truly brings you here, my friend?" Samir asked.

"Something was stolen from me," Aelzandar said. "Do you remember the Tears of the Divine, Samir?"

The merchant let out a whistle. "Ah yes, of course. Such a treasure you found, Aelzandar. And so well protected. Who could have stolen it? Who would manage such a feat, but another spellweaver?"

"Yes, Ivellios. We are following him north. We believe that he is headed towards Skurj."

"Ah. Such a long journey you are undertaking my friend. From Macrodonia to the very fringes of the northern wastes, from sand to snow. Tell me then, were you intending to pass through Qar Arrid?"

"Well I hadn't given it much thought," Aelzandar admitted, "but it seems that Ivellios has stopped there for reasons of his own."

"I am not surprised. If one is to cross the mountains into Lerid and from then to Skurj then you will pass through Qar Arrid as you leave the Caliphate. And effendi, no doubt you remember the famous library in that city." Aelzandar nodded, and Samir continued. "No doubt Ivellios knows of it as well."

A look of realisation spread across the archmage's face. "Of course."

"So you see why you too must visit Qar Arrid."

Polnygar cut into the conversation. "I don't understand. Why do we need to visit this library? Ivellios is ahead of us if we fall behind then..."

Samir smiled broadly. "Your master has remembered a certain book that is held in Qar Arrid's library. A book that now, more than ever, contains things that he must know, especially if this Ivellios seeks the secrets too."

"What book?" asked Polnygar.

Samir's expression grew dark. "A blasphemous and forbidden tome, so steeped in heretical thought that the Caliph declared it off limits. Seized from the possession of the sorcerer Ralur after his death two and a half centuries ago and kept under lock and key ever since. *The Tome of Divine Metaphysics*."

"It is the only book I know of that contains any information on the Tears of the Divine," Aelzandar said. "Or so I have learned. No one alive has ever read it, though. Not even myself. Its guardians keep it closely secured from everyone. But it contains all that Ralur discovered of the Soldara. Knowledge that would rival that of the long-dead Cassian."

"Is Ivellios after this book?" asked Polnygar.

"Perhaps. But getting access to it would be an astonishing feat for anyone," Aelzandar mused. "And if it contains information about the Tears..."

Samir looked humble. "I am by no means astonishing, effendi, but as a close, personal friend of Omar al'Dazhi, Emir of Qar Arrid I have laid eyes on this book. The contents are to me unreadable, but I am sure that I can persuade the emir to allow you to see the book, just as I have."

Polnygar looked at the archmage. For the first time since she had known him, he actually looked excited. Samir opened his arms and smiled at them both. "So, effendi, are you willing to have one more traveller in your company?"

CHAPTER 7

"I have found us a guide," Aelzandar told the others.

Augustin did not look impressed. "Another tag-along?" he snorted.

Polnygar bristled at his words. She did not like Augustin reminding her on how she had joined up with him in the first place. She was little more than a stowaway on his ship, having secreted herself aboard to escape the staid life in Aderilund with her mother. Despite a lingering sense of shame at the deception, she did not regret her choice.

"Polnygar," Aelzandar said. "I must apologise for Samir's earlier behaviour. The ways of his people are different to us, and sometimes difficult to comprehend. I will make sure that he is never that rude again."

Polnygar appreciated Aelzandar's apology but did not want to seem entirely helpless. "Thank you, because if he tries something like that again, he'll wish he never laid eyes on me."

"Why do we need this buffoon anyway?" Augustin said with scorn.

"Samir has travelled the path from here to Lerid many times," Aelzandar said. "I cannot think of a better guide. He also has many friends in high places in the Caliphate. Such contacts can only make our journey smoother."

"That's assuming we can trust anything the fat human says," Hebu said with disdain.

Aelzandar waved away the Nemoi's concerns. "I trust Samir implicitly. He may be a flatterer and prone to exaggeration, but he is always true to his word. He will be a great asset on our way to Qar Arrid."

"Qar Arrid? Why on earth are we going to Qar Arrid?" Augustin said.

"Knowledge, my dear Baron. We are travelling in darkness, and a little knowledge might well light our way."

"Speak plainly, damn it," Augustin snapped.

Aelzandar quickly explained why and how the tome could be of great use in their pursuit of Ivellios. Augustin seemed annoyed at the extra stop they had to make, but he wasn't about to protest if it meant being able to foil whatever Ivellios had planned.

"You don't ask for much, do you?" Augustin said bitterly.

Aelzandar smiled. "Prepare yourself, Baron, we leave in the morning. Come Hebu, we must meet Samir and finish gathering supplies for the journey."

As Aelzandar left, with Hebu trailing close behind, Augustin turned to Polnygar. "You think he's right? That the Tears of the Divine could be connected to these cultists of the Horned God?"

Polnygar tapped the palm of her hand. "They *knew*, Augustin. They knew that I would get this scar. How?"

Augustin scratched his chin. "Beats me. Maybe they were looking for something else."

"I don't think so," Polnygar said.

Augustin frowned. "Well, whatever the truth, I'm sure it will come to light. I just hope it isn't too much of a distraction from us pursuing Ivellios. I have a score to settle with that elf." He rubbed the stub of his arm as if to emphasise his point.

The rest of the afternoon passed with little of note. Aelzandar and Hebu returned, and the group shared supper together, a traditional Selvara spiced meal that set Polnygar's tastebuds on fire. Shortly after that, they retired to the simple traveller's lodgings Aelzandar had organised, to get some much-needed sleep before they continued their journey the next day.

Before she could go to sleep, however, Polnygar found herself summoned by Aelzandar, who arrived at her room with a smile on his lips. "Ah, my dear, you are not asleep yet. Good. Come with me, I need to show you something."

Polnygar yawned. "What is it?"

"Something wonderful," was all Aelzandar would say as he beckoned to join him outside.

As they walked, Aelzandar explained. "There is a special ceremony that the Selvara have – part of their own interpretation of the Art. I have heard much of it, but never witnessed it myself. It happens only on special occasions and very rarely are strangers invited to join. Tonight we have that opportunity. Are you interested, my dear?"

"Sounds interesting," Polnygar said. "Let's do this."

"Excellent," Aelzandar said, clasping his hands together. "I knew you would be eager."

They travelled to the Tree of Life in the centre of Selvarial, where a circle of Selvara had surrounded the giant tree. The Selvara stood hand in hand with their eyes closed and appeared to be chanting something in their own dialect of the elven language.

"The Selvara call it the Spirit," Aelzandar whispered. "They believe it

113

can connect them with the power of the Tree of Life."

A Selvara mystic, naked and covered head to toe in tattoos gleamed in the moonlight. He watched them with a critical gaze as they approached.

"Greetings brother," Aelzandar said, giving a short bow. Polnygar gave her own greetings and bowed as well, but she did her best to keep her gaze above the Selvara's waist.

"Greetings brother, greetings sister," the Selvara said. "It is rare indeed that Eldara outsiders are given the chance to join the Rite of Life, but such is the reputation of the Great Archmage that we have extended to both of you this great honour. Please join the circle."

As she approached the circle, Polnygar realised that it wasn't just the first Selvara who was naked. The rest of them in the circle were unclothed as well. Polnygar's hair stood on end and she felt very awkward. She whispered to Aelzandar, "They're naked. They're *all* naked. Please tell me I don't have to be as well."

The Selvara overheard her. "You may keep your clothing if you wish."

"Thank you," Polnygar said with some relief.

The two of them took their places and, holding hands with each other and the Selvara on either side, they closed their eyes.

"What happens next?" Polnygar whispered.

"Let yourself relax my dear, and become one with the Rite," Aelzandar said.

Polnygar tried to clear her mind, pushing out everything – the journey, Ivellios, the Tears of the Divine, the Heir of Lydin, Aelzandar, Augustin – until she was alone with her mind, free of any distractions. The chanting continued, penetrating into her innermost thoughts. She felt serene, at peace and for a moment she thought that might be it.

It started – that familiar sensation. For a second she thought she was having another uncontrolled outburst of the Art, but she realised this was different. This was not the sudden exhilarating rush that had accompanied such events before, but the slow, smooth build up of positive energy, suffusing her entire being. She felt as if she was being purified from the inside out, that the very energy of life was permeating every fragment of her body. The energy filled her up and just when she thought she might burst with it all, the chanting stopped and Aelzandar let go of her hands.

She opened her eyes. It appeared the ceremony was over. She felt rejuvenated, healed of all the cares and worries of the last few months, almost as if she had been born anew.

Aelzandar looked at her with a smile. "The Tree of Life, Polnygar." He turned to the Selvara. "Thank you, my brothers. It was indeed a most holy and sacred experience. It was an honour to share it with you."

The Selvara bowed in appreciation.

"Come Polnygar," Aelzandar said. "I think it's time to get some rest."

As they returned to their lodgings, Polnygar pressed Aelzandar for more information. "What was that? What happened? It almost felt as if I could hear the chanting of the Selvara inside my head. Was that the Tree?"

"It was the power of the Tree, yes. Why do you ask?"

"Is it possible to communicate like that with the Art?"

"Indeed it is, my dear," Aelzandar said. "The Art is a path to many abilities. What you speak of is known as far-speaking. Spellweavers use it to communicate amongst themselves without being overheard by those without the Art."

"How is it done?

"I can show you if you would like. Take a seat."

Aelzandar folded his hands. "First, you must put your mind into a state of readiness. You must relax, and open your mind to me."

Polnygar tried to clear her mind once again.

"Don't overthink it Polnygar, just relax."

She felt her mind clear, and Aelzandar, seemingly able to read her face, smiled. "Good, now, let us make the initial connection."

He placed his hands on either side of her head. "Good, I can sense your mind. Can you feel my presence?"

An image of the archmage seemed to coalesce in her thoughts. "Yes," Polnygar said. "What happens now?"

"I am here." Aelzandar's words registered in her mind, but the archmage's lips did not move.

"I can hear you but you are not speaking," Polnygar said.

"Indeed. Now you try."

"I don't know how," she said.

"The connection has been established between us. Simply form the words in your mind, and they will travel to mine."

Polnygar nodded and closed her eyes. *"Hello?"* she thought.

Aelzandar's voice echoed in her mind. *"Excellent, my dear. I have heard you loud and clear. Now, let me show you what else far-speaking can do."*

A blur of images appeared in Polnygar's head, images of deserts, and pyramids and dusky-skinned men and women. Macrodonia. But these were not memories – no, they were images of places Polnygar had never been to, people she had never met.

"What is this?" she asked.

"A sending. I am giving you some memories from my own mind. It is another thing that may be accomplished with this power. Spellweavers use it to share their knowledge. Now you try."

Polnygar tried to focus on a single memory. A young man took shape in her mind, seventeen years of age with a fair complexion, dark hair and a scar adorning his lip.

"Your brother, Bellaydin, yes? You both look quite alike, in many ways."

Her focus began to slip, and other memories began to crowd her thoughts, forcing their way down the link with the archmage. Her departure from Aderilund and arrival in Macrodonia, the attack in the bazaar, Augustin's enchantment, the journey to Ralom, her battle with Ivellios. The trickle gushed into a torrent, and she felt overwhelmed.

The connection broke. "I think that's enough for a while," Aelzandar said, holding up a hand.

Polnygar tried to read the archmage's expression. "Did I do something wrong? Suddenly I couldn't control it."

Aelzandar smiled. "A sending can be difficult at the best of times, my dear. That was very good for a first attempt."

Polnygar felt her head spin and stumbled. Aelzandar caught her arm. "I feel faint, what's wrong?"

"Tapping into the Art is no different to using any other muscle in your body, and strenuous use can tire one easily. And just like a warrior who fights on when his sword arm tells him to stop, a mage who tries to use the Art when his mind is overtaxed is likely to pay the consequences."

"Exhaustion?" asked Polnygar.

"Death," Aelzandar corrected her with a grim expression. "And worse."

Polnygar's mouth twitched. "What could be worse than death?"

"Power always has a price," Aelzandar said. "Sustained use of the Art takes its toll on mortal flesh. I have seen mages grow addicted to the Art, so much so that they lose all sense of identity and purpose. They eventually destroy themselves, becoming little more than walking corpses. Do you know what a lich is?"

Polnygar shook her head.

"Consider yourself fortunate," said Aelzandar. "Liches are malevolent creatures dependant on the Art for their continued existences. This is what a mage without restraint can become. It is not a fate that anyone should hope for."

Polnygar shuddered. "It sounds horrible."

"You are a long way from that fate, my dear. And I would never believe you one to choose such an end." He stood and picked up his staff. "You will find as you improve in skill and experience, the Art will prove less taxing and reaching your limits will take longer. Regardless, I believe that may be enough for tonight. We should all get some rest."

***

That night, Polnygar dreamed.

She floated in an insubstantial place, outside the world as she knew it. She was in a void, a nothingness only disturbed by the appearance of Ivellios's sneering visage.

"Mal-halyth!" he hissed. "The joining of Eldara and Human blood is an abomination. It should never have been allowed."

As Ivellios spoke his features began to change, melting from his face as if they were but a mask covering the true face beneath. Soon all that remained was a grotesque and alien face, horned and demonic in appearance.

Two eyes, cold as night, focused on Polnygar. "Your blood is tainted. Your blood and the blood of all your line." The voice was no longer that of Ivellios. It was deeper, oddly sonorous and spoken with a strange inflection. "Give me the power that should have been mine. Give it to me, or I will take it by force."

A clawed hand reached out for her, she tried to escape, but there was nothing she could do. She could feel the clawed black fingers on her throat when she woke up suddenly.

Panting, her skin lined with sweat, she rose from her bed and noticed light streaming in from outside the tent. It was morning.

She washed her face, and dressed quickly, before heading outside to meet the others.

Augustin noticed her. "Are you alright, girl?" he said. "You look a little pale?"

"Bad dreams," she said. She spied Aelzandar and Hebu near them, in discussion with Samir.

"What do you think is going on there?" Polnygar asked.

"I have no idea, but Aelzandar seems unusually excited." Augustin said. "He must really want to read this book. By the way, I thought I saw you and Aelzandar slip out last night. Did you do anything interesting?"

Polnygar flushed red, and before she knew it she was recounting the night's events at the Tree of Life.

"Naked?" Augustin asked Polnygar after she had finished her story. "All of them?"

"Yes," Polnygar whispered. "I've never felt so awkward in my life. Why would they do that?"

Augustin chuckled. "I take it you don't have much experience with these sorts of elves."

"What's that supposed to mean?"

"They can be different to the stuffy types in Aderilund and the north. Let's just say they're the subject of a lot of stories. Many of them quite lurid."

"And I think we best leave those lurid myths where they belong, Baron," said Aelzandar as he joined the two of them. Hebu stood next to him.

"I'm sure the baron has never personally read any of these Selvara stories, has he?" The Nemoi's tone was sarcastic.

"I hear things," Augustin feigned ignorance – unsuccessfully, in Polnygar's opinion.

Aelzandar moved the conversation on to other matters. "I was just finalising the final arrangements with Samir here. We are merely awaiting his bodyguards."

"Bodyguards?" said Polnygar as Samir approached them, smiling warmly.

"My beautiful lady," Samir said, bowing his head. "It shames me to admit that though I am skilled in the art of the deal, my talents in the arts of war have always been lacking, so I have been forced to take on mercenaries for my own protection. The route from here to Qar Arrid is, unfortunately, a dangerous one, and bandits are known to prey on the unprepared."

Augustin touched the sword at his hip. "We are hardly unprepared."

"I would not question your skill in arms, my friend," Samir said. "Nevertheless, I would feel safer with my own guards. Shapur and Sharbhaz have served me well for many years. Ah. Here they are now."

Two lumbering Ahktarran Lizardmen marched towards them. They were lightly armoured and robed in the manner of desert warriors, their hides crisscrossed in scars. Their ears were pierced many times over and their arms heavily tattooed.

"Greetings?" gulped Polnygar to the two towering Ahktarra, who did not respond, instead merely glaring straight ahead.

"They will not speak, my lady," Samir said. "They have both had their tongues cut out, I am sorry to say."

"That's horrible!" Polnygar said.

"It was not my doing, it happened long before they came into my service." Samir sighed. "'Tis the fate of all slaves, I'm afraid."

"You have slaves?" Polnygar said, shocked.

Augustin sounded disgusted. "No one would ever dare own a slave in Emparia."

"But we are not in Emparia, Baron," Hebu cautioned. "Or do you believe everyone in this world should think as you do?"

"Are you saying this is acceptable?" Polnygar demanded of the Nemoi.

"Such high-minded hypocrisy from you two. I expected better. Ask the average Emparian peasant if he feels much freer than a slave," Hebu said. "These things are a matter of cultural perspective."

"A person's freedom shouldn't be a matter of cultural debate," Polnygar persisted. She looked to Aelzandar for silent support, but while his usually friendly face wore an unusually dark cast, he did not look at her.

Samir looked confused. "My dear friends, I am sorry if this offends you. But I give you my word that I did not enslave them or harm them in any way. Before I purchased them, they were bound for the arenas, where they would have fought until they died. I have at least given them purpose."

"Yes, *your* purpose," Augustin said.

Aelzandar looked annoyed and waved his hands. "Please. None of this. This bickering is pointless. I favour slavery no more than you do, Believe me." Polnygar thought she spied anger in his eyes, but his voice took on an allaying tone. "Samir has explained to me his needs. He has given me assurances that he does not mistreat his guards in any way."

Samir nodded. "I would not mistreat anyone I had entrusted my own life to, friends."

Augustin looked at Polnygar and shook his head, but said nothing more on the matter.

They left Selvarial soon after. With Samir joining them they formed their own caravan, the horses and camels they had brought with them from Ralom refreshed and supplemented with Samir's own herd. They made good time after leaving the gates of Selvarial and soon enough were back travelling through the familiar dunes of the desert.

The desert between Ralom and Qarld was known as the Desert of Despair, a name that did not exactly fill Polnygar with confidence that their trip across it would be uneventful. The cultist attack outside Ralom still preyed on her mind and she still expected them to jump out from behind every cliff-face or stunted bush that the group passed. Despite her worry, her fears turned out to be mostly unfounded, and they encountered no one else on the road except fellow travellers, including a group of Sarrisites undertaking a religious pilgrimage to a distant holy site.

Aelzandar had told Polnygar that the borders of Macrodonia had once extended far past Ralom, and she could see evidence of this around here, whether it be crumbling monoliths covered in hieroglyphics or broken statues depicting long-dead pharaohs peeking out from underneath the sand.

Now, however, all this land belonged to the Caliphate, an empire dedicated to the Infinite Faith of the long-dead prophet Sarrius. The Caliph ruled from far-away Qar Udel, the so-called City of a Thousand and One Delights. She knew little of their ways or customs, but if Samir was any example of the average Sarrisite, then the religion's edicts and practices were only laxly followed this far away from the Caliph's gaze.

Despite her anger at his ownership of the two slaves, and his unwelcome flirtation when they first met, Polnygar found it difficult to truly hate the fat merchant, as Samir was too good-natured and witty for anyone to dislike. She consoled herself that Shapur and Sharbhaz did seem to be well-treated by the merchant. He never used force to scold them and the pair always received a full ration portion, just like the rest of them. She also spied Samir talking to them as he would the others, and witnessed no signs that the merchant believed himself superior to the two Ahktarra. How they felt about their lives was impossible to know, as they spent most of the journey patrolling the edges of the caravan, their attention focused elsewhere. Their faces did not betray even the slightest flicker of their inner thoughts. She was a little disappointed by Aelzandar's dismissal of her concerns but perhaps she should have expected it as it was unlikely that someone with as privileged a life as the archmage would know much of the suffering of a slave.

Samir spent much of the trip next to Polnygar, quizzing her incessantly about the Art. His fascination with the world of magic seemed endless, and he seemed quite interested to know exactly what feats Polnygar could perform. She demonstrated a few simple tricks with fire, which she later regretted since it only increased Samir's fascination with her. Thankfully there was no more unwelcome advances, but the merchant stayed close to her and peppered her with endless questions.

Augustin rode beside her while she spoke with Samir, but hardly got a word in edgeways against the excitable merchant. After riding next to her for a while in sullen silence, Augustin seemed to give up and joined Hebu and Aelzandar at the front of the caravan.

Samir didn't seem to notice Augustin's departure, continuing his conversation with Polnygar without missing a beat. "In the lands of my people, sorcery is the power that the Infinite has granted to women alone. It is the Infinite's gift to them to compensate them for not being born a man."

Polnygar felt herself burning at the suggestion that any woman would need compensation for being born a woman, but said nothing. If they needed Samir on their trip, she was going to have to learn to tolerate his remarkably different beliefs.

"Of course," Samir said. "I cannot hold this to be true, not since I have journeyed among the world at large and seen so many men with the talent. Though most of my countrymen would argue that such men have the hearts and minds of women." Samir looked at Aelzandar, who shook his head in disapproval. Samir quickly backtracked. "Not that that would be something to be ashamed of."

"If more men had the minds and hearts of women, perhaps the world wouldn't be in the state it's in," Polnygar commented.

"You are most accurate, my lady. There have been quite a few sorceresses in the history of the Caliphate. Did you know that, my sweet green-eyed lady?" Samir asked. "Fatima al'Naif was even the one who taught the archmage Kelloccio the White everything he knew. She was both powerful and beautiful, so the stories said. When she was a young woman, the Caliph of the time asked for his hand, but she rejected him. He spent the rest of his days pining for what could have been and never took a wife of his own."

Samir had a seemingly inexhaustible supply of stories, most of which featured doomed yet romantic love matches. Augustin scoffed at quite a few of the tales, but the merchant always insisted every one of them was true.

There were other matters troubling Polnygar. The dream she had the night before was so vivid, and terrifying that it had remained in her thoughts even as they left Selvarial. The rational part of her mind told her that it was just her anxieties about Ivellios and the Horned God manifesting in her subconscious. Despite this she couldn't help wondering if it was some sort of portent. There had been those dreams she had on the way to Ralom, about her brother and cousin and about the Heir of Lydin. Her thoughts drifted towards dark places. She needed answers, and she knew only Aelzandar could provide them.

"I need to ask you something," she said.

"Of course my dear," said Aelzandar. "What is troubling you?"

"I've been having dreams lately," she said after she caught up to the archmage. "Very strange dreams."

"Most dreams are, my dear."

"I know," Polnygar said quickly. "But these are different. Most dreams disappear from my mind moments after I awake. These stay with me. I can't help thinking that there's something more to them."

Aelzandar looked thoughtful. "That is a possibility. Have you heard of the *Dreaming?*"

Polnygar shook her head.

Aelzandar looked sombre as he spoke. "It is another realm, separated from the one we know. Some call it the fey-realm, others, the land of nightmares. It is said to be a place of restless spirits and unimaginable horrors. Most of us only ever see it in our dreams, and the memories of such a place are fleeting, disappearing from our minds when we wake. Sometimes, however, there are those of us who have a deeper connection with this place."

Polnygar craned her head closer. "Is this like the Art?"

"In some ways. Sometimes the connection to the Dreaming is not innate, and the dreams are in fact sendings from others. You remember what I showed you in Selvarial, yes?" Polnygar nodded, and Aelzandar continued. "Other times the Dreaming can be touched spontaneously, even outside of sleep. This has been called the *Sight*, and I have seen many who claim to possess such a power. Of these, many are in truth, frauds, making a living swindling the gullible. There are also those for whom the power is real. These moon-seers, as they are called, are a rare breed."

Polnygar directed more questions towards the archmage. "Do you have this power? Have you ever had dreams that turned out to be true?"

"No," said Aelzandar. "But I once knew a young woman who did. Her name was Vanaja and she was about your age, tremendously skilled in the

Art. She dreamed of far off places, of terrible secrets hidden in the darkness."

"What happened? Did she find what she dreamed of?"

Aelzandar looked grim. "Yes, she did. Vanaja followed the visions to her own death."

Polnygar's face fell. "That's not what I wanted to hear."

Aelzandar sighed. "The problem with visions is you never know *who* sends them, or what purpose is behind them. Sometimes chasing such things can be dangerous. Sometimes your dreams can kill you."

The archmage said nothing more, instead gazing out to the horizon, looking lost in his own thoughts.

CHAPTER 8

To Polnygar's relief, after many weeks of scorching days followed by freezing nights, their journey through the desert came to an end. They came within sight of a valley bisected by a river that snaked down from the mountains to the north.

"The river Arrid. We are close, friends, Qar Arrid is not far from here," Samir said.

"Good," said Augustin, wiping the sweat from his forehead. "I've had just about as much as I can take of wandering through the desert."

"Well then my friend, I hope you are ready for good food, relaxation and hot baths. You will find that Qardleean hospitality has no equal."

"No chance of a drink at all?" Augustin asked.

"For most folk, no," Samir smiled. "But when you know the right person to ask, effendi, all things are possible."

The desert gave way to farmlands and small villages and after that a grand city, seated on the turn of the river, with wide, tree-lined streets and tall buildings glistening white in the sun. Samir led the caravan down the path that twisted from the cliff-face to the city, and through the tall gates of Qar Arrid.

The city's inhabitants were a cosmopolitan mix. The bulk were Qardleeans, tan-skinned and bearded, but Polnygar also noticed a number of Ahktarra and some darker-skinned men and women.

"The Shadrish," Aelzandar said to Polnygar. "Folk from the archipelago that marks the Caliphate's western border."

Minarets towered above the city's skyline and the emir's palace dominated the centre of the city. Surrounding the palace was a ring of elegant and colourful gardens. Water danced playfully in each of the many fountains.

A great marble statue stood on a plinth near the palace. It depicted a magnificent dragon, its tail snaking around to join with its mouth. "Bahamut, Herald of the Infinite," Aelzandar explained to Polnygar. "The faithful of the Caliphate hold that it was Bahamut who revealed to the Prophet Sarrius the will of the Infinite."

"So they say. The story has never particularly convinced me," said Hebu. Aelzandar only responded with a weary sigh.

"I guess we should find the nearest traveller's inn," Augustin mused.

"Nonsense, my friends," Samir said, placing one arm around Augustin's shoulder and the other around Polnygar. "I am a close personal friend of the emir, may he serve faithfully. I will not have my new friends stay in the travellers' quarters. No, we must continue to the emir's palace. He will receive us, my friends, do not worry."

The opulence of the palace impressed Polnygar. It stood on the slopes of a small hill in the centre of the city, surrounded by date palms. A long, broad boulevard, elegantly tiled, led up to the palace's courtyard where half a dozen soldiers stood guard. Clad in mail and with helmets that concealed their faces, they were an intimidating presence.

"So tell me, Samir, how do you know the Emir of Qar Arrid?" Aelzandar asked the merchant as they approached the palace.

"Ah my dear Archmage, that is indeed a somewhat florid tale. And perhaps too scandalous a tale to be told when ladies are present." He looked at Polnygar as he said those words. "Suffice to say in my role as purveyor of exotic goods I happened upon the extract of a certain flower, known for its stimulating aroma, and found that it was in much demand in the palace of Qar Arrid."

"So you provided the emir with this extract?" Polnygar said.

Samir smiled. "Ah now my dear, sweet lady that would be telling."

The guards saw them coming and two of them moved in front of the palace gates, crossing their spears to bar entry.

"It doesn't look like they recognise you," Augustin noted drily.

Samir laughed nervously. "I'm sure it's just a misunderstanding. Let me talk to them for a moment."

The merchant approached the guardsmen and spoke to one of them. Polnygar was not able to hear the words being spoken, but Samir appeared quite animated. At the end of the conversation, one of the guards opened the palace gates. Samir turned back to his companions. "See? Just a misunderstanding. We should have no problem now."

The guards led the group inside the palace, and Polnygar was amazed by its size and grandeur. Delicate mosaics covered the walls and floors, and the doorways and ceilings were inlaid with fine gold leaf.

"The emir will see you now," said one of the guards, and he escorted them into the throne room. The room was a large, open chamber with a tall domed roof. A fountain dominated the centre of the room, and to one end was a raised dais. Atop this dais was a padded throne that was currently empty; whoever its usual occupant, they were nowhere to be seen.

A Nemoi, richly dressed in robes of silk with a finely made turban, approached them "Greetings to you again, Samir. I see you returned and this time you have brought with you some strangers. Might I ask why?"

"Is that what I think it is?" Polnygar whispered to Augustin while glancing at Hebu.

"A Nemoi?" he asked, his voice low. "They can be found here as well, but not as prevalent as in Macrodonia."

Polnygar nudged Hebu, but all she elicited in response was a withering glance. Despite this, she did notice the newcomer's eyes linger over Hebu critically for a moment, before turning back to Samir.

"Vizier Baruch," Samir said, bowing to the Nemoi. "It is my most humble pleasure to meet you again. I am here to speak with the emir."

"Are you sure he wishes to speak with you, Samir?"

"Please do not speak for me, Baruch, I am quite capable of doing so myself." Polnygar turned to the new voice; another man had entered the room, accompanied by several guards. Dripping in jewels and gold trim, the newcomer's outfit made the vizier's look like a pauper's. He did not appear to be much older than Polnygar and had a kind face with an easy smile. "Samir, my old friend. Who are these strangers you bring before me?"

Samir dropped to the ground in reverence, and the vizier turned to the others. His face was taut, and without humour. "Show some respect, foreigners. This is the Emir Omar al'Dazhi. Favoured of the Caliph and Prince of the Righteous."

Aelzandar got down on his knees, alongside Hebu. Polnygar quickly did likewise, but a frowning Augustin stayed standing.

"Kneel, you fool," hissed Hebu. "This is not the time for your stubbornness."

"Emparians do not kneel to foreign princes," Augustin said, folding his hands.

"Don't be difficult, Baron," said Aelzandar.

The emir, sensing the confusion, waved a hand, "Please, none of you need kneel. You are guests here, and I will not have it said that I neglected my hospitality." He climbed the stairs and eased himself into the throne, and the guards came up to stand on either side. The vizier joined the emir on the dais shortly after.

Aelzandar rose to his feet. "It is much appreciated, Your Eminence," he said, inclining his head.

The emir smiled broadly enough for Polnygar to see his dimples. "So, Samir, who are our guests?"

Samir rose to his feet, dusting himself off and straightening his wrinkled clothes. "Allow me to introduce my companions, Your Eminence. Aelzandar of Macrodonia, Archmage and Lord of the Nine Orders, and his companion, Hebu."

"Your fame precedes you, archmage," the emir said, acknowledging Aelzandar. "Your name is legend in the Caliphate. There are few here who have not heard of the legends of Cassian and Aelzandar, especially the fall of the Night Dragon."

Aelzandar inclined his head. "I assure you that not all they say about me is true, Your Eminence."

The emir smiled knowingly. "I would hope not my friend, many of the legends call you an enemy of the Infinite Faith. And the rest of you?"

Samir motioned to Augustin. "This is Baron Augustin Bauer."

The emir looked at Augustin with a critical eye. "We receive few Emparian visitors here, but you are welcome all the same, Baron."

Polnygar realised that the emir was looking directly at her. She flushed and tried not to return the gaze. His eyes seemed to twinkle as he gazed at her. "In the name of the Infinite and Eternal, who is this vision of exquisiteness that you have brought to me, Samir? Such eyes, green like emeralds. Hair, as black as the night sky, and skin like ivory. A goddess, walking amongst us."

"Your Eminence, you do indeed have a keen eye for beauty. Born of the union between an Emparian sire and an Elven dam, this is Polnygar Ap'Lydin – the exotic flower of the south."

Polnygar wasn't sure she appreciated Samir's description of her, no matter how well-intentioned. She felt like she was being compared to some sort of prize mare. The emir, however, looked impressed. "You do not exaggerate, she is indeed another Zohra. Easily worth twice any other woman." He clapped his hands, "Ah, my friend, I am happy to host you and your companions for as long as you wish to stay. You shall be my honoured guests."

Aelzandar made a small cough, glancing towards Samir.

"Ah yes, Your Eminence, there is one other thing, a favour we beg of you," Samir said.

The emir leant forward on his throne, looking at Samir expectantly. "Yes, my friend?" As the emir spoke, his vizier glared at Samir, eyes flinty with suspicion.

"My companion, the archmage, wishes to visit your most glorious library while he is staying in Qar Arrid."

The emir looked confused. "Of course," he said. "But you need not receive my permission for that, Samir. The library is open to all."

"Actually, Your Eminence," said Aelzandar. "There is certain book in particular that I wish to read."

The emir raised his eyebrows. "Oh?"

"*The Tome of Divine Metaphysics.*"

The Slaves of the Horned God

There was a silence. The emir frowned and the vizier looked scandalised. "That is forbidden!"

The emir waved a hand at the vizier. "Enough Baruch." He turned to Aelzandar. "*The Tome of Divine Metaphysics* is a blasphemous work, archmage. It is full of heresy and vile ideas. Why would you wish to read such filth?"

"I assure you, Emir, that the theories within this work are not what interest me. But I believe that this book has information that I need."

"Information?" the emir ventured. "What information?"

"A rival of mine, a spellweaver named Ivellios has come into possession of a powerful relic known as the Tears of the Divine. I believe there is a connection between this relic and the tome."

The emir leant back in his throne and thought for a moment. "I will consider your words, archmage," he said. "In the meantime, I encourage you to explore the pleasures Qar Arrid has to offer. I am sure you will find your stay to be most pleasurable. Try the palace baths. You will not regret it."

"I thank you, Your Eminence," said Aelzandar. "You have been most generous."

The emir turned to his vizier. "Show them to their rooms, Baruch."

The vizier nodded respectfully and descended the dais. He led them through the palace until they reached a complex of rich and luxurious rooms. A number of sleeping chambers were connected by a single, spacious common area. Light and airy, the rooms were furnished with colourful and exquisite rugs and tapestries. Servants had laid out clean clothes and bowls of hot water for washing. "Make yourself at home," the vizier said. "If you need anything, there is a bell to call for a servant."

Polnygar noticed that Hebu and the vizier's eyes met once more before the vizier departed without further comment, leaving them alone.

"Well, that was an interesting experience," Hebu remarked.

"Do you two know each other?" Polnygar asked.

"Who, myself and the vizier?" Hebu said, eyebrow raised. "Yes, of course. All Nemoi know all other Nemoi, no matter the geographical distance between them."

"A simple no would have sufficed," said Polnygar.

"Now where's the fun in that?" Hebu asked.

"I have dealt with Baruch in the past," said Samir. "He is self-important, and likes to believe he controls access to the emir. Unfortunately for him, the emir doesn't see things the same way. I have always found the emir most reasonable for one of his position."

"Do you think you'll be allowed to see the book?" Polnygar asked Aelzandar. "He did say he would think about it."

"Indeed, my dear," Aelzandar said. He rubbed his chin. "His reaction surprised me. He seemed less shocked at the request than I expected him to be."

"I don't trust him," Augustin said. "Nor that vizier."

Samir shook his head. "Baruch is harmless, more bombast than anything else. The emir is a great man, generous, pious and merciful. He will allow us to see this book, just you wait."

A veiled servant entered their chambers. "I am looking for the one known as Polnygar."

Polnygar looked at her companions, her surprise mirrored in their faces. "Um...that's me."

The servant produced a flower placed in an elegantly crafted tube. "A gift from the emir. He says, 'To the Flower of the South. A blossom almost as beautiful as she.'"

Polnygar flushed red. "Ah, thanks. I guess." The servant bowed and departed.

"What in the name of the gods does he think he is doing?" Augustin demanded.

"My friend, there is no harm intended. He is merely complimenting our lovely friend."

"Whatever you say. I am going for a walk," Augustin grumbled.

"What's wrong with him?" Hebu asked.

Aelzandar just smiled and waved a hand. "I think it might be best to let him cool off for a bit. As for myself, I do believe I might have a lie down for a while. Today's efforts have drained me."

Polnygar yawned, and realised she herself was feeling rather tired, and the idea of a short rest did sound rather appealing. "I think I might have a rest myself," she said, excusing herself. She found one of the beds, diligently made up by the servants in preparation for their arrival, and tossed the excess cushions to the ground before laying her head down on the pillow.

CHAPTER 9

Polnygar's brow was coated in perspiration when she woke up. Another nightmare had interrupted her sleep. She had seen men with dead white eyes surrounding her, trying to push her down into an icy lake. Behind the men stood Ivellios, looking at her and laughing at her misfortune. She had called out to Augustin to save her, but the baron had frowned and turned his back on her. The dream had felt vivid enough that though awake now she shivered as if she could still feel the chill of the ice. Seeing the afternoon sunlight streaming in through the window comforted her, and she shook off the tendrils of dread.

Just a dream, she thought. *Not a premonition.* All the same, however, she felt the need to clear her head. She tossed back the blankets and emerged from the bed. Her hair was most likely a tangled mess, and she made a half-hearted effort to fix it, before giving up and tying it back behind her head.

Leaving the bedroom she discovered the rest of the guest complex to be empty except for Hebu and Samir sitting at a small table.

"Aelzandar just left," Hebu said. "He is meeting with the emir. He will be back soon." He turned to Samir. "I believe it is your move." The pair were playing a game of Shatranj; Polnygar could tell from the shape of the board and the playing pieces. The pieces were far more elaborate than those she had seen in Macrodonia. She approached the table to get a closer look.

Hebu noticed her interest. "The game is played a little differently in the Caliphate to what we have in Macrodonia. Qardleeans like to recreate famous wars when they play and have special playing pieces for when they do."

"I can see that," said Polnygar. Samir's pieces were white, and carved in the shape of warriors and priests from the Caliphate. Hebu's on the other hand, were black, and had traditional Macrodonian designs. His king-piece was a powerful mage, garbed in robes and was depicted unleashing some sort of fiery vengeance on his foes."

"So what war is this one then?" Polnygar asked.

Samir held his hands out and spoke with a flourish. "We are playing the campaign of the dreaded Jaguseti, a dark sorcerer who ravaged the lands of the Caliphate and ruled with an iron fist until the power of the Infinite brought him low."

Hebu gave the Qardleean a withering look. "What Samir *means* to say is that he is playing the Caliphate, whereas I am Jaguesti, King of Anacoilis and Dracacoilis, Lord Archmage and first Pharaoh of Macrodonia. And just as Jaguesti before me, I am having a rather successful campaign." He moved one of his pieces, knocking one of Samir's off the board. The Qardleean frowned.

"And will the Infinite bring you low too?" Polnygar asked with a smile.

Hebu snorted. "If you mean will I die quietly in my sleep after a two-hundred-year reign, with my empire at its height, then yes, I truly hope that the Infinite brings me *just that low.*" Samir laughed heartily and the pair continued with their game.

The Slaves of the Horned God

Polnygar decided to explore outside the palace, reasoning there must be something of interest in the city-proper to divert her attention for a few hours. She negotiated the unfamiliar corridors in the palace, before finding herself in the sumptuous entrance hall. The emir's throne was empty, and the vizier was nowhere to be seen. Polnygar was glad they were not there. She would have found herself addressing nobility on her own and she didn't expect Baruch would have been very forgiving if she made unwitting gaffes. She strolled through the palace gate with a sense of freedom and purpose. The path wound its way from the gate down a hill before joining with the paved paths of Qar Arrid.

Of all she had heard of the famed library of the city, she expected it would not be too difficult to locate. After about an hour of walking about she found it – a grand building in the richer district of the city. Great mosaics covered the outside walls, depicting several Caliphs from the distant past. One in particular caught her attention, and while the young Caliph's face seemed undamaged the images of the two women who stood on either side of him had been defaced. Someone had excised their faces in a deliberate attempt to erase their identities. There was no sign of any attempt at repair and since there was no damage to any other part of the mosaic it would seem to have been a deliberate state-sanctioned defacement. She wondered idly who the women were and then walked inside the library

She was greeted by a tremendous collection of shelves, each groaning with books of every description and theme. She didn't know where to start, so she lingered near the entrance, unsure as to where to head next. Noticing her uncertainty, an elderly man in a robe gave her a kind smile.

"Ah, hatun. You must be one of the foreign guests of the emir. My name is Huramosh. I am the librarian here."

"Polnygar Ap'Lydin," Polnygar said. "I'm looking for something to read,"

"*Ibn Lydin*," the librarian said, translating her name into its Qardleean equivalent. He said the name as if he were familiar with it. "I have just the book for you." He went to one of the shelves and scanned a row of books before he pulled one out. "Here you go, hatun," the librarian said. "I hope you find it most diverting. I thought of it as soon as you said your name."

Polnygar read the title on the book. "The Siege of Ralom: A History of the Most Glorious Campaign to recapture the Holy City from the Infidels of Caruillin."

The librarian turned the book to a particular page, indicating a part for Polnygar to read. For a brief moment the writing seemed little more than gibberish, but then, as if a veil had been drawn, the characters became familiar to her. She touched the enchanted bracer on her wrist. Aelzandar had given it to her in Macrodonia and it had proved invaluable in helping her understand and communicate in foreign tongues. It translated the Qardleean characters for her, making the book as easy to understand as if it were written in her birth tongue.

The first passage described a war over the city of Ralom some seventy years or so ago. At this time the city was under the control of the Empire of Caruillin, but the Infinite Caliphate desired to regain control of the city, having ruled it another seventy years before the battle, losing it after a disastrous war with Macrodonia. In an attempt to fight off the Qardleean attack the Empire of Caruillin had requested assistance from an Emparian expeditionary service led by Prince Alusine Ran-Tyron, Duke of Emperor's Palace.

"Now this part, hatun," the librarian said, turning to another page. The next passage described how the allied forces succeeded in driving off the Qardleeans, but then had turned on each other in an attempt to control Ralom. The Qardleean author seemed to take much satisfaction in this betrayal, and there were many snide remarks that this was the sort of thing to be expected from infidels. Eventually, the Emparians had driven out the Empire as well as the Caliphate, leaving Ralom as an independent city-state, which it remained until now, judging by Polnygar's recent visit there.

However it was not the details of the battle itself that piqued Polnygar's interest – rather it was the identity of one of the Emparian commanders, a knight serving under Prince Alusine. *Sir William Ap'Lydin*, Polnygar thought. *My grandfather.* Excited, she let out a tiny yelp.

"Ah, so you see why I thought you might be interested in it," the librarian said.

Polnygar nodded. "Make I take this back to the palace to read further?"

The librarian smiled. "Of course," he said. "The emir will ensure it is returned once you have left Qar Arrid, of that I have no doubt."

The title on one of the nearby books caught her eye. "*The Tragedy of Belial'ad-Din.* What's that?"

"An old Qardleean tale. It is the story of the son of a Jinni, whose demonic blood drives him to darkness and evil, despite his attempt to live a holy life. Why do you ask?"

"It sounds like my brother's name, Bellaydin."

The librarian seemed amused. "I do know that the story of Belial'ad-Din is known outside the Caliphate, perhaps the tale is told differently in such places. I would not name my son after such a figure, but the ways of you outlanders are a mystery to me."

"And yet you do not care to find out, Huramosh? Have you forgotten the words of Sarrius?" A veiled woman came into view. "'*Knowledge is the elixir of life*.'"

Upon seeing the woman, the librarian paled, bowing his head and clasping his hands together in the manner of a supplicant. "Apologies, my lady. I did not see you there. You have shamed me with your most pertinent reminder of my spiritual shortcomings."

The woman raised a hand. "Pay it no heed, Huramosh. Go, and may the Infinite guide your steps."

The librarian bowed again, before hurrying off out of sight. The woman turned to Polnygar. "So, you are one of the outlanders I have heard about. Tell me, child, what is your name?"

Something about the woman's voice seemed to engender trust in Polnygar, and she felt completely safe in revealing her identity. "My name is Polnygar Ap'Lydin."

The veiled woman nodded. "Ah yes, the young half-elvish girl. Come Polnygar, sit with me here. Let us speak somewhere away from prying eyes."

The veiled woman took her to a private booth and, after pulling the privacy curtain across, she lifted her veil, exposing her face to Polnygar. The woman was elderly, older than Polnygar had guessed and her green eyes twinkled with an inner spark. "My name is Um Badr," she said. "I hope you are enjoying your visit to the Caliphate. It can be a confronting experience for foreigners, particularly women."

"It is different, I will say that," Polnygar admitted. "Are you a local?"

The woman smiled. "Not to Qar Arrid. I have come from the capital, as many do. My journey takes me from here to the Shadrish Archipelago, but I imagine that would not be your destination."

"No, I..." Polnygar was about to tell the woman that she was travelling to Skurj, but thought better of it. "We're headed towards Lerid."

"As I expected," Um Badr said.

"Earlier you said that the Caliphate was a confronting experience for women. I certainly agree, based on what I've experienced so far. But the librarian certainly treated *you* with deference and respect. You must be someone of great importance."

Um Badr patted Polnygar's hand. "Don't confuse his fawning with respect. I have certain connections back in the capital, family members who might make life difficult for him. Fear is a powerful motivator. No, the sort of men who rule the Caliphate these days have no time for a woman's opinion."

Um Badr leaned closer to Polnygar. "It wasn't always like this, you know? Women once ruled the Caliphate. We were the mighty Sha'eera, advisors to the Caliphs themselves. We ruled in their name. But that was centuries ago. Now we are made to keep to the places they decide for us. They claim it is the Prophet Sarrius' will. *The Art is the Infinite's gift to women, but such a gift was meant to serve man, not to rule him.*"

"Sarrius said that, did he?" Polnygar said.

Um Badr laughed, stopping only when Polnygar gave her a perplexed look. "See how they are? You have heard that name, but not once has anyone told you that the Prophet was a woman. It is a piece of history I'm sure many of the sheikhs and emirs wish they could change – that a woman was given the words of the Infinite. So they do their best to ignore that unsettling fact. Just like all men do when confronted with something that troubles them."

Polnygar smiled, but Um Badr's expression turned serious. "You should look after yourself in Qar Arrid, Polnygar," Um Badr said. "You are a long way away from home and being watched."

"Watched, by who?"

"The emir's vizier trusts no one. He has his spies watching you at all times. And there are others." She gave Polnygar a mysterious look. "You know who I am referring to."

"My lady, we are needed elsewhere," a voice outside the booth side.

"I am coming," said Um Badr. The old woman turned to Polnygar. "Remember what I have told you, and be vigilant."

After Um Badr was gone, Polnygar left the library. She took a different route back to the palace, hoping to explore some more of the city. Um Badr's words stuck in her mind. She was being watched by the vizier. That much she expected – he had not disguised his distrust of them when they arrived. And there were others, Um Badr did not specify, but Polnygar knew she was referring to cultists of the Horned God. Were they here, working even in the Caliphate?

She passed through the bazaar. Merchants crowded around her, hawking their wares. The aroma of spiced meats drew her attention.

"What is this?" she asked, pointing to a selection of roasted meat on skewers.

"It is called kabab here, hatun," said the merchant. He stroked his beard, neat and oiled. "Are you interested in some?"

Polnygar nodded, and offered some coins from her belt.

He waved a hand. "No charge, hatun," he demurred. "I am honoured to serve a guest of the emir."

"Thank you," she said, and felt awkward as the man passed her the skewered meat. He continued to stare at her while she ate.

"You must protect yourself, hatun."

Polnygar stopped chewing. "What?"

"Your skin, it is like ivory," the merchant said. "It would be wise to cover your face when outside, lest the desert wind age you before your time. A woman like you must be careful, there is danger here. The followers of *Dhul-Qarnayn* are – "

He suddenly cut his words short and stared with a panicked expression at something behind Polnygar. "Apologies hatun," he stammered. "May the Infinite guide you."

The merchant returned to his stove. Confused, Polnygar turned around. A heavily armoured palace guard stood there, his fingers tightly gripping his spear. Polnygar stepped back and glanced about her. The other merchants watched the guard warily, and did their best to ignore Polnygar. She decided that moving on might be the best decision.

A crowded street opened up to her right, a shingle depicting some esoteric symbol hanging above it. Intrigued Polnygar walked down the alleyway. More merchants lined the street. These merchants, robed and dripping with jewellery, offered a glittering array of trinkets and baubles, claiming all sorts of miraculous and potent effects. Polnygar declined as politely as she could, and kept moving, pushing the throne of supplicants.

"You have made the right choice, hatun," said a woman, swathed in robes "None of them could help you. None of them had the Sight." The woman wore a loose veil over her hair but her dusky skin was of a darker complexion than most people Polnygar had seen in the city. Her clothing glittered with jewels, but of such size and quantity that Polnygar doubted the gems were real.

"And you do have the Sight?" Polnygar said, irritated.

The woman smiled, her dark eyes flashing and gestured to the sign above her. It depicted the all-seeing eye – a Macrodonian symbol for knowledge – and the writing underneath indicated that the woman was a fortune-teller.

Polnygar waved her hand. "I'm not interested, really."

The woman raised an eyebrow. "Oh, is that so? Well, then Polnygar. I will leave you in peace."

Polnygar's mouth dropped. "You called me Polnygar? How do you – "

"You are Polnygar Ap'Lydin, are you not? Polnygar Milael Ap'Lydin?"

Polnygar narrowed her eyes, her natural scepticism taking over. "Who have you been talking to?"

"Daughter of Saegralanna li'Saegras and Alusine Ap'Lydin?"

"Yes, but –

"These things were not revealed to me by any man, Polnygar. I have the

Sight. And I have seen you with it. For some of us, the veil that separates us from the dreaming is thin. With the Sight, we can see through it with ease."

The Sight. Could this woman truly have it? Or is she one of the charlatans which Aelzandar had warned me of? "So you know me," Polnygar said. "What else can see?"

The woman smiled and held out a hand. "Much more. If you wish to find out, you must step inside."

Polnygar was hesitant, but her curiosity won out, and she entered the woman's shop. Inside it was dimly lit and cluttered, but Polnygar glimpsed strange and exotic shapes in the gloom. The air was heavy with the scent of burning incense. Shelves crowded with glass vials of queer coloured liquids stood over pots of rare and valuable herbs and ritual ingredients. The ceiling was covered in an array of shining stars and a dazzling portrayal of the four moons of the night sky. Curiously, all four moons were depicted as full, an occurrence that was incredibly infrequent in the outside world.

"The moons are a potent enhancement to the Sight, particularly when they are full. But you know this already, don't you? It is the same with the Art. Please Polnygar, this way." The woman ushered Polnygar to a table with two seats. "Come, sit. I am Madame Noor," the woman said. "Let us see what the cards can tell us."

She took a deck and shuffled the cards. "You are familiar with the Wistarni Deck, are you not?"

Polnygar nodded. "A little. They're the Macrodonian ones, yes?

The woman nodded. "Yes. There are six suits, each linked to one of the Ancient Ones, as well as to one of the six cardinal elements."

"Six elements?" Polnygar questioned, as she watched the cards shuffling between the woman's hands. "I thought there were only four elements, the same number as the moons in the night sky: Water, Wind, Fire and Earth."

The fortune teller's eyes twinkled. "You have neglected the two elements that stand apart: The Ether, and its opposite, the Nether. Now, if you are ready, we shall begin. First, the cards will speak of the past."

She pulled the first card from the deck and laid it on the table. It depicted a young woman, surrounded by fire. "This card represents who you were. The Nine of Fire. The symbol represents passion, enthusiasm and restless energy. For a long period of your life, you have been possessed by a yearning to explore, to seek out new horizons, to see what lies beyond the comfortable borders of home."

The fortune teller nodded and glanced at Polnygar. "The next two cards are of people from your past. Those whose influence has shaped you." She drew two new cards from the deck and laid them on the table. One depicted a young man gazing at a distant horizon. The other, a woman of middle years, sitting in a homely setting. "These two are closely connected, family perhaps. I see a young man, shy and introspective, and a woman, kind, caring and with a great love for you."

Polnygar smiled. "Mother and Bela, of course."

The fortune teller smiled a knowing smile. "The next card is who you are." She placed a new card on the table. It showed a figure seated at a table, deep in study, with stars twinkling in the background.

"The Five of Ether. The card of the student. You have taken on an academic pursuit, and are learning things you have never known before. The next two cards represent those who are influencing your life the most at this moment." Two more cards came from the deck. One depicted a knight, deep in battle against many foes. "The card of the Myrmidon. A great warrior, proud of his strength and courage, yet troubled by a wound that will never heal." The next card depicted a man of power, with three eyes. "The Master of Ether, also known as the Archmage. This represents a figure of awesome power and skill, and mastery over the Art. It is this man who has the most to teach you." The fortune teller paused, as if to give Polnygar time to consider the cards.

"Now, my child," the fortune teller continued. "We shall see what the future holds for you." She drew a card and placed it on the table. It depicted a skeletal figure holding an hourglass. "Death will surround you. There are those close to you know who may not survive this journey."

Polnygar drew an audible breath. "Someone is going to die?"

The fortune teller spoke evasively. "Perhaps. Perhaps not. But none shall come out unchanged. There are forces ranged against you. Let us see who they are." She placed a card on the table. "The Charlatan. The card of a traitor. The one who this refers to is your enemy, though he may have once purported to be your ally. Betrayal is all he knows. As has he betrayed you, so shall he betray others."

Polnygar nodded. She wondered who that card could mean. *Ivellios? But he never pretended to be an ally.*

"But he is not your true enemy," the fortune teller said. "There is one, working in the shadows behind the charlatan. Let us see who the true architect of all this is..."

She placed the final card on the table. The card was ominous, nearly totally black, with a shadowy indistinct figure and a pair of sinister red eyes peering from out of the vague form. Even the fortune teller shuddered when she saw the card. "The Great Old One. A malevolent force of eldritch and ancient pedigree. A power not to be trifled with, but which has now set its eyes upon you, and others you hold dear."

Polnygar looked at the card. There was something deeply unsettling about it. "Who is this ancient power?"

The fortune teller grew quiet. "I cannot tell you. The cards have revealed all that they will. All I will say is that you are being watched, Polnygar. Hold those you care for close and prepare for the confrontation that will come."

Polnygar pressed for more information but the fortune teller bowed her head and held out her hand for payment and Polnygar, knowing she would get nothing more from her, placed a gold coin in her palm and departed.

As she came outside of the fortune teller's she felt the hairs on the back of her neck prick up. She had the oddest sensation that she was being watched, as Um Badr and Madam Noor suggested she would be. She looked around just in time to see a cloaked figure poke its head back around the wall of a nearby alleyway, look around, and then disappear from sight. Intrigued she was about to take a look when she noticed Augustin Bauer walking down the same street. He looked about cautiously, then disappeared down the same alleyway.

Suspicious, Polnygar followed Augustin and the mysterious figure down the alleyway they had disappeared into. She looked around with utmost vigilance as she did, mindful of what had happened the last time someone followed her – in Macrodonia, Horned God cultists had nearly killed her and Augustin. They would have both been dead had it not been for Polnygar's spontaneous development of the Art.

The alleyway was narrow and deserted. Assorted rubbish littered the cobblestones and a mangy dog was busy rummaging through a pile of garbage for food. The alleyway curved about to the left and, her hand clutching her sword, Polnygar followed it.

As soon as she turned a corner she found herself surrounded by a group of cloaked men, all pointing swords at her throat. She cursed herself for falling into the same trap again, but this time she knew, as she felt a sensation building within her, that any use of the Art to escape would be intentional on her part.

"Polnygar, what in the name of the gods are you doing here?" It was Augustin. His mysterious cloaked associate was standing next to him. Both came towards her. "Have you been following me?"

The cloaked figure issued a command to the others. "Stop. I don't think she's going to cause us trouble." The accent was certainly not Qardleean. For that matter the swords pointed at Polnygar's throat were not Qardleean scimitars either. The cloak figure turned to Augustin. "Is she your travelling companion, Augustin?"

"Of sorts," said Augustin. "For Kytilas' sake, Céline, get your boy to put that damn sword away. Polnygar, did anyone else see you?"

Polnygar was wary of answering and instead turned to the cloaked figure. "How do you know Augustin?"

The woman pulled back her hood to reveal a striking head of blonde hair. "I am Captain Céline de Lerid of the Leridian Chevaliers," she said. "Augustin and I are old friends. I met him recently while your group was in Forestown. He mentioned you."

"Me?"

"I might have said something in passing," Augustin said.

"Well, he mentioned you along with the archmage and some gnome, but it was you he was most voluble in his description of." She pursed her lips and darted her eyes at Augustin. "Though, might I say, even that does not do justice to your beauty."

"You Leridian women," said Augustin, rolling his eyes.

Polnygar felt flattered, but retained enough self-awareness to be suspicious of Céline's friendliness. "Why are you here? And why were you watching me?"

"We are passing through Qar Arrid on our return to the Empire. Unfortunately the Caliphate has no love for those of us who serve King-Emperor Anton so a measure of discretion was required. Hence, the cloaks. I contacted Augustin, asked him to meet us here. When I saw you come out of the library I was not sure whether I recognised you. I believed it was not wise to risk being discovered, so I ran. You followed regardless. That was brave, and your courage should be rewarded. During our journey here we have discovered some information that might be of use to you."

"And what is that?"

"Augustin mentioned that you have tangled with a group known as the Cult of the Horned God, yes?"

"Go on," said Polnygar.

"We have reason to believe that they may be active here, in this very city."

Augustin was surprised. "In Qar Arrid? Are you sure?" Céline nodded.

Polnygar remembered Um Badr's warning. The old woman was right.

Céline continued. "We were ambushed just outside the city limits by a group we thought must have been bandits. But these 'bandits' fought savagely, and to the death. When we examined the bodies, well, Augustin mentioned a certain mark that the Horned God's worshippers have – these men had it. Here, I have drawn what we saw." She passed Polnygar a scrap of paper with some rough lines drawn on it. Despite the crudity of the picture it was clearly the sigil of the Horned God.

"We'll tell the others," Polnygar said to Augustin.

"We must be on our way, we have no desire to stay here any longer than we must," Céline said, "and I leave you with this advice: trust no one here. If I am right, and the cult is active here, there is no telling how much it may have infiltrated Qar Arrid."

Polnygar nodded. "Thank you, I will be careful. And we will pass on to Aelzandar what you have told us."

"Augustin, there is more," Céline said. "You said you are trailing a spellweaver named Ivellios."

Augustin looked interested. "Indeed we are. What of it?"

"He has been seen here, in Qar Arrid. Not long before you arrived."

Polnygar was surprised. Ivellios was here? She looked at Augustin, who likewise showed interest. "Where?"

"He was last seen heading to a set of old ruins at the cliffs, just outside the city proper. The locals call it the Shrine of the Ancients."

"Shrine of the Ancients, eh?" Augustin remarked. "Any ideas why he would be headed there?"

"None, I'm afraid."

"You don't think he's still there, do you?" Polnygar asked.

Augustin shrugged. "I don't know, but there's a chance, and I'm not passing up the opportunity to deal with him. Céline, can you come with me?"

"Miss me already?" Céline's familiarity with Augustin agitated Polnygar, but she said nothing. "Sorry to disappoint you, sweetheart," Céline continued. "As I have said, I must be leaving."

"Understood," said Polnygar plainly.

Céline nodded to Polnygar, then gestured to her companions. "Come on men, to the pass, and then on to Lerid. Farewell to you both." She playfully blew a kiss towards Polnygar and Augustin. "Don't get into too much trouble." The chevaliers departed, leaving Augustin and Polnygar alone.

"Well, let's get going. We need to get to these ruins as soon as we can," Augustin said.

"What? Don't you think we should go back to the palace first?" Polnygar said, "Shouldn't we tell Aelzandar what we've learned?"

Augustin looked frustrated. "By the time we do that Ivellios could be long gone."

"If he's still there," Polnygar added.

Augustin waved his hand. "My mind is made up. You do what you want."

Polnygar hesitated as Augustin started to leave. She took out the piece of paper Céline had given her and looked at the symbol of the Horned God. Frowning, she stuffed the paper back into her pocket and made her after Augustin. "Augustin, wait."

"There's no point, Polnygar," Augustin said. "I have to do this. That damn bastard turned me into a puppet and cost me my arm. There's no way I'm going to leave him to anyone else, even Aelzandar. Ivellios is mine. And he's going to pay."

"I know," said Polnygar. "Let me help."

Augustin's face softened with a smile. "Good. Glad to have you along."

CHAPTER 10

It had been hours since Polnygar and Augustin left the city. Finding their way to the shrine was easier than expected, as most citizens of Qar Arrid had heard of the place and could give directions. At the same time, however, the locals cautioned Polnygar and Augustin from making the journey, as the ruins were believed to be cursed. Augustin had scoffed openly at this, causing Polnygar no end of embarrassment as the Emparian insulted the Qardleean who had told them.

Polnygar sighed.

"Something wrong?" Augustin asked.

"I've been wondering," Polnygar said. "If Ivellios is at this shrine, what are we going to do? What's our plan?"

"What do you think?" Augustin patted the sword on his belt.

Polnygar gave him a quizzical look. "That's not much of a plan."

"Does it need to be?"

"He nearly killed both of us last time," Polnygar said.

"Yes," Augustin growled. "But this time I'm ready for him."

Polnygar didn't continue the discussion any further, but her concerns over their strategy remained. They reached a ravine, so deep that its bottom was not visible, instead there was just an endless black void spanned by a crumbling stone bridge. On the other side of the ravine was the temple, carved into the side of the cliff. Six colossal statues, weathered with age, flanked the central entrance.

Polnygar became aware of another's presence in her mind. Aelzandar. *Where are you? I cannot find you in the palace.*

Polnygar pushed him from her thoughts with difficulty and focused on the task at hand.

"This must be the place," Augustin said.

"It looks Macrodonian," said Polnygar. "But even more ancient."

Augustin waved a hand at the statues. "I thought I recognised these fellows. The gods of Macrodonia, aren't they?"

Polnygar nodded.

"Looks like we'll have to find another way in," said Augustin. The entrance had been completely sealed with stone. This stone was of newer vintage than the rest of the temple and was inscribed with script.

"Can you read it?" Augustin said.

Polnygar was about to shake her head, when her hand moved subconsciously to the bracelet. The words on the slab came into focus, and she could read them aloud. "Sealed in the name of the Great and Eternal Pharaoh, Jaguesti, First of His Name, King of Anacoilis and Dracacoilis, and Lord Archmage. Flee, traveller. This place is damned for all time. Only death awaits you here."

Augustin chuckled. "Well, that certainly sounds inviting. Is there no way in?"

Polnygar ran her fingers over the stone. "It's sealed tight."

"I don't believe Ivellios would have come all this way without getting inside. Is there no way to open it?"

Polnygar touched the slab again. She felt something – magic, if ever so slightly. It was little more than an echo. "I think the slab has been moved before. By someone skilled in the Art."

"Magic?" Augustin said. Polnygar nodded. "Can you move it?" he asked.

"I can try," Polnygar said. She placed her palms on the slab and began to concentrate. Deep in the recesses of her mind, she felt the energy of the ether begin to stir, and her arms and hands started to tingle. They heard the rasps of scraping stone, and the slab began to move.

"Some help would be nice," Polnygar grunted as the slab began to push forward. Augustin came to her, leaning his weight against the slab, and helping to push it out of the way.

Polnygar took down her hands and relaxed, panting for breath.

"Nicely done," Augustin said.

The entrance was open now, but they could see nothing but darkness inside.

Augustin frowned. "Looks like there's going to be a lot of stumbling around."

Polnygar snapped her fingers and created a small ball of light above her hands. With a flick of her wrist, she sent it ahead of them, illuminating the way.

Augustin laughed. "It certainly helps to have a woman of your talents around."

They descended into the temple, moving down a set of crumbling stone stairs. After a descent of almost ten feet, they reached a large domed chamber. A musty, ancient smell hung in the air and shadows clung to every corner.

Polnygar flung the ball of light ahead of them, propelling it high in the room to cast more light. Before them was a startling scene. A battle had taken place in the chamber, but the combatants were not human.

Men of metal stood around the room, cobwebbed and frozen in place, some still brandishing weapons splattered with dried blood. Their apparent foes were stranger still, and their corpses lay in various states of dismemberment and decay about the chamber. They were of flesh, but their appearance so loathsome and hideous Polnygar could scarcely rationalise what she was seeing. Their bodies were vaguely human-shaped, but instead of human hands and feet they possessed clawed appendages like those of a reptile. Their tattered clothes, little more now than rags, looked like they once might have been robes of alien design, but it was their heads that troubled Polnygar the most. In essence, they resembled a cephalopod – bald, and grey-skinned, with large opaque eyes, no visible nose and a number of tentacles clustered about a tiny beak-like mouth.

"Ugh," said Augustin. "What in the name of the gods are these things? I've never seen anything like them."

"Nor I," said Polnygar, "but these metal men seem to have been fighting them."

"Lucky for us I think they managed to kill each other," said Augustin, looking at the dusty battleground. "But here's something..."

"What is it?" Polnygar asked.

"Footsteps in the dust. I'd wager Ivellios. Let's see if he's still around."

Polnygar was about to tell Augustin that they should wait until they had Aelzandar, but after the Emparian's previous reaction, and seeing the grim look of determination on his face, she thought better of it.

They followed the footsteps to another chamber, smaller than the first. There was an altar on a raised dais at one side of the room, flanked by two immobile metal men like in the chamber before. Surrounding the altar was a stone arch, carved with dusty, ancient inscriptions.

"Is that elven?" Augustin looked at Polnygar.

She moved closer, bringing the light towards the arch. "I think so, but I've never seen it written like this. It looks so archaic."

"So? This place must be centuries old." Augustin gestured around in the darkness. "I'd expect old writing."

"You don't understand," Polnygar shook her head. "The Eldara are long-lived and conservative. Eldaric hasn't changed for millennia. Any living Eldara can read writing from the time of Lideros without any trouble at all. But Lideros was almost *six thousand* years ago."

Augustin whistled.

"So, this writing isn't just old," said Polnygar. "It is positively pre-historic."

"Do you know what is says though?"

"I think so," said Polnygar. The words were readable, but she wasn't sure if it was her own knowledge of Eldaric that gave her understanding, or the magic of Aelzandar's bracer.

"The gods weep, and heaven is overthrown."

Augustin was quiet for a moment. "So, any idea what that might mean?"

Polnygar shook her head.

"The footsteps end right there," said Augustin. "But there's no other signs of Ivellios."

"He must have come here," Polnygar said. "But why?"

She looked at the altar, the only other item of significance in the small room. A small metal frame sat atop it, covered with the dust of ages. She reached out a hand to touch it but immediately flinched.

Augustin turned to her with concern. "What's wrong?"

Polnygar rubbed the scar on her palm. "My hand. It hurt again. It's still stinging."

Augustin frowned. "That's odd. What do you think caused it?"

"I don't know. All I did was reach out to the altar. Towards that frame."

"This frame?" Augustin said. He reached out for it. As he did Polnygar heard the clanking of metal and turned around just in time to see the metal hand of one of the previously dormant metal men reaching towards her.

"Duck!" Augustin yelled, and Polnygar did so, narrowly avoiding the wide sweep of the metal man's sword. Augustin pulled his sword from its scabbard and swung at the metal man, his sword clashing with the metal man's. Augustin feinted to the left, catching the thing off-guard but his sword just rang off its metal skin and his opponent barely registered any reaction to the blow. The battle continued, with Augustin grunting and sweating as he fought, but despite the Baron's efforts none of his attacks seemed to be able to dent the metal man's metal skin.

"The bloody thing's unbreakable." Augustin shouted. "Now would be the time to do something if you can."

Polnygar stepped back, out of the range of the metal man's swings, and held two index fingers out a few inches in front of her face. Torrents of flame erupted from her fingers, engulfing the metal man. Unfortunately, it seemed to shrug off the attack, with only a few scorch marks visible for all Polnygar's troubles.

"It seems resistant to the fire," Augustin called out over his shoulder. He dodged to his left. "I hope you know of something else."

Polnygar recalled Aelzandar once telling her that fire was not the only power that a mage could summon. Apart from fire, however, there was only one other type that she had used before, and that was only once. Aelzandar had taught her a spell to summon lightning. It was worth a try.

The Slaves of the Horned God

What had the archmage said? *Sometimes the words are not enough. Sometimes we must visualise what we are attempting through the Art. For example, if I want to call forth lightning from the heavens, perhaps I would try and visualise the darkening clouds of a thunderstorm, and the power forming within.*

Polnygar tried to picture a thunderstorm, but the image eluded her.

But sometimes we need something more direct. Consider this: Picture a piece of amber, and then a cloth, and in your mind, rub the amber with the cloth. Take that image, keep it in your thoughts. Sustain it. The mind will make it real.

This time it felt different. Polnygar summoned up tendrils of the Art. As she pictured the amber sparks in her head, electricity began to dance at the end of her fingers. She flung her hands forward and directed the energy towards the metal man. As the sparks connected the metal man began to jolt and gyrate.

"It's working, keep it going," an elated Augustin said.

Polnygar drew back her fingers and willed another bolt of lightning towards the automaton and shuddered again before collapsing to the ground, all life and movement gone.

"Nice work," Augustin said. "I think you destroyed it." He frowned. "Are you alright?"

Polnygar felt dizzy. "I'm not sure. I feel faint. I think I need to sit down for a moment."

Augustin moved towards her quickly and took her arm. With tender care that seemed unlike him, he helped her to a ledge on the wall where she could sit. He watched her with concern. It wasn't until a few minutes later when he spoke. "How are you feeling now?"

"Better," she said. "Using the Art can sometimes be draining."

"I never noticed before. Aelzandar never said anything."

Polnygar blushed. "He has centuries of experience. His limits are far beyond mine."

Augustin nodded. His gaze moved to the metal man lying on the ground. "What was that thing? And what was it doing here?"

Polnygar shrugged. "I don't know, but..."

"What?"

"It's strange," Polnygar said, "but it's oddly familiar."

Augustin gave her a quizzical look. "You've seen one before."

"No, that's the thing. But it feels like something out of a dream I had."

She remembered the odd dream she had experienced on the way to Ralom. At the time she had dismissed it as nothing more than a nightmare, but after seeing these metal men again, she wondered about the words Aelzandar had shared with her in Selvarial. *Was that more than a dream? Was it a vision of the future?*

"I don't know," she said. "I can't make sense of it."

Augustin shook his head. "It's strange, I'll certainly give you that. And ancient, by the looks of it. Although it's not the only strange and ancient thing in here." He jerked a thumb towards one of the grotesque octopus-headed corpses. "How do you think these ended up here?"

"I don't know. I don't want to know. They make me shiver just looking at them."

"Ugly buggers, I'll say that – Wait, what was that?" Augustin turned his head.

"I heard it too," Polnygar said, looking around. As she did, her mouth went dry. All about the room the metal men were slowly coming to life, their cobwebbed limbs clanking and creaking as they turned their faces to Augustin and Polnygar.

"This doesn't look good," Augustin said. Polnygar drew close to him, but he tried to push her away. "No, Polnygar, get out of here, save yourself."

"Don't be stupid," she said. "We can deal with them. Just keep them busy while I ready the spell."

"Right!" Augustin drew his sword with grim determination and moved to engage the nearest metal man. Within moments others joined the melee and Augustin found himself fending off several metal men at once. One swung at him, and he barely dodged its blow, instead colliding with another metal man with a clang. It tried to grab him but Augustin managed to wrench himself from its grasp.

"Don't take too long," Augustin said in between ragged breaths. "This is not as easy as it looks."

Polnygar recited a few words in Draconic and felt the lightning erupt from her fingertips, surging towards the metal men. As she did, however, she stumbled, feeling a great tide of fatigue wash over her. Panicked thoughts began to overwhelm her. *What is happening?* She tried to pull back, to reserve what strength she had left. The lightning died on her fingertips.

In the shadows there was clanking and whirring as more metal men emerged from the darkness, heading towards Augustin. Their crystalline eyes flickered in the darkness like stars against the night sky.

"We're not done yet," Augustin said, dodging another metal fist. He swung towards the walking statue with his sword, knocking it to the ground with a clang. The others began to crowd around him, stomping towards him with slow but relentless movement. A single metal man lunged towards him, but Augustin ducked, and the metal man's fist connected with the wall, sending a shower of dust and stone fragments through the air.

One of the men came towards Polnygar, its joints groaning and creaking as it did. She took a step backwards, and then up on to a ridge near the wall as it swung wildly at her, its metal arms flailing in the darkness.

"Do it," Augustin grunted. "Do it now!"

Polnygar's eyelids were heavy and her mind felt subsumed in fog. Still, she fought back, found her resolve and pushed through the weariness. *I can do this,* she thought. She searched inside herself, pulling from reserves she didn't know she had. The power welled up inside her and again she summoned the static discharge from her hands, flinging it towards the metal men. Just as before, she felt drained and though some of the metal men crumpled to the ground, the others were still a threat.

The ground shifted beneath her feet. At first she thought it was just the fatigue, but then it shook again. Sand and dirt fell from the ceiling onto her head. *What is happening now?* She shook her head, trying to clear out the fog. All around her, the room shook, as if from some giant explosion. In her state, she couldn't tell if the blast was above her or a figment of her imagination. Another quake settled the matter and rocks and sand toppled from above her, light pouring into the cavern. Above her a hole had opened up, and in the shaft of light coming from it she saw a number of ropes come down.

She heard the ringing of metal on metal nearby. Augustin was hard pressed against a pair of metal men. She flung two quick bolts of lightning towards them, slowing them enough to allow Augustin to evade them and come to her.

"Something's blown a hole in the roof," Augustin panted. "Look, coming down on the ropes." There were newcomers in the cavern, armoured guards, who had moved to engage the metal men. They wore the distinctive clothing of the palace contingent.

The emir's men? How did he know we were here?

"Thanks the gods," Augustin gasped. "Help is here. Polnygar, just hold on a little longer." Someone muttered something in the darkness, and Polnygar heard Augustin swear. "Don't worry about me, help her!"

She heard whirring and clanging and someone yell out in pain. Reacting quickly, she summoned every bit of energy she had left and let loose with another flow of lightning from her fingertips. Immediately another wave of exhaustion hit her, stronger than the last. Her knees buckled, and she felt someone's hands grab her around her waist.

The last thing she saw before she collapsed was Augustin's panicked face.

CHAPTER 11

Polnygar opened her eyes. She felt awful. It was as if she'd fallen off a mountain. Every limb ached and she felt a hammering inside her head.

"Don't get up. You need rest," came a gruff voice.

Slowly her vision reasserted itself. She saw a bald, dark-skinned face in front of her "Hebu?" Polnygar said weakly. "What are you doing here?"

"Looking for you," the Nemoi said. He fumbled with his medical kit.

Polnygar rubbed her forehead. "How did you know?"

"The archmage became concerned when you broke off the mental link," Hebu said. "Luckily he could glean enough from your surroundings to find out where you were headed. He sent me on ahead to fetch you both." Hebu placed the back of his hand against her forehead and pressed two fingers to Polnygar's wrist. He nodded and stood up. "She's fine."

As the Nemoi moved away, putting his medical kit back in its pouch Polnygar glimpsed a black dagger tucked into his belt. She was surprised she had never noticed it before. It was quite distinctive, with an elaborate hilt carved in the shape of a dragon's claw. Polnygar wondered why a scribe needed such a finely made weapon. *A gift, perhaps?* The thought was not much more than a guess. She tried to move, and immediately regretted it, feeling a wave of nausea and dizziness.

As if sensing her discomfort, Augustin came to Polnygar. His face was etched with concern. "Are you alright? What happened? You collapsed."

Polnygar groaned and rubbed her head. "I think I overtaxed myself. Aelzandar did warn me that could happen. What happened in the temple? How did we get out?"

Augustin sat down next to her. "It could have been very bad, but Hebu blew a hole in the ceiling, and several of the emir's soldiers came down and fetched us out. The metal men are still in there, but with the seals on that place, they aren't getting anywhere."

Polnygar rubbed her forehead. She looked over at the Nemoi, who was examining the remains of an automaton. "You blew a hole in the ceiling?"

Hebu didn't even turn around. "Tarkenese smokepowder. Courtesy of our friend Samir."

Nearby came a voice. "Ah, my ears are burning. Did someone say my name?" Samir looked down on Polnygar, his face a picture of genuine concern. "Oh my beautiful Polnygar, thank the Infinite that you are unharmed. Aelzandar will be most pleased."

"Just how did you get your hands on smokepowder?" Augustin remarked. "The Tarkenese never sell that to outsiders."

"You are correct, my friend. Normally they don't, and outsiders are never let into Tarken to procure it for themselves. I myself was lucky to meet some exiled Tarkenese alchemists, hoping to buy passage to distant lands. I persuaded them to sell me some of their stock so they might have enough coin for their trip."

Augustin sounded sceptical. "And where was it these alchemists were headed?"

"Emparia, Baron," Hebu said. "Believe it or not, your own homeland. Perhaps they hoped to find employment under your queen."

"Right," said Augustin. From the tone of his voice it was obvious Augustin did not believe a single word of Samir's tale.

"Where is Aelzandar?" Polnygar asked. The others were here, and the archmage's absence seemed most conspicuous.

"He is with the emir at the moment. Come, we are not far." Augustin looked to Hebu, who nodded in confirmation.

"Here, let me help you up," Augustin said. He lifted her with ease, and Polnygar felt a strange sense of relief and comfort as he carried her to the horse.

They soon met the emir and Aelzandar, but the archmage did not say a word upon seeing Polnygar. He merely frowned and then patted her hand, but this gesture lacked his usual warmth. The rest of the trip back to the city, he did not speak to her, instead spending his time in hushed conversation with the emir. Polnygar felt as if she was being silently chided. After what seemed like an interminable passage of time, the silence was finally broken.

"You should have let me in when I attempted to far-speak," Aelzandar said. He did not sound pleased.

"I'm sorry," Polnygar said.

"What you did was incredibly dangerous. You could have both been killed."

"I couldn't let Augustin go alone," she protested. "If I hadn't been there he could have died."

"If you two hadn't gone there at all," Aelzandar said, "there wouldn't have been any danger to begin with."

"I know. I'm sorry."

Aelzandar sighed. "It is fine. I am just glad that you are unharmed."

"I passed out," said Polnygar. "I overextended myself again, didn't I?"

Aelzandar nodded. "Yes, but you are still new in the ways of the Art, and not used to channelling such power. With time and practice you will improve, and you will find yourself able to push your limits further and further."

"What were those things that attacked me?"

"Automata," said Aelzandar. "Constructs of the Soldara."

Polnygar's responded quickly. "So you have seen these automata before? Where?"

"In my youth there were hundreds in Liderial," Aelzandar explained. "The secret to their construction was lost with the Soldara, and all the spellweaver caste could do was continue to maintain those that still existed. Eventually, however, even doing that proved beyond their powers. Only a handful of automata remain now, in the king's palace. What these ones were doing in this cave, I cannot imagine."

"There was as a connection between this place and the Tears of the Divine," Polnygar said. "I could feel it. My scar – the one I got when the Tears burned me – it itched again."

Aelzandar looked thoughtful. "A connection you say? Entirely possible. It is probably why Ivellios came here. What exactly he found out, I cannot say. Hopefully when and if we are given access to *The Tome of Divine Metaphysics*, more shall become clear to us."

"A most remarkable piece of craftsmanship, these automata," said

Hebu. He had recovered a discarded arm that had once been affixed to one of the metal men. The Nemoi ran his fingers across its surface with appreciation.

"What are you planning on doing with that?" Polnygar asked.

"I'm not sure yet," said Hebu. "But I'm sure it will be of use eventually." He held it up to the sun. "Augustin, your arm, does it trouble you?"

The Emparian responded in a gruff tone. "It's still gone, if that's what you're asking."

"And that is a continuing inconvenience to you?"

Augustin said nothing but just glared at the Nemoi.

"I will take that as a yes, shall I?" Hebu tapped his fingers on the automaton arm. "I believe I may have a solution to your dilemma. I will explain further once we are back in the palace."

For the rest of the journey back Hebu refused to elaborate any further, staying silent as they entered the Qar Arrid's gates and while they rode through the city's streets back to the palace. When the stable workers helped them dismount, Hebu practically leapt from the ground and rushed back to their quarters, metal arm in hand.

"Someone's excited," said Polnygar.

"Who knows what he's up to," said Augustin. "But I will admit I'm curious as to how this relates to my *inconvenience*, so to speak."

As Polnygar and Augustin entered, they saw Hebu at one of the tables. "Fetch me my pack," he said to Polnygar, pointing at a leather bag. She passed it to him and the Nemoi withdrew several thin, metal tools.

"You still haven't told me what you're doing," said Augustin.

"I believe I know what Hebu has in mind," said Aelzandar. The archmage had just entered, an enigmatic smile on his face. "Am I to assume you will require my assistance, at the very end at least?"

"If you're not too busy," said Hebu as he tinkered with the arm.

"Happy to help," said Aelzandar.

An hour passed before Hebu had finished and Polnygar could see that the Nemoi had cleaned away some of the excess debris from the end of the automaton arm and attached a series of leather straps on the end.

"Hold out your arm," Hebu said to Augustin. The Emparian did, but Hebu shook his head. "No, your *other* arm. The one missing a hand."

"Why?"

Hebu sighed. "I'm fixing it for you."

Augustin looked doubtful, but held out his other arm, Hebu carefully attached the automaton hand, pushing the end of it against Augustin's stump. Once it was in place he carefully buckled the straps. Augustin looked at his new, metal hand critically. "Very nice. It's not a lot of use if I can't grip anything though. I'd just be lugging a hunk of metal around."

Hebu looked up at the Emparian and shook his head. "Did I say we were finished?"

"Patience, Baron," said Aelzandar. "This is where I come in." He placed one hand on the metal arm, and murmured a few words of the Art. The automaton hand glowed briefly and moved.

"Whoah," said Augustin. "I don't believe it." He moved his arm around and the metal hand's fingers flexed. He moved to the table, and picked up a bottle with ease. "How did you do that?"

"Many things are possible with the Art, Baron, you know that," said Aelzandar.

"Of course, the Art." Augustin rolled his eyes but he looked at Hebu with barely concealed glee. "Thanks. I mean it." The Nemoi just inclined his head.

"We will be eating supper soon," Aelzandar said, changing the subject. "And after that, I suggest we all get a good night's sleep. Tomorrow Samir and I will be doing our best to persuade the emir to let us see the book."

Augustin folded his arms. "Just how successful do you expect to be with that?"

"The emir is a wise man. He will see reason," said Samir. "I am sure of it."

"Well, let us hope so," Hebu said. "For all of our sakes. Otherwise we will have wasted our time here."

"I'm beginning to think we already have," Augustin said under his breath.

CHAPTER 12

Days passed, each much as the one before it.

Bellaydin found himself in a funk, torn between conflicting feelings on the matter. In his own mind he knew that Edgar had deliberately antagonised him with comments intended to provoke a reaction. If Bellaydin would not rise and defend his family's honour, who would? But then was the other sensation, the painful knowledge he knew he had let down Haakon terribly. The duke had been kind to him ever since they had met in Wishapton, and had done nothing but show encouragement and render assistance wherever Bellaydin needed it. The incident in the forest had clearly broken that bond of trust and the duke had obviously taken it as a personal betrayal. Bellaydin felt this keenly, though he too felt somewhat betrayed himself by the duke's reaction. That stung Bellaydin as well, and his emotions flipped from guilt to resentment and back again.

Bellaydin's lessons passed with their usual monotony, and he saw Rhiannon less frequently than he had before. Her mother had impressed on her the importance of her duties within the castle, and so she had less time to spend chatting with Bellaydin. Instead now she mostly gave him a meal, exchanged a few pleasantries and then continued with her duties.

Edgar's behaviour was not improved since their scuffle. If anything he was even more sullen and spiteful than he was before, but he directed most of his barbs at Otto and Kurth, and barely acknowledged Bellaydin's existence. In any case, Bellaydin was mostly withdrawn from his time with the squires, paying little attention to their arguments.

Bellaydin visited Rhiannon in the kitchen, only to see the girl frantically greet him as he entered.

"What's wrong?" he asked.

Rhiannon's words tumbled out. "Haven't you heard the news?" she said. "About the war? About the Earl of Warding?"

"What about the war?" Bellaydin asked. He'd felt he was a bit out of the loop lately, though more through his fault than anyone else's.

She placed some food on the table for him and filled a mug of ale. "The Earl of Warding is dead, and his army has been destroyed by the Goriinchians. It was a total rout, they say. There are bodies littering the hills for miles."

"What?" Bellaydin was shocked. He had seen the army the Earl of Warding had set off with. It was enormous, much larger than the garrison that had successfully defended Wishapton. "How did this happen?"

Rhiannon whispered. "Everyone's saying that the Earl walked into a trap, that the Goriinchian war chief goaded him into battle when he was not ready. The Privy Council have been recalled, they're all arriving here tonight."

Anson Mainstream, the Earl of Warding, was dead. Another noble killed in the war in the space of a year. Anson was also Squire Otto's father, and Bellaydin knew what effect the death would have on the boy. He was hardly strong at the best of times. This would devastate him.

"I wish I knew more," Bellaydin said.

"Well, it's a pity you can't hear what they will discuss in their council meetings then," Rhiannon said.

"No, the meetings are private. Only the highest ranks nobles are allowed to attend, which I'm sure doesn't include squires like myself."

"Well, what if there was another way?" Rhiannon said enigmatically.

"What do you mean another way?" Bellaydin asked.

Rhiannon leant closer. "Shhh...not so loud. Meet me near the west wing in fifteen minutes. I'll show you."

"Show me what?"

"The west wing. Fifteen minutes," Rhiannon repeated and returned to her duties.

Bellaydin left the kitchen and headed to the west wing to wait for Rhiannon. When she arrived, she looked about to make sure no one was watching and then grabbed Bellaydin by the arm.

"Where are we going?" he said.

"There's an alcove near the roof in the west wing which opens up into a small crawlspace. If you get in there you can crawl straight ahead until you are right over the council chamber. Then you can overhear things to your heart's content."

"How do you know about this?" Bellaydin asked.

"Growing up in the castle makes you privy to all sorts of secrets," Rhiannon said. She led him to the alcove and, removing an old wooden board, exposed the crawlspace to him. "There you go," she said.

"When is the council meeting on?"

"Much later tonight, once the nobles arrive. I think it's too long for you to wait unless you like sitting in dark enclosed places. No? As I thought."

She placed the board back on the crawlspace. "I'd better get back to the kitchen," Rhiannon said. "See you later, skinny."

Bellaydin returned to his room to wait for the arrival of the nobles. As he did he overheard scattered conversations of other residents of the castle. Everyone was talking about the loss of the Earl of Warding and his army, and the threat that the Goriinchians posed to Emparia. There was widespread panic that the Goriinchians would cross the border any day and that Emparia was defenceless.

It wasn't long until the sounds of trumpets outside his window announced the arrival of the nobles of the Privy Council. First was the Duke of Oldharbour, Wulfric Highcrown, followed by the Duke of Georgeton, Oswin Zalltor and finally the Earl of Tyronsville, Alfred Bauer, and the Countess of Genio, Maria Ap'Lydin. As the last of the nobles and their retinues arrived at the castle Bellaydin left his room quietly and headed to the crawlspace. Once there he waited until he saw the nobles enter the council chamber and then, taking the cover off the crawl space, he entered the small dark tunnel. Malken was there, sleeping soundly, but Bellaydin pushed past the cat, crawling on his belly until he reached a spot where a series of tiny holes gave him sight to the council chamber below. He could see the herald introducing the queen and the various nobles, and could see them take their seats.

"We all know why we are here," the Duke of Emperor's Palace said. "The Goriinchians have slaughtered our army in the field. A few stragglers made it to the border but for the most part the Goriinchians have destroyed the army. The Earl of Warding is missing, presumed dead. There is also the matter of this note, sent to us via messenger, purporting to be from the Goriinchian Prophet-King Ygarak to Her Majesty Queen Amaryllis. Normally this missive would be for the queen's eyes only, but Her Majesty has graciously given her permission for me to share its contents with you. Shall I, Your Majesty?"

"Yes please, Edmund," said the queen. "Go ahead."

The Duke of Emperor's Palace unfurled a scroll and cleared his throat.

The Slaves of the Horned God

"From the Prophet-King Ygarak, Lord of Karlicia, Voice of the Horned God, Confounder of Infidels, to the so-called Queen of the Enparrans, Amaryllis; Lo, you have tried to make war on the sons of the Horned God, lo, you have sent your Pig-Lord and his army against us. Did you believe that the Horned God would allow such blasphemy? Did you believe that he would let you spill holy blood on holy ground?

I have sent my great general, Aonghus of Clan Culainn to meet your challenge and lo, the Horned God willing, you have seen what has been accomplished. We have met your army on the fields of battle and as the Horned God wills we have made widows of your wives and orphans of your children. We have killed the Pig-Lord as he led his soldiers to death, we have sent him back to you so that his skin reflects his soul.

Never again shall Enparrans taint the lands of Karlicia, never again shall you cross the mountains. For when next we meet it shall be your cities that fall, your children that feel our blade, your women that become ours. We shall take back the Karlicia that you have occupied, and send you back across the sea whence you come. In this the era of Prophecy, the Horned God has decided that your time is at an end."

The duke curled up on the scroll. "This note was found by soldiers near the town of Drakeford. A single rider approached them after the battle was over, and when he came closer they noticed it was the earl's horse. Atop it was a bloody corpse, the head removed, and the head of a pig stitched on in its place."

"Was it the Earl of Warding?" asked one of the nobles. Bellaydin was not able to tell who it was – perhaps the Earl of Tyronsville.

"Impossible to say, due to the state of the body, but the note seems to indicate it was."

"The Goriinchians are heathens," said an old man, dressed in clerical robes – the Archbishop, no doubt. "It was a mistake to let this cult spread again to our lands. We must forbid it once again, else we must contest with ever more spies and traitors who masquerade as men of faith."

"With all due respect, Your Grace," said Haakon. His voice sounded agitated. "You go too far. There is no evidence of treachery here, but it is true that the battle was a disaster. How in the name of the gods could this happen?"

"The gods have abandoned us," said the archbishop. "Punishment for our heresy."

"Nonsense," said another noble. It was Wulfric Highcrown, Duke of Oldharbour. Bellaydin was not surprised Wulfric attended court when the matter of the war against Goriinchia became an issue. "It was plain for all to see. The Earl of Warding was not suitable to lead any army, let alone plan an invasion into Goriinchia."

The Duke of Georgeton cut in. "It was clearly the decision of the council, and of Her Majesty, I might add, that the Earl of Warding was the best choice to take the attack to the Goriinchians. You were at the council, Your Grace."

Wulfric responded plainly. "Indeed I was Oswin, and it was you that was the leading voice for your puppet I recall."

Oswin took umbrage, and the council meeting degenerated into a shouting match.

"Please, Your Graces," the Duke of Emperor's Palace said. "There is no need for this. We need to decide what our next plan of action is."

"Are we in real danger?" the queen asked.

"I do not think so, Your Majesty," said the Duke of Georgeton. "The Duke of Oldharbour is exaggerating things for his own reasons."

Haakon tried to steer the conversation to a solution. "Clearly a new army must be gathered. We must punish the Goriinchians."

"That will take time," said the Duke of Georgeton. "Is that a luxury we can afford? What of the regional forces, can we not just fortify the major cities and wait for any Goriinchian counter-invasion? Georgeton can ill-afford to contribute any more soldiers."

"If you had listened to me in the first place, Your Grace, and not given command to an incompetent like Anson Mainstream," Wulfric said, "there would be no need for any more soldiers and the Goriinchians would already be defeated."

The Duke of Georgeton cut in. "Is that so? I notice that Oldharbour did not send any of its troops with the Earl of Warding's forces. Why was that, Wulfric?"

"My reasons were well known. The Earl of Warding was not a suitable commander. I said that loud and clear. I saw no reason to waste the lives of the soldiers of Oldharbour."

The Earl of Tyronsville raised his voice. "So the men of Tyronsville died so that Your Grace could keep his hands clean?"

The nobles started to argue amongst themselves again and the council descended into a farce. Bellaydin had heard enough. He crept back through the crawl space and out into the alcove, replacing the board over the crawl space entrance.

The squabbling of the council disappointed Bellaydin. They were destroying William's legacy with their bickering. The hard-fought victory at Wishapton, which William had paid for with his own life, meant nothing now as the Goriinchians had scored a far more crushing victory against an even larger Emparian force. Wishapton was theirs for the taking, if indeed they even wanted the tiny frontier town. Much richer targets were now in their grasp – Genio, perhaps, even Oldharbour. Bellaydin's mind went to even darker places. *What if the Goriinchians made it to the capital?*

Despite his superior attitude, Wulfric Highcrown was just as bad as the rest of them. Bellaydin didn't know that the duke had gone to the extent of refusing to commit his troops to the army being led by the Earl of Warding. It seemed selfish and petty, particularly when the safety of the realm was at stake. How was Maria ever to grow into her position of countess with role models such as these?

Bellaydin felt sorely aware of William's absence. William would have never let this travesty happen. He would have made sure the borders of Emparia were safe. He would have fought with the army, even if it meant serving under a non-entity such as Anson Mainstream.

He heard the sound of someone sobbing nearby."Who is it?" Bellaydin called into the darkness. There was no response, but as Bellaydin came around the corner he saw Otto slumped against a wall, tears running down his cheeks.

"I suppose you've heard too," said Otto, between sobs. "Everyone else has by now."

Bellaydin nodded. "Otto, I am so sorry."

Otto wiped his nose and let out a great sigh, "I was told to steel myself for this possibility when my father left with the army. But when it actually happened I realised that there was nothing that could have prepared me for this. You would know this better than me."

Bellaydin sighed. "I was so young when my parents died. My memories of them are so few. That made it easier for me than it must be for you."

"I suppose," Otto said. He looked towards Bellaydin and a tone of indignation entered his voice. "There are some who are saying my father deserved to die, you know?"

"That's horrible. Who would say such a thing?"

"I have heard it around the castle, but none will say it to my face. Except for Edgar, of course. My father may not have been a great warrior or leader, but he was still my father." His voice wavered. "A good, honourable man, who just wanted to serve his queen. He did not deserve death."

"Few do," Bellaydin said."Your father's death wasn't his fault. The Goriinchians murdered him, Otto. Just as they did William. They will pay the price for their savagery."

"I hope you are right," said Otto. He stood up, straightening his tunic. "Thank you, Bellaydin. It felt good to talk to someone. Rhiannon has been kind, and comforted me, but the other squires haven't come at all. Sometimes I feel very alone in this place."

"You're not the only who feels like that," Bellaydin acknowledged. "If you ever need to talk…"

"Thank you." Otto smiled, and then took his leave, disappearing back towards his own quarters. Bellaydin did the same, heading off in the direction to his room.

As he walked past the kitchen, he stopped. It was late now, and the kitchens would be closed for the night, remaining dormant until the staff rose early to cook the morning meal, still, Bellaydin hoped he might find Rhiannon still there. It would be good to speak with her before he retired for the night.

The kitchens were dark, quiet and seemingly abandoned. Bellaydin was about to leave when he heard a laugh. It sounded like Rhiannon's. He walked to the source of the laughter – the pantry entrance at the other side. A small shaft of light came from under the door. He also heard another voice, male. He opened the doors.

Rhiannon screamed in shock. "Oh, gods, Bellaydin, haven't you ever heard of knocking?"

Bellaydin was unable to speak. Another head poked up from under the sheet next to Rhiannon. "Oh, hello Ap'Lydin," said Kurth Bauer.

Bellaydin moved his lips but no words came out. Rhiannon looked at him expectantly.

"How long has this been going on?" he eventually said.

"A while," Rhiannon said. She looked at Bellaydin, "Oh, don't be like that."

"Like what?" Bellaydin asked,

"Stop pouting," Rhiannon said. "I like you too, just not as much." She looked at Kurth. "What do you say, Kurth, room for one more?"

Kurth looked at her in shock. Rhiannon looked back at Bellaydin and raised her hands in dismay, "Sorry. I tried."

Kurth was grabbing for his clothes. "Listen Ap'Lydin," he said. "Best this remains our little secret, yes?"

"Who would I even tell?" Bellaydin said.

"Don't say anything to anyone," Kurth said. "This whole thing is a complicated situation."

"What does that mean?"

"What he means," Rhiannon said, wrapping the sheet up around her body, "is that he is the son of an earl, and I am the daughter of a cook, and if his father were to know he and I were *sharing the pantry*, so to speak, he'd likely find himself out of an inheritance."

Kurth shook his head darkly as he pulled his clothes back on. "Just keep it to yourself Ap'Lydin. No gossip."

Rhiannon's eyes followed Kurth as the squire left.

"I can't believe you didn't tell me about this," Bellaydin said.

Rhiannon smiled cheekily. "Oh, dear Bellaydin, are you jealous?"

Bellaydin blushed. He was, in fact, jealous, but he felt it better to deny it to avoid looking like a fool.

"Of course not," he said defensively.

"Oh, Bela, Bela," she said, touching his face. "I can handle the nose, but I like a man with a bit of meat on him." She squeezed his arm for emphasis. "I'd worry you'd snap under the strain."

Bellaydin felt incredibly foolish and embarrassed, and Rhiannon must have noticed. "Oh, I'm sorry my skinny squire, I didn't mean to upset you. Give me a moment to dress." She waited a moment. "That means eyes on something else, squire."

"Sorry." Bellaydin stepped back, closing the pantry doors. Within a few minutes the doors opened again and Rhiannon emerged, clothed in her usual attire.

"So, how did it go with your spying on the council?" she asked as she poured him some ale.

Bellaydin looked at the mug with a frown on his face.

"Go on, drink," said Rhiannon, "it'll make you feel better."

Bellaydin took a swig from the mug and then, thinking again, downed the whole thing in one gulp.

"Steady there," Rhiannon said.

"I heard the council alright. It's true, the Earl of Warding is dead, the army was destroyed and at any moment Goriinchians are going to swarm across the southern border."

Rhiannon frowned. "Well, aren't you the bearer of good news. What are those high and mighty nobles going to do now?"

"Nothing much, by the sounds of it. They're all busy blaming one another."

"That's what they do," Rhiannon said, filling Bellaydin's mug again. "So we're all just going to sit here until the Goriinchians decide to show up?"

Bellaydin waved a hand. "There was something about each noble mobilising his own forces, but unless they can agree on someone to lead the combined forces I don't know if it'll be enough."

"So what are you saying, we should all brush up on our Goriinchian for 'Long Live Ygarak, Praise the Horned God'?"

"Wouldn't hurt," said Bellaydin, and he didn't entirely mean it as a joke.

***

Bellaydin returned to his room in a low mood. Seeing Rhiannon with Kurth had sparked a seed of jealousy within him, and he wasn't exactly sure why. He didn't feel infatuated with Rhiannon. In fact, he felt of her as more a good friend than anything else, and it wasn't as if Kurth was the worst squire she could have chosen to sleep with. He briefly imagined catching her with Edgar de Morcor and a cold shudder of revulsion went down his spine.

Still, whatever the reason, he felt personally wounded that, coupled with what he had heard at the council meeting and the current rift with Haakon made him feel very isolated and alone. He wished Polnygar was there with him. She was always able to say something to cheer him up. Unfortunately, she could be anywhere by now - Carurlonia, back in Aderilund, perhaps even in Emparia. Augustin Bauer was the younger brother of the Earl of Tyronsville. Might Polnygar end up in Emparia after all?

He pushed all thoughts from his mind and lay down on his bed, hoping for a long, restful sleep. Tomorrow things would improve. He was sure of it.

CHAPTER 13

Pennants fluttered in the wind.

Bellaydin had never been to a tournament before, but one had been organised later that week to celebrate the Duke of Emperor's Palace's eighty-fifth birthday, and the squires of the royal court were given the honour of attending as the duke's guests. Common folk crowded the list fields near Castle Emparia, clustering around the great wooden stands that had been erected for the nobles. Pavilions were scattered in the surrounding fields each of them housing one of the numerous knights who had made the journey to the capital to participate.

Bellaydin sat with the other squires, watching the action in front of them. Two armoured knights, locked in close combat, fought each other with brutal ferocity. The crowd followed every swing and dodge with awestruck fervour and reacted to every blow as if it had been personal. From his vantage point he could also see the royal box. The Duke of Emperor's Palace sat next to the queen, who was flanked on her other side by the Duke of Alariat. Still smarting from embarrassment, Bellaydin was unable to look Haakon in the eye, so turned his attention back to the skirmish below. The tournament was a welcome respite from recent stresses and, strange as it seemed, watching the combatants brawl distracted him from his concern over the direction of war with Goriinchia.

"Who are we watching?" Kurth asked, craning his neck to try to see the battle. "I must have missed their names."

Since Bellaydin had caught Kurth with Rhiannon, the squire had been doing his utmost to pretend that the situation hadn't happened by talking about every possible topic *except* the girl from the kitchens. Kurth did his best not to look Bellaydin in the eyes, which only made his behaviour even more awkward.

"Sir Poul de Barry, sworn sword to the Duke of Alariat," said Otto.

Kurth sighed. "I was hoping to see Sir Bastion Theed. We must have missed him. Who is Sir Poul's opponent?"

"I think he is fighting Sir Euan." Otto was putting up a brave front but he said the words with little enthusiasm. His father's death had deeply affected the Mainstream squire and it didn't take much for Bellaydin to notice the still fresh tears that were staining his cheeks.

"Sir Euan? Who's that?" asked Kurth.

"He's the queen's uncle, on her mother's side," said Otto. "He came here when King Henry married his sister. Sir Euan de Dilmun."

"Piggy means Sir Euan the Hungry," corrected Edgar. "He's been serving under your father, hasn't he? No wonder he's hungry. What's left to eat in Warding when you've been at the stores, Piggy?"

Otto didn't respond. He continued to stare straight ahead, a faraway look in his eyes. Next to him, Kurth shook his head and muttered something.

Sir Euan and Sir Poul put on quite a show, but eventually one of the warriors had battered the other into submission and the duel was over. Edgar laughed and clapped. "And down goes the Hungry Knight," said

Edgar. "Easiest silver I've ever made."

A herald, clad in the livery of the royal house, introduced the next combatants. "Announcing the next competitors. Sir Dallen Withers, sworn sword of the Duke of Georgeton." The crowd offered applause and Bellaydin recalled his encounter with Sir Dallen. The knight had perturbed Bellaydin, though he couldn't quite say why.

"And facing Sir Dallen will be Sir Geoffrey Keslin, sworn sword of the Countess of Genio." The crowd clapped, Bellaydin among them. Hearing Sir Geoffrey's name had surprised him. Bellaydin was unaware that the knight was in the capital. Why had he not come to visit? Bellaydin felt a little forgotten.

The sigils of both knights were displayed prominently. Geoffrey Keslin's family shield depicted a dragon, its tail curled around its legs. A grey skull on a black field symbolised his opponent, Sir Dallen Withers. Bellaydin had seen it when he met Sir Dallen, and even then had found it an unsettling crest.

The combatants emerged onto the field in full armour and faced the royal box. Sir Dallen was the first to speak. "I, Sir Dallen Withers will win this battle for the honour of my liege lord, Oswin Zalltor, Duke of Georgeton. Long live the Queen!" He raised his sword in salute.

Sir Geoffrey approached the royal box. "I dedicate my performance to the two most beautiful ladies in the kingdom: my gracious liege lady, Maria Ap'Lydin, Countess of Genio, and of course, our fair Queen, Amaryllis, First of Her Name. Long Live the Queen!" Sir Geoffrey blew a fatherly kiss to the countess and took a long bow.

Both combatants mounted their horses before moving to opposite sides of the field, ready to begin the joust. Bellaydin strained his neck, trying to see Geoffrey better.

"Keslin's got no chance," said Edgar. "I've got ten silver pieces riding on Withers."

"Sir Geoffrey is a champion of the list fields," said Otto.

Edgar scoffed. "Maybe in Genio or Warding, Piggy. This is the capital, not some provincial backwater. I've seen Sir Dallen fight. He's defeated some of the best warriors in the realm. The only thing Geoffrey has defeated is an ale keg."

"So, who is this Sir Dallen then?" Bellaydin asked.

"He's my father's right-hand man," Tancred added. "He's unbeatable."

"Never heard of him," said Kurth.

"You wouldn't have," Edgar said. "Not all the way out in your haystack."

"I'll take your bet, Edgar," said Bellaydin

"You'll what?" Edgar said.

"Ten silver, right? Sir Geoffrey's going to win."

Edgar laughed. "You must be joking."

Bellaydin fished inside his tunic for his coin pouch, and emptied it, showing the coins to Edgar. "I'm good for it. Ten silver says that Sir Dallen loses."

"Alright then, Ap'Lydin. Easy money for me."

"Ap'Lydin, don't bet on Keslin just because you know him," Tancred said. "He's outclassed."

"I'm not," said Bellaydin. "It's *because* I know him that I know you've underestimated him. "

The herald sounded the horn and the two knights wheeled about to face each other. They raised their lances, and galloped full pelt towards each other. The two knights collided with terrible force, and though the blow threw Geoffrey back in his saddle, neither knight toppled from their horse. They rode to their respective ends before circling around and, to the sounds of trumpet, charging at each other again. This time Geoffrey's lance struck true, toppling Sir Dallen from his horse. Geoffrey's blow didn't deter Sir Dallen, however, and the knight got to his feet quickly, drawing his sword and holding his shield ready.

Bellaydin shot a glance to Edgar, but the squire barely looked his way. "It's not over yet, Ap'Lydin. Withers will eat Keslin alive."

Geoffrey dismounted to meet Sir Dallen, drawing his own sword as a page brought him a new shield. Barely a moment later Sir Dallen lunged at Geoffrey with a roar, his sword smashing against Geoffrey's shield. Sir Geoffrey ducked and swung about, trading blow for blow but Sir Dallen blocked with ease, snarling as he did. He swung at Geoffrey, and his blade caught the other knight's tunic, tearing the fabric and cutting through the mail. First blood. Geoffrey wheeled about and dodged the next blow, sending Sir Dallen stumbling towards the dirt. The knight righted himself just in time to block Sir Geoffrey's next swing. The crowd reacted with cheers and groans as the battle hung in the balance, and Sir Dallen and Sir Geoffrey circled each other warily.

"Keslin's looking tired, Ap'Lydin," Edgar said. He gave a smug look and chuckled under his breath. Both fighters, in fact, seemed to be wearying, but they fought on, drenched in sweat.

Sir Dallen, obviously frustrated, sought to end the duel and thundered towards Sir Geoffrey, smashing the knight with his shield. Dazed, Geoffrey attempted to recover, but Sir Dallen's attack was relentless, and he drove Geoffrey to his knees.

"It's all but over," Edgar commented. Bellaydin did not respond.

Sir Dallen went for the knockout blow when Geoffrey unexpectedly shifted to the left, and Sir Dallen's sword connected with nothing but dirt. Dust filled the air around them and by the time Sir Dallen could react it was Geoffrey who was on the offensive. He drove Sir Dallen back with a flurry of lightning-quick blows. The crowd reacted with amazement, cheeringly wildly. Sir Geoffrey seemed to have summoned energy out of nowhere. Bellaydin knew better. It had all been a feint. Geoffrey had used the same trick in Goriinchia. Soon Sir Dallen had fallen to the ground, bloodied and bruised with Sir Geoffrey's sword at his throat.

"Yield," Geoffrey commanded.

Sir Dallen looked at him. "Yes, gods damn it, alright. I yield. I yield!"

Smiling, Geoffrey offered his hand and helped the other knight to his feet. As the pages arrived to help Sir Dallen, Geoffrey held his sword high above his head and acknowledged the crowd, who cheered and shouted his name. The Countess of Genio, ignoring protocol, jumped to her feet, clapping loudly. Sir Geoffrey approached and kissed her hand tenderly. He bowed to the queen and then left the field.

Edgar would not meet Bellaydin's eyes but handed over the coins that they had agreed to. "Lucky."

In spite of himself, Bellaydin smirked. "I told you not to underestimate him."

***

"Uncle Bela!" Maria almost leapt into the air as she saw Bellaydin, hugging him tightly without prompting. As if remembering her rank she let him go, smoothed down her dress and smiled awkwardly. "I hope you're well."

He was still at the list fields outside the castle. The tournament was over now, and all about him servants scurried about removing banners and pennants, clearing the decorations and accruements that were no longer needed. Maria was smiling widely and almost jumping up and down with excitement, quite different to the demure spectator he had seen at the joust. Behind her Sir Geoffrey Keslin stood protectively. At the knight's side was the Eldara Talthas, his fingers twitching on his longbow.

Bellaydin laughed and held his arms out, returning the hug that Maria had given him. "I am well, Maria," Bellaydin said. "How is Genio? How is the life of a countess?"

"Urgh," she said, twisting her lips. "Boring, to be honest. I spend my days talking politics with old men, and my nights doing needlework with little girls and ageing spinsters. How is it with you?"

Bellaydin shrugged. "I spend my days in lessons where I prove my ineptness on a regular basis."

"Give yourself time," Maria said. "What are the other squires like?"

"They seem to be doing better. I expect they've been taking such lessons their whole life."

"Are they good people? Do you get on well with them?"

"Some of them are good people," Bellaydin said.

"And the others?"

Bellaydin just gave her an enigmatic smile.

"I think I saw one of them before the joust," Maria said. "Who is the blonde boy?"

Bellaydin's dark eyes flashed. "Edgar."

Maria touched her hair. "He's handsome, don't you think?"

"I hadn't noticed," Bellaydin said. "Don't judge a book by its cover, though."

Maria laughed. "Oh Bela, aren't you over-protective? Don't worry, I already have a handsome, blonde attendant, don't I, Sir Geoffrey?"

Geoffrey chuckled heartily before greeting Bellaydin himself.

"That was some performance out there," Bellaydin said, clasping Geoffrey's hand.

"I never had any doubt, Bela," Maria said. "Genio's finest would beat any of those so-called champions from the great duchies."

Geoffrey smiled humbly. "I try my best. Sir Dallen is feared on the battlefields, and rightly so, but he also needs to learn that it's not strength alone that wins battles. Still, even I've got to admit that he nearly had me there at one stage." He turned to his left and realised he'd forgotten something. "Oh, you remember Talthas, don't you?"

Bellaydin extended a hand, which the Eldara accepted and shook firmly. "Sir Geoffrey has been kind enough to take me on as his own sworn sword."

"Or sworn bow, at any rate," Geoffrey said. "It was no big ask. These Eldara can fight, as I'm sure you know, Bela. And the countess was happy to have Talthas come on board."

"More than just happy, Bela. I'd never seen an elf before," Maria said. "Tell me, you lived with them. Are they all this friendly?"

"Not in the slightest," said Bellaydin. Amusingly, Talthas seemed to shrug and indicate his agreement.

"Well, I'd still like to see more of them I think," Maria said. "Would you take me to where you grew up, Bela? I'd like to see it."

"One day, of course," said Bellaydin.

Geoffrey placed a hand on Maria's shoulder. "Once the war with the Goriinchians is done I'll take you myself, milady."

"How does the war go?" Bellaydin asked Geoffrey.

"Not well, I'm afraid." He drew close to Bellaydin. "You heard about the Earl of Warding, didn't you?"

Bellaydin tried to be nonchalant. "In passing." He didn't want to tell Geoffrey he'd been spying on the Privy Council.

"The whole thing was a bit of a disaster. Most of the forces from Georgeton and the eastern earldoms were tied up in that attack. Losing all that, along with the Earl of Warding himself, well..." Geoffrey trailed off. "One of your fellow squires is the earl's son, isn't he? How is he holding up?"

"Better than expected," said Bellaydin. "But he's still devastated."

"Unsurprising. The earl's death is keenly felt, despite what some might say. I expect they'll have to call up the rest of the armies eventually. This will include Genio's."

"When will that be?" Bellaydin asked.

"No idea. It will all depend on what the Duke of Emperor's Palace decides. He is Lord Chancellor, after all. He has to keep the queen and the other nobles happy. I know Wulfric's been trying to have himself named as new commander of any Goriinchian invasion force, but the Zalltors have never been fond of him, and they'll petition the Lord Chancellor heavily to make sure that doesn't happen. Unfortunately there are few other willing candidates left. Until the deadlock is resolved, nothing much will happen, I wager."

He placed a hand on Bellaydin's shoulder, and drew him aside. "What's wrong, Bela? You look troubled."

"Oh, it's nothing really. One of the other squires. He's been saying things about my parents."

Geoffrey furrowed his brow. "What sort of things?"

"Filthy lies," Bellaydin said. "I know my parents didn't marry for love, but this went further. He made out that my father was a cuckold, and my mother was a...well, you know. I don't really want to say."

"Which squire said this?" Geoffrey raised his voice. "Who's been telling him such things?"

Bellaydin felt taken aback by Geoffrey's passionate response, but it was understandable that Geoffrey might feel slighted. He was close to William, after all.

"It was Edgar. I don't know where he's been hearing such things, but he certainly implied it was widely held."

Geoffrey's face relaxed. "Maybe they circulate such rumours amongst his household, but there's a reason his branch of the royal family are not held in high esteem. Put it out of your mind."

Bellaydin nodded, but one thought still troubled him. "But what if it is true, Geoffrey. What if my parents did break their vows to each other? I don't know how I would feel about that."

Geoffrey gave a gentle smile. "Bellaydin. It does none of us any good to judge another while on the outside looking in. Only those within a marriage can know what truly happens between a husband and wife. Your parents were good people, Bela, and they both loved you. That is more than many people can hope for."

"You're right, Geoffrey," said Bellaydin. "Thank you."

"Don't let Edgar get to you." At the sound of trumpets from nearby. Geoffrey turned to the countess. "My lady, I'm afraid we must get going. It is time."

"Already?" Maria said.

"I'm afraid so." Geoffrey turned to Bellaydin "Bela, next time I'm in the capital, why don't we catch up for a drink? I'd love to talk more."

"I'd like that," said Bellaydin.

"Goodbye Uncle Bela," Maria said. "Come and visit me in Genio when you are able."

Led by Geoffrey and Talthas, Maria departed towards her carriage some distance away. Once they were out of sight, Bellaydin returned to the castle. The gates and castle doors were open, with servants and attendants coming and going at a steady pace. Bellaydin moved past the throng, climbing the stairs to his own chambers. As he reached the top he almost collided with Rhiannon, who was running down the corridor. "There you are," she said, out of breath. "I've been looking for you. Did you see him?"

Bellaydin frowned. "See who? Sir Geoffrey?"

Rhiannon wrinkled her nose. "Who? No, the earl of course." She paused, realising the confused look on Bellaydin's face. "You haven't heard, have you?"

"Heard what? What about the earl?" Bellaydin did little to hide the irritation in his voice.

Rhiannon rolled her eyes and grabbed his hands dragging him over to one of the balconies where they could look over to the lower level of the castle. To Bellaydin's amazement, against all odds, the Earl of Warding was not as dead as most had thought. In fact, he was standing below them, with a few of his personal bodyguards, bedraggled and much the worse for wear but most certainly alive.

"He arrived barely an hour ago," Rhiannon said. "What do you suppose happened?"

"News of his death was obviously exaggerated," Bellaydin said. "I just wonder whose corpse that was that the Goriinchians mutilated and sent back to us."

The rest of the castle was agog, and a crowd of nobles and castle servants had gathered to look at the earl and his retinue. The steward soon arrived and after having a few words with the earl, he escorted the new arrivals towards the great hall.

"He's off to explain himself to the queen, and I have to get back to the kitchen," Rhiannon said. "See you later, skinny."

Bellaydin waved Rhiannon goodbye and turned to walk back to his room.

A voice interrupted him. "Bellaydin," said Haakon, "I was hoping to catch you."

"Your Grace," Bellaydin said, bowing his head.

"I'm assuming you saw the earl's return," Haakon said, looking over his shoulder.

"I thought the Goriinchians had killed him," Bellaydin said. "I must have been wrong."

"It seems we were all mistaken," the duke told Bellaydin. "The mutilated corpse the Goriinchians sent us was not the Earl of Warding. It was Sir Bors Thornton who the Goriinchians had defiled in such a way. His widow has since identified his remains from some personal effects."

"Did the Goriinchians know who it was?"

"Unlikely. I think the simplest solution is the most credible. The Goriinchians expected the earl to be leading the army into battle, to be fighting at the vanguard of the force just as their own war chiefs did, but most likely the earl stayed to the back and delegated the role to Sir Bors. When the tide of the battle turned, the earl made good his escape."

"That doesn't seem exactly honourable," Bellaydin said, though he had to admit the earl's decision was probably the most rational in the circumstances.

"Indeed it does not. Many of the other lords are furious, and Wulfric is calling the earl a craven coward. Luckily for the earl, however, the Duke of Georgeton will protect him from any serious repercussions. I do think that Anson Mainstream will take a long time to live this down, and we will hear little from Warding for the rest of the war." The duke sighed. "Listen Bellaydin, I didn't come here to talk about the Earl of Warding."

"No?"

Haakon gave Bellaydin a rueful smile. "No, I came to offer my apologies. I was short with you when we last met, and that was unfair. I understand that what happened on the hunt was not entirely your fault and I am sorry for overreacting."

"It's alright. I probably did overreact. He was trying to provoke me, I knew that. I should have ignored him. I know it is difficult for you, he is your cousin's son."

"*You* are also my cousin's son, Bellaydin, and I should have shown you more loyalty, especially since you have done far more to deserve it than Edgar ever has."

"Thank you, Your Grace," said Bellaydin. "That means a lot to me."

The duke smiled and patted Bellaydin on the shoulder gently. "I will see you later, Bellaydin. Be well."

"You too, Your Grace," Bellaydin said as Haakon departed.

Bellaydin continued down the hallway and had almost reached his room when he passed by the chambers of the Duke of Emperor's Palace. A soft miaow caught his attention, and Bellaydin looked down to see a ginger shape move by his legs.

"Malken." Bellaydin knelt down, scratching the cat behind its ears and chin. "Have you been in the duke's chambers again?"

Malken looked at Bellaydin, blinking at him with its wide yellow eyes. "Well? What do you have to say for yourself?" The cat purred, bumping its head against Bellaydin's hand. With a whip of its tail, it moved towards the door, which was already ajar.

"Malken, back here," Bellaydin said, following the cat. "You know you're not supposed to be in there." The cat ignored Bellaydin, and slipped through the gap in the door.

"Sorry, Your Grace, I couldn't catch him." Bellaydin called out loudly, but there was no response. "Hello? Your Grace? Are you in there?"

Bellaydin pushed open the door. "Your Grace? Hello?" There was nothing but an eerie silence from within, so it was with caution that Bellaydin entered the duke's sitting room.

Inside it was dark and freezing, quite unlike the warm and inviting atmosphere that had greeted him on his last visit. In the shadows, Bellaydin saw the fire pit had long since burned out and the floor around it was dusted with charcoal. On the table was a clean set of cutlery, a plate of food, uneaten and going cold in the frigid, and a single goblet, still filled with wine. Bellaydin saw the back of the duke's favourite chair and spotted the fabric of the duke's sleeve hanging over the edge. Malken sniffed the duke's arm, then hissed, giving off a terrible howl before bolting back out the door.

The cat's behaviour unnerved Bellaydin, but with some hesitation he moved closer to the chair. "Your Grace?" There was no response, so he came around to the front of the armchair.

Slumped before him was the duke, one hand holding a goblet and the other hanging limply by his side. "Your Grace?" He approached the duke and shook him with his left hand. There was no response, though the goblet dropped to the ground, falling from the duke's limp grasp. As Bellaydin drew near the duke's face he could see a blue tinge to his lips.

"Oh no..." said Bellaydin. He touched the duke's hand. The man's skin was cold to the touch. Bellaydin felt a sudden sense of dread. He dropped the duke's hand and called out. "Help! Help me. Something's happened to His Grace!"

Bellaydin stepped back, almost tripping, and then ran to the door. "Help! Come quickly!" He kept yelling for help. After a while he heard another man's voice, and someone running quickly towards the chambers.

"Squire, what's wrong?" It was the steward, Martin. He looked at Bellaydin with a baffled expression. "You're loud enough to wake the dead."

Bellaydin felt sick in his stomach. His words tumbled out in a frantic mess. "Something horrible has happened to the duke, come quickly."

"What?" Martin looked alarmed. "Where is he? Show me."

Bellaydin brought Martin to the duke's body. As soon as he saw it, Martin slumped to his knees.

"No, it can't be." he said. Tears in his eyes, he embraced the duke's body. "What happened?" he demanded of Bellaydin. "What did you see?"

"Nothing," said Bellaydin. "I came in and he was already like this. He had a goblet in his hand."

Martin saw the goblet on the floor and picked it up. "This one?" he asked. He looked inside and then took a sniff, before almost gagging.

"What is it? What's wrong?" Bellaydin asked. "Poison?"

"That does not smell right, whatever it is," Martin said. He looked in another direction and bent down to pick up a small leather pouch. After examining it for a moment, Martin slipped it into his clothes. "We must alert the rest of the Privy Council. They should be downstairs. You must fetch them quickly. I will remain here."

Bellaydin rushed out the door and hurtled down the stairs at great speed. He ran through the lower level of the castle and found the nobles assembled outside the council chambers, chatting amongst themselves casually. He could see Haakon and Wulfric, as well as the Duke of Georgeton and the Earl of Tyronsville. Maria and the Earl of Warding were not there. It appeared the meeting of the Privy Council had not yet begun. The men talked with each other freely, evidently not noticing Bellaydin was there.

"I don't suppose we expect to see the Earl of Warding today," the Earl of Tyronsville said.

The Duke of Georgeton sniffed the air and stroked his beard. "Anson needs some time to recuperate. He sends his apologies."

"It's the Duke of Emperor's Palace," Bellaydin panted. "Upstairs, come quickly."

The nobles looked at each other. Bellaydin gestured with his hand for them to follow and in short order he led the Dukes of Alariat, Oldharbour and Georgeton, and the Earl of Tyronsville to the duke's chambers.

"What is this, Bellaydin? What has happened?" the Duke of Alariat asked as they climbed the stairs.

"Something terrible has happened to the Duke of Emperor's Palace," Bellaydin said, out of breath, "You need to follow me."

The nobles exchanged a few worried looks as they reached the duke's chambers. Bellaydin led them to the sitting room, where Martin was, standing next to the duke's body.

"Martin? What's going on?" said Haakon. "Edmund…"

Martin fell to his knees by Edmund Tallcastle's limp form. "I am sorry, Your Grace. It seems that our noble lord, Edmund Tallcastle, Duke of Emperor's Palace and Earl of Garns has passed on to his reward." The other nobles looked shocked. "There is more," Martin said. "I do not believe his death was natural."

He passed the goblet to the Duke of Oldharbour, who smelled it gingerly. "Poison. The distinctive smell of the Tarkenese lotus blossom."

"What's that?" Bellaydin said.

"A powerful narcotic," Haakon said. "In small doses, it is an effective aid to sleep. In doses such as this, it is fatal."

"Perhaps the old man just put too much in his nightcap?" the Earl of Tyronsville suggested.

Martin's face made it plain that the steward thought little of that possibility.

"So I presume that this was an act of murder then?" Haakon said.

"This is ridiculous," the Duke of Georgeton said. "Who would want to poison the Duke of Emperor's Palace?"

"Anyone with an interest in seeing the realm weakened," Wulfric said. "And looking to advance their own interests at the same time."

"Are you alluding to a traitor within this castle, Wulfric?" asked Haakon.

"I am not alluding to anything, Your Grace," Wulfric said. "I am merely stating the facts as they appear."

The Duke of Georgeton stepped back. "A Goriinchian sympathiser, I suppose. We must secure the castle at once. No one should be allowed to leave until we have searched the entire structure top to bottom."

"Agreed," said the Earl of Tyronsville. "But be quick about it."

"The queen must also be informed," said Haakon. "I shall do so myself immediately."

The decision being made, Bellaydin left the duke's chambers and hurried back to his own. Knowing that the castle guards would soon start searching the castle for any sign of a Goriinchian sympathiser, Bellaydin remembered that he had a Goriinchian holy book hidden under his bed. Finding such a book in his quarters, along with him being the first person to discover the duke's body, might lead to some awkward questions. He got down on his knees and searched under his bed, looking for the book.

He found nothing.

Panicking, he looked underneath the bed, even pushing the whole frame aside, but there was no book there. He stood and, in shock, began tossing his other possessions aside seeing if he had put it somewhere else. It was not anywhere in his room.

Someone has taken it. Who would have done it? And why? Do they hope to accuse me of being a Goriinchian sympathiser?

Troubled, he sat back on his bed with his head in his hands. Someone was plotting something, Bellaydin could see that, but was he even the target? And was the duke's death part of the plan, or merely happy coincidence? What were they hoping to achieve? Was it to assist Goriinchia in the war, or was there something even more sinister still to come?

He was still musing over these later as he passed through the west wing on his way to the mess hall. He heard voices, coming from the crawlspace. He wondered if the Privy Council was in session. Moving with haste, he removed the board covering the crawlspace and entered, moving himself to the secret vantage point. He could see into the council chamber below and saw the highest nobles in the land engaged in a shouting match.

"What does it matter how it happened?" the Duke of Georgeton shouted. "There's a murderer within these walls, capable of killing the Lord Chancellor and escaping without a trace. Of course, we're in danger."

"Who would want to kill old Edmund anyway?" The Earl of Tyronsville seemed to be taking the matter rather casually. "And why use poison? The old man was hardly going to put up much of a fight, he hasn't seen his feet for the past decade."

"Have you been drinking, your lordship?" asked Haakon. The Earl of Tyronsville, sheepish, tried to look elsewhere.

"Your Graces," said Wulfric. "I believe we all suspect the culprit here. We have a Horned God worshipper hiding amongst us, I am sure of it."

"I agree with the Duke of Oldharbour," said the archbishop. "We should have driven out these heathens when had the chance."

"Garamond, Wulfric, do these deranged lunatics frighten you?" said the Duke of Georgeton. "Worshipping the Horned God is no crime, and hasn't been for a year. What reason would any of them have for murdering Edmund Tallcastle? It was the duke who enforced the edict of tolerance more than any of us."

"The duke was also the greatest peer of the realm," Wulfric said. "And the linchpin of our defence against Ygarak. Any of the Horned God's acolytes would have seen him as a prime target."

"You're mad," said the Duke of Georgeton. "You're obsessed."

"Your Graces," said Haakon. "Enough of this. Arguing gets us nowhere. We have important matters to discuss. You have all read Edmund Tallcastle's will."

The other nobles nodded and muttered. "Aye," said the Earl of Tyronsville. "Who would have guessed the old man had a son. *FitzGarns*. The mark of a bastard son. Didn't think he had it in him."

The archbishop looked about the room. "Does Martin know, Your Graces?"

"That he is the illegitimate son of the highest noble in the land?" Haakon said. "I cannot say. But his father has never acknowledged him publically. Until now."

"A fortunate turn of events for our friend the steward," said Wulfric. "He won't inherit the duke's title, but much of the rest of the duke's wealth will go to Martin directly."

"What are you implying, Your Grace?" The Duke of Georgeton came face to face to Wulfric, staring into the other man's eyes.

Wulfric gave a rather unsettling smile. "Nothing. Just stating the facts, Your Grace. I will leave it to the rest of you to draw whatever conclusions you wish."

The nobles sat down and started to talk too softly for Bellaydin to hear, so he crawled back out and went back into the hallway, replacing the plank as he left.

Martin was the duke's son. A strange turn of events, and quite possibly linked to the reason for the duke's death. He was still deep in thoughts when he arrived at the great hall for the meal. Bellaydin saw Otto Mainstream as he entered, already eating.

"I'm glad your father turned up alive, Otto," Bellaydin said. To be honest, he didn't really care that the Earl of Warding was alive, but he felt that Otto needed to hear a friendly bit of support. *Gods know he won't get it from any of the other squires.*

Otto for his part smiled widely, relief evident in his face, before concentrating on his meal. Nearby Kurth Bauer also ate slowly, trying to avoid eye contact with Bellaydin. Odds were the squire was still feeling awkward about Bellaydin catching him with Rhiannon.

Edgar de Morcor and his ever-present companion, Tancred Zalltor broke the silence with their arrival. As the two squires entered the great hall, Edgar had a broad smile on his face

"I have good news, my friends," Edgar said disingenuously. He knew very well that none of the other squires would have used that word to describe their relationship with them.

Kurth picked at his food. "Let me guess. You're secretly the son of a wagon driver, and the shame of your true origins means you will now retire to a monastery and never bother us again?"

"Very funny, Bauer," Edgar said. "No, my good news is that they have found the duke's murderer."

Bellaydin was stunned. *They'd found the murderer already? How?*

"Who was it?" Bellaydin asked.

"You wouldn't believe it," Edgar said. "That slut of a serving girl. What was her name, Tancred?"

"Rhiannon," Tancred said. "Ap'Lydin's friend." He eyed Bellaydin coldly.

"That's right," said Edgar. "Turns out she was a secret Horned God worshipper the whole time. They detained her about an hour ago in the castle prison."

Rhiannon? It seemed impossible. As for her being a worshipper of the Horned God, secret or not, Bellaydin knew that was nothing more than a lie. He looked towards Kurth, who, though red-faced, had said nothing, picking through his food nonchalantly.

"I don't believe it," Bellaydin said. "She wouldn't murder anyone."

"And you know this how exactly, Ap'Lydin? I knew you liked to muck about with the common folk in the kitchens, but I never thought I'd hear you try to defend them. What is it, are you sweet on her or something?"

"No, she's a friend," Bellaydin said. "Just why did they decide it was her, anyway?"

"They found the holy book of the Goriinchians amongst her possessions. No one who wasn't a worshipper of the Horned God would keep that book." Tancred said the words matter-of-factly, as if there was no other explanation for it.

"The slut tried to deny it," Edgar said. "As any filthy Goriinchian would."

"That proves nothing," Bellaydin insisted.

Edgar screwed up his face. "How much proof do you need? Goriinchians are all the same. Say, Ap'Lydin, that's a Goriinchian name, is it not? Is this why you are so eager to defend her?"

Bellaydin looked at Kurth again, expecting the boy to speak up, but he was ignoring the other squires, staring intently into his plate.

"If you'll excuse me, I have lost my appetite," Bellaydin said, rising with indignation.

"Go on Ap'Lydin, run away. Your kind always does," Edgar shouted after him as Bellaydin stormed off to his room. Bellaydin slammed the door so hard it nearly fell off its hinges, and then collapsed on his bed.

His head felt like it might explode. Rhiannon was no Horned God worshipper, and she was certainly no murderer. It was abundantly clear to Bellaydin that the book they had found her with was not hers; shortly after his own copy of the holy book of the Goriinchians goes missing, the castle soldiers find Rhiannon with a copy of the very same book. *Quite a coincidence, if true.* Bellaydin didn't believe for a moment that it was.

There was a knock on the door. "What do you want?" Bellaydin called out testily.

"It's me, Otto," came a voice.

Bellaydin stood up and opened the door. "What do you want?" he repeated.

Otto looked at him nervously. "Do you really believe that Rhiannon is innocent?"

Bellaydin blinked. "There's no way she could have done it. Someone has framed her."

Otto nodded. "I agree. There are others, too. Meet me at the hunting lodge in the royal forest. One hour." The squire looked around, checking to see if anyone was watching, and then added, "And bring anyone else who has an interest in justice being served."

The squire departed, leaving Bellaydin to think over his words. As far as Bellaydin was concerned there was at least one other who should share his disgust with how the nobles were treating Rhiannon.

He went to Kurth's room and rapped loudly on the squire's door. "Kurth! Open up, it's Bellaydin."

There was no reply, but he heard movement behind the door. He knocked again. "Come on!" The door opened and Kurth looked at him wearily.

"What do you want, Bellaydin?"

Bellaydin pushed Kurth inside the room and shut the door. He poked the squire in the chest. "Your lover has been imprisoned on trumped up charges and planted evidence, and you don't give enough of a damn to speak up in her defence?"

"I told you, I can't risk having my father find out about her," Kurth said defensively.

"I can't believe I'm hearing those words come out of your mouth," Bellaydin said. "This is someone's life we're talking about. That is far more important than your family's damn honour. Get a sense of perspective."

"It's not that simple," Kurth protested.

"I know you're not a coward, Kurth," Bellaydin said. "I don't understand why you insist on acting like one."

Kurth said nothing.

"Look, Otto and I are going to meet at the hunting lodge in the royal forest in one hour. If you give a damn about Rhiannon at all, you'll be there too. I leave it in your hands." Bellaydin left Kurth alone to think about. He hoped he'd done enough.

CHAPTER 14

Twilight bathed the forest.

Bellaydin was on his way to meet with Otto, having slipped out of the castle without attracting too much attention. As the shadows grew longer, Bellaydin lit his torch, giving himself enough light to view his surroundings. He saw the hunting lodge ahead. It was a rather simple wooden structure, reserved for the queen's party and built by her father, King Henry, during his own reign. The old king had been a rather keen hunter and falconer but had not passed the enthusiasm for the hobby to his daughter, she mainly kept it up for social standing amongst the nobility.

He saw Otto standing near the lodge, waiting for him. The fat squire saw Bellaydin, and smiled. "You made it," he said.

Bellaydin nodded. "I had to come. She's a friend."

Otto smiled. "She was always kind to me."

There was a rustling in the undergrowth nearby. Bellaydin wheeled about, his hands going to the sword on his belt. "Who's there?"

"It's only me," said Kurth Bauer, as he pulled himself through the bush he had been momentarily entangled with.

"Congratulations Ap'Lydin," Kurth said. "You managed to shame me into doing the right thing."

"Better than letting your pride convince you to do the wrong thing," Bellaydin said.

"Shall we go in?" said Otto. He knocked on the door of the lodge and announced himself.

The door opened, and standing in the doorway was Rowena, Rhiannon's mother and the castle cook. She looked at Otto and then at Bellaydin and Kurth.

"Thank you for coming boys," she said, her diction still tinged with a Goriinchian accent. "It is good to know that Rhiannon still has some friends." She led them inside to the lodge, offering them seats by the roaring fire. "My husband will be with you shortly."

Bellaydin was intrigued. In all the times he'd been to the kitchen to see Rhiannon, he'd only ever seen her mother, not her father, and she never really spoke about him at all. He warmed his hands by the fire as he waited. Next to him was Otto, and Kurth sat at the end, fidgeting in his seat.

"It is good to see you again, Bellaydin," said a familiar voice.

"Martin." exclaimed Bellaydin, "You are —"

"Rhiannon's father," Martin said. "Yes I am." He took a seat next to his wife, smiling at Rowena.

"You never mentioned it," Bellaydin said.

"I prefer to keep my personal life to myself," Martin said. "My wife, Rowena, is Goriinchian. There are those in the castle that might use it against me."

Bellaydin's thoughts swirled. "But that makes Rhiannon and the duke... She's his..."

"What are you talking about, Ap'Lydin?" asked Kurth.

Martin sighed. "I am Martin FitzGarns, the Duke of Emperor's Palace's bastard son. Rhiannon is my daughter, meaning that she is accused of killing her own grandfather."

"What?" Kurth sounded shocked, which didn't surprise Bellaydin. Though he couldn't tell if it the shock was made greater by the revelation that, illegitimacy aside, Rhiannon was technically of better stock than Kurth himself.

"Now you can see why this situation is doubly stressful for my wife and I," Martin said. "We know Rhiannon did not do this, but I cannot understand how it came to be that she was framed."

Bellaydin felt his gut churn. He decided to be honest. "The book they found Rhiannon with. It wasn't hers, it was mine. Someone stole it from my possessions and planted it among your daughter's belongings."

The steward's expression turned grave. "Why on earth did you have the Goriinchian holy book in your room?"

"It was a gift to me, from…someone who once helped me." Bellaydin felt it wise to avoid complicating matters by explaining his connection to Morgan Culainn, only daughter of the warchief whose army was currently threatening Emparia.

"How did anyone find out you had the book?" Otto asked.

Bellaydin found himself stumped. The portly squire had made a good point. Just how did someone know where to find the book?

"We can worry about that later," Martin said. "I need to know that you are all willing to do what it takes to prove Rhiannon's innocence."

Bellaydin and Otto nodded, and then Kurth did as well, after some hesitation.

"Good," said Martin. "Now it is clear that my father was poisoned, and most likely with the Tarkenese lotus blossom, particularly with what we found in the duke's chambers. Show them the pouch, my dear." Rowena held up a small pouch, opening it to reveal the petals of a lotus blossom.

"May I see that pouch?" Bellaydin asked. Rowena passed it to Bellaydin, and he turned the leather pouch over in his hand. It was embossed with a sigil depicting a grey skull. "I recognise this sigil. This belongs to Sir Dallen Withers."

"Indeed it does," said Martin.

"The knight from the tournament?" asked Otto.

Martin nodded. "Withers is the sworn sword of the Duke of Georgeton. The finest knight in service of House Zalltor."

"Do you think the Duke of Georgeton is behind this?" Bellaydin said.

Martin shook his head. "Oswin Zalltor is many things, but a murderer is not one of them. But Sir Dallen Withers on the other hand..."

"Why didn't you show the other dukes this?" Kurth asked.

"I did. They all claimed to not recognize it. Even the Duke of Georgeton."

"He must know something. Why would he pretend to not recognize the sigil of his own sworn sword?" Bellaydin said.

"Exactly," said Martin.

"What do we do?" asked Kurth. "We can't just stroll up and ask him if he knows who poisoned the Duke of Emperor's Palace. He'll just clam up."

Martin shook his head. "No, we must try a subtler approach, and concentrate on finding evidence to exonerate Rhiannon. Do you know of the duke's apartments within the castle? He uses them whenever he visits the capital. His entire retinue stays with him. If there is any link between this crime and House Zalltor we shall find it there."

"What are you suggesting?" Bellaydin asked.

"I need you squires to break into the Zalltor apartments and see what you can find." Martin said the request very plainly, as if he were asking them to do something totally innocuous.

"Are you serious?" Kurth said. "What if they catch us?"

"I am steward of Castle Emparia, remember? I will ensure that whatever happens, a reasonable explanation will be provided to Her Majesty."

"What exactly are we looking for?" Otto stated his question plainly.

"Whatever you can find that will exonerate my daughter. A note, more of the lotus blossoms – anything. Please, this is our only hope."

"I'm not sure," said Bellaydin. It sounded like a dangerous plan.

"We'll do it together," Kurth said. "All three of us – you, me, Piggy. For Rhiannon."

Otto turned and repeated, "Yes, for Rhiannon."

Bellaydin sighed. "Alright. For Rhiannon."

Martin nodded and produced a large key. "This will open the rooms of House Zalltor. Once you are done you must return it to me immediately. No one must know I gave it to you."

Bellaydin frowned. "But Rhiannon is your daughter. Won't others make the connection themselves?"

"That is why I must keep my involvement to a minimum. If anyone asks, one of you stole the key. It is well known that the Duke of Georgeton's sons are careless when they've been drinking."

The squires returned to the castle later that night, ready for the next part of their plan. They were to await a signal from Martin, who would alert them as to the best time to enter the apartments. In the meantime, they readied themselves, dressing in light, unremarkable clothes that would hinder others identifying them, at the same time enabling ease of movement.

Eventually, the call came, and Bellaydin, Kurth and Otto met in the gloom outside the Zalltor apartments. The sigil of an owl, House Zalltor's symbol, hung over the ornate double doors.

"Alright, one of us should stay outside to watch for anyone returning," Bellaydin said.

Otto raised his hand. "I'll do it."

"Give us a shout if anyone comes near," Kurth said. "And keep your dagger handy."

Otto widened his eyes.

"You never know." Kurth shrugged. "Come on Bellaydin, let's do this."

Bellaydin inserted the key Martin had given them into the lock, before pushing the doors open. Inside, the room was dark, satisfying Bellaydin that no one was in there. As he and Kurth stepped inside, they stood for a moment fumbling around in the dark, until Kurth produced a torch from his belt. Striking flint to steel he lit it up and illuminated their surroundings.

Kurth made an impressed noise as he surveyed the rich surroundings. "I mean, you always hear that the Zalltors are rich, but you never really know what they mean by that until you see it."

Bellaydin was inclined to agree. Priceless furniture and art packed the sitting room, and finely made tapestries lined the walls.

Kurth whistled. "Meanwhile in Tyronsville we make do with a leaky castle, sodden farmlands and patched clothes."

Bellaydin looked around. "Start looking."

"Right," said Kurth. They began rifling through cupboards and opening drawers, hoping to find something that might help them. Bellaydin found a few gold coins, many clothes, and a ring or two, but nothing unusual or incriminating.

"Anything yet?" Bellaydin said.

"No, nothing," Kurth said.

"I'm going to check the next room," Bellaydin said.

He walked into one of the other chambers. It appeared to be the duke's private chambers. He began to search it, as he had the sitting room, taking care to not mess up the room too much – it would lead to too many questions if the duke returned to find his room ransacked.

"Please, give me something, give me anything, give me…" Bellaydin froze. He felt like there was someone behind him. "Kurth? Is that you?"

"Unlikely," said a raspy voice.

Bellaydin turned around just as a blade swung through the air towards his face, he dived to the ground just in time. "Wait. Stop."

"Who are you boy, and what are you doing here?" said Sir Dallen Withers. The knight's voice was a strangled whisper.

Bellaydin stood, and dusted himself off. "Ah, nothing, I was just, looking for something," Bellaydin babbled, looking for an escape route.

Sir Dallen's eyes flickered as he looked at Bellaydin and then towards the overturned chest. "You should not be here," the knight growled. "How did you get in?"

"The doors were unlocked. I was only looking," Bellaydin said.

"And what do you expect to find?"

Bellaydin swallowed, but found the courage to continue. "The duke was murdered. I think you might know something about it."

Sir Dallen's eyes narrowed. "And what makes you think that?"

"We found your pouch. The one that held the poison."

Sir Dallen's mouth twitched, and Bellaydin knew that the knight realised he'd been caught out. Sir Dallen lunged at Bellaydin, swinging his sword above his head, and Bellaydin dodged to the left to avoid the blow. The knight's sword caught the edge of the bed, sending splinters flying.

"Kurth, Otto! Help!" Bellaydin cried out.

"Die!" Sir Dallen said, spittle flying. He kicked wildly, and Bellaydin managed to dodge all the blows but one, which caught him in the stomach, knocking the wind from him. He staggered backwards from the blow. Sir Dallen sneered, swinging his sword in the air as he approached Bellaydin with slow and deliberate menace.

"Don't…please, don't…" Bellaydin pleaded, stepping away from the advancing knight.

"At least die with dignity, squire," Sir Dallen said.

Kurth grabbed Sir Dallen from behind, causing the knight to drop his sword. Kurth wrestled with the knight, attempting to overpower him. Kurth was young and strong, but Sir Dallen was a behemoth of a man, and pretty soon the squire was finding himself outmatched. Regaining his composure Sir Dallen smashed his fist into the front of Kurth's face, sending him flying to the ground. As Sir Dallen flung Kurth to the ground, Bellaydin grabbed the knight's sword, bringing it up protectively in front of his face.

"Brave of you boy," Sir Dallen said. "But do you even know how to use of one those?"

"I guess we'll soon find out," he said.

Sir Dallen snickered and continued to move towards him. Bellaydin swung at him, but the knight twisted his body, and Bellaydin's blow hit him on his armour. The knight reached out with his right arm and grabbed Bellaydin's sword arm by the wrist, squeezing it tightly. The man's strength was immense – almost inhuman – and Bellaydin's eyes watered from the pain as Sir Dallen's grip threatened to break his wrist.

Yelping with pain, Bellaydin's grip loosened, and the sword clattered to the ground. Sir Dallen punched Bellaydin in the face, and Bellaydin felt a sharp pain in his jaw and tasted blood. Another blow, this time to Bellaydin's nose, and he felt blood trickle down his face.

Soon Sir Dallen was pummelling him, again and again, and just when Bellaydin felt he might pass out from the pain, the attacks stopped. Bellaydin opened his eyes and saw Sir Dallen struggling to move, Kurth and Otto were both holding on to him tight. The knight thrashed about violently, concentrating all his strength on trying to throw Kurth and Otto off him.

"Hit him with something," Kurth yelled out. "Do it."

Bellaydin picked up the sword.

"No," Otto yelled. "We need him alive."

Bellaydin nodded, turning the sword so that the flat of the blade was facing Sir Dallen and then with one mighty blow he smashed the knight in the face with it. Sir Dallen's eyes rolled up to the back of his head and, his legs buckling, the knight crumpled to the floor, unconscious. Bellaydin breathed a sigh of relief and collapsed with exhaustion himself. "We got him. Thank the gods."

Kurth kneeled next to the knight's body. "He's out cold, but not for long I'd wager."

"We need to find Martin," Otto looked about nervously. "The guards will be here soon."

"Go on then, Otto. Find Martin, bring him here," Bellaydin said wearily. Otto looked at him hesitantly. "Go!" The squire did as Bellaydin asked, and quickly ran off to find the steward.

"Are you alright?" Kurth said. "You got beaten pretty bad."

Despite his aching body, Bellaydin managed a smile. "Thanks for reminding me." He winced. "I think I'll be sore for a long time."

Kurth sat down next to the partially destroyed bed.

"Give him another whack if he looks like he's waking up," Bellaydin said.

Luckily it didn't prove necessary because as Sir Dallen began to stir Martin had already arrived. The steward carried a sturdy rope, and with his help, the three squires tied Sir Dallen securely to a chair. Groggily, the knight slowly awoke and, realising his predicament, became immediately enraged, struggling against his bonds and trying to escape.

"Easy now, Sir Dallen," Martin said. "You won't be escaping that easily. Not until you tell us everything."

The knight screwed his face up in disgust and then spat straight in Martin's face. "I do not answer to boys or bastards," Sir Dallen sneered.

Bellaydin was shocked. The knight seemed to know that Martin was the natural son of the duke. Despite overhearing it from the Privy Council, Bellaydin had been under the impression it was not widely known. He'd assumed the contents of the duke's bequest had not been disclosed outside of a few. Apparently, he had been mistaken.

"Why did you poison the Duke of Emperor's Palace?" Martin demanded. Sir Dallen did not answer, so Martin hit the knight across the face. "Answer me."

The knight merely chuckled, showing his bloodstained teeth. "You'll get nothing out of me, bastard."

Martin turned to Bellaydin. "We will have to try some alternate methods of persuasion. Otto, go to my room, and fetch the blue phial in the cupboard."

Otto nodded and did as asked, and in a few minutes returned with the blue phial. "An alchemical formula, brewed by Qardleean mystics, and intended to force the truth from the unwilling," said Martin as he held it up. "Hold him while I give it to him."

Bellaydin and Kurth restrained Sir Dallen's head as Martin poured the liquid down his throat.

"Easy now," the steward said. The knight thrashed against his restraints, trying to spit out the drink, but they forced it down his throat.

"Now, Sir Dallen, again we must talk," Martin said.

The knight stared ahead blankly and then nodded slowly.

"Do you know who killed the Duke of Emperor's Palace?" asked Martin.

Sir Dallen nodded slowly and then pointed to himself.

"You did?" asked Martin.

Sir Dallen nodded but then added, "There were others."

"Others, what others? Who else was involved?"

Just as Martin said those words the door behind them swung open. It was the Duke of Georgeton, Oswin Zalltor, and his three sons. "Steward. What is the meaning of this?" the duke demanded.

Martin turned. "I apologise for the intrusion into your private rooms, Your Grace, but I heard a scuffle and screams for help, and came to investigate."

The Duke of Georgeton looked at the restrained knight, his eyes narrowing. "What is Sir Dallen doing here?"

"It appears he attacked these squires. Strange behaviour, Your Grace. Most unbecoming for a knight."

The Duke of Georgeton looked at Martin through slitted lids. "I suppose it is. Is there another reason that you have incarcerated my sworn

221

sword, steward?"

"Well yes, actually," said Martin. "Sir Dallen was just telling us some rather interesting information Your Grace, about the murder of the Duke of Emperor's Palace. It appears he may have been involved."

The Duke of Georgeton looked shocked. "Sir Dallen, is this true?"

The knight nodded, his grin disconcerting. One of the duke's sons spoke up, "He's fading, father. We need to get him to the healer's if he's going to survive to tell us the truth."

Another of the duke's sons whispered in the duke's ear. "Quite right, Reynald," the duke said. "Martin, thank you for your work here. You and the squires are dismissed. We shall deal with this from here."

"Your Grace, with all due respect, I wish to remain."

The duke waved a hand. "You are not required, Martin. Surely you have other duties to return to? Do not worry, if Sir Dallen is guilty, I will ensure that your daughter is released."

Martin nodded. "Come on boys, we've been asked to leave."

Bellaydin and the other squires followed Martin from the rooms. Once outside, Bellaydin turned to the others.

"Well, his arrival seemed awfully convenient," Bellaydin noted.

Martin nodded. "Yes, just as Sir Dallen was about to tell us that there were others involved."

"What do we do now?" Kurth asked.

"We must wait," said Martin. "There is nothing we can do. If the duke is true to his word, Rhiannon should be released."

"But what of these others Withers mentioned?" asked Bellaydin.

"We may never know the truth of that," Martin admitted.

"But we can't just let – "

"Enough Bellaydin," Martin said. "It is out of my hands. Believe me when I say I am no more pleased than you are, but that is where we are." The steward looked annoyed, and Bellaydin could read the frustration evident in the man's face.

Martin placed a hand on Bellaydin's shoulders. "Thank you, boys," he said to the squires. "You have been of great help to me, and to Rhiannon."

***

For the next few days, they did as Martin had bid them, and waited to see what would happen. At first, it seemed that Bellaydin's distrust of the duke was ill-founded, as the nobles quickly released Rhiannon from imprisonment, gave her a royal pardon, and reunited her with her family, apparently none the worse for wear. There were other signs that were less encouraging. Sir Dallen Withers had been taken into the Duke of Georgeton's custody and from there he heard little more, except for a brief proclamation from the Zalltor family that they'd expelled Sir Dallen from their favour even before the murder, and he had committed the crime entirely of his own volition. Bellaydin found that difficult to believe, particularly since Sir Dallen lacked any sort of motive for the murder entirely.

Despite his suspicions, Bellaydin found there was little he could do about it. The Privy Council quite clearly believed that the matter was resolved, and Oswin Zalltor returned to the capital acting as if the whole series of events had nothing to do with him. It was as if the whole incident had never happened. Still, there was at least some good to come of the squires' efforts. One day he entered the kitchens and someone surprised him with a tight hug.

"Thank you, Bellaydin," Rhiannon said, tears in her eyes. "Kurth told me all the help you gave him finding the real killer. Thank you, you're a good friend."

Bellaydin felt a bit sore at Kurth, who had evidently exaggerated his own role in their little quest and diminished Bellaydin's, but this was mitigated by the sheer sense of relief he had at seeing Rhiannon again. The girl in the kitchen had been one of the few bright spots of Bellaydin's experience in the capital.

"You seem even thinner than I remember," Rhiannon chided. "No one fed you while I was away?"

Bellaydin rubbed his stomach self-consciously. "I think I might have been too busy."

Rhiannon smiled. "Well, now that I'm back we'll have to see if we can't fatten you up again."

Bellaydin's reunion with Rhiannon was brief, as he was soon summoned to the great hall with the other squires. When he arrived, Bellaydin saw the Duke of Oldharbour there. It was the first time in months he had seen Wulfric, and judging by the sour expression on the noble's face, he had not mellowed in the interim.

"Squires," Wulfric said as Bellaydin sat down. "With the unfortunate passing of the Duke of Emperor's Palace it now falls to me, senior duke of the realm and Lord Constable, to organise the defence of this kingdom. As a consequence, I shall be leading a new expeditionary force to the south to bring the fight to the Goriinchians."

"And what of the last army?" scoffed Edgar de Morcor. "How do we know this new one won't meet the same fate?"

Wulfric looked perturbed at the comment. "The Earl of Warding's forces were unprepared. This time we know what we are facing and have formed the strategy we need to deal with the Goriinchians."

"Why are you telling us?" asked Kurth. Bellaydin was wondering the same thing.

"I am telling you this because it has been decided that you squires are to join the army, and experience the responsibilities of a knight first hand. You will be attached to my command, where you will learn the art of tactics and the chain of command."

There was a hushed silence. Bellaydin knew that that Wulfric had intended for him to spend a few months attached to the army of Oldharbour, but Bellaydin had never suspected that the duke would intend for this to happen midway into an invasion of Goriinchia. The other squires looked surprised and a little apprehensive. Otto looked particularly concerned. As if anticipating the reaction, Wulfric raised a hand. "You have nothing to fear, you will not be in the vanguard of the fighting. This is merely to give you a taste of what you can expect when you are fully fledged knights. Now go and pack your things. We leave tomorrow."

The squires rose and returned to their quarters. Bellaydin was about to do the same when Wulfric stopped him. "Just a moment, Bellaydin."

Bellaydin stopped. What Wulfric might say worried Bellaydin, the duke was never one for casual conversation.

The duke pulled a book from his robes and handed it to Bellaydin. "I believe this belongs to you." It was the Goriinchian holy book Morgan Culainn had given him and that had disappeared from his room in the castle.

Bellaydin swallowed. "How did you know?"

"I knew there was only one person in this castle naive enough to keep such a book amongst their belonging. Take it, and if you know what's good for you, you'll destroy the damn thing."

Bellaydin flushed. Wulfric's words stung.

"These things, books like this," Wulfric said, "they are not to be taken lightly. It is not a game, Bellaydin. And the Horned God does not relinquish his slaves without a fight."

With those words still ringing in his ears, Bellaydin returned to his quarters to gather his possessions. Placing the Goriinchian holy book back with the rest of his things, he wrapped them once again in a piece of cloth. As he did so, there was a knock on the door.

"Hello, anyone there?" It was Geoffrey's voice.

"Geoffrey," Bellaydin said. "What are you doing here?"

"About to go to war, from what I hear," he grinned. "Good to see you, Bela." He crushed Bellaydin with a bear hug.

"Are you joining the duke's force?" Bellaydin asked.

"The entire army of Genio is. Due to our losses at Wishapton, we stayed out of the Earl of Warding's little expedition, but with the failure of that force, we're needed again."

"It'll be good to fight alongside a familiar face."

Geoffrey nodded. "There's someone else here who wants to see you as well."

There was a quiet voice from behind the doorway. "Uncle Bela?"

"Maria?" said Bellaydin.

"Uncle Bela," the girl ran into the room and embraced him. "I've missed you."

Bellaydin squeezed her tightly. "How have you been?"

"Oh, they've kept me busy," Maria said. "They barely let me leave Genio; they say I need to learn how to be a countess."

"Someone has to do it," Bellaydin said. "I hear your army is going into battle."

"Oh yes. Isn't it exciting? They're not letting me go with it, though. They say war is no place for a lady." She made a face. "Sometimes I think boys have all the fun. Geoffrey is going to be in charge."

Geoffrey gave a slight bow. "And I will do my best to bring glory to your name, my lady."

Maria leant over to Bellaydin and kissed him on the cheek. "For luck," she said.

Bellaydin blushed. "I'm not going to be involved in any fighting."

Maria looked happy. "Well, all the better as I'm concerned. You're my only family left. I don't want to lose you too."

"Oh, I think your cousin's going to be around for a long time yet, my lady," said Geoffrey. "Come, let's leave the squire to get ready."

Maria and Geoffrey departed, leaving Bellaydin alone with his thoughts. His time at the capital was at an end, and though the thought of marching off to battle wasn't something he relished, he still felt a rush of excitement. He would be heading south again – would he see Wishapton? At the very least he would be with Geoffrey, Wulfric and Kahlaf again, some familiar faces after the strangers of the capital.

But most of all he hoped that they would settle the score with Cathan Culainn and the other Goriinchians – the followers of the Horned God and the murderers of Bellaydin's cousin. This time, they would be on the defensive. He hoped that that now it would be the Goriinchians who would know fear.

CHAPTER 15

Rose petals rained from above.

Once again an army departed from Emperor's Palace. Once again the city folk honoured the soldiers by lining the streets to see them off. This time the army marched under the banner of House Highcrown – the twisted serpents.

The troops of Georgeton, Warding and Tyronsville had already been pledged to the previous force, led by the disgraced Earl of Warding, Anson Mainstream. This new army was comprised solely of forces from Oldharbour and Genio. Duke Wulfric Highcrown was the overall leader but the forces from Genio were under the command of Sir Geoffrey Keslin, acting in the stead of the young Countess of Genio, Maria Ap'Lydin.

Bellaydin rode with the other squires. To his left were Kurth Bauer and Otto Mainstream; to his right, Edgar de Morcor and Tancred Zalltor. Edgar and Tancred rode close together, deep in conversation. Every so often Edgar glanced at Bellaydin with a superior smirk on his face, but otherwise, the pair ignored the others. Kurth, for his part, spent his time gazing at the countryside as they passed, whereas Otto made a few attempts to engage the others in conversation but, receiving no real response, eventually gave up and stared straight ahead.

The Ahktarran Kahlaf el'Lahn rode ahead of the squires. The duke had given the Lizardman the role of overseeing the squires and keeping them away from any real danger. The look on Kahlaf's face told Bellaydin that he was not pleased with this arrangement, and he spent most of the journey with an unpleasant scowl etched on his features.

The army was moving quickly, and with a sense of purpose, and they were now some distance from Emperor's Palace. Bellaydin estimated that they would soon be as far south as Wishapton. Thinking of the town brought back memories – of the battle, of William's death, and he tried to push them from his mind. He didn't want to experience that pain again.

"You, Lizard," Edgar called out. "How much longer?"

Kahlaf didn't turn around. "Eager to see others fight and die, little prince?" The Ahktarran laced his words with contempt. "Don't worry, we shall be there soon enough."

Bellaydin strained his neck, trying to look through the mass of soldiers to the front ranks where Geoffrey and Wulfric led. Since their departure, Wulfric had not spoken to him, and even Geoffrey had only given a half-hearted distracted sort of greeting. It was clear to Bellaydin that the challenge to come preoccupied their minds. The Goriinchians had already annihilated one Emparian army, Bellaydin prayed that that would not be the fate of this army as well. At least the sheer size should give the Goriinchians pause; Wulfric was obviously not taking the threat lightly. Behind contingents of heavy cavalry came armoured men-at-arms, rows after rows of billmen and a good number of archers. The majority wore the colours of House Highcrown, with the remainder showing their allegiance to House Ap'Lydin and the Earldom of Genio.

A few hours later sunset caused the army to call a halt to the march and set up camp for the night. After they had assembled their tents, Bellaydin and the other squires sat with Kahlaf around a campfire, sharing their bland army rations. After the splendid food they had enjoyed at Castle Emparia, the dried and heavily salted meat was scarcely edible. Otto looked particularly miserable, a fact which Edgar de Morcor noticed and used to his advantage.

"What's the matter, Piggy? Miss the days of them filling up your trough?" Edgar looked about the other squires, expecting laughter or some sort of reaction of that kind but found only blank stares, even from Tancred.

"So," said Kurth, changing the topic, "what do you think we're up against?"

"Death," said Otto.

"My father says the Goriinchians are no match for Emparian soldiers," Tancred ventured.

Kurth laughed. "How well has your father been paying attention, Tancred? Those 'filthy barbarians' just routed the largest Emparian army assembled since the civil war."

"Unfortunately," said Tancred, "my grandfather put his trust in the wrong man to lead the army." His eyes came to rest on Otto rather accusingly.

Bellaydin noticed Kahlaf's eyes flickering as the Ahktarran looked from squire to squire, his brow furrowed.

"I don't think the blame lies with Otto's father alone. Everyone underestimated them."

"Oh?" said Edgar. "What makes you a sudden expert, Ap'Lydin? This time last year you were still prancing around with elves, were you not?"

"Maybe so, but it was not long after that that I was a prisoner of the Goriinchians. I even met their Prophet-King."

"You met Ygarak?" asked Otto. "What was he like? I've heard stories-"

231

"Believe them," Bellaydin said. "He was frightening. Inhumanly tall, clad in armour and with a horned helmet that gave me no view of his face."

"He's a man, like any other," said Edgar. "One sword thrust and he dies like any other."

"So you hope," Kurth said. That remark seemed to unsettle Edgar somewhat, as he coughed nervously.

"What do you say, Kahlaf?" Bellaydin asked. "You were there with me when the Goriinchians captured us."

Kahlaf looked at Bellaydin and then to the other squires. "The Goriinchian threat is not one to be taken lightly. They are numerous, they fight with great tenacity and their war chiefs are men of great ability."

Kurth nodded. "And what of Ygarak? Is he, as men say, unkillable?"

Kahlaf gave a thin-lipped smile. "Unlikely. I have not met any man or creature that is."

"Just as I said," Edgar said, grinning.

Kahlaf continued. "Do not delude yourself little squire. There is still a vast gulf between unkillable and defeatable."

"Maybe for you, Lizard," said Edgar. "But we have an army."

"The Earl of Warding had an army too," Kahlaf said. "And it did not save him."

"This time it is different," Tancred said.

Kahlaf looked at him, unblinking. "If you insist."

"Cowardice does not become you, Lizardman," said Edgar. "I didn't expect one of your kind to be so craven."

Kahlaf looked with scorn upon the young squire. "Think what you will. When the battle arrives, you will all be tested. And we shall see whose resolve holds."

The Slaves of the Horned God

***

Some distance away, in the command tent, Geoffrey leant over a table of maps and battle plans. The Eldara archer Talthas li'Lyros stood beside the knight, his eyes following Geoffrey's. The Duke of Oldharbour regarded both men carefully.

"I trust the situation is clear to you then, Sir Geoffrey?" said Wulfric. The duke reclined in his chair, a goblet of wine in his hand.

"The Goriinchian losses from the Battle of Wishapton were not as great as we hoped," Geoffrey noted, his finger on a scout's report. "I really thought we'd hit them hard."

"Much of their strength was held in reserve," Wulfric said, "And in spite of my efforts in lifting the siege, I was unable to prevent the Goriinchians from executing an orderly retreat."

"It also looks like they've been strengthened with new recruits as well."

"Yes, and after successfully annihilating our first expeditionary force they have only suffered minor casualties. They have now crossed the border, and hold much of the marches. From here they threaten border towns such as Wishapton and Drakeford, and if not dealt with, Genio and Oldharbour will be next."

Geoffrey's eyes flickered at the mention of Drakeford. He picked up his goblet and had a drink. "So what is your plan? Surely you have some strategy in mind?"

Wulfric nodded, putting down his goblet and standing up. "Warchief Aonghus Culainn is waiting for us at Goriinch Hill. He expects to lead us into a trap, just as he did to the Earl of Warding. We shall be disappointing him and will ruin his plans. The River Drake lies between us and the Goriinchians. There are two bridges that cross the river. The Goriinchians will expect us to cross at the northern one. It is larger, and will carry more of our men."

233

"I remember that bridge. So we *won't* be crossing there?"

"*You* shall cross there, but I will take my forces further, and cross at the lesser known ford south of Drakeford. While the Goriinchians face your forces, believing themselves to have taken you by surprise, I will outflank them from the south, and between us we will catch the Goriinchians in a pincer, crushing them before they know what is happening."

Geoffrey looked thoughtful. "A well thought out strategy, Your Grace, but it is not without risks. Especially for myself and my men. The countess would not be pleased if this plan backfires."

"I am well aware of the danger this strategy poses for our forces, Geoffrey, but we cannot risk a frontal assault, not with the Goriinchians as entrenched as they are. Catching them by surprise is our only chance."

"Our timing will have to be perfect," Geoffrey said. "If you don't arrive in time..."

"I have taken that into consideration. Rest assured Geoffrey, that I have timed this exquisitely."

Geoffrey shook his head in wearied resignation. "Well, you're the commander. And your reasoning is sound. I have to admit, it sounds better than the Earl of Warding's plan."

"The Earl of Warding had no plan," said Wulfric.

"Exactly. It is agreed then?" Wulfric asked. "Good. Sir Geoffrey, we may have had our differences, but I knew I could count on you to see reason when the time came."

Geoffrey nodded in acknowledgement. It was as close to praise as he was going to get from the Duke of Oldharbour. "And what of Bellaydin and the other squires?"

"They will accompany my forces. It would be too dangerous to leave them with you. Not that I don't trust your abilities, Geoffrey, but I would not like to explain to the titled heads of Emparia's greatest houses that their sons were killed in a military manoeuvre."

"Right then, I suppose I better go talk to my men then."

Wulfric sat back in his chair. "It would be wise."

Geoffrey bid Wulfric farewell and left the tent. As he returned to his own tent, he mulled over his thoughts. The duke's plan was solid, and certainly seemed necessary to defeat the Goriinchians, but at the same time, Geoffrey couldn't shake the nagging worry that came with being the one taking all the risks. Despite the duke's assurances, Geoffrey did not feel confident in their ability to synchronise their attacks. What if the Goriinchians attacked his army before Wulfric crossed the river? Geoffrey shook his head. No sense dwelling on it. This was the sort of thing he had to be prepared for as a knight, even if this was his first real command. The important thing was that Bellaydin and the other squires were safe. He owed it to William to see that the latter's cousin didn't throw his life away recklessly. The Goriinchians had certainly chosen an interesting place for a battle. Goriinch Hill – every Emparian knew that place. It was where the last of the Tyron kings had fallen in battle to Henry de Morcor over thirty years ago. He wondered if the Goriinchians knew of the place's significance and had chosen it deliberately.

"Talthas, your thoughts?" Sir Geoffrey asked the Eldara.

The Eldara looked around. "You wish to hear what I have to say on this?"

"I'd be interested to hear your counsel," said Geoffrey. "Is the duke's plan sound?"

"For the most part yes," the Eldara said. "But it also carries a great deal of risk. If the Goriinchians were to attack either our forces before the duke is ready..."

Geoffrey cut him off with a wave. "You fought with us at Wishapton.

How do you judge the Goriinchians in battle?"

"Ferocious, and without fear," said Talthas. "Their faith in this Horned God of theirs makes them scorn death."

"Reckless then?"

Talthas frowned. "I would not say that. Their commander at the siege of Wishapton had a firm grasp of tactics. He did not spill his own soldiers' blood without just cause."

"They are at Goriinch Hill," Geoffrey said. "They will have the high ground."

"Their archers will be more effective than ever. They already rival us Eldara in skill."

Geoffrey sighed. "This is starting to sound like a bad idea."

"Why not pull back, and wait for them to come to us?"

Geoffrey sighed. "The Privy Council is expecting a great victory. The duke will not retreat, not now."

Talthas shared resigned looks with Geoffrey.

"Sir Emeric," Geoffrey called out.

A young knight, hearing his name, came up the hill. "Yes, Sir Geoffrey?"

"Make ready," Geoffrey said. "Tell your men that we are moving out."

Sir Emeric looked pleased. "Has the duke decided it is time?"

Geoffrey nodded. "Yes, but he will not be joining us yet. The army of Genio will be alone. The duke will rejoin us for the battle."

"As the duke commands," said Sir Emeric, saluting Geoffrey.

As the younger knight went to talk to the other lieutenants, Geoffrey reflected for a moment and made a silent prayer that Wulfric's plan would work. "I hope you know what you're doing, old man."

***

"Alright you squires, enough rest, it's time to get moving." Kahlaf moved from sleeping squire to sleeping squire, kicking each in turn until they woke from their slumbers.

"I'm awake, I'm awake," Bellaydin said. The sun had barely risen over the horizon, and the camp was still bathed in twilight.

The other squires groaned, either crawling from their tents or trying to protest the hour.

"It's too early," Kurth protested. "I'm going back to sleep."

Kahlaf did not look impressed. "I would not advise that, squire. The army is moving out."

"I thought we were not leaving until tomorrow," Otto said.

"There appears to have been a change in plans," Kahlaf said. "The army of Genio will be moving on without us. We are to accompany the forces of the Duke of Oldharbour."

Kahlaf's announcement shocked Bellaydin. It appeared that Wulfric was splitting up the great military force he had brought together. He began to pull down the tent. "We can't let Geoffrey face the Goriinchians alone."

Kahlaf gave Bellaydin a look. "It is not our place to question His Grace's motives. We have orders, we carry them out."

Bellaydin silently packed the tent away and slung it over his shoulder. The other squires had already got into line behind Kahlaf, and Bellaydin joined them. Before long they were on the road again, travelling south along the banks of the river.

"We are nearing Drakeford," Kahlaf said to the squires. "You should steel yourself."

For what? Bellaydin thought. He soon saw what Kahlaf was referring to.

They rode through a scene of carnage. All about them were bodies of men in varying states of decay. Carrion birds wheeled about the sky above them. Weapons lay scattered about, along with the occasional tattered cloth bearing the symbol of a boar.

"The Army of Warding," Kahlaf said solemnly. "An object lesson in not underestimating the Goriinchians."

As they passed through the battlefield, not one of the squires said a word. Even Edgar was unusually silent, his head bowed in respect. There were tears in Otto's eyes, as if the boy felt some sense of responsibility for all the death that had happened here.

Kahlaf looked at the boy and said gruffly, "The sins of the fathers do not pass to the sons." For the first time, Bellaydin saw softness in those reptilian eyes.

"Are we safe here?" Edgar asked, his eyes darting about.

"The Goriinchians have moved on by now," Kahlaf said. "We are safe. For the moment."

The town of Drakeford was just ahead. It was in a sorry state – the settlement's walls were scorched and broken, and debris and corpses littered the ground outside the city walls. They passed through the town gate, marvelling at the destruction. The sacking of the town had been merciless and without restraint. Barely a building remained standing. A trickle of survivors, their faces bleary and their wounds bloody, staggered past the group. Bellaydin found himself avoiding their gaze.

"The Goriinchians destroyed everything. Barbarians!" Kurth spat. "Look, even holy places are not safe from desecration."

In the centre of the town stood a shrine to the Divine Martyr. It had been violated and ransacked, profaned beyond recognition. The symbol of the Horned God had been daubed with paint on what remained of the shrine.

Bellaydin shook his head. *Geoffrey's home town, destroyed. Lucky he's not here to see this.*

"Where is everyone?" asked Kurth. "Not all dead, surely."

"Sir Edric Keslin is liege lord of Drakeford," Kahlaf grumbled. "Last I heard his soldiers were patrolling the marches. With the bulk of the forces tied down there, the Goriinchians were able to overwhelm the town's defence. Look there, on the hill. Even the fortress has been put the torch."

"There's nothing left for them to come back to," said Bellaydin.

"*If* they come back," Kahlaf said. It seemed a depressing thought.

The squires continued through the town before the army reached the river. It was far too wide and deep to be crossed by foot. A great bridge spanned the water, ancient and weathered, dating back to the days of Ancient Davorea. Great stone columns rose from the water, supporting the bridge. Cracks lined the stonework, clearly they were just the latest army of many to have trod the stonework over the centuries.

In order to cross the bridge the army squeezed into a narrow file, and amidst the confusion Bellaydin and the other squires found themselves pushed closer to the front. A loud sound, like the banging of distant drums, reverberated in Bellaydin's ears. All about him, people stopped, looking around. Another bang rung in his ears, and the bridge beneath him began to quake. Cracks began to appear on the stonework, widening with every second. Soldiers started to panic. One of the other squires – Kurth perhaps – called out. The stone beneath Bellaydin's feet gave way and he plummeted down, falling rapidly through many feet of air. Screams and shouts filled his ears, along with the sound of debris hitting water until he felt himself hit the river below. Icy cold water filled his lungs. He couldn't breathe. He struggled in the water, weighed down by armour and his pack, as he tried desperately to surface for air. His limbs began to weaken and a sense of despair filled him. Just as he was about to black out he felt strong hands grab his chest, and pull him up, towards the surface.

Bellaydin flopped onto the shore unceremoniously, gasping for air.

"Easy, breathe," Kahlaf spoke with a gruff sort of concern.

"What happened?" Bellaydin spluttered in between gasps.

"I'm not sure. Something – or someone – undermined the bridge. It collapsed as soon as we were on it."

"Maybe it was just old," Bellaydin managed as he tried to breathe normally.

Kahlaf did not look convinced. "That bridge has stood for thousands of years. It has carried far more men in the past than it did today."

Bellaydin saw Kurth, Otto, Tancred and Edgar nearby, panting and wheezing as they recovered from being pulled out of the water. Their clothes and hair were all soaked through.

Bellaydin panted, still trying to regain his breath. "At least we're all safe."

"Short-sighted as always, Ap'Lydin," Kahlaf said. "Of the soldiers that fell into the river, we here are all that have surfaced on this shore."

Bellaydin looked towards the river. "No others? They're all dead?"

"Not all. Some were close enough to the other side to pull themselves out, but there is no sign of the rest."

"You found me. We can find them too," Bellaydin pled.

"It is too late."

Bellaydin looked across the river. Tiny figures milled about on the other side – the rest of the army, and the duke himself. "It's too far. We'll never make it across."

"Correct," said Kahlaf. "We must make our way on foot."

"Are you mad? This whole area is crawling with Goriinchians," said Edgar, and Tancred quickly echoed him. Edgar waved a hand at the thick forest that stood before them. The air was still and quiet, but Bellaydin had the nagging suspicion that Edgar was right, that there were people watching them from within the woods.

"There must be settlements nearby, somewhere we can get help," Kurth said.

"The Goriinchian army has come through here already. Likely any village they encountered has now suffered the same fate as Drakeford." Kahlaf came towards the squires. "Our only hope is to press on, and join up with the forces of the Earldom of Genio. We must reach Sir Geoffrey Keslin. If we don't, all our lives are forfeit."

The river was calm, the raging waters that had swallowed the duke's armies having subsided. All that remained of the bridge was crumbling stonework on either side of the river. The rest of it lay somewhere in the deep blue water on the riverbed below, interspersed with the corpses of hundreds of soldiers. Easily a quarter of the Emparian strength, taken without a fight.

Bellaydin thought of their loved ones back home, who had lost fathers, brothers or sons. It could have just as easily been him to perish in that river were it not for Kahlaf. The other squires were bedraggled and miserable. Bellaydin reckoned the same thoughts were going through their minds. Kahlaf, on the other hand, looked just as stoic as ever, his attention focused on the challenges ahead.

"The duke was planning to encircle the Goriinchians," Kahlaf said. "With the bridge out, that plan is in ruins. He has no way to reach the Goriinchian army without backtracking and returning whence he came. Without the duke's support, Sir Geoffrey's forces will be annihilated."

"We must get moving," Kahlaf said. "Are you all able to walk?"

"I think so," said Bellaydin. The other squires murmured their assent.

"Who put you in charge, Ahktarran?" said Edgar.

241

Kahlaf reared up to his full height, towering over the squire. "The Duke of Oldharbour, if you recall. If you wish to continue enjoying life, I suggest you do as I ask. Do not think that your age and inexperience will spare you if the Goriinchians find us." Edgar glared at Kahlaf with contempt, but said nothing more.

The group continued on foot, Kahlaf leading the way as they followed the contour of the river. They headed north-east, intending to rendezvous with Sir Geoffrey's forces before he faced the Goriinchians. They encountered a few lost soldiers on the way, but none deigned to speak with them, most of them looking like they were trying to flee the area as quickly as possible.

Tancred asked about them. "Are those the duke's men?"

"Deserters," scowled Kahlaf, his lip curling in disgust.

Edgar seemed to agree with the Ahktarran. "The craven cowards were probably looking for any opportunity to save their own skins."

Bellaydin wasn't so sure. The collapse of the bridge was a shock for all of them, and many soldiers had drowned in the river. If it hadn't been for Kahlaf taking control of the situation, Bellaydin would most likely be acting like these other survivors – panicked, and looking for any hope of survival. They walked by a few soldier's corpses, washed ashore from the river, bloated and foul-smelling, their faces and the horrific nature of their death etched on their pale, haunted features. It chilled Bellaydin's spine to think he was seconds away from meeting the same end.

Kahlaf raised a hand, and the rest of the group stopped dead in their tracks. The Ahktarran looked around suspiciously and sniffed the air. "Someone is coming."

"Enemies?" asked Kurth.

"I cannot tell," said Kahlaf. "Be on your guard."

They waited, hiding as a group of figures approached. Leaning against a tree Bellaydin took shallow breaths, hoping to stay out of sight. He risked a quick glance at the approaching figures and saw a peasant woman and her two adolescent children. Bellaydin breathed a sigh of relief.

The woman stopped in her tracks. "Hello? Anyone there?" Her accent sounded Emparian. She was of middle years, her dark brown hair tinged with grey, with wrinkles around her eyes. Kahlaf came out of the shadows, sword at the ready, and upon seeing that the newcomer was unarmed, lowered his weapon, and waved for the other squires to show themselves. The woman's eyes widened as she saw the Ahktarran's full form and her children stared open mouth.

"Who are you?" Kahlaf demanded. "What is your business?"

The woman stammered for a moment, lost for words.

"Answer me."

"Myfanwy. Myfanwy Ap'Morten. Don't hurt us."

"Goriinchians," said Tancred.

"No," Bellaydin said, "they're from Wishapton. Aren't you?"

Myfanwy nodded.

"What are you doing here?" asked Kahlaf.

"They killed my husband because of our faith."

As Myfanwy spoke, Bellaydin's felt a shiver go up his spine. He was there when the villagers murdered Dugald Ap'Morten. Bellaydin's cousin, William, had been furious but was too late to stop the crime. Bellaydin still remembered the sound the corpse made as it swung on the rope.

"After my husband's death I feared for my safety," said Myfanwy. "And that of my children. We fled our home, travelling south, looking for safety."

Edgar sounded surprised. "Safety? In the Marches?"

"They are trying to reach the Goriinchian army," Kurth deduced.

"Traitors!" shouted Edgar.

Kahlaf snorted. "Is this true?"

Myfanwy raised her hands. "Yes, but please, we mean no harm. We just wish to survive."

Kahlaf looked thoughtful for a moment and then waved the family on.

"Thank you, thank you." Myfanwy ushered her children past the group.

"You're not just going to let them go, are you?" Edgar said. "They're damned traitors."

"A frightened woman and two children, Edgar?" said Kurth. "Is this what you consider treason?"

"They're going to our enemies," Tancred added. "They may be passing on vital information."

"Do they look like they know anything of value?" Bellaydin said.

Neither Edgar nor Tancred deigned to respond, and by now Myfanwy and her children were long gone. Kahlaf spoke to Edgar and Tancred. "We have enemies enough here, squires. It does not make sense to go making more."

"I think we can all agree on that," said Bellaydin. "Which way, Kahlaf?"

"Goriinch Hill is to the east. If we are to meet up with the army of Genio, without encountering any Goriinchians, we will need to head further north before turning south again. We should continue along the river."

"Well," Bellaydin braced himself. "Let's keep going then."

***

The air was still as Geoffrey climbed to the vantage point, Talthas close behind. Ancient pieces of rusted metal lay embedded in the soil, remnants of a battle long past.

"Goriinch Hill," Geoffrey said, his foot nudging the rusted remains of a man's helmet.

Talthas looked at him. "You know this place?"

He nodded. "Everyone in Emparia does. This is where it all began."

"Where what began?"

"The civil war." He pointed north. "On that side was the loyalists, with the king and his son, on the other, the rebels, led by the Duke of Alariat."

"And you?"

Geoffrey smiled. "Not born yet. But I've heard the stories so many times I can picture it in my mind. Duke Henry's forces fortified near the forest, the mad charge of the Earl of Warding, the breaking of Prince Alusine's host. The Royal Guard, fighting to the last man. Heroism not seen since."

"There were many heroes that day, I'm sure," Talthas mused.

"Yes," said Geoffrey. *Heroes on both sides,* he thought. *If I close my eyes I can see them: The king, Alusine the Last. His son, the Silver Prince. Brave Sir Faustin and the Laughing Blade. The Grey Eel's reckless charge. The Earl of Genio, Caradoc Ap'Lydin, slain by his brother. William was just a child when his father died...*

Talthas gave him a look of concern. "Are you alright, Sir Geoffrey?"

"Yes, I'm fine." Geoffrey wiped his eyes and looked towards the shadow on the horizon.

"They seem well prepared," said Talthas. "And numerous."

Geoffrey nodded silently. The lines of the Goriinchians stretched as far as he could see. His own forces seemed meagre by comparison. He cursed under his breath. Where was the duke? Geoffrey's chances without Wulfric's reinforcements were slim. His army consisted of foot-soldiers from Genio and the surrounding lands, supplemented with crossbowmen. His strongest warriors were Sir Emeric and the other knights, but Geoffrey could see that they chafed under his command; They could not be trusted to follow orders consistently. He had heard stories from other battles of knights disobeying orders and charging impetuously, believing their individual courage enough to win the day. He hoped the knights with him were not that foolish.

"No sign of the duke, Sir Geoffrey," Talthas said, "what do we do now?"

"Nothing. We wait until his forces arrive."

"And if the Goriinchians attack first?"

"Pray to all the gods for deliverance." Geoffrey turned his horse. "Pull back. We must make camp and be ready. For now, we watch them."

"Very well, sir."

Nearby some of the knights had gathered. Sir Emeric was amongst them. "What is happening, Sir Geoffrey? Why are we not attacking?"

Geoffrey repeated to the knights what he had just told Talthas.

A black-haired and burly man scoffed. "You are showing your yellow-streak, Sir Geoffrey. These are Goriinchians – barbarians, primitive folk. They will rout at the first sight of real soldiers. We should attack now, while we have the element of surprise. Instead you stand here, pissing in your armour."

Geoffrey shook his head. The knight's arrogance was unsettling. "Goriinchians are hardly primitive or barbaric, Sir Fulk. Have you ever faced them in battle? They are cunning foes." Geoffrey himself had once called the Goriinchians barbarians. After Wishapton his feelings on the matter had changed.

"Have you been in your cups, Sir Geoffrey?" said Sir Fulk. "Or are you somehow fond of these savages? They are no match for any Emparian."

"Perhaps a match for those of us without the courage of a true knight,"

Sir Emeric said.

"There is a difference between courage and foolhardiness," Geoffrey said. "And I don't want any of you doing something stupid. Wait for my signal. None other."

"I had expected a knight of Genio to be made of sterner stuff," said Sir Fulk. "But what can be expected from a commander who shuns his brothers in arms, and spends his time with an elven sellsword. You should be down here with us, not alone in your tent with your new friend."

Talthas' fingers twitched towards his bow.

Geoffrey's voice was low. "Careful with your words, Sir Fulk."

"He speaks the truth," said Sir Emeric. "This mercenary is not a knight, yet you treat him as if he was."

"Is that what worries you?" Geoffrey said in an exasperated tone. "Right. Time for drastic measures. Talthas."

The Eldara snapped to attention. "Yes, sir?"

"I need you to kneel."

Confused, Talthas did as ordered, kneeling in the mud in front of Geoffrey. The knight drew his sword. Talthas's eyes widened and he flinched slightly as Geoffrey brought down his sword and lightly touched the Eldara on his shoulder.

"Talthas li'Lyros, do you swear to serve Queen Amaryllis, First of Her Name, her heirs and successors, to fight bravely and with honour, and to protect the common folk until your strength fails you?" Geoffrey looked at the Eldara expectantly.

"I do," Talthas said quickly.

Geoffrey moved the sword from left to right, touching each shoulder in turn. "In the name of the Unconquered Sun, the Silver Lady and the Divine Martyr, I dub you Sir Talthas of Goriinch Hill. Rise, sir."

Talthas, mouth open in awe, did as Geoffrey commanded. The other knights stared at Geoffrey darkly.

"There," said Geoffrey, putting his sword back in its scabbard. "Now that we're all knights, no one can claim anyone is getting ideas above their stations."

Sir Fulk snorted. "What farce is this? You cannot knight a man in the mud just to prove a point."

"I think you'll find I can," said Geoffrey. "Any knight can create a knight. The location is irrelevant."

Sir Emeric looked disgusted. "But he's an *elf.*"

"Also irrelevant," said Geoffrey. He folded his arms. "Will there be anything else? Or shall we get on with fighting the *bloody Goriinchians?*"

The other knights regarded him warily but said nothing more. Eventually, one by one they moved away, muttering under their breath. After they were gone, Talthas turned to Geoffrey. "Thank you, Sir Geoffrey. You have done me a great honour."

"I need at least one knight here who knows what he's doing," said Geoffrey. "Sir Emeric and Sir Fulk will drive me insane if I let them. They're a pain in my arse, but I need the bloody bastards." Geoffrey sighed. "Now then, *Sir Talthas,* I want to get a better idea of what we're facing. You're the best scout we have, and the only man I trust. I need you to take a look around, get as close to the Goriinchians as you can without them noticing."

Talthas nodded. "I'll see what I can find out."

"Scout the surrounding area too, if you can," Geoffrey said. "I want to know if there's anywhere which might give us the edge against the Goriinchians.'"

"Understood." Talthas readied his bow, and jogged off, a determined look on his face.

Geoffrey watched the Eldara as he left. In the past few months, Talthas had proved his worth. He was capable, loyal and with a keen tactical mind. *Give me an army of Talthas and this war would be over. But no, what do I get instead?*

He gazed out towards the camp where Sir Emeric and Sir Fulk were standing close to each other, speaking in hushed tones and intermittently shooting Geoffrey disdainful glares. After their conversation the two began an impromptu sparring session, and the energy they put into the bout clearly showed that the pair were eager, even impatient, to see action on the field of battle. The rings of steel on steel began to attract attention from the rest of the camp, and slowly a small group of soldiers came to watch. Sir Fulk and Sir Emeric began to show off for the crowd, utilising a series of aggressive and theatrical attacks against each other. The soldiers cheered the two knights on, which only enticed the pair of them into ever more outlandish moves. Sir Fulk leapt backwards from one of Sir Emeric's thrusts, landing square in the middle of one of the tents, pulling it down and finding himself cocooned in its canvas. The crowd roared with laughter.

Geoffrey shook his head at the pair. *Their eagerness will get us all killed.*

Geoffrey spent the better part of the next hour and a half pacing about the camp. When Talthas returned, it was with a grim expression.

"The Goriinchians are well entrenched, Sir Geoffrey. It will not be easy to dislodge them."

"Just as I thought. A frontal attack would be suicidal."

"There's more," Talthas said, his voice low. "I saw movement on the higher ground."

"Archers? We already know about that."

"There are more of them hidden in the forest. I believe we might be encircled."

Geoffrey muttered under his breath. "Are you sure?"

Talthas nodded.

Geoffrey shook his head. "Why would there be archers posted on the higher ground if they didn't know we were…" He trailed off as he began to realise the full weight of the situation. The Goriinchians were not about to fall into his trap; on the contrary, they were about to spring a trap on him. The Duke of Oldharbour's tardiness no longer appeared to be mere coincidence.

"Damn it, damn it to the Underworld," Geoffrey said. "They know what we have planned. We've walked into a trap. And we're completely exposed."

"Perhaps not sir," Talthas offered. "I have discovered a network of caves. Very defensible, and the Goriinchians won't be able to follow us."

"Why not?"

"Because they are not just normal caves. They're tunnels of Eldara design and sealed by commands in the Eldaric tongue. I can open them for us, and seal them once we're inside."

"Leaving us trapped still?"

"Eldara tunnels always have more than one entrance. It should lead us out of danger."

"Hopefully we won't need it. But it's good to know."

Their conversation was cut short by the sound of shouting nearby. Geoffrey and Talthas moved quickly down to the soldiers milling about.

"What in the name of the Underworld is going on?"

"It's Sir Emeric and Sir Fulk sir," a soldier with tight red curls said. "They're charging the enemy, they've ordered their troops to come with them."

"We must get them to call it off," Talthas said.

"It's too bloody late," Geoffrey said. The men watched as Sir Emeric, Sir Fulk and odd knights galloped towards the Goriinchian army. Sir Emeric and Sir Fulk charged ahead, their swords pointed towards the Goriinchian lines as their infantry followed suit, screaming in defiance and with their weapons held aloft. None of them paid the slightest heed to the forested hills on either side, where Geoffrey now knew hundreds of archers lay hidden, waiting to loose a rain of arrows on the Emparians.

"They have no idea what they're facing. They'll be massacred," Talthas said.

"Sir, should we join the attack?" the curly-haired soldier asked. His hands tightened on his weapon.

Geoffrey furrowed his brow. "No. That would just waste more lives on a futile assault. Besides, our orders from His Grace were clear." He turned to Talthas. "These caves you mentioned, are they close?"

"Just over the hill. Are you considering a tactical retreat, sir?"

"If they are defensible as you say it may be our only option. The Goriinchians will surround us given the opportunity and I am less confident with every moment that I will ever see the duke's reinforcements."

Talthas nodded gravely. "I think you're right, sir."

"Good. Go to the caves. Be ready to get them open. Wait for my signal."

"Yes, Sir Geoffrey." The Eldara ranger moved off quickly in the direction of the caves.

"Men! Defensive positions!" Geoffrey barked orders to his soldiers. "Whatever happens, hold the line and watch for my signal." His hand moved to his belt, patting the signal horn there. This would take careful timing. He watched Sir Fulk and Sir Emeric dwindle into the distance, their soldiers streaming behind them. Geoffrey silently swore in frustration. *When will men like them learn the difference between courage and stupidity?*

***

"Get down," Kahlaf cautioned.

"What is it?" Kurth asked.

"Soldiers nearby."

"How many?" Bellaydin asked.

Kahlaf reached out with his sword and parted the foliage in front of them. Below them stretched a Goriinchian army numbering well into the thousands. "More than enough to annihilate any number of challengers. This is the army the Emparians are seeking, no doubt."

"They haven't seen us, have they?" Edgar asked.

Kahlaf gave the squire a withering look. "If they had we'd be already dead. Look up there on the ridges. Saldarri archers."

The Ahktarran was correct. Camouflaged Saldarri were hidden amongst the trees, their bows nocked and ready.

"There are more of them there, look," said Otto, pointing at the valley below. Sure enough there were Goriinchians waiting to catch the advancing Emparians by surprise. "What are they doing?" said Kurth. "They're going to get themselves massacred."

"Trust Keslin to do something this stupid," Edgar was livid.

Bellaydin squinted down at the knight leading the charge. "That's not Geoffrey," he said.

Kahlaf said. "I didn't think it would be. Geoffrey may act like a child sometimes, but he has a keen tactical mind. He would not lead such an impetuous charge as this."

As the Emparians grew closer the line of Goriinchians parted, funnelling the Emparians through the middle of their lines. At the same time, the Saldarri archers released their arrows, and a black rain of death fell upon the Emparians. Confusion reigned amongst the Emparians but they still pushed forward. Bellaydin caught sight of a single figure in the Goriinchian line, tall, clad in armour, wielding a sword that shone with a blue light. *Kaltban*, Bellaydin thought, recognising William's sword, taken by the Goriinchians before he died. His hearth thumping, Bellaydin leant forward, squinting in the sunlight. *Who is wielding it?* The Goriinchians had started chanting as the figure strode forward ready to engage Sir Fulk. "Culainn. Culainn. Culainn."

Morgan's father. "It's the Warchief Aonghus Culainn," Bellaydin said to his companions.

"Are you certain?" Kahlaf said. "Seems odd for him to fight at the front of his lines."

"I know it's him."

Sir Fulk attempted to charge Culainn but with one blow the Goriinchian killed Fulk's steed, unhorsing him. Another tremendous swing sent the Emparian's head flying across the field. At the sight of this, the remaining soldiers turned and fled; the Goriinchians swarmed after them.

Kahlaf urged the squires. "Come, this is our chance. We need to move."

With Kahlaf leading the way they made their way down the ridge. The sound of battle filled the air as the Goriinchians and Emparians clashed a short distance away.

"Quickly," the Ahktarran barked, ushering the squires past him. Three Goriinchians challenged them – stragglers, cut off from the main force. Kahlaf skewered one with his sword, while the others came for the squires.

"Otto, watch it," Bellaydin yelled to the other squire as a Goriinchian raider lunged towards them. Otto stood frozen, sword in hand until Kurth grabbed him and pulled him to safety. Kurth thrust upwards with his own sword, felling the Goriinchian in a spray of blood.

Someone cried out in pain. It was Edgar. "He's been wounded," yelled Tancred.

"Damn it," said Kahlaf. Edgar was still standing but had gone white. His hand was clutched at his side, stained with blood.

"We need to find shelter," said Bellaydin.

Kurth seemed unconvinced. "Where? There are archers behind us, and a battle ahead of us."

"Edgar won't last long if we don't," Tancred warned.

Bellaydin briefly wondered if that would be such a bad thing, but immediately felt guilty for the thought. As his gaze met those of the other squires, he knew he wasn't the only one to harbour such thoughts.

Kahlaf tried to keep them moving. "Let us go see what we can find."

They walked on, their speed somewhat reduced by Edgar's injury. All kept their eyes peeled for a cave, or shelter in the foothills – anything that might offer them some sanctuary from the battle that raged ahead. It was Otto who finally spotted what he first took for a cave.

"It's not a cave," Kurth corrected him. "It looks like...a door?"

Carved into the rough, rocky cliff was a pair huge stone doors, sealed shut and with no discernible way of opening them. Carved script curved its way around the outline of the doorway. The remains of two vaguely human-shaped statues stood on either side, broken and weathered from the passing of many centuries.

"Looks to be sealed shut. Any ideas?" Kurth asked.

"There appears to be some sort of writing on it," said Otto. "But I can't read it."

"It's Eldaric," said Bellaydin. "The elven script."

"Can you read it?" said Kahlaf.

"Yes," Bellaydin said. "It appears to be some sort of riddle."

"Riddle?" Tancred said. "There's a riddle written here? Why?"

Bellaydin tried to remember what he had been taught as a child. "It's a spellweaver puzzle door. They are sealed with a passphrase only known to those allowed entrance. They write the riddle to provide a clue to jog the memory of those who might have forgotten the phrase. Reciting the word in the elven tongue should open the door."

Kahlaf shook his head in disbelief. "Elves."

"So what's the riddle?"

Bellaydin read the words aloud. "I never was, am always to be, none ever saw me, nor ever will, and yet I am the confidence of all who live and breathe."

Edgar laughed weakly. "What in the gods' name is that supposed to mean?" His laugh degenerated into a hacking cough.

Bellaydin had never heard a riddle like that before; the answer eluded him. Neither Kurth nor Tancred offered any solution, and Kahlaf remained silent. "A person, perhaps," Bellaydin mused aloud.

"Person? It would have to be some sort of invisible, non-existent person," said Kurth.

"Yes, Bauer, do you have any of those in Tyronsville?" Though frail, Edgar's tone was caustic. He started to chuckle but then winced in pain.

"We need to try something," said Kahlaf. "Our enemies will be upon us if we tarry."

"No, please. Just take your time," said Edgar, "I'll just die here while you fools try to solve a riddle."

Tancred ignored Edgar's sarcasm. "It sounds like a guardian spirit of some sort."

"Try 'ghost' then," said Kurth.

Bellaydin spoke the Eldaric word for ghost, but nothing seemed to happen. "Any other ideas?" he asked.

"I think you are thinking too literally," said Kahlaf.

"What do you mean?" asked Kurth.

"I doubt that the answer is an individual. What being, or even god, could possibly claim to hold the confidence of all who live?"

Kurth nodded. "I think Kahlaf's right. It must be a metaphor of some sort for something abstract. Not an object you can hold, or even point to. But a quality or a characteristic, maybe."

Tancred's eyes flickered. "Like courage, you mean."

"Well 'courage' doesn't fit the riddle, but something like that," said Kurth. "Something you'd possess."

There were shouts and the sounds of footsteps from nearby. Kahlaf reached for his sword. "We are running out of time."

Bellaydin turned to others, hoping that at least one of the squires had had a flash of sudden inspiration. There was silence as each of them shot a hopeful look at one another.

"I think I know this," said Otto.

"You do?" asked Bellaydin.

"Yes," said Otto. "Think about it. 'Never was, always to be'. It's 'Tomorrow'."

Bellaydin approached the doors and repeated the word in the elven tongue. They heard an echo from inside the stone wall, the wheezing and groaning of machinery and the scraping of stone on stone. The doors swung open, eliciting a collective sigh of relief from the young squires.

"I guess that was the right answer," Kurth patted a beaming Otto on his back.

Kahlaf grunted, and then gestured for the squires to enter. "Quickly now. I can hear soldiers approaching."

They all entered quickly and once the last of them was through, the stone doors swung on their hinges and shut tight. Bellaydin's heart leapt within his chest. He hoped there was a way to open the doors again from the inside.

All about them was darkness. Slowly Bellaydin felt his eyes begin to adjust to it and the interior of the chamber began to take shape. Everything was indistinct at first, but details became clearer with each passing minute. After one such minute, he realised there was an arrow nocked and pointed directly at his face.

"Hold there, all of you. Who are you, and how did you get in here?" The Eldara ranger held the arrow, ready to loose it at a moment's notice. In the dim gloom, Bellaydin realised he'd met this Eldara before.

"Talthas?" Bellaydin said. "Talthas li'Lyros?"

The Eldara's face softened as he squinted at Bellaydin Then his eyes widened in recognition. "The Ap'Lydin squire? What are you doing here? Who are these with you?"

"I'll explain later." Bellaydin said. "For the moment, we have bigger problems."

Kahlaf helped Edgar forward. "This boy needs the attention of a healer."

Talthas nodded. "I'll call for someone. Quickly, come this way."

The Eldara led them down a dark corridor which opened into a large, vaulted chamber. Great columns lined the walls, carved with ancient and intricate designs. The walls bore dusty and faded mosaics, depicting mysterious figures wielding the Art. The imagery reminded Bellaydin of the mosaics he had seen in an ancient ruined temple when he first travelled through Goriinchia with Geoffrey and Kahlaf. These were somehow even older, yet less crude.

Soldiers milled about inside the chamber, some injured, most weary. Talthas called out for help, and two soldiers ushered Edgar away to be tended to. "I'll go help them," Otto told Bellaydin. As Bellaydin watched Otto follow Edgar and the soldiers, he spotted a familiar face.

"Geoffrey," Bellaydin exclaimed.

"Bela?" he said. "Kahlaf? What are you doing here? You should be with Wulfric's army."

Bellaydin and Kahlaf exchanged looks causing Geoffrey's face to fall. "What's wrong? What's happened?"

"We were on our way to the rendezvous point as we crossed the bridge," Kahlaf began. "Then it collapsed under us. We were lucky enough to be able to swim to the shore."

"The bridge didn't collapse," said Kurth. "The damn thing exploded."

"Exploded?" Geoffrey raised his eyebrow in disbelief. "What in the Underworld do you mean?"

"The squire is correct," Kahlaf said. "That was no ordinary structural collapse that the bridge suffered. Someone deliberately engineered such a disaster."

"How?"

"There are alchemical compounds that when used in the correct quantities can achieve such feats. In the Caliphate, Tarkenese mercenaries used to use them all the time. It was one reason that the Caliphate never conquered Tarken."

Tancred spoke up. "How would the Goriinchians get their hands on such things?"

"I would not know," said Kahlaf. "Presuming, of course, it was the Goriinchians."

"Who else would it have been?" asked Tancred.

Kahlaf said nothing, but his lip curled up in the semblance of a cynical smile.

Geoffrey put a hand to his brow. "Well whatever happened, this puts us in a very difficult situation. Am I to assume that we are without reinforcements?"

Kahlaf narrowed his eyes. "The duke will still come, Sir Geoffrey. He will do what he can."

"Even if that were true he will be significantly delayed. The Goriinchians have over-run Goriinch Hill and the lands around it. Drakeford is no more. We are surrounded."

"Can they reach us in here?" asked Bellaydin.

"Not unless they know Eldaric," Talthas said.

Geoffrey didn't look convinced. "Still doesn't do us much good. Our supplies are low. Eventually we'll have to get out. Talthas tells me that there should be another exit to these tunnels."

Talthas confirmed, "I've never heard of an Eldara building that had only one way out."

Geoffrey waved a hand. "These corridors here are confusing, they seem to go on forever. We haven't explored much beyond the main chamber, and I don't want to march our tired and injured soldiers through the tunnels without knowing where they'll lead. I need to know if there is an exit, and which is the quickest way out."

"I'm ready to start looking for an exit whenever you want," Talthas said.

"No, Talthas, I need you here with me in case the Goriinchians breach the gate. We need your bow."

"I am willing and able," Kahlaf said, his hand moving to his sword.

"I am sure you are, Ahktarran," said Talthas, "but can you read Eldaric?"

The Ahktarran shook his head, then looked at Bellaydin. "Bellaydin got us in here, he can open the exit if he finds it."

Bellaydin suddenly realised that everyone was looking at him. "I don't know if I'm the best person to go, Geoffrey."

Bellaydin could not quite pin down what it was, but he felt very uneasy. *Being stuck in a cave while bloodthirsty Goriinchians could break in probably doesn't help* he thought.

"None of us is safe here, Bela," Geoffrey said. "The Goriinchians will each break through or, failing that, try to starve us out. At least in the tunnels, you have a chance."

"What if I get lost and can't find my way back?"

"We have chalk with our supplies. Mark out the way you came, so that you can return without incident."

Kahlaf was apprehensive. "Sending a boy here on his own though, Sir Geoffrey?"

"I don't intend to send him alone."

Talthas looked around. "We can't spare many soldiers as it is."

"That's fine. We don't want too large a group," Geoffrey said. "It will only slow them down, and time is of the essence."

"We could send the squires together," Kahlaf suggested. "I can accompany them if you wish."

"I need you here, Kahlaf," Geoffrey said. He turned to Kurth and

Tancred. "You boys go. Stick together, help each other out. Find the exit and return."

Bellaydin looked at his fellow squires as they took in all that Geoffrey was telling them. He felt comfortable with the idea of being accompanied by Kurth, who he knew to be resourceful and a skilled warrior, but Tancred was another matter. Bellaydin knew practically nothing about Tancred, outside of his loyalty to Edgar de Morcor; even now as Bellaydin studied Tancred's face he couldn't read it. He hadn't objected to being sent on the mission. *Maybe you're not just Edgar's shallow puppet.*

Geoffrey looked at Bellaydin, his eyes grave. "I know this is a lot to ask of you three, but this is where I need you most."

"I understand," Bellaydin said. "When do we leave?"

"Soon," Geoffrey said, "but not right at this moment. You need to recover your strength before you go."

Bellaydin and the other two squires were brought food and drink. The food was bland, with texture like wet parchment, but in Bellaydin's ravenous state he hardly noticed the taste and finished it within minutes. The water was odd tasting and cloudy but drinkable. Once all three of them had eaten and drunk, Geoffrey ordered more food packed into parcels, and filled their flasks with water. Within the hour, they were ready to head off.

"Good luck," Geoffrey said. "We're all relying on you."

CHAPTER 16

The tunnel was dark and cramped.

"I can't see a damn thing, Tancred," said Kurth. "Bring the torch closer." Even in the flickering light Kurth's annoyance was still visible. "So, left or right?"

"Left takes us back to where we came from," Tancred said.

"Are you sure?"

"I've been paying attention, haven't you, Bauer?"

The two squires had been bickering with each other for the past hour. For someone who rarely said anything at all, Tancred was exceptionally talented at riling Kurth up. The young squire from Georgeton was more selective in his barbs than Edgar de Morcor had been.

Kurth turned to Bellaydin. "Any of the writing here mean anything to you, Bela?"

"Not really." Bellaydin squinted at the script covering the walls. Despite his fluency in the elven tongue, reading this script was no easy task. The writing on the walls was a complicated archaic form of the Eldaric tongue.

What little Bellaydin could translate spoke of strange persons and intricate histories he knew nothing about. Then there were the few which were puzzling and obscure pieces of structured verse. Jumbled and strange imagery was interspersed with these writings, depicting tall figures like the Eldara, but taller and more alien. Here and there were depictions of things even more bizarre, possessing anatomy that defied understanding – humanoid, but with the features resembling that of an undersea mollusc, combined in ways that seemed horrific. It made the hair on Bellaydin's neck stand up.

"Let's just keep moving," he said to the others.

After passing through several more dark tunnels the trio reached an open chamber, no bigger than a sitting room. Four lanterns, placed equidistant around the room's circumference, provided an eerie blue illumination to the space. Bellaydin had spent enough time around Eldara to recognise arcane lamps, light sources powered by the Art and favoured by spellweavers. In the middle of the room was a large latticed metal frame with an opening in its centre. Judging by the shards on the ground around the frame, it had once held a large crystal but some calamity had caused its shattering.

"What do you reckon this is for?" asked Kurth.

Bellaydin had no idea as to the purpose of the device, but judging by the size of the chamber it was important enough to be the focal point of the whole network of tunnels. There were only two doorways in the chamber – the entrance that they had currently came through, and the exit on the other side.

Kurth gestured to the walls. "Any of the writings here give you any clue?"

Bellaydin glanced about. "Not really. These are just parables about death and the passing of souls."

"What are these?" asked Tancred, pointing to a series of pictures on the wall. They were renderings of the same Eldara-like beings from earlier, killing human figures. Another series depicted these beings standing next to expressionless figures; unlike the flesh tones given to the human and quasi-Eldara, these figures were drawn with metallic hues.

"I don't know," said Bellaydin, "but I'd wager it has something to do with this room."

"This whole place reeks of sorcery," said Tancred. "And of things unnatural."

"Calm down, Zalltor," said Kurth. "It's just some old twisted metal and some broken crystal. Whatever this thing was, I'd say it's been a long time since it last functioned."

Bellaydin, his curiosity overcoming him, picked up one of the larger crystal shards. It felt cool in his hand as he placed it inside his tunic.

"If you're finished souveniring, you might want to take a look at this," Kurth said, pointing to a foot-long piece of metal sticking out of the wall.

"It's got to be some sort of lever," said Tancred as Bellaydin moved to where they were. Tancred's hand moved towards the lever before Bellaydin or Kurth could offer any words of protest. At once, it seemed to thunder in the chamber as the walls vibrated around them.

"The doors!" yelled Kurth. Stone barriers were descending in each doorway, blocking off every opening. The three squires lunged towards the closest exits, squeezing under them before they were trapped in the room. It was not until he was through and the stone door had slammed shut that Bellaydin realised he and Tancred had gone through the opposite door to Kurth.

"Kurth!" Bellaydin pounded his fists on the stone slab, but there was no response. He turned to Tancred. "Do you see any way to open it? Is there a lever anywhere?"

Tancred shook his head. Bellaydin searched around the walls frantically and tried one last time. "Kurth!" There was no response.

"We should keep moving Ap'Lydin," Tancred said. "If we can find the exit, perhaps we can find a way to open this door later."

Bellaydin sighed. The other squire was right. Kurth would make his way back to Geoffrey and the other soldiers if he hadn't already left. It was up to Bellaydin and Tancred to continue. He took out a piece of chalk from his belt pouch and placed a mark on the wall. "Let's go."

They continued, feeling their way through dark tunnels, the weak glow of their torches illuminating little more than their immediate surroundings. Bellaydin glimpsed long-forgotten frescos and writing, worn by the passage of the ages. Broken arcane lamps hung on the walls, ruined in some long ago calamity. The passages were littered with cobwebs, and on several occasions Bellaydin almost panicked when he mistook the distorted shape of a spider for something more sinister. Every time Bellaydin or Tancred spoke, their voices echoed down the empty and forgotten halls.

"The maze goes on forever," said Tancred. "Who would build such a thing?"

"Elves," said Bellaydin. "But not elves like the ones I knew." He had thought this building was the work of spellweavers, but with every step his certainty faded. Even the most obdurate spellweaver has tastes and desires that an ordinary human might realise. But whoever built this strange, twisting place of madness was of a realm beyond even the spellweavers.

The minutes turned into hours until Bellaydin lost track of time completely. Still, they pressed on. The darkness began to play tricks on his mind. He found himself disorientated. *Did we just pass through this corridor? Is that our chalk mark? We are going in circles, surely.* Just when Bellaydin thought he might be lost in dark tunnels forever, they turned into a very faintly lit corridor. They picked up their pace a little, and another turn brought them into another corridor; this one opened into a large chamber and the gloom lifted. Before them was a large archway illuminated on either side by two functioning arcane lamps.

Bellaydin noticed Eldaric script was engraved over the top of the archway. "Look," he said to the other squire. "Elven writing."

"What does it say?" Tancred asked.

"Master's Chambers," Bellaydin said, reading it aloud. "No," he said, correcting himself, "Magister's Chambers."

"Is this what we're looking for?" Tancred asked.

Bellaydin sighed. "I sure hope so."

Through the archway was a magnificent vaulted room, shaped like a hexagon. A raised dais topped with an elaborate black stone throne dominated the centre of the room. A table, carved from the same black stone stood, just in front of it. Crystal, like Bellaydin had seen shattered in the room he had been in with Tancred and Kurth, was embedded in the throne. On either side of the throne stood inanimate suits of armour, helmeted and carrying great swords. These cobwebbed men of metal stared silently at the newcomers. It struck Bellaydin that they were the same kind of as the metallic-coloured figures he had seen in the earlier murals. But it wasn't just from the murals that the metal figures evoked a memory. Half-remembered dreams began to surface in his mind. *Didn't the Seeress cause me to dream of metal men that day that Morgan led me to her?*

"Well, this is a little unsettling." Bellaydin approached the table, which was covered with intricate carvings. As his eyes roamed over them he noticed Eldara script at various points.

"Any idea what it says?" Tancred asked.

Bellaydin pointed to one point on the table. "This here says Magister's Chambers, just like the archway outside." A sudden realisation came to him.

"It's a map. See, this is where we are now....," he pointed to a spot on the table, and then another. "This is where we were before."

As he touched the carvings on the table they lit up with a blue glow, and in the distance, they heard the whirring of gears and the rumbling of stone.

"What was that?" asked Tancred.

"It sounds like a door opening, and I suspect it's the door to the room where we lost Kurth."

He rubbed his chin.

"Maybe we should head back, see if he's still there."

"No," Tancred cut in. "We need to find this exit first, no point returning without accomplishing that."

Tancred was right. Bellaydin turned back to the map. "This room we are in, it appears to be on the edge of the map, I wonder if..."

He touched the map's edge. Immediately, one side of the wall began to groan and whirr before receding and allowing light to pour in from outside.

"I think we found it. Let's head back."

Tancred raised a hand. "We should take a look outside first. Make sure that it's safe."

"That's a good idea."

The opening led to a sheer cliff covered with scattered vegetation. Upon exiting, Bellaydin turned to the open entrance. Two great statues flanked it, the carved features of the spellweavers they depicted eroded and barely recognisable. Bellaydin went to the edge and looked down the cliff. A dizzying sense of vertigo assailed him as he did. The cliff had to be between twenty feet to thirty feet high. Small footholds and stunted shrubs dotted the cliff face but the drop was otherwise a straight plunge.

Tancred came next to him. "That's quite a drop."

Bellaydin peered further down the cliff, and as he did he lost his footing and slipped off the ground. He frantically reached out and was able to grab onto a jutting rock, but just barely. The weight of his body and the fear he was feeling made it extremely hard for him to hold on. Tancred rushed to the edge of the cliff and looked down at Bellaydin in shock.

Thank the gods, Bellaydin thought. "Tancred, help me."

Tancred got down on bended knees, shook his head and, much to Bellaydin's horror, started to laugh heartily.

"I was looking for a chance to be rid of you, and you've saved me the trouble."

"Did Edgar put you up to this?"

Tancred chuckled. "That vacant little shit?" He wagged a finger at Bellaydin. "Though I can't imagine it'd displease him to see you dead."

"No, please. Why?"

Tancred eyed Bellaydin with disdain. "Same reason I do everything else. For House Zalltor. Sometimes, Ap'Lydin, pawns have to be sacrificed so the worthy may rise. You, those oafs back in the cave, the Duke of Emperor's Palace."

"*You* killed the Duke?"

Tancred smirked. "Do you really think Sir Dallen would have the brains to slip poison into a man's goblet undetected?"

"The truth will come out," Bellaydin said, straining to hold on. "You'll never get away with any of this."

"Oh, Ap'Lydin," Tancred's eyes gleamed with a dark intelligence.

"I already have."

He pushed Bellaydin off the cliff.

CHAPTER 17

Polnygar rose from her bed. It had been almost two weeks since the incident at the Temple of the Ancients, and they seemed no closer to seeing the book they had come for. Though Aelzandar preached patience, Augustin had been getting agitated and Polnygar sympathised. Every day wasted in Qar Arrid put them further away from Ivellios. *Why is the emir keeping us here so long?*

Their quarters were quiet. "Where is everyone else?" she asked Hebu. The Nemoi was buried in quiet contemplation with the pile of scrolls he had brought with from Macrodonia.

"Away," the Nemoi said. "The archmage and the merchant have gone to speak with the emir. Baron Bauer said he was going for a walk. I've found something more productive to do than go with any of them. You should too."

Polnygar couldn't argue with that, but wondered what task, productive or otherwise, she could fill her morning with. As she stretched, she noticed her back felt stiff and sore, likely due to sleeping in an awkward position. It was with that in mind that she approached the nearby servant, who was busy arranging fresh clothes for the guests.

"Excuse me. The baths, do you know where they are?" The servant nodded, and pointed Polnygar down a hallway. "Thank you."

Qardleean baths were renowned the world over for their luxury and elegance, but to others, they were a byword for decadence and considered to exemplify everything wrong with Qardleean culture. As far as Polnygar felt about the matter, she could certainly see the attraction, particularly after the sort of long journey she'd been on. She'd been wearing the same clothes for months and relished the thought of actually being clean again. Growing up in Aderilund she'd certainly been accustomed to regular bathing, but for the Eldara it was a strictly functional pastime, and they would bathe in cold water as frequently as warm. In Qarld they bathed for pleasure.

As she came around the corner she nearly collided with Aelzandar. The archmage was strolling through the halls of the palace at a gentle pace, deep in conversation with the emir. Samir and a contingent of guards walked with them.

"Ah, Polnygar," said Aelzandar. "How are you feeling?"

"I'm feeling better, yes," she said, distracted.

"Are you looking for something?"

"I thought this was the way to the baths," she said.

"Indeed they are, Flower of the South," said the emir. "But if you are not in a rush, why not walk with us for a moment?"

Polnygar hesitated but the emir smiled at her, and seemed to plead with those hazel eyes of his. "Are you enjoying your time in Qar Arrid?" the emir asked Polnygar. "I hope you have taken some time to explore the city."

"Yes, I have," Polnygar said. "It is not what I was expecting."

The emir eyed her with interest. "Oh?"

Polnygar demurred. "Well, I'd heard some stories about the Caliphate."

The emir chuckled. "Oh, is that so? Let me guess, did these stories seem to paint a land with ranting clerics and endless religious prohibitions and rules?"

Polnygar nodded, though she felt awkward doing so.

The emir spread his hands wide. "There are places like that in the Caliphate, as there are in most places in the world. But here in Qar Arrid, we wear our faith lightly. We are a long way from the Caliph and his court, we do things our own way here. We prefer to see the voice of the Infinite as a guide, not a lord and master. That is what Sarrius taught."

"I hope I have not offended you," Polnygar said.

"Not at all, Flower of the South," said the emir. "The world can be a perilous place, and it always helps to be cautious. Samir has told me that you have faced danger between here and Ralom. What was the name of the wretched cult who attacked you?"

"The Cult of the Horned God," Polnygar said. She saw Aelzandar look at her oddly and wondered why.

"They sound positively vile," the emir said. "But I should have expected such superstitions from the lands of the infidel. Rest assured though that I believe it unlikely for such ruffians to be in Qar Arrid. You may consider yourself safe here."

"I hope you're right," said Polnygar. She remembered Céline's words. The Leridian seemed to be adamant that there were cultists in the city. "What if there were some here?"

The emir touched her hand gently. "Never fear, Flower of the South. If by some chance some have infiltrated this city, I will find them and deal with them as the law demands. You have my word."

"Thank you," Polnygar said.

"No need for thanks," the emir said. "It is the duty of the faithful to correct evil wherever they see it. I pity these cultists, in truth. After their demise they will never achieve the blessed reward. They will never become one with the Infinite. No, instead these sinners are doomed to wander as restless spirits, in pain for all eternity." The emir glanced at Aelzandar. "I see the archmage looking at me expectantly. Perhaps he wishes to talk about some book again. We shall leave you to the baths. If you continue down this passage, and take a left and then a right, you will be right there."

After some fruitless meandering trying to follow the emir's rather vague instructions, Polnygar finally found the entrance to the baths. A large archway opened up into a spacious courtyard decorated with marble mosaics on its floor. The stuccoed walls sported scenes from a mountain panorama and gold stars and celestial imagery including a long, serpentine silver dragon adorned the sky-blue domed roof.

She looked around. The room was quiet, there was no one else in the baths. She worried that there would be others present, particularly since she had heard stories that Qardleeans had slaves to attend to them while bathing and Polnygar wasn't particularly enthused about the idea of being naked in front of strangers. Satisfied that she was alone, she carefully disrobed, placing her clothes in one of the alcoves and drawing a towel about her body. She took one of the bars of soap from the shelf. It had a faint aroma of olive oil. Qardleean soap was white, unlike the black ash and fat derived product that predominated in most of Carurlonia.

She departed the main chamber through one of the archways and was immediately met with a blast of hot air. Polnygar breathed out and gave out a relaxed sigh. The room contained a series of benches around the wall and a large hot pool in the centre. Steam rose from this pool, and so Polnygar dipped a toe into the water to test it. Judging it a good temperature, she dropped her towel and slipped into the pool.

The hot water was soothing to her tired muscles and did much to alleviate the aches and pains she had acquired during the many weeks of travel between Ralom and Qar Arrid. She realised she hadn't experienced this sort of comfort since she left Macrodonia, which seemed a lifetime away. Thinking of Macrodonia made her reflect on all that had transpired since she had left Aderilund and thinking of Aderilund made her think of her brother.

She felt a pang of regret when she realised how much she missed Bellaydin. If only she hadn't been so eager to leave Aderilund, maybe she could have waited for a time where they could have both left together, and seen the world as brother and sister.

Sighing deeply, she tried to clear her mind of regrets and enjoy her bath. It didn't take long before she realised she was beginning to relax a little too much. She caught herself almost falling asleep. Reasoning it was time to go, she emerged from the pool, dripping wet, and reached for the towel. She dried herself only superficially. Most Qardleean bathhouses had both a hot and cold bath area, and she reasoned that the cold room must be the other archway in the main chamber. She decided that she would have a quick swim in the cold bath before dressing and returning to her chambers to meet with Aelzandar and the others.

As the approached the cold room, she heard a voice. There was someone else here. A male. Wrapping the towel tightly around herself she approached the cold room with caution. The man in the cold room was singing, but she couldn't quite make out what the words. Curiosity got the better of Polnygar and she peered through the archway.

In the cold pool in the centre of the room sat an unclothed man, facing away from her. He was lean, but well muscled and Polnygar couldn't help but admire his physique, though she felt a little voyeuristic for doing so. He was singing to himself in Emparian. Just then he emerged from the pool, his taut, muscled legs dripping water as he reached out with one arm to fumble for a towel. Not finding it, he tried to turn around, and that was when Polnygar finally realised who she was staring at. At the same time, the man spotted her looking at him.

"What the- oh, gods damn it," Augustin yelled, and grabbed his towel.

Flushing he wrapped it quickly around his waist, covering his nether regions, unfortunately, a little too late for preserving his modesty.

"Polnygar? How long have you been there?" Augustin said, shocked.

Polnygar flushed bright red in turn. "Um…not long. I'm sorry, I thought I was the only one here."

"Obviously not," Augustin said. He alternated between looking directly at her and trying to stare at the wall.

"I'm sorry, I didn't mean to embarrass you," Polnygar said, putting a hand to her mouth and trying to quell her own embarrassment, which was growing by the second.

Augustin merely waved a hand, not making eye contact.

"I'll see you back with the others," Augustin said and shuffled past her.

"Alright," she said. As he neared the archway, Polnygar added, "Just so you know, you have nothing to worry about. Believe me."

She wasn't sure why she said that last part. It just felt right. Augustin gave her a sheepish smile as he left, and she found herself smiling in return. After he had left, she dropped her towel to the floor, and slipped into the cold pool for a while before she herself dried off, and returned to the main chamber to dress again. Trying to be nonchalant she returned to their rooms without looking like she had experienced anything was unusual. She assumed that Augustin would feel too awkward to bring up the incident if she ignored it.

As she anticipated, Augustin looked at her as she entered, but his expression was unreadable and he avoided direct eye contact. Polnygar didn't think it was productive to try to talk to him about it.

"Where have you been?" asked Hebu, without taking his eyes off the scroll he was reading. He and Aelzandar were sitting at a table together, both absorbed in their own study.

"Why do you ask?" Polnygar said innocently.

Hebu looked up at her with a withering expression. "Your hair is dripping water all over the floor. Just as the Baron was dripping when he came in twenty minutes ago."

"Must be a coincidence," Polnygar said breezily, and smiled and walked away.

Samir entered the chambers, smiling from ear to ear. "I have some good news, friends," he announced, clapping his hands together. "The emir has announced that he will grant the archmage access to the *Tome of Divine Metaphysics.*"

Aelzandar was visibly pleased. "That is excellent news, Samir. When can we leave?"

Samir held up a hand. "My dear friends, a moment if you will. The emir has a request of his own."

Aelzandar looked sceptical. "And what is this request?"

"He is captivated by the beauty of our dear friend and travel companion Polnygar. He wishes to dine with her."

"Me?" said Polnygar. "I don't really think – "

"Please, my dear lady," Samir said. "He would be most grateful if you would accept his offer. I am sure he would do whatever was in his power to assist us in our quest. And of course, no one would expect you to dine alone."

"What do you mean?" asked Polnygar.

Samir smiled, and touched her hand lightly. "I would be overjoyed to be your chaperone if you feel uneasy at the prospect of dining alone with a strange man, even one as honourable as the emir."

"No, no, no," Augustin said. "There is no way that I am leaving you alone with that emir. I don't trust him."

"Of course, my friend Augustin, if you would prefer to act as chaperone yourself then —"

"Yes, I would, actually," Augustin snapped.

"Can everyone be quiet?" Polnygar interrupted. "I haven't agreed to any of this yet."

Samir and Augustin closed their mouths and did not say another word, though Augustin glared at the Qardleean.

"Look, before I say yes to anything, I just need to know what I am agreeing to," Polnygar said.

"Merely a meal, and some conversation," Samir said, shrugging.

"And you say that this could help us?" Polnygar asked.

"The emir is always generous to those he favours," Samir said.

"What do you say, Aelzandar?" Polnygar asked.

"Well my dear, I would never presume to tell you what you should or shouldn't do," Aelzandar pontificated.

"I know. I just want to hear if you think it could help us."

Aelzandar sighed. "I agree with Samir. And I fear that the offer to view the *Tome of Divine Metaphysics* may have been conditional on this request being agreed to. But I leave the choice to you."

Polnygar sighed. "Look, I'll do it. It's one meal, how bad could it be?"

"If you're going to do it, I'm going to be there. I want to keep an eye on him… and you."

"I'm sure you will," Polnygar said pointedly. She noticed Augustin turn a shade of red, and quickly change the subject. "So the rest of you are going to the library?"

"If I am not needed here," Samir said. "I will accompany the most esteemed archmage and his assistant to the library. They may need assistance locating the book they seek."

"I guess that it is settled then," Aelzandar said. "When do we leave, Samir?"

"Right away," the merchant said. "I have been told you are to be escorted there immediately."

Aelzandar turned to Polnygar. "I thank you, my dear, for doing this. I do hope the experience will not be too stressful for you. Hebu and I will be back shortly, and, I hope, with the information we need. We will leave for Skurj the next day."

Polnygar smiled and nodded. Aelzandar kissed her on the forehead and then departed with Samir and Hebu.

"You didn't have to agree to this, you know," said Augustin, leaning against the wall.

"I know," Polnygar said, "but I'm hoping it might help us."

Polnygar noticed he was still avoiding eye contact with her, but thought she noticed his eyes hover over the rest of her briefly, before turning away again to look at a random wall.

Two servants interrupted Polnygar and Augustin's rather awkward and stilted conversation. One was a large, dark-skinned burly male, the other a slighter, tan-skinned young woman.

"Effendi, hatun," the male servant said, "it is time. We are here to dress you."

Augustin tried to bat them away. "I don't need help to – What sort of clothes are these?"

Polnygar looked at the elaborate clothes that the servants were both holding. She had the feeling that, despite Augustin's protestations, he wouldn't find it easy to dress in such unfamiliar garb.

"Please effendi," the male servant said, indicating that Augustin should follow him, "I will help you dress."

Augustin begrudgingly did as he was told, and disappeared to one of the adjoining rooms.

The remaining servant motioned for Polnygar to take a seat, and once Polnygar did so, the servant began fussing with her hair, applying oil to it and undoing the various knots and tangles.

"You are very beautiful, hatun," she said. "Your parents must have been blessed by the Infinite."

"Maybe," Polnygar said.

The servant worked on her hair, applying more oils and scents, and then she began to carefully braid it. It had been a very long time since anyone had braided her hair, and the only memory she had of such an event was back when she was just a child. She was still living with her father in Emparia, and one of his servants had given Polnygar an elaborately plaited hairstyle.

As the servant pulled Polnygar's hair back she noticed Polnygar's pointed Elven ears. "You are elf, hatun? Like those in the desert?"

"My mother's the elf," Polnygar said. "My father was from Emparia. I don't know what that makes me."

The servant smiled and continued working on her hair. She took several gold threads and weaved them into Polnygar's hair.

"Hatun, are you ready to get dressed?"

Polnygar nodded, and the servant helped her remove the rather plain traveller's clothes she had worn since Macrodonia. With that done, the servant produced an elegant and beautifully embroidered red and silver gown and helped Polnygar into it, completing the ensemble with a similarly embroidered tight fitting blouse.

The servant then fetched a piece of polished metal, and Polnygar could see how she looked. She was pleasantly surprised; the outfit actually looked quite fetching and was more comfortable than she expected.

Augustin emerged from the room nearby, holding out his arms.

"How do I look?" he asked. He was wearing a similarly opulent looking tunic that reached to below his waist and was decorated with gold embroidery. The pants were long and baggy and caught at the ankle.

Polnygar smiled. "It's different, but you know, I think it suits you."

Augustin smiled uneasily, but his expression soon turned serious. "I hope this dinner isn't a mistake. It doesn't feel right to me."

"Well, it's probably too late to back out now," Polnygar said. "Let's just hope we don't have to spend the whole night there. Maybe it's as low-key as Samir said."

Augustin held out his arms. "Does any of this look low-key to you?"

***

Hebu's legs ached.

In the streets outside the palace, the Nemoi struggled to keep up with Aelzandar. "Master, please," the Nemoi said, "What is the great rush?"

"Knowledge awaits, Hebu," Aelzandar said. "I can almost taste it."

The Nemoi shook his head in dismay and picked up his pace. Aelzandar walked ahead of them, with Shapur and Sharbhaz not far behind.

Samir rushed behind Aelzandar as well, sweating in the late afternoon sun. "Please. Great archmage, let us just rest for a while."

"Oh, very well," said Aelzandar in an irritated tone. He halted and waited for Hebu and Samir to catch up with him.

"What is so exciting about this book anyway?" Hebu asked. "And why

281

do you expect to find information about the Tears of the Divine within?"

Aelzandar took a seat on a nearby stone bench and motioned for Hebu and Samir to do likewise. "More than two centuries ago, the Qardleean city of Qar Dal was conquered by a malevolent foreign sorcerer, who then used the city as his base of operations. He was killed a few years later, dead as a consequence of his attempt to steal the power of the jinn. The name of the wizard was a name I'm sure you've heard yourself – Ralur."

Hebu nodded. Ralur was one of the most infamous sorcerers of the past few centuries. His rapid rise and even more rapid fall was the stuff of legends.

"Now before he took control of Qar Dal, Ralur had ransacked the ancient Tower of the Magi in Goriinchia. I know this, because I was there when the tower fell." Aelzandar was quiet for a brief moment, before continuing. "I know he recovered many items of great magic from that tower, but it was said that his true goal had eluded him. Some relic he sought was no longer in the tower and as a consequence he was forced to improvise, leading him to pen down his knowledge of this relic in a book. This book was his manual to his hoped-for divine apotheosis, the book we know now as *Divine Metaphysics*. It was recovered by soldiers of the Caliphate in the ruins of Qar Dal after Ralur's defeat."

Hebu stood and stretched. "And what does this have to do with the *Tears of the Divine*?"

Aelzandar tilted his chin. "When the tower fell I had no idea that Ralur sought anything in particular. Now, I have begun to believe differently."

"So, he was looking for was the *Tears of the Divine*?"

"Indeed," said Aelzandar. "The very same relic that Ivellios has stolen a piece of. If my deductions are correct, this book will tell us the true power of the relic and allow us to know exactly what Ivellios might be planning."

"*If* we find anything of use," said Hebu. "Ralur was little more than a jumped up prig, a boy meddling in things he was too young to understand. How can we assume that this book contains anything of use?"

"Where would we be without your cynicism, Hebu?" Aelzandar's annoyance was plain to hear. "Why not try to be as accommodating as our friend here?"

Next to them, Samir was panting. "I am -very glad that - I was - able to - help you."

Aelzandar smiled, slapping Samir on the shoulder. "Come Samir, onwards to the library." The merchant groaned and hauled himself off the bench. The group continued walking until they reached the library, a tall ornate structure built of white stone and topped with the same onion domes that were common in Qardleean buildings.

"This is it my friends. Inside..." Samir leant against the stone steps to catch his breath, "Inside, *Divine Metaphysics* awaits us."

Samir bowed to both Aelzandar and Hebu, waiting for the pair of them to enter before he made his own way up the steps after them, exchanging a few words with Shapur and Sharbhaz before he did so. The Ahktarran guards remained outside the library, at the steps.

The library itself, like many public buildings in Qar Arrid, had no actual door, rather a number of open entries, allowing the breeze to alleviate the heat of the day. Burly guards posted about the exterior of the building were sure to dissuade any troublemakers. Hebu's eyes flickered over the mosaics inscribed on the walls. Qardleean art was colourful and quite beautiful, but this piece someone had defaced this piece, and quite deliberately.

"Wishing to wipe away the memory of Soraya el'Fumat, I understand," he muttered to himself. "But to take out the face of Fatima al'Naif? The woman who saved the world? Such a pity."

Inside the library was a spectacular collection of shelves upon shelves upon shelves, each filled to the brim with scrolls of papyrus and parchment, and a good number of bound books. As the trio moved past them, Hebu could read a few words here or there or catch a glimpse of the titles. Some works were treatises on medicine or the natural world, others were political or religious tracts, and still others gazetteers of realms both far and near. There were even a few musings on the arcane mysteries of the Art, though Hebu wondered who they were intended for since he saw little evidence wizards were at all common in Qarld. Citizens of Qar Arrid milled about the library, browsing through the shelves. By the looks of it, they were firmly from the upper echelons of their society, with quite a few priests among their number. He certainly noticed that Aelzandar was trying hard to resist the urge to stop and read everything that was available.

"Look Hebu," the archmage said, his voice tinged with excitement. "The epics of Jorjuramur Tiin, and over here, Foss the Wrathful's tales of regicide."

Hebu barely gave the books a second glance. "Both incomplete, I see."

"Of course," Aelzandar muttered. He ran his fingers over the spines. "But still…"

"This way friends," Samir said, as he urged them further on.

They continued to walk until they reached a large steel door with guards stationed on either end. Qardleean script both above and below the door gave ominous warnings, promising great spiritual risk and moral degradation to any who wished to go through the door.

Upon seeing them, the guards unlocked the door, opening it wide and allowing the group to enter the final chamber. The room behind the door was simple enough, with clean white tiled floors and walls. A small plinth stood in the middle of the room, and upon it was a worn and scorched book. It was heavily damaged, but the strange arcane symbols upon its cover were still visible.

"Yes...yes. This is it!" said Aelzandar. His hands trembling, he approached the book and opened it.

The Slaves of the Horned God

"*On Ascension: The Tome of Divine Metaphysics*," Aelzandar read the title out aloud, "by Ralur of Skurj."

He opened the book and drew in a breath. "This will take some time. Most of the writing is barely legible, and what can be read seems to be a cryptic combination of Eldaric, Draconic and archaic Davorean."

Hebu sighed, "Let me get some chairs then."

***

Polnygar looked at the meal arrayed before her with dismay. She had heard of the Qardleean reputation for elaborate and decadent feasts, but until now she'd never appreciated the lengths a Qardleean would go to impress a guest. The emir had laid out a banquet with enough food for forty men, even though there were only four of them at the table. Racks of spiced lamb and roasted pheasant sat next to bowls of dates, almonds and piles of exotic fruit the likes of which Polnygar had never seen. Delicate deserts of infinite complexity competed for table space with baskets of flat bread and plates of fine cheeses.

In front of them was a dazzling array of entertainers. Scantily-clad dancing girls vied for space with jugglers and Ahktarran fire-breathers. Despite the diversions in front of him, the emir seemed preoccupied with Polnygar, staring straight at her with his brilliant green eyes.

"Come, my friends, eat," the emir said. "The Infinite has blessed us with this bounty, and it has been a long time since I have had guests from so far away."

Polnygar nodded with a weak smile. She picked up a piece of cutlery and considered the array of food before her, then decided it would be better to grab something than just sit there wordlessly. Across from her, a frowning Augustin put some lamb on his plate. He was obviously having trouble hiding how he felt about the whole thing. The vizier Baruch was staring at her without blinking, suspicion in his gaze. Polnygar tried to avoid making eye contact. It was certainly one of the most awkward meals she'd ever eaten.

"I have noticed that new and magnificent metal arm you have friend," the emir said. "Where ever did you get it?"

Augustin's mouth twitched. Polnygar knew he would not be foolish enough to reveal everything that had happened at the Temple of the Ancients.

"It is something that the archmage gave me. It is his power that makes it function."

"Fascinating," the emir said. "The things one can do with the Art. Aelzandar truly deserves his awesome reputation. I am glad that he has come to the Caliphate in peace."

The vizier was the next to say something, and his tone was not friendly. "So, Baron," Baruch asked. "How well do you know your companions? Do you believe you can trust him?"

"Who are you referring to? Aelzandar?" asked Augustin. "He saved my life."

"Mine too," Polnygar agreed.

Baruch shook his head, "I am not referring to the archmage. He is a known quantity, despite a history of antagonistic relations with the Caliphate."

The emir nodded. "Alas, there has been bad blood in the past, but his late master, Cassian, was far more conciliatory. I have heard the stories."

Baruch gave a slight incline to his head, "Of course, Emir. But it is not Aelzandar I speak of. No, I am referring to the other one who travels with you."

"Samir?" Augustin said. "I don't see anything to doubt he's a merchant, just as he says."

"I am referring to the Nemoi." Baruch's voice was tinged with annoyance.

"Hebu?" asked Polnygar.

"The gnome is harmless," Augustin said. "He does little more than carry Aelzandar's books and complain all the time. He's just a scribe."

"How little you foreign barbarians see," Baruch said. "Hebu has many secrets, you will see that. And he is far from just a simple scribe."

Augustin looked sceptical. "What do you mean by that?"

Baruch's eyes gleamed. "Have you ever heard of the Black Talons?"

Augustin shook his head.

Baruch's voice was low. "The Black Talons are a group of rebels..."

"Brigands," corrected the emir.

"Yes, Emir," Baruch said. "Brigands who fought against the Caliphate when it ruled Macrodonia as a satrapy. They destabilised our rule there with violent and criminal acts. When the Macrodonians revolted and threw out our governors, their new line of Pharaohs co-opted the Black Talons as their own private secret police."

"Pah," said the emir, "you mean assassins."

"I don't see what any of this has to do with Hebu," Polnygar said.

Baruch narrowed his eyes at her. "Your friend is without a doubt a member of the Black Talons, sent by his Pharaoh as an agent to achieve the Macrodonian kingdom's goals in this region."

Augustin laughed out loud. "Hebu? An assassin? A hand-picked agent of the Pharaoh? I think you must be spending too much time with your hookah, Vizier. What evidence do you even have?"

Polnygar chuckled herself. The whole idea of the diminutive Nemoi as any sort of assassin was ridiculous to her.

"I have no evidence but my own suspicions," Baruch said. "But I know that the Black Talons are said to carry a certain type of weapon, a dagger carved with the claws of a dragon. I don't suppose either of you has seen him carry such a blade?"

Polnygar's smile faded. She had noticed just such a dagger on Hebu earlier when he was treating her. Could the vizier be right about him?

"I haven't seen anything like that," Augustin said. "The desert sun has driven you mad."

"And you?" Baruch asked Polnygar.

She shook her head. "No, I haven't seen anything."

The emir laughed. "I must apologise for my vizier. He can be paranoid, seeing enemies in every corner. He worries for my safety. I should be flattered I suppose."

Baruch bowed his head. "I live to serve you, Your Eminence."

"Good, Baruch, now, let us turn to more fulfilling matters." He turned to Polnygar. "I find your face most fascinating, lady," the emir said. "You must tell me how it is your parents met and fell in love. I am sure it is a tale worthy of poetry."

Polnygar gave a non-committal smile and drank some tea, to buy herself some time before to answer. "I think my grandfather was the Eldara ambassador to Emparia, so I guess my mother was there with him. She and my father would have met at the royal court some time or another. They weren't together for very long anyway. I was only three or four when the king requested my father enter into a marriage of convenience with a rival family. That's how I ended up with a younger half brother."

"Oh, I see," the emir said. "Such a disappointing end to what was I am sure a love story to rival any of those in the Caliphate's history."

Augustin rapped his fingers on the table impatiently. "No one wants to know about how my parents met?"

The emir smiled insincerely. "Do you really wish to tell us?"

"Not particularly," Augustin smiled incongruously as he stabbed his knife into a piece of meat.

"I apologise for my curiosity, Lady Polnygar," the emir said. "But you are a most exotic treasure for us here. Such pale skin and light eyes, with such dark hair. You are beautiful as Zohra, and one does not see loveliness like that more than once a century."

"You compared me to Zohra when we first arrived," Polnygar said. "Who is she?"

The emir leant back in his chair and smiled. "Ah, Zohra... one of the many tales of romance that one might hear in the Caliphate. Zohra was one of the Infinite's finest creations, a woman of such exquisite and radiant beauty that men would fall under her spell with but a single glance. Many pursued Zohra, but few obtained her, and tragedy followed wherever she went."

"Tragedy?" Polnygar asked.

The emir's tone was grave. "There was a curse attached to her, you see. It was said she was under a spell from a jealous jinn and that this enchantment would kill any man who she fell in love with."

"That's horrible," Polnygar said.

"Indeed," the emir continued. "This spell followed her entire life, leaving a trail of misery behind her. She even went to the Holy City of Ralom, to seek absolution from the Infinite, but the curse remained and she died alone. The people, the hearts touched by the tragic tale of her life, built her a magnificent tomb so that she might finally be at rest, and laid her within. To this day it is a popular place of pilgrimage, especially for young lovers. It is said that in death, Zohra can bring the same happiness to others that she never achieved for herself."

"It's a sad story, but lovely epilogue," Polnygar said, looking at her plate.

"Sad, yes, but one of my favourites," the emir said. He looked at her intently. "So, tell me, my lady, do you have a love in your life?"

"What?" Polnygar said. The emir's question had caught her off-guard.

"A lover. Someone you feel close to, a man who has caught your heart?"

"No, no, not really." Polnygar stammered.

"Oh? I had assumed that the baron and you…"

Augustin's eyes widened.

"No. No, nothing like that," she said, flushing red.

"Oh? Well, I am happy to be wrong then. I may court you without embarrassment."

Polnygar's knife clattered to her plate. Across from her, Augustin stared intently at the lamb on his plate, stabbing it with such vigour that the other serving bowls near him shook. The emir did not seem to react, merely calmly taking a sip of his tea.

"I cannot lie to you, Flower of the South," the emir said. "Ever since I first gazed upon you, your face has not left my mind. You are the most beautiful creature I have ever seen, and I think if I cannot have you then I will never live to see another dawn. I will not have you depart here without speaking my heart's will. I wish for you to be my wife, and remain here with me in Qar Arrid. You will be showered with both wealth and respect here, as my beautiful young bride, and you will bear me a tribe of strong sons."

Polnygar nearly choked on her food. Even Augustin had stopped eating and was staring at the emir. "You've got to be joking," the Emparian muttered.

The emir looked surprised. "Joking? How could one joke about such things? No, I am completely sincere. I have been most taken with your young friend." The emir looked at Polnygar expectantly.

"I thank you for the offer," she tried to sound as polite as she could. "But I am sorry, I do not wish to be your bride."

"Come now, my dear," said the Emir. "Don't be so hasty to dismiss my proposition. There is much I can offer you. You would have all you desire here, and much more. Think of the life that would await you as the wife of an Emir. You would live in a palace, dine on the finest foods, wear the most splendid gowns. You would be honoured above all other women in Qar Arrid and safe from danger."

Polnygar tried to be diplomatic. "I don't think it would suit me, really."

"Don't be too sure, sweet Flower of the South. You have enjoyed our library, have you not? It is one of the finest in all Carurlonia. If you were to become my bride it would be yours and yours alone. No other man on earth could offer you such a gift. And there would be more, jewels and treasure, servants to attend to your every need. Whatever luxury you needed would be provided."

"She said no," Augustin said, slamming his fist on the table. There was silence in the chamber as the Emir's attention moved from Polnygar to Augustin.

"My friend," the Emir said. "This does not concern you. I wish to hear from the Flower of the South."

"The answer's still no," said Polnygar. This time she did not even attempt to disguise her annoyance. "Now leave me alone."

The emir's face darkened. "Is that so?" he said, his voice quavering. "I had expected more wisdom from one so beautiful. You do know I cannot let you leave here until you come to your senses. Guards!"

A detachment of soldiers came up towards the emir. "Take the lady back to her room, and guard her well. She is not to leave the room unless she comes to me. As for him—" The emir motioned to Augustin. "Take him to the dungeon and let him cool his heels there. Perhaps the lady merely needs some motivation to give the correct answer."

Augustin stood from the table and tried to move, but the guards grabbed him, and in the ensuing tussle, knocked him unconscious, before dragging him out of the room. Polnygar too tried to run, but a guard grabbed her by her arm and though she struggled she was escorted back to her chambers.

CHAPTER 18

Hebu had never seen Aelzandar so excited. The archmage was seated next to Hebu, with the book on a table in front of him. Samir paced about behind them. The librarian had left the vault, giving them the privacy the archmage had requested.

"This is fascinating. Fascinating!" the archmage exclaimed as he pored over *The Tome of Divine Metaphysics*. "There is more here than I expected."

Hebu looked at the archmage with what he hoped was a withering expression, but if Aelzandar noticed, the archmage ignored it, choosing instead to continue reading the book. Hebu decided that since indifference didn't seem to work, he would try instead to feign interest instead. "Tell me then, what have you discovered?"

"There is much information here. Unfortunately a substantial amount seems to be irrelevant for our purposes – there are fifty pages on soul-transference alone."

Hebu was unfamiliar with the term. "Soul-transference?"

"An alleged skill the Soldara had learned through the Art, a method whereby one might transfer the soul and mind of one being to the body of another. It's pure conjecture of course, and most mages consider it little more than legend. I don't believe it was ever possible outside of the dreams of certain unethical practitioners. "

"Thank the Infinite," said Samir. "It sounds truly foul."

Hebu sighed. "So is there anything in that book on the Tears?

"Indeed there is," said Aelzandar. He turned the pages rapidly. "According to the research of Ralur, the Tears of the Divine did reside in the Tower of the Magi." Aelzandar stroked a finger across his chin. "While some wizards considered them a creation of the ancient Soldara, Ralur thought otherwise."

Hebu moved towards the archmage. "What then?"

Aelzandar ran a finger along the page. "Ralur claims to have discovered ancient documents that describe the Soldara bringing the Tears from another place to the tower. This place is said to be linked to the Ancient Ones, the five companions of Aldion."

Hebu twisted his fingers around his beard. "I wonder, that shrine that Polnygar and Augustin discovered. It seemed to have links to both the Soldara and the Ancient Ones. Could it be where the Tears were created?"

"That supposition has merit to it, Hebu, but I would not be comfortable saying that for certain."

"Understood," said Hebu. "What else does the book say?"

"Regardless of how they were created, the Soldara first unlocked the powers of the Tears and used them as a repository for eldritch power."

Hebu craned his neck, trying to look at the book. "What sort of repository?"

"Ralur had the theory that energy siphoned from the ether itself could be stored within; energy that could be used to enhance the practice of the Art. Alternatively, it could be used for more profane purposes."

Samir had been listening in silence, but now he shook his head. "You are starting to use words that worry me, effendi. What do you mean by profane purposes?"

"Well, the work inside this book is all supposition, but the basic idea is that instead of focusing the power outwards, the power instead could be focused inwards, to the owner of the Tears themselves, who could then attempt to absorb the power. Doing so would give him tremendous power and invulnerability. It would make him, for all intents and purposes, divine."

"A god you mean?"

"Of sorts. A living, breathing god mixing with normal folk on the mortal plane."

Samir shook his head again; he seemed scandalised. "Such a blasphemous idea, my Lord Archmage. It is no wonder that Ralur destroyed himself then. Meddling with forces like that, forces that he could never possibly hope to understand, let alone master."

Aelzandar looked a bit perturbed at Samir's comments. "Well, whether you consider it blasphemy or heresy or anything of the sort, Ralur's theories were sound. If he did destroy himself it was through some other mistake. Perhaps he was unable to correctly focus the ethereal energy, or perhaps something else prevented him from doing so.

"But master," said Hebu, "something does not make sense. You owned the Tears of the Divine. If there is such great power within, how were you never able to detect it or use it yourself."

"I possessed merely a single fragment of the Tears. According to Ralur's research, only the whole relic reunited can perform the feats he describes. One would have to gather all the pieces – four, according to Ralur's book – before one would be able to channel the power."

"So is that Ivellios' plan?" Hebu asked. "Trying to find all the pieces so that he can acquire the power within?"

"Perhaps," Aelzandar mused. "I can't help but feel there is something we are missing in all of this..."

Samir coughed. "Ah, friends," he said nervously. "Did either of you notice that it's suddenly very quiet in here. Very quiet indeed."

"What do you mean, Samir?" Aelzandar asked.

Hebu looked around. It was indeed quiet and furthermore, the other patrons of the library had disappeared. "Curiously, we seem to be the only ones here," he noted.

"What?" Aelzandar closed the book and put it under his arm. "Are you sure, Hebu?"

Hebu walked out of the vault into the rest of the library. It was abandoned. He moved towards one of the windows and looked out into the city streets. "There's more," he said. "Guards outside. Lots of them." There were shouts and the sounds of swords clashing outside.

"What's happening?" Samir said.

"Your two bodyguards are attempting to bar entry," Hebu said, "but the soldiers are not taking a no for an answer."

"We need to leave," Aelzandar said. "Now. Both of you help me barricade the door."

Combining their strength, the three of them pushed one of the free-standing bookshelves in front of the doors.

"What of Shapur and Sharbhaz?" Samir said.

"There is nothing we can do for them," Aelzandar said. "But they can buy us time. Quickly, Samir, our lives may depend on this. Do you know of any other way to escape this library?"

"The basement. There's a secret tunnel there that leads to the palace."

Hebu gave Samir a quizzical look, and the merchant was quick to explain. "The current emir's grandfather liked books, but hated people."

"It sounds promising," Aelzandar said. "Do you think you know how to get it open?"

"Possibly. The emir showed me once – I – forgive me, friends, it was a long time ago."

"It's our best chance," said Aelzandar. "Take us there now."

Samir motioned for them to follow. They passed through a series of small antechambers until they reached a small chamber, bookshelves lining each of the walls. "If I recall, there is a secret passage hidden behind this wall, opened by pulling on one of the books."

"Which one?" asked Aelzandar. "Quickly."

Samir scanned the shelves. "Here it is." He pulled on a book - *The Life and Times of the Fourteenth Caliph* – and the trio heard the grinding of stone as the entire bookshelf flipped open on a hinge, revealing a tunnel behind it.

"We may need a torch but I don't know where we might find one."

As Samir looked around the chamber, Aelzandar smiled and snapped his fingers. A small sphere of light burst into life, hovering above his fingertips.

"Of course, archmage, I forgot who I was talking to."

There was a crash followed by the sound of splintering wood from behind them. "Move. Quickly," Aelzandar ordered. "Into the tunnel."

Hebu did as ordered, but Samir hesitated for a moment before he too did so.

"Pull it closed behind us," Aelzandar said.

"But what if we—"

"Do it," the archmage said firmly.

297

With a sigh, Samir did as he was told, and sealed the wall shut. Hebu heard shouts from inside the library, but it was not apparent if the soldiers had seen the secret passage or not.

"What is going on here?" Hebu whispered. "Why are we suddenly under attack?"

"My friends, I am sorry, I had no idea, you must believe me. This is a mistake, it has to be," Samir said, holding up his hands.

Aelzandar waved away Samir's apologies. "It does not matter. All that should concerns us now is surviving this."

"What's our next move?" said Hebu.

"We must find Polnygar and Augustin," Aelzandar said. "They may already be in danger."

"Back to the palace?" Hebu asked. "Do you think this was the emir's plan all along? Was giving us access to this book a trap?"

"I don't know," Aelzandar said with irritation. "But it certainly seems that way."

"And what shall we do with the book then?" Hebu asked.

Aelzandar looked thoughtful. "We shall take it with us. If the emir has betrayed us, then this book is in the wrong hands. That could be extremely dangerous."

"Let's hope then that ours are the right hands, master," Hebu said, and strapped the book to his belt.

"Samir, do you know where the horses and camels are?" Aelzandar said

"In the palace stables."

"Can you get there easily?"

"Certainly."

"I need Hebu and yourself to go to there as quickly as you can," said Aelzandar, placing a hand on Samir's shoulder. "You must retrieve our mounts, and what possessions of ours you can and prepare yourself to depart. Take the camels to the outskirts of the city, I will meet you there."

"And where shall you be, archmage?" Samir asked.

"I will be in the palace, fetching Polnygar and Augustin." He turned to Hebu. "If it transpires that we have not returned by dawn tomorrow, you must leave without us, understood? You travel north to the Leridian Pass, and from there on to Skurj. We will join you whenever we can."

"Good luck, master," Hebu said.

***

At the palace, Polnygar sat in the room. She was a prisoner. Outside her chamber stood the vizier Baruch, who tried to convince her to accept the emir's proposal. They had manacled her in an attempt to prevent her using the Art to escape.

"You underestimate the grandeur you might experience as wife to an emir," the vizier said through the door. "You would be feted above all other women."

"Let me go!" Polnygar shouted.

"You have fire," the vizier said. "That is good. The emir likes that in a wife. It will make breaking you all the more rewarding."

She banged her fists against the door in fury, but the vizier and the guards surrounding him did not budge. "This can all be over in a moment," the vizier said. "All you have to do is accept the emir's most generous proposal."

Polnygar just kicked the door in response.

As the hours passed, Polnygar grew increasingly frustrated and desperate. Her avenues of escape were limited, Augustin had been taken by the soldiers to an uncertain fate and she was unsure if Aelzandar was returning or not. She was on her own. Reasoning with the vizier seemed a futile task, and her chance of overpowering them was unlikely; the manacles made sure of that. She would have to find an alternate way to escape one that would involve playing on her enemies' weaknesses. A plan began to form in her mind. Calming herself, she approached the door.

"Alright," she yelled. "I'll do it. Take me to him."

There was a brief silence on the other side before the door opened. The vizier looked at her sceptically.

"Is that so? We shall take you to him then. But I am warning you, no tricks."

Polnygar held up her hands in resignation. "No tricks." She sighed.

Apparently satisfied, the vizier motioned to the guards, and two of them grabbed her by each arm and held her roughly. "Let us go and meet His Eminence then, shall we? And he will see firsthand how enthusiastic you are."

Polnygar swallowed hard as she was half-dragged, half-pushed through the corridors of the palace until they reached the private chambers of the emir. The emir was waiting for her, dressed in finery, a sinister smile on his face.

"Ah, Flower of the South, you have perhaps reconsidered my offer?"

The guards let go of her, practically flinging her forward. Polnygar looked about the room. The emir eyed her expectantly, and the vizier was glowering at her, practically daring her to prove his scepticism right.

"I…have," she said, swallowing hard.

"Excellent news, my beauty," the emir said. "Guards, remove my intended's shackles."

The guards unchained her. Polnygar was tempted to use the Art, but with the number of people around, she was not sure if she would actually be able to defeat them all. She decided to wait and see how things played out but stayed cautious nonetheless.

The emir smiled greasily, opening his arms wide. "Let us embrace."

Before Polnygar could react he had pulled her into a rough clasp. As he pawed at her, Polnygar stiffened her body. Her head felt hot with anger and shame, and though she didn't want them to, the tears were dripping fast and furious down her cheeks. The emir pulled away and leered at her; he ran his hands up her body from her thighs to her breasts."

"Yes, you shall bear me many fine sons, there is no doubt of that."

Polnygar thought she was going to be sick. She pushed at his chest in an attempt to free herself but he grabbed and pulled her close again. His malodorous body odour, inexpertly masked with a sweet perfume, permeated her senses so deeply she felt she could taste it.

"You know," he whispered into her ear, "there is another reason that I want you as my wife."

Polnygar jerked her head away, refusing to face him as he smiled greasily.

"I would never turn down an opportunity to meld my bloodline with that of the Heir of Lydin. It was foretold, you see."

Polnygar froze. When she found her voice, it arose in a gasp. "We never told you... how do you know?"

The emir chuckled unsettlingly. "Oh, I know about the Heir of Lydin, Flower of the South. How could I not, when it is a holy prophecy of my faith."

"Your faith?"

The emir reached for his turban and unwound it, exposing his forehead and the tattoo on it. A tattoo that Polnygar had seen many times before –

the symbol of the Horned God.

Polnygar was floored. "But you...how?"

"I have not followed the Infinite Faith for many years now," the emir said. "I follow only Dhul-Qarnayn. The Horned God."

The vizier Baruch looked horrified. "Your Eminence? You can't abandon the Infinite Faith! The Caliph will not be pleased."

"Baruch. I tire of your incessant questions and your blind adherence to that faith."

"Your Eminence, please..."

The emir turned to the guards. "Silence that fool. Permanently."

"What? N-No!" The vizier stepped back, holding his hands up as the guards advanced on him, scimitars drawn. Polnygar tried to pull away from the emir again in the confusion, but he grabbed her arm.

"See how the Horned God deals with those who have outlived their usefulness," he proclaimed.

The vizier screamed as the guards hack away at him; he slumped against the far wall within seconds, his blood pooling on the floor below where he fell.

"Now my dear," the emir said, his eyes blazing with lust, "where were we?"

Polnygar's face boiled once again with disgust, fear and anger. Beneath those emotions she felt a familiar surge of power begging to be released. Grabbing the emir's arm with her free hand, she directed the energy towards him, her eyes glaring right into his.

The emir screamed in pain as his flesh sizzled and burned underneath Polnygar's touch. In shock and horror, he released her, stumbling backwards onto the floor. One of the guards ran to help him up, but the emir pushed him away. "Grab the girl."

The guards came towards Polnygar, scimitars drawn, but she held out two fingers, and traced a line in the air above the floor. Immediately a line of flames burst into being, pushing the guards back. With the guards distracted, Polnygar fled the room.

She ran through the corridors of the palace, nearly tripping over the dress she was wearing as she tried to evade the sight of guards or others who might be sympathetic to the emir. She had to find Augustin, but unfortunately, she had no idea where the emir's guards had taken him.

A guardsman lunged towards her; his scimitar slashed wildly at her. Polnygar attempted to dodge his attacks but her dress was too cumbersome. The guard's scimitar slashed through her dress, snagging itself in the resulting tear. Fortunately for Polnygar the elaborate ornamentation and heavy padding of the dress meant she avoided injury. As the guard struggled to remove his sword, Polnygar let fly with a powerful kick to her assailant's head, sending him crumbling to the ground and his helmet flying.

The guard was out cold, but his eyelids were still open, and Polnygar saw to her horror that his eyes were pure milky white, much like Augustin's when he was under the power of the spellweaver Ivellios. *What's going on here?* Polnygar wondered if perhaps the emir had powers like Ivellios', but she had seen no sign that he knew anything about the Art. *Is someone else doing this? Ivellios?* Apart from his rumoured visit to the Temple of the Ancients, Polnygar had seen no other sign that the spellweaver had even been in Qar Arrid.

As she freed the guard's scimitar from her dress, his armour gave her an idea. Taking stock of her surroundings she noticed a small alcove, hidden away from the corridor. After checking to make sure that she was alone, she dragged the body to the alcove. She quickly stripped the guard of his remaining armour, and then took off the embroidered dress she was wearing. She dressed herself in the guard's armour as swiftly as she could, including the face-concealing helmet. She was lucky the guard had not been a particularly tall man, so the armour actually fitted her quite well.

She put the scimitar back in the scabbard and strapped it to her waist. Emerging from the alcove, she took a look around at her surroundings. Disguised, she now had the chance to search the palace with less immediate danger, but she still had to find the dungeon entrance.

Before she could contemplate her next move, she heard a soft, agonised moan behind her. As she turned, she saw a trail of blood in the hallway. The trail led to a crumpled body, half propped up against a wall. It was the vizier, Baruch. Despite what she had seen earlier he had survived his emir's betrayal, at least for now.

As Polnygar approached the Nemoi's eye, though glassy and unfocused, seemed to regard her. For a minute, Polnygar considered leaving him to his fate, a just reward for his part in her ordeal with the emir.

"Let me see what I can do," she said instead, trying to find his wound. Blood soaked most of his clothes.

He pushed her gently away, smiling weakly as he did. "It's too late." He thrust something into her hand – his signet ring and a scrawled note. Polnygar read it. "Dhul-Qarnayn."

The vizier nodded. "The Caliph must be informed."

"I can't."

He pointed. "Upstairs. The aviary. A message must be sent." His voice was fading.

"There's no time," Polnygar said, "I need to find the others."

The vizier's hand grasped at her arm. "You must, or others will die." His tone was pleading, punctuated with pained gasps.

His eyelids closed shut as his body went limp. Wasting no time, Polnygar stood, and went in the direction the vizier had indicated. A narrow spiral staircase led upwards to one of the towers. Just as the vizier had indicated it was an aviary, housing a multitude of birds. Polnygar knew enough about messenger pigeons to recognise them when she saw them. The tower had large, open balconies, perfect for the birds to fly out of but also potentially dangerous for any unwary visitor who stepped too close to the edge.

There were voices coming from below. Polnygar looked around vainly for a place to hide, finally ducking behind one of the pigeon boxes just as two armed soldiers reached the top of the stairs. Taking them by surprise she lunged forward, sticking one guard straight through the belly with her scimitar. The other one thrust towards her, his sword slicing through her sleeve without drawing blood. Polnygar side-stepped his next attack and then barrelled into him. The soldier fell back and, losing his footing, toppled off the edge of the balcony. He barely had time to scream before he hit the ground.

Polnygar looked out into the city below. Soldiers marched through the streets, civilians scattering in their wake. She looked towards the library, hoping to catch a glimpse of Aelzandar and the others, but all she saw were soldiers surrounding the building. She saw one of the soldiers dragging a corpse from the library steps. From a distance, it was difficult to see much but the corpse was definitely not human. It was Ahktarran. *Shapur or Sharbhaz then. But where are the others?*

Polnygar was running out of time. Working quickly she grabbed one of the pigeons and tied both the note and the ring to its foot before releasing it. The bird flew off quickly and soon disappeared from sight. Polnygar made a silent prayer that it found the intended recipient without trouble, then retreated down the stairs.

She spied a group of guards patrolling the corridors and tried to look innocuous by giving her best impression of a guard marching on patrol. As the other guards passed her, Polnygar observed that they were headed to a corridor off the main living quarters. The corridor descended at some slope. *This looks promising.* After the guards had gone, Polnygar followed them, attempting to emulate their gait and stance as she walked. The last thing she wanted was for one of them to notice her.

Her instincts proved correct, as the corridor did indeed lead below the palace and into the dungeons. However, much to her dismay, the dungeons themselves were as maze-like as the palace above, and furthermore, they were so poorly lit as to make navigation impossible. Different corridors branched off in every direction, each of the cobwebbed passageways leading to prison cell after prison cell. She had no idea which way to head first.

To Polnygar's alarm, a small glowing orb emerged in the distance. She could just make out the shadowy outline of a figure next to it. She thought it looked familiar, but could not be certain. The figure seemed to have noticed her, and drew a large curved sword but otherwise made no other movement. Polnygar drew her own scimitar and likewise made no effort to get any closer before she could determine the newcomer's intentions.

"I have no quarrel with you, friend," he said. "Let me through and we shall go our separate ways in peace, but if violence is your desire, then let me warn you – I am no easy prey and you will find yourself outmatched."

Polnygar's lowered her sword arm. "Aelzandar?" she said.

The other figure lowered its own blade. "Polnygar?"

The archmage moved forward, the glowing ball of light travelling with him. He looked at Polnygar sceptically. "Is that you?"

Polnygar took off her helmet, her long hair tumbling out.

"Thank the gods," Aelzandar said. "We were ambushed at the library, I feared the worst. Where is Augustin?"

"They took him here somewhere. I'm trying to find him. What happened at the library?"

"The emir betrayed us. I believe his offer to show us *The Tome of Divine Metaphysics* was merely bait for the trap he always intended to spring."

"Did Samir know about this?" Polnygar asked.

"I do not believe so. He was as much a victim as we were. He took the whole thing as a rather personal betrayal."

"The emir turned on us when I would not accept his so-called proposal of marriage," Polnygar said.

"Please forgive me, Polnygar," his tone was contrite. "I did not expect for this to happen. I would not have asked you to dine with him if I thought it would."

Polnygar frowned. "There's more. I think he has other reasons for pursuing me than just lust. I saw a tattoo of the Horned God's symbol on his forehead when he removed his turban."

Aelzandar's eyes widened. "A follower of the Horned God?"

"He confirmed it himself. He wanted to…" Polnygar felt her throat go dry at the memory. She swallowed hard. "He wanted to merge his bloodline with that of the Heir of Lydin. By force if necessary."

Aelzandar looked revolted. "I am glad you escaped. I am sorry for putting you in that situation, my dear."

Polnygar avoided looking directly at Aelzandar. "Let's just focus on finding Augustin and getting out of here. Where are Hebu and Samir?"

"I have sent them ahead to organize our escape from Qar Arrid. They will meet us outside the city limits."

Polnygar nodded but then heard the voices of guards coming from one of the corridors. A moment later she heard agonised moaning. *Prisoners.*

Aelzandar turned to her and whispered. "We need to avoid being discovered." He waved her onwards. "I will wait for you to bring Augustin here. It will probably be easier for you to move about unencumbered on your own."

Polnygar placed the helmet back over her head and nodded at Aelzandar before heading towards the voices. Moving carefully about the dungeon tunnels, she overheard a conversation from the guards in front of her; they were talking about the "golden-armed infidel". Polnygar knew that they could only be referring to Augustin. She trailed the other guards, passing prison cells filled with all manner of bedraggled prisoners. In one cell an emaciated Ahktarran stared at her balefully, in another, a Selvara in rags showed sign of brutal torture. Unshed tears rimmed the Selvara's eyes and he had the stare of a man who had given up on all dreams of freedom. Polnygar's heart ached to leave them there, but she knew she could not afford to unmask herself. Not until she found Augustin.

Eventually, she came to a filthy cell away from the others, and inside she saw the Emparian. He was still wearing the clothes he had worn at the feast, but they were filthy and torn. There were fresh wounds on his exposed chest, covered with dried blood. Polnygar balled her fists as she thought of what the emir had done to him.

She rattled the doors of Augustin's cell and he looked towards her groggily. "Back again?" he asked. "I told you before. I am not going to tell your master anything, so you can just stop trying. It's a waste of both our time."

Polnygar looked about to make sure that there were no other guards nearby. Once she noticed that she was alone, she removed her helmet.

"Polnygar?" Augustin said, his voice cracking. "How did you-"

"No time to talk," Polnygar eyed the lock of Augustin's cell. "I need to get you out of there."

"The guard captain has a key, maybe you should…"

Polnygar shushed him. She placed her fingers on the lock and focused on it. The familiar exhilaration that accompanied the use of the Art travelled through her. Within moments the lock was glowing red and hot. Using the hilt of her scimitar she smashed the smouldering lock out of place and the door swung free.

"Or you could just do that," Augustin said. "Sometimes I forget you have a whole other toolkit to use."

"Are you alright, can you stand?" Polnygar asked.

"I might need a bit of help," Augustin said, struggling to stand on his feet. "They beat me pretty hard, you know. But I think they were only hurting me to hurt you."

Polnygar flushed. "I think they're going to learn that I don't appreciate it when people hurt those I care about."

Augustin smiled, then grimaced. "The leg isn't feeling too good."

"Don't put too much weight on it. Aelzandar's outside. We're going to get out of here now."

"I take it things didn't go any better at the library than they did at the dinner," Augustin said, and Polnygar nodded grimly. "What about you?" he said as Polnygar put her arm around his shoulder to help him out of the cell. "He didn't hurt you, did he?"

Polnygar felt a lump in her throat at the mention of the emir but she refused to think about it. She decided to not tell Augustin the full extent of her mistreatment. There would be time for that later. "He certainly tried. But I think he's going to regret laying hands on me."

Augustin's look hardened. "Just let me at him."

"There's more," Polnygar said. "It seems the emir is a follower of the Horned God."

Augustin looked shocked. "Are you sure?"

"I saw his tattoo. It was a perfect match to the mark we saw on the bandits. He admitted his allegiance. He certainly saw no need to hide it from me any longer. In fact, I wouldn't be surprised if he knew we were coming."

"Well, I doubt any of this is a coincidence. Samir certainly seemed eager to help us, didn't he?"

Polnygar brushed away Augustin's suspicions. "We don't suspect Samir was involved with the plot. Aelzandar said Samir was as shocked as he was."

Augustin looked at her. "I know you respect the archmage, Polnygar, but don't forget that Samir is an old friend of his. Friends are often incapable of seeing the bad in each other."

Polnygar nodded but said nothing. She had to admit that Augustin was making a good point.

"Come on, let's go," she said.

The other guards were gone, having walked past Augustin's cell, but Polnygar knew that their patrol would soon bring them back, so she led Augustin back quickly the way she had come. When they reached the stairs to the palace, Aelzandar was there waiting for them. He looked relieved when he saw them both.

"It is good to see you, Baron," Aelzandar said. "I had feared the worst, but at least you still live. I must apologise to you. I feel responsible for this debacle."

Augustin closed his eyes and waved a hand weakly. "You were not to know."

Aelzandar put Augustin's arm around his shoulder. "Easy there."

"We need to leave," Polnygar said. "Is there another way out?"

Aelzandar shook his head. "Only through the secret tunnel I took to reach here. I fear going back that way would be running straight into danger. The emir's guards would have no doubt discovered the tunnel already. I am sure of it."

"It looks like the only way is up and out," Polnygar said. "But the palace will be crawling with guards by now."

"Back into the lion's den," Augustin said. He clenched his good hand. "Find me a sword and I'll be good."

"Do not overexert yourself, Baron," said Aelzandar. "

The three of them made their way to the top floor. Again, they did not encounter any guards in the dungeon as they made their way through the corridors. The ones Polnygar had seen earlier must have returned to the palace proper, most likely to search for her.

They moved quickly through the palace corridors, Polnygar leading the way with her guard helmet on to not arouse suspicion. Augustin was in the middle since he was still injured, and Aelzandar took the rear, his sword *Sakkaru* drawn to face any oncoming threat.

They rounded a corner, and three guards spotted them. Shouting threats and brandishing scimitars, they charged at the trio. One made a clumsy attempt on Polnygar, but she twisted away from his sword and dispatched him easily. The other two fell to Sakkaru, and Aelzandar finished them off with a grim expression.

"I think we just found you a sword, Baron," Aelzandar said, nodding to the dead guards.

Augustin picked up one of their scimitars and gave it a practice swing. Nodding his head in appraisal, Augustin kept it with him.

"Look, let me show you something," Polnygar said. She went to each of the guards and removed their helmets. Both of the dead men stared back with lifeless completely white eyes.

Aelzandar looked thoughtful, but Augustin gave a look of repulsion. "Gods above, what happened to their eyes?"

Aelzandar looked at him. "Yours were much the same when you were under Ivellios' spell."

Augustin went quiet for a moment before saying, "I don't remember any of it. So are these men under a spell as well? Was Ivellios here?"

"No doubt they are under a similar enchantment, but I can't be certain its Ivellios. Too much here still eludes us."

Augustin nodded. "Regardless, we should go. Now."

"The courtyard is just here," Polnygar said.

With Polnygar leading once more, the three hurried through the remaining corridors and made their escape into the courtyard, which seemed to be just as abandoned as the palace.

"This does not bode well," Aelzandar said.

"Suspicious…" Polnygar said. "What do we do?"

"Continue with the plan," Aelzandar said. "We must reach Hebu and Samir and leave Qar Arrid."

Polnygar nodded, and the three of them, careful to check for any lurking guards, navigated quickly through the courtyard, out of the palace grounds, and into the city proper. The city streets were not as quiet as the palace, but the people of Qar Arrid paid no real heed to the three of them walking briskly through. Polnygar saw a handful of guards patrolling the streets, but curiously these guards made no attempt to intercept the group.

"This seems far too easy," Polnygar said.

"I'm not complaining," Augustin said.

Aelzandar pointed in the distance. "Hebu and Samir await us on that ridge. But we must hurry. It will be sunset shortly, and we will miss them if we tarry."

The gates of the city were open, as a large stream of travellers were departing on pilgrimage. The three of them insinuated themselves into the crowd, drawing the hoods of their cloaks and covering their faces to disguise their foreign features. They were jostled to and fro by the sheer mass of people; the guards on the walls did not notice and they passed through the gates without issue. Before long they were outside the city limits, having peeled off from the group of pilgrims with surprising ease. The sun was sitting low on the horizon, and dappled shadows covered the hills.

"This way," Aelzandar said to Polnygar and Augustin. "We need to move quickly."

Aelzandar led the way and Polnygar and Augustin moved closely behind as quickly as they could, though both of them shot the occasional glance over their shoulder. Polnygar was worried that their escape had been noticed, and Augustin obviously shared her concern, but no Qardleean followed them. They reached the rendezvous spot – an old, gnarled tree next to a menhir, surrounded by forested cliffs. Tall cedars cast shadows on the ground below hiding the setting sun.

"Is something wrong?" Polnygar asked.

"They're not here," Aelzandar said. "Where are they? It is not yet the appointed hour. Why have they already left?"

Polnygar heard a noise – the clink of metal on metal – and the shadows broke to reveal hundreds of waiting soldiers, armed to the teeth. They stepped out from the hiding place in the trees and trained their weapons on Polnygar and her companions.

A familiar voice issued out a command.

"Archmage. Heir of Lydin. Baron Bauer. Do not move. You are completely surrounded."

CHAPTER 19

The Emir of Qar Arrid sat atop a magnificent white stallion, on a vantage point overlooking the menhir and the tree. He wore his finest silken robes, paired with an elaborate jewelled turban. Around the emir dozens of his personal guard lined up, each with a composite bow trained upon the three fugitives below.

Aelzandar, Polnygar and Augustin exchanged quick looks with each other.

"Look at the guards," Polnygar whispered to Aelzandar. "Their eyes are white, just like the one we saw in the palace."

"Your Eminence," Aelzandar called out to the emir. "I must apologise. We didn't have time to say goodbye. I'm so glad you caught up with us."

The emir laughed. "It was a courageous effort, archmage, but all for nought, I am afraid. Do not be so foolish as to try to cast a spell, Aelzandar," he warned. "My men are well-trained, and will stick you full of arrows before you so much as speak a single word."

"We have no more business with you, Your Eminence," Aelzandar said, spreading his arms in a conciliatory manner. "We merely wish to be on our way."

"I'm afraid it's not that simple, archmage," the emir said. "You have stolen from me, and the penalty for theft in the Caliphate is severe. Common theft earns the loss of a limb. Grand theft," he drew a sword from his belt, "death."

Aelzandar did not flinch. "Of course Your Eminence, those are your laws and we will not question them. But what is this theft we are accused of?"

The emir leant forward in his saddle, "You have stolen two things from me – two things of great value. The first is *The Tome of Divine Metaphysics*. It is no longer in the library, and I have no doubt that this blasphemous tome is now in your hands."

"If it is so blasphemous then you should be glad to be rid of it, Your Eminence," Aelzandar said. "But I assure you, my hands are empty and I do not carry your missing book." He raised his arms up, exposing his palms.

The emir did not look convinced. "I never thought you would keep it on your person, Aelzandar. You are far too cunning for that."

"Tell me then, what else is it that I have stolen?"

"My bride, the half-breed Flower of the South and Heir of Lydin," the emir exclaimed. "She belongs to me, yet you attempt to spirit her from the Caliphate."

Polnygar glared at him. "I would rather die than remain here with you."

"I have no doubt," the emir said. "But a woman's opinions are of no consequence. You shall be my wife, even if I have to kill all your companions to force the matter."

"No one, man or woman, should be a slave to another," Augustin said, brandishing his sword. "It demeans them both."

The emir laughed. "What fanciful ideas you Emparian barbarians have come up with in your damp little land. You are most amusing."

"You cannot kill us, Your Eminence," Aelzandar said. "We have done nothing to warrant it, despite your bombast, and the Infinite Faith curses those who kill others while offering them hospitality."

The emir laughed again. "You think any of that concerns me anymore? The Infinite Faith is a lie. I forge my own path."

"Your path, or that of the Horned God?" Polnygar called out.

"Dhul-Qarnayn has opened my eyes, my bride-to-be. He has shown me the falsehoods that the clerics wove around me from the moment I was born. When I first heard His voice I was born again."

Aelzandar challenged the emir. "Does the Caliph know of your apostasy? What do you hope to achieve?"

"The Caliph is a doddering corpulent pustule of flesh who cannot rise from his bed unless his vizier commands it. In the new order that is to come, the weak shall be swept aside, and with the Horned God's guidance, I will fashion a new Caliphate, one dedicated to the True Faith that shall endure for thousands of years. The people of Qarld will embrace their new destiny as slaves of the Horned God."

"I see many here are slaves already, Your Eminence." Aelzandar gestured towards the guardsmen. "Was this your work, or that of another?"

The emir smiled. "Oh, Aelzandar, still seeking answers, even at the end. Since you shall die anyway, I will tell you that, yes, the spellweaver Ivellios did pass through here, and yes, he did render me assistance. In return, he only asked that I ensured you and your companions never left Qar Arrid."

"Why help him?" Augustin demanded.

The emir merely smirked in response. "Enough of this. I tire of your questions. It is time for the sentence to be carried out."

"Whatever amazing plan you have ready, archmage," Augustin whispered to Aelzandar. "Now is the time."

"No plan, Baron."

"Damn…" Augustin said.

The emir raised his hands, signalling to his men. They pulled back their bowstrings, training them on the trio below.

Polnygar took a step back, ready to shield herself as best she could. Some distance nearby, a tree spontaneously burst into flames, and a huge explosion rang out.

The emir turned his horse around to the sound, and as he did, Aelzandar thrust his staff forward, and then wrenched it back just as suddenly. The emir toppled from his horse but instead of falling to the ground he found himself hovering in the air for a moment, before being pulled forward at high speed towards Aelzandar, still suspended in mid-air.

"Help…Help!"

"A little word of advice to you, Your Eminence. Never turn your back on an archmage." Aelzandar struck his staff forward again and the emir collapsed on the ground in front of him. He scrambled to his feet only to see Polnygar and Augustin's blades pointed right at his face.

"A strange thing about an army of puppets, Your Eminence," Aelzandar said. "They are useless without their puppet master." He motioned up on the hill, where the hundreds of Caliphate soldiers still stood with their bows trained on the group, but otherwise had not moved. "I wonder then, if Ivellios is pulling your strings too, or is there another player in this game?"

The Emir's face twisted into a sneer but he said nothing.

"Polnygar, Augustin – we are leaving," Aelzandar said, and then turned to the emir. "And you are coming with us."

Polnygar pressed the blade into the emir's back and felt some small satisfaction when the man gave a small yelp of pain. "Move," she said firmly.

The emir did as Polnygar demanded. "What are you hoping to accomplish?" he said. "My soldiers will come for me wherever you take me."

"They'll be finding your corpse if you don't shut your mouth," growled Augustin. He turned to Aelzandar. "What in the name of the gods are we going to do with him?"

"He will have to come with us as far as the border," Aelzandar said. "We can't risk him escaping and bringing his troops after us."

Polnygar said. "We should restrain him, tie his hands with something."

Augustin held the emir firmly, ignoring the man's struggles. "That would be a good suggestion if we had something to tie him with."

"Indeed," said Aelzandar. "For now, watch him closely."

Augustin tightened his grip on the emir. The group continued to climb the hill, moving away from the mass of soldiers. As the three of them walked, Polnygar said to Aelzandar. "That burning tree was a nice touch."

"Indeed it was, but I had nothing to do with it."

"You didn't cause that explosion?"

"No, but it was a most serendipitous turn of events. Distracting the emir so I could deal with him."

"Then who was it?"

As if in response to Polnygar, a voice came out from over the next hill, "Effendi, Effendi." They quickened their pace and saw Samir waving at them. Hebu was next to him, along with their camels, loaded with their supplies.

Samir came up and hugged Aelzandar. "Effendi. You're fine. You are all fine. Excellent! That is excellent." He hugged the others in turn. "I trust my little demonstration was a success?" Samir asked.

"Demonstration?" said Augustin.

Samir looked surprised. "The Tarkenese smoke powder I set off? It was Hebu's idea. He saw it amongst my trade goods and thought it might provide a necessary distraction to help you escape."

Polnygar eyed the Nemoi suspiciously. The sight of him had brought to mind what the emir had told her about Hebu. Could he really be a Black Talon? An agent of the Pharaoh? She found little reason to trust anything the emir had said, but he had been right about Hebu's knife. If nothing else, she was convinced that Hebu was more than just a simple scribe.

"How long have you been here?" Polnygar asked him.

"We have been waiting here for you to arrive since we left the city," Hebu said.

"Yes, and you were supposed to wait for us until sunset," Aelzandar said.

Samir bowed his head. "Yes, I know effendi, and I apologise, but the city was in an uproar and we thought they might close the city gates on us. The emir had gone mad."

There was an unsettling laugh from their prisoner. "Mad? You know so little," the emir said. "Soon the Horned God will rule over all and you will rue the day you decided to make him your enemy."

The emir twisted about in Augustin's grasp and sunk his teeth into the baron's wrist. Augustin gave a cry of pain and rivulets of blood trickled down his arm. He let go of the emir, just for a second, but it was enough time for the emir to escape Augustin's grasp. He reached out to grab the emir, but his metal fingers closed on a piece of the emir's clothes. The material tore, the emir pulled away and fled down the hill, running and then sliding down the steep slope.

"Gods damn it," Augustin clenched his metal hand around the wound.

"Quickly," Polnygar said, her voice urgent. "After him."

"No," Aelzandar said, grabbing Polnygar's hand. "There is no time. And it could prove fatal. His troops are likely nearby and already rushing to meet him. The emir will also now be wary of our attempts to use the Art. We surprised him before, he will not make that mistake again. We need to get to the Leridian border. How far away are we?"

"Not far," Samir said. "A few hours at the most. Can you not feel that the air has become much cooler?"

"Let's get moving," Hebu said.

"Move, move," Samir said, urging the camels forward. The foothills of a set of towering, snow-capped mountains loomed towards them. Polnygar thought it would be nice to stop and see if they could put on something warm, but time was a luxury they could not afford. They moved as fast as they could, and in a matter of hours they were at the entrance to the Leridian Pass.

"Through here and we have left the Caliphate," Samir said.

Polnygar heard voices from behind them. Faint, but growing louder. "They're coming," she shouted. The five of them scrambled up the mountain pass, the camels galloping on ahead, creating dusts of snow.

"Make sure we don't lose them, friends." Samir said, but the rest had other things on their mind than the safety of Samir's trade goods. As if to punctuate the point, an arrow flew past Polnygar's head.

"Go. Go. Go," Augustin yelled as he followed them up the mountain path. Polnygar heard battle cries from behind them as three guards, part of the vanguard of the main force, charged towards them. One of them caught up with Augustin, but he swung back with his scimitar and decapitated the poor lout with a single blow.

Polnygar climbed the mountain, too focused on her own flight to notice the others, and it was not long before she found herself alone. The path was still visible, however, so she pushed on ahead.

A soldier came at her from behind, but Polnygar twisted around and thrust the scimitar into his belly. He died with little more than a gurgle, collapsing as his blood painted the snow red. She could hear the shouts of more soldiers behind her, and attempted to double her speed, but as she did so she realised the sounds of battle were also ahead of her now. Had she been surrounded?

She tripped on a rock, falling head first into the snow. Cursing her luck she scrambled to her feet, only to find herself facing two soldiers coming out of the forest towards her, weapons drawn. Someone else was with them – the emir.

"So my love," he said, his lips twisting as he said the words. "It seems after all that nothing will keep us apart. It is not too late for you to fall into my arms and beg forgiveness. If you do so I can promise that your punishment will not be too severe."

Polnygar took a few steps back, her hand on her sword. "I'll take my chances."

"I had hoped not to force you, my love," the emir said. He nodded to the two soldiers; they drew their swords and ran towards her. Polnygar readied herself as the two men came to her and, when they came within reach, she lashed out with her sword, catching one at the side and the other with her elbow. The first soldier fell to the ground, blood gushing from his side while the other, though winded for a moment, swung back at her. She dodged his blow and held out her hand, sending tendrils of flame towards his face. The sound of sizzling flesh filled the air and the soldier collapsed screaming; his burning flesh hissed as he hit the snow-carpeted ground.

Polnygar held out her sword to the emir and sneered. "There's still time for you to beg forgiveness, Your Eminence. I can promise you that the punishment will not be too severe."

"My men will have surrounded you by now," the emir said. "There is no escape."

Polnygar looked about. "I see no one coming to your aid. I think your men have abandoned you."

The emir's brow furrowed; then scimitar raised, he charged towards her. "Praise the Horned God. Death to all unbelievers!"

Polnygar dodged the emir's first blow and parried the second with some effort. She swung at him with her own weapon and gave him a wicked wound across the chest but the emir, swept by fanatical frenzy, shrugged off the injury. He attacked a surprised Polnygar with his weapon, slicing her unprotected arm and drawing blood. With a battle cry, Polnygar summoned all her strength and pushed the emir back to a tree, smashing his hand against a branch and causing him to drop his weapon. Undaunted the emir reached out towards Polnygar's throat and began to squeeze the air from her lungs.

Struggling for breath, Polnygar raised a hand up, and with her last strength held it against the emir's cheek, willing for flames. Soon the emir began to scream, and there was an awful smell as his cheek began to burn. Still, he did not let go of her throat, so she intensified her concentration. Finally, just as she had nearly slipped into unconsciousness, she felt the emir's hands loosen and his body slumped to the ground. His head was a smoking and blackened mess, and even though she despised him, the sight of his corpse made her feel sick. She wrenched over and vomited into the snow. Resting against the tree she recovered her breath. Hearing the sounds of more soldiers coming, she realised she had to get away as soon as possible. There was no telling what the soldiers would do if they chanced upon her near their emir's body.

There was blood in the snow ahead of her. At first Polnygar thought it had come from the emir or one of his guards but it was too far away from their bodies, and there was no sign of splatter. As she followed the trail the snow became more and more soaked with blood until it terminated at a grisly sight. Half a dozen bodies lay in the snow, piled atop one another. Blood had seeped from the pile into the snow, pooling beneath it, the warmth turning the snow to mush. As Polnygar drew closer she saw dozens of stab wounds. One corpse's eyes seemed to have been gouged out.

"I see we have found each other," said a voice. It was Hebu. The Nemoi stood nearby, hands on his hips. His clothes were splattered with blood.

"What happened here?" Polnygar said. "Did you kill these guards?"

The expression on Hebu's face didn't change the slightest. "Me? Oh no. I wouldn't think so. I'm just a scribe. These men must have met with a rather unfortunate accident."

Polnygar caught her breath. She didn't believe him for a second, but she couldn't quite picture him slaughtering six guards on his own either. "A rather serious accident, by the looks of it."

Hebu looked over the bodies. "Well, the mountains can be a treacherous place. There are wolves and all manner of creatures here that prey on humans."

Noting Polnygar's stunned face, Hebu smiled. "I expect the same fate has befallen the emir. Unfortunate, but the Caliph at least can be assured that his kinsman's demise was entirely accidental. We should leave, find the others. This is a dangerous place."

Hebu began to walk up a nearby ridge, almost casually, Polnygar thought. She followed the Nemoi cautiously. *Oh, yes.* She thought. *More than a simple scribe.*

As they walked Polnygar began to hear the sounds of combat. The clash of metal and the shouts of men assailed her ears. As they crested the top of the ridge she could see that the mountain pass had become a battlefield. All around her were the soldiers of Qar Arrid but they were locked in battle with another set of soldiers who appeared to be just as fierce in combat but with the advantage of being fresh to the battle. Many of them bore elaborate coloured surcoats, some with the symbol of a black eagle and others with a blue fleur-de-lis. She saw Samir and Hebu trying to avoid being caught in the crossfire while Augustin and Aelzandar battled alongside these new troops. Whoever they were, they had come just in time, and they were certainly no friends of the Caliphate.

"Polnygar," Augustin yelled, spotting her. "Thank the gods."

She ran towards him, dodging the clumsy attack of a Caliphate soldier as she did, and soon they were fighting back to back. "Who are these?"

"Soldiers of Caruillin. Luckily for us, they were stationed at the border. The Caliphate soldiers were getting too close to Imperial lands, so…"

Blood splashed Polnygar as an Imperial soldier butchered a soldier from the Caliphate right in front of her.

Augustin grimaced. "You get the picture."

***

Before long the tide of battle had turned, and the might of the Qardleean soldiers broke. Their minds addled by the power of the Horned God they fought to the death, refusing to surrender even when their strength failed them. Polnygar winced as many were beheaded where they stood. After the bloody work was done a knight approached them, clad in fine mail and with a blue fleur-de-lis emblazoned on the surcoat.

"Augustin Bauer," she said, removing her helmet. "Fancy meeting you again."

"Céline," Augustin exclaimed. "What in the name of the gods are you doing here?"

"Saving your lives, of course," the Leridian smirked. "And killing a few Sarrisite dogs at the same time." She paused, and her eyes roamed over the man. "By the way, that's a beautiful new arm you have, Augustin. I like how it shines in the sun. Very pretty."

"Thanks." Augustin muttered. He glanced at Polnygar, who in turn, looked away. "We're lucky you were here."

Céline smiled. "Not luck, my sweets. I've been keeping tabs on you and your friends. It seems the emperor is concerned you might be connected to some trouble up north."

"What trouble might that be?" Augustin inquired.

"Unrest in Skurj of all places. Apparently your friend Ivellios has arrived in Liderial and his presence is unsettling the relationship between Alfheim and the Empire's northernmost province."

"Why am I not surprised…" Augustin noted.

"There's more," Céline said. "You mentioned in Forestown that you had experienced trouble with the Cult of the Horned God?"

"Yes, what of it?" Augustin said.

"There is an old temple of the Horned God in Skurj. It has been abandoned for centuries. Abandoned, that is, until now. The locals are saying the cult has returned. Do you know anything about that?" Augustin shook his head and Celine frowned. "Pity. Would have made my job a lot easier."

For her part, Polnygar found herself alarmed at the revelation that the Horned God had a presence in Skurj. She wondered if Aelzandar knew. *Is that why he seemed reluctant to bring me there? Straight from the frying pan, into the fire.*

Aelzandar arrived just as Polnygar thought of him, with Hebu and Samir in tow. The merchant opened his arms wide upon seeing Polnygar and Augustin, his face contorted in dismay. "Baron Augustin, Polnygar, friends. Have you seen my camels? I fear I may have lost my goods in the battle."

"I believe some introductions may be in order?" Céline asked.

Augustin complied and acquainted Céline with his companions. While she greeted the rest with courtesy, it was Polnygar who received her warmest smile. She took Polnygar's hand and kissed it. "Delighted to meet you again, Madame," she said to Polnygar, who smiled, blushing slightly.

"Alright, alright, that's enough," Augustin said, taking Polnygar's hand away from the Leridian.

Samir looked at Céline with a pleading expression. "Please, hatun, can you help me?"

"Of course." She looked around, and shouted to one of her soldiers. "Would somebody come here and help this Qardleean look for his damn camels?"

"Thank you, hatun," Samir bowed.

"I must thank you, Captain," Aelzandar said, "your arrival was most fortuitous."

"As I was saying to our mutual friend here," Céline said, indicating Augustin, "luck had nothing to do with it. Sinister forces are afoot, and I believe your presence here may be the cause of it. Unfortunately, this invasion of Imperial territory by soldiers of the Caliphate has complicated matters. I have no choice but to detain you until this is sorted out."

"What?" Augustin said. "You can't be serious, Céline."

"This is outrageous," said Hebu. "We have important work to do."

"As do I," said Céline. "My men will escort you to camp. You are to wait there until I come for you." She steered her horse away as she went to examine the battlefield.

***

Polnygar and the others were summarily taken by the chevaliers to a nearby military camp. The camp, little more than a cluster of tents around a campfire, did little to ward off the cold mountain air, even with the blankets that Céline supplied them with.

"Stay here," said one of the chevaliers.

Polnygar didn't like the soldier's terseness. "For how long?"

The chevalier raised a hand. "For however long the captain wishes."

"Just let me talk to her," Augustin called out after them, but the chevaliers didn't even turn to acknowledge him. He went to move but both soldiers raised their blades.

"You are to remain here. The captain has authorised us to use force, if necessary."

"I'd like to see you try," Augustin reached for his sword. Immediately both chevaliers adopted defensive poses.

Aelzandar laid a hand on Augustin's metal arm and gave him a reproachful look. "Baron, please. Let's not resort to violence. Friends, we will await your captain."

"Your friend is wise, Augustin," the chevaliers said. "You should listen to him."

"No, you oafs should listen to…" The words died on Augustin's lips as he realised that the guards had turned their back towards them. None of them were paying any attention to him.

"Gods damn it, what is she playing at?" Augustin kicked the dirt about. "Every day we spend stuck here Ivellios gets further ahead of us. We're weeks behind him as it is."

"I understand your frustration, Baron," Aelzandar said, "but we have little other option than to be patient."

With nothing else to do, they waited. From time to time Polnygar spied Céline from the tent. Once she saw her deep in conversation with an unfamiliar knight. The newcomer was young, in fact he seemed little older than Polnygar herself, and wore a surcoat emblazoned with a black cross.

Céline and the knight spoke in hushed whispers with both of them occasionally glancing towards the tent where Polnygar and the others were confined. After their discussion, both Céline and the knight disappeared into one of the other tents, and Polnygar saw no more of them for quite a while.

Finally Céline returned, and this time she had different company. Four Qardleean soldiers accompanied her, along with a veiled woman. "How are we all?" Céline asked.

Augustin stared at her. "You've had us detained here for gods know how long. How do you think we are?"

"An end is in sight, handsome," she said cheekily. "If you and your friends would accompany us to the command tent."

The soldiers snapped to attention, and led the group towards the centre of the camp, where a large tent stood. The flags on the top bore a blue fleur-de-lis, the symbol of House Lerid.

"Take a seat," one of the soldiers said gruffly. Aelzandar did so, and Polnygar followed his lead. Samir and Hebu did likewise but Augustin held back. The soldiers pushed him forward.

"You too, handsome," Céline said. She rested a hand on his shoulder and Augustin reluctantly sat down. Céline introduced the newcomers. "These are emissaries from the Caliphate. They have travelled a long way to arrive here in time." Céline indicated the veiled woman. "This is Um Badr, mother of the Caliph. She claims to have a message for us."

Polnygar was shocked. It was the woman from the library in Qar Arrid. She was no mere traveller.

Samir went white as a ghost. "My lady, I should have recognised you!" He dropped to his knees. "My most humble apologies, please forgive this humble servant. May the Infinite bless you, and eternal life to the Caliph – May he live forever."

"No need for that," Um Badr snapped. "We aren't in Qarld, Samir. We are guests of the Empire. It would not do to create a spectacle." She lifted her veil, revealing a pale, wrinkled face with glittering green eyes. "My son wishes to convey his apologies to both the emperor and your guests here."

Céline inclined her head. "That is kind of your son, but one wonders why he couldn't deliver this message in person."

Um Badr's voice never wavered. "Qar Udel is a long journey from here, and my son was not confident that he would arrive before the situation deteriorated further. I myself was closer, so the message has been entrusted to me."

"I thought Qardleeans were resistant to sending their women on missions such as these."

"Normally yes," Um Badr said. "But I am old enough that my son no longer worries that some wicked infidel would take advantage of me." Her tone was droll. "Besides when finesse is required, a woman's touch is always better, wouldn't you say?"

Céline gave a half smile. "So," she said, "what is it the Caliph wishes to convey to us?"

"The actions of the emir were deplorable," began Um Badr. "But he acted alone. The Caliph had no part in them. Furthermore we have testimony from our late and most trusted servant, Baruch ben Omri, that the emir had betrayed the Infinite Faith for the worship of Dhul-Qarnayn, the Horned God."

Céline looked sceptical. "So this invasion of Imperial territory was not the will of the Caliph?"

Um Badr shook her head. "He and his soldiers were acting of their own volition, not on any order of the Caliph."

"And what of this emir?" Céline said. "If he has betrayed us both, why is he not before us in chains?"

"His body was found not far from here," Um Badr said. Her eyes came to rest briefly on Polnygar. "It appears that he became disorientated, and fell prey to the savage beasts that roam these mountains. Justice has been done."

Augustin scoffed. "Why should we believe you?"

Um Badr nodded to two of the soldiers, who brought a large, ironbound chest forward. "As a token of his deep regret, the Caliph is willing to offer payment in gold. We hope that this alleviates any animosity on behalf of the emperor."

"I imagine it couldn't hurt." Céline smiled. She bent down and opened the chest. The sun glinted off the piles of coins and treasure within. After running her fingers through some of it, Céline closed the chest. "Very well then, I shall convey this to the emperor as soon as possible."

"Let your emperor know that no more soldiers will violate your borders. You have the thanks of the Caliph and may the Infinite smile on you, Captain Céline."

Céline called for one of the chevaliers. "Make sure our guests here are well-looked after, and provisioned for their trip home tomorrow."

Um Badr glanced at Polnygar as she departed. "It is good to see you in one piece, Polnygar. I told you to keep your wits about you in Qar Arrid."

As Um Badr and her soldiers left the tent, Céline turned towards the others.

"So, are you satisfied then?" Augustin spoke tersely. "It looks like war with the Caliphate has been averted."

Céline sighed. "Satisfied? Almost. The Caliphate was only one of my concerns. There are other matters. Emperor Anton is deeply concerned with what is happening in Skurj."

Aelzandar adopted a quizzical look. "And just what is happening in

Skurj, Captain?"

"It seems your rival, the mage Ivellios, has begun to make trouble between the elves of Alfheim and the men of Harralin. And now I hear rumours that the Cult of the Horned God has returned to its temple there. Both problems point back to your little group, archmage."

Aelzandar blinked. "I hope you are not suggesting that we are the cause of that …"

Céline waved her hand. "I am not suggesting you alone are the cause of Skurj's problems – but for this situation at least, you may be the solution."

"We're not your minions, Céline," said Augustin.

"Relax, handsome," Céline said. "I'm not here to give you instructions. But I do have to meet with Count von Sterrenberg upon my return, and that old tyrant has the emperor's ear." She cleared her throat. "And so, by decree of His Imperial Majesty Anton II, you are to be escorted to Skurj without delay. There you will be met by Grand Master Keller of the Knights of the Crux Caruillin." Céline pulled back the tent's flap, and the knight Polnygar had seen earlier stepped through. "This handsome young man is Sir Holger Keller, Knight of the Crux Caruillin and nephew to the Grand Master. Though I am reluctant to let him leave so early, he will be your escort to Skurj."

The young knight nodded, and gave an awkward smile as he stepped forward.

"You need not do this, Sir Holger," Aelzandar said. "We were on our way to Skurj anyway."

Sir Holger shook his head. "I have my orders from the emperor himself. He considers this matter of utmost importance. He had writs issued to ensure no delays on our journey. "

Céline cut in. "Sir Holger was only instructed to bring the archmage, Baron Bauer and the Ap'Lydin girl. The Qardleean merchant is free to go about his business."

"You are most kind, hatun," Samir said. "I have goods I hope to sell in Dilmun. I do not fancy a trip to Skurj. There is little profit in it."

"Skurj offers little for anyone these days, except trouble," Celine looked at the others. "Say your goodbyes. You leave in an hour." Céline shouted instructions to her soldiers to bring horses.

Aelzandar sighed. "I do not like the idea of compulsion in this matter, but I cannot deny that an Imperial escort will prove most useful in speeding our journey to Skurj."

"I don't care, the sooner we find Ivellios the better." Augustin rubbed his arm, right at the point where the flesh met the metal and Polnygar once again felt a surge of guilt. She too wanted to find Ivellios, but she wondered how much of that was to assuage her own sense of responsibility for Augustin's injury. She laid a reassuring hand on his arm and smiled at him. He smiled back, if only for a moment.

Some soldiers arrived with Samir's camels and fresh horses for the others. The merchant clasped the hands of one of the soldiers "At last. Thank you, my friend. Thank you."

The soldier walked off as Samir searched through the saddlebags. "Here, my friend," he said to Aelzandar, "I shall return to you all that is yours." He handed over several books and scrolls. "And here, take some of my supplies. You will need them for the journey. There is no charge, I owe you all that much."

Aelzandar exchanged a salaam with Samir. "Goodbye old friend, I hope we shall meet again soon."

Samir nodded. "I am sure of it, my friend. Probably when you least expect it."

"Farewell Hebu, Prince among Nemoi," Samir said, crouching down to exchange a salaam with the diminutive scribe.

"Goodbye Augustin, I am sorry we didn't become closer," Samir said, clasping the baron's hands.

"Probably my fault as much as yours," Augustin said, giving a small, guarded smile.

"And Polnygar, my dear, sweet Polnygar. With a mind to match her beauty. I will miss you most of all." Samir kissed her hand and held it against his heart.

"Our journey awaits us friends," said Sir Holger.

"Attention," shouted Céline. "Men, time to move out."

Samir looked around. "Well my friends, it looks as if it is time for you to depart. Fare thee well, and good journey to you."

"Goodbye Samir," Aelzandar said, mounting one horse with Hebu riding behind him. A soldier helped Augustin into the saddle of his horse and Polnygar mounted last of all.

"Onwards then," Aelzandar said. "To Skurj."

CHAPTER 20

I'm alive.

Bellaydin opened his eyes. He was lying at the bottom of a ravine. His head was spinning and his body ached with bruises all over, but by some miracle he had escaped serious injury. He dimly recalled his body rolling and hitting the cliff as it went down. Perhaps his fall had been broken.

He lifted his head up to look around. The ravine was forested on all sides and there was no other person to be seen. Gingerly, Bellaydin tried to stand. As he did so, he immediately regretted it. A sharp bolt of pain went from his foot up his leg. A sprain. He leant on a nearby rocky outcropping to steady himself and catch his breath.

Tancred had betrayed him. When he thought of it, his eyes felt hot and he clenched his fists. He was furious at himself for ever trusting the snake. Others had spoken of the Zalltor family's duplicitous ways, but Bellaydin had shrugged it off as part of the regular squabbling and distrust. Even with the obvious link between the murder of Edmund Tallcastle and House Zalltor, Bellaydin had not suspected anything from Tancred. The squire was so quiet and unassuming. Edgar had been the one they thought as the dominant of the pair, but it now seemed that Tancred had been pulling the strings behind the scenes. He had been too concerned with the wrong squire.

Bellaydin knew that Tancred had likely returned to the others by now, no doubt spinning some tall tale of them getting separated in the tunnels. Would Tancred inform the rest of the exit they had found? *Likely not*, he thought. *Why else would he need me out of the way? He doesn't want Geoffrey and his men to find the exit.*

Though boiling with anger, he put the anger he was feeling and thoughts of revenge out of his mind for now. Survival was the most important thing. He was alone, in an unfamiliar place, separated from his allies, and close to a hostile army. He had to figure out what to do.

He briefly considered attempting to scale the cliff-face, but with his injured foot he knew he wouldn't get far. Besides he was never particularly good at climbing and heights had never agreed with him. He would be much better off travelling on the ground, but there was still the matter of his injury. He searched around nearby and found a large fallen tree branch, just the right size to act as a makeshift crutch. Now he just needed to work out where he should be going. He looked up at the cliff. There must be another way up; perhaps a gentler path nearby.

Bellaydin took a tentative first step. Pain coursed through his foot, just as before. He felt like someone had driven a nail into his ankle. He clenched his jaw and curled his fists, attempting to distract himself from the agony and managed, after much sweating and grunting, to move himself forward a few feet. He felt helpless. He could barely move at all with this injury, let alone with any speed. He didn't even want to think about what would happen if the Goriinchians caught up with him.

Bellaydin heard voices nearby. There was no time to hide, and his injured foot didn't make moving easy. He tried to lie down behind some rocks, but even as he did so he realised how futile it was. He prepared himself for the inevitable – shouts and curses in Goriinchians as the soldiers found him, and then death – but instead there was nothing. He looked up and saw a woman and her children. The same woman he had met earlier – Myfanwy Ap'Morten.

"Please," Bellaydin begged, "I'm injured. I need help."

The woman looked at him wide-eyed. "You...you are one of the squires with the Lizardman."

"Yes, yes, that's right. We did not harm you, remember? We let you pass, please, I need help. My leg..." His arm moved towards the crutch.

She looked uncertain.

Bellaydin looked at her. "Please."

The woman looked thoughtful and then turned to her children. "Ciarán, Siobhán," she said, "help the young man up." The two adolescents did as their mother asked. Bellaydin thanked them profusely and leant on his crutch.

"Where are your friends, young man? We cannot take you far," Myfanwy said.

"I just need to get away from here, somewhere where I can get my leg looked at."

"We will do what we can. If anyone asks, you are Donal Ap'Morten, my eldest son. Your late father was Dugald Ap'Morten and we have left Emparia because of the death of your father."

The image of Dugald Ap'Morten, lynched by the villagers of Wishapton suddenly entered Bellaydin's mind. He remember the way the corpse's eyes bulged and the horrific expression on the unfortunate man's face. *If she knew I was there when he died, would she think differently of me? Would she be as kind?* He swallowed, trying to clear his mind.

"Is that clear?" Myfanwy's voice brought Bellaydin back into the moment.

Bellaydin nodded. "Understood."

"Good." Myfanwy looked around. "Come, children, let us leave quickly, before others arrive."

Gingerly, Bellaydin leant on his crutch and, with the support of his newfound "siblings", he was on his way.

***

By the time Kurth had returned to the camp, Edgar had recovered enough to start protesting about his treatment.

"Where is Tancred, gods damn you? Why I have been left in the care of this fat oaf?"

If Otto was insulted he didn't show it. Instead, he greeted Kurth with a weary smile and nod.

"Where is Sir Geoffrey?" Kurth asked.

"With Kahlaf, going over defensive strategies," Otto said. "Where are Bellaydin and Tancred?"

"We got separated," Kurth said. "They're still out there."

"Oh no," said Otto, putting his hand to his mouth. "Are they alright?"

"I honestly don't know. I'm hoping they aren't trapped there. I'm going to ask Sir Geoffrey if I can get help to find them."

"You lost Tancred? What have you done Kurth, you hayseed?" Edgar said, clutching his side. "We need to find him, he might be injured." He attempted to stand, but Otto held him back.

"Edgar, you're not well enough," said Kurth. "Let me talk to Sir Geoffrey."

The knight was deep in conversation with Kahlaf, maps scattered over a makeshift table, but he looked up and smiled when he saw Kurth approach.

"Ah the Bauer squire," Geoffrey said. "Kurth tell me, were you successful? Wait, where are the others? Where is Bellaydin?"

"We were separated, Sir Geoffrey," Kurth said, staring at his feet. "I'm sorry, I lost the others."

The colour drained from Geoffrey's face. For a while he said nothing and when he did speak it was only to utter two words.

"I see."

Talthas, his face stern, stepped forward. "Sir Geoffrey, you must send me to find them. There is no one else."

Geoffrey rubbed his face wearily. "You're right. Something might have happened to them. We can't leave them there by themselves. But we need you here, Talthas."

Talthas smiled. "The wolves are not yet at the door, Sir Geoffrey, and I shall return."

"Go then," said Geoffrey. "Find them, quickly."

"Our markings are still on the wall, Talthas," Kurth said. "Let me come with you."

"No, squire. You have been put in enough danger, and I will move more quickly alone. Sir Geoffrey will have need of your strength here."

Kurth nodded silently as Talthas departed.

"So, squire, how are you with a sword?" Sir Geoffrey asked.

"Fair, Sir Geoffrey. We were all trained during our time at the palace."

"Good, we'll need every one of us to do our part if the battle comes. What of the others?"

"Edgar is skilled but his injury will probably slow him down, even if he does recover by then. Otto..."

"Yes, what about Otto?"

Kurth decided to be diplomatic. "Well, I don't think he'll embarrass himself."

"Good. Is that your assessment as well, Kahlaf?" The Ahktarran looked up and with a grunt and nod, confirmed his assent. Geoffrey looked satisfied. "You are dismissed squire, go back and join the others."

Kurth did as Geoffrey asked and returned to his fellow squires. Edgar was sitting up, trying to fend off Otto's treatment and scowled at Kurth as he arrived.

"Well," said Edgar, "what has Sir Drinks-A-Lot said?"

"He's sending Talthas to look for them."

"The Eldara?" Edgar said, scoffing. "Is that all?"

"Eldara scouts are the best pathfinders in the known world," Otto said.

Kurth nodded in agreement before adding, "I don't think they can spare more than one person anyway."

"Typical," Edgar muttered under his breath, "always an excuse."

Hours passed and the squires spent the time playing simple games to stave off the boredom. Kurth had a pair of wooden dice, which they took turns betting on. They didn't have any actual coin with them, so they instead used small stone chips until Edgar tired of the game and demanded they stop.

A soldier yelled out near them. "Newcomer."

Kurth stood up. "What's going on?"

A group of soldiers came towards them. "It's one of the missing squires, he's just returned."

"What? Where is he?"

A rather bedraggled looking Tancred Zalltor came towards them. Dirt and grime covered his face and his clothes were torn at the edges. He was walking with a slight limp.

"Tancred," Edgar said. "Thank the gods. I feared we had lost you." He shot Kurth a dirty look. "No thanks to these incompetents."

"Where's Bellaydin?" Kurth demanded.

Tancred rubbed his arm, his eyes darting about the room. "We were separated. I lost him."

Kurth grabbed him by his shoulders. "Where?"

"I don't remember."

"Did you find the other exit?" Otto asked.

"No," Tancred said, "I don't think it actually exists."

"Talthas seemed to think so," Otto said.

"Elves are well known for their inscrutable ways, Piggy. They like to confuse us. It amuses them." Edgar did not hide his scorn.

"He's gone to look for you both," Otto said to Tancred. As soon as Otto spoke, Tancred turned rather pale.

"What? Has he left?"

"Yes, a few hours ago. I'm surprised you didn't pass him in the tunnels," Kurth said. "Tancred, are you alright?"

The squire rubbed his forehead. "Yes, I just feel a little tired, that's all."

Edgar moved across. "Piggy, make some room, will you? Kurth, get him something to eat and drink. Sit down, old friend."

This rare display of kindness from Edgar to another took Kurth aback; he wordlessly went off to get some food and water for Tancred.

While Edgar clearly appreciated having his only friend back, Tancred's behaviour made Kurth suspicious. There was something odd about the way he had reacted to Talthas going to look for them. Kurth's thoughts turned to the conspiratorial. *Has something happen to Bellaydin that Tancred doesn't want Talthas to find out?*

***

Bellaydin groaned. The journey felt a lot longer than it actually was, as he had to stagger the whole way on a makeshift crutch. Bellaydin and his new companions passed through the battlefield, where the corpses of the slaughtered Emparian troops still lay. Carrion birds had descended to feast, and they tore at the human remains hungrily, leaving little more than exposed bones in their wake. But even more gruesome were the corpses of Sir Emeric and Sir Fulk, the two knights who had led the charge. Both were decapitated, and their heads and bodies separately impaled. Flies buzzed about the bodies, attracted by the rotting flesh.

"Wars are a brutal thing," Myfanwy said. "If you are wise, you will leave here as soon as you are able."

"I won't abandon my friends," he said, trying to avoid looking at the scene of carnage.

Myfanwy smiled. "Let us pray that your courage does not kill you."

Finally, they arrived, and the sight in front of Bellaydin did not comfort him.

"This is the Goriinchian camp," Bellaydin said. "This is not safe."

Myfanwy touched him on the arm. "Shhh. It will be alright. You will be safe as long as they all believe that you are my son." She looked at him. "We just need to disguise you. Here, take this." She took her cloak and draped it over Bellaydin, covering the squire's outfit. It also hid his sword, which also could attract undue notice.

Bellaydin studied the Goriinchians milling about. There were soldiers, grim-faced and armed to the teeth, but also civilians of all type, including women and children. Most were at work with domestic duties: cooking, cleaning and other, less savoury pursuits.

Myfanwy grabbed a scarf and a few more items of clothing and gave them Bellaydin to put on. She tore the exposed part of his sleeves, completing the disguise.

She looked satisfied. "There. I think that should be enough."

"I don't have a forehead tattoo like everyone else here," he said.

Myfanwy faced him. "Neither do I nor the two young ones," she said. "We grew up in Emparia. That explanation will suffice for you too. Come, let us get you looked at."

She guided to him a tent, and left him in the hands of a healer, a wizened old Goriinchian man, so bent with age that he looked as if he might snap under the weight of his years. Muttering words that Bellaydin did not understand he grasped the young man's leg firmly and pushed at the bones. There was an audible crack, and another sharp pain up Bellaydin's leg, but then the pain eased. The leg, though it still throbbed, felt substantially better than it had before. The old man muttered a few more words at him, and then thrust a mug of steaming, black liquid into his hands, indicating that he should drink. Though he tried to decline, the old man was insistent and eventually, if a little tentatively, Bellaydin drank the concoction.

He immediately regretted his decision, as the foul-tasting liquid was bitter, and burned his mouth like fire. Coughing and retching he stumbled out of the tent.

Myfanwy thumped Bellaydin's back a few times. "It tastes foul, but it should help the healing." With a taste like that, Bellaydin seriously doubted it. Myfanwy gave him a motherly smile. "You should stay overnight before you think about going anywhere on that leg. Come, you can scrub the pots while we cook."

With few other options available, Bellaydin sighed and got down to work. The cast-iron pots were old and battered, and some were lined with rust, but they were for the most part still serviceable. He grabbed the nearby stiff-bristled brush and took the first pot to the bucket of water. The first one was hard work, but after a while, he got into the rhythm of things and found the arduous duties a welcome distraction from his current predicament.

The sound of voices brought him back to reality, followed by the wailing of bagpipes. "What's going on?" he said. He dropped the brush to look around The camp had become frantic, with soldiers and camp-followers rushing about. "That noise. Are we under attack?"

"It's the warchief," Myfanwy said. "He must be returning to camp."

A group of armed and fierce looking warriors strode towards them, led by the war chief Aonghus Culainn. Bellaydin recognised him from their previous encounter, back when he first arrived in Goriinchia. But the warchief seemed different. Where he had once boasted a healthy, florid complexion, Aonghus now possessed a pale and sickly tinge to his skin. His hair seemed dull, faded, so unlike the vibrant red Bellaydin remembered. But it was his eyes that were most disturbing. Where they were once blue, now they were pure white, giving him an inhuman, blank stare. Next to him strode his brother, the cleric Cathan Culainn. The priest was unchanged from how Bellaydin remembered, and his expression, that horrid mixture of hate and fanaticism, was just as it had been before. Bellaydin's heart skipped a beat when he realised that the party was headed straight towards him.

"They know me," he hissed to Myfanwy.

Myfanwy tried to brush him off. "Keep working. Don't do anything suspicious."

Aonghus came first. Grunting he took the food offered to him and said nothing. He seemed to move his head towards where Bellaydin sat furiously scrubbing a pot, but his blank gaze was directed straight ahead and he made no other reaction.

After Aonghus, Cathan came to accept food. He exchanged a few terse words with Myfanwy but he didn't so much as glance in Bellaydin's direction. Most likely he thought to notice the work of a pot scrubber was below his position.

Bellaydin breathed a sigh of relief once both men had moved away and the other members of their retinue came to receive their meals. If Aonghus and Cathan did not recognise him, then he felt sure that his presence would remain undetected. He looked up, just as he heard a familiar voice, and found himself staring straight into the eyes of Morgan Culainn.

Bellaydin gave a silent curse. *How could I have been so stupid?* The girl stared right at him, and Bellaydin knew for sure she had noticed him. She tried to avoid his gaze and accepted her meal with a few words of thanks to Myfanwy. Even after she moved on, Bellaydin was too stunned to think of anything else. Would she give him away? She had saved him once already, Bellaydin reasoned, perhaps she would so again.

Eventually, the warchief's entourage had their fill and moved on. Morgan left without saying a word to Bellaydin. As darkness fell on the camp, Bellaydin tried to ponder what Morgan's look had meant.

"She knows me, Myfanwy. If she tells her father or uncle I am as good as dead."

Myfanwy lay a comforting hand on his shoulder. "If she were going to tell it would have happened already. I think we can say you are safe. You should get some rest."

Weary, Bellaydin agreed and found himself a quiet corner to lie down on. Myfanwy offered him a blanket, thin and scratchy but better than nothing, which he took without complaint. Exhaustion began to overtake him and within moments he found himself nodding off.

CHAPTER 21

Bellaydin awoke to something sharp pointed against his neck.

"Don't move, Enparran," said a voice. "If you so much as make a sound, this goes through your throat."

Bellaydin's eyes flung open, and he saw Morgan holding a dagger against his throat. She was so close that all he could see was her wide blue eyes, and he could feel the warmth of her breath on his cheeks.

Without a word Bellaydin slowly raised his hands. As he did, Morgan motioned with the dagger. "On your feet."

She led him away from the sleeping Ap'Mortens to a place where they were alone. "What are you doing here, Enparran? This is not a safe place for you to be."

"I was injured," Bellaydin rubbed his cheek. "There was nowhere else to go."

"And why are you at this place to begin with? Have you come with those infidel armies?"

"Yes," Bellaydin said. Realising what he had said, he hastily amended his original statement. "It wasn't exactly voluntary."

Morgan raised an eyebrow.

Bellaydin tried to elaborate. "They made me a squire. I have to go where I am told."

Morgan looked thoughtful. "Perhaps it is the will of the Horned God that we meet again."

"I don't think so."

Morgan frowned and shook her head. "Why do you continue to hide from the truth, Enparran?" she said. "The Horned God is your god, just as he is mine. You are but a wayward sheep, waiting for a shepherd to guide you back."

"I don't think I'd ever like to be called a sheep," Bellaydin said. "And if you think I'm just waiting to be led to the Horned God, you are sadly mistaken. I wouldn't expect you'd find many Emparians who would be enthusiastic about that offer."

"The Horned God's priests tell us that in the lands of the Enparrans, your heathen priests know the truth, that their gods are a lie, and the Horned God rules over all. At funerals they whisper the truth to the dead, hoping that the Horned God will take pity and speed the deceased into the afterlife."

Bellaydin scrunched up his face.

Morgan narrowed her eyes. "Is this not true?"

"I was at my cousin's funeral. The priest didn't whisper anything to his corpse."

"Maybe you just didn't hear it."

Bellaydin sighed. The girl was stubborn. "Despite what your priests tell you, Emparians aren't all chomping at the bit waiting for conversion. Especially not me."

"Did you not read the holy book I gave you?"

"Yes, I read it."

"None can read such sacred and beautiful words and not be moved by them."

Bellaydin shrugged. "They didn't seem all that beautiful to me."

"Perhaps not to an unenlightened barbarian."

"I'm not unenlightened. I've read beautiful literature and poetry before. I grew up with elves. Their talent with language is astonishing."

Morgan clicked her tongue in displeasure. "The Fey are unnatural creatures, far from righteousness and the Horned God's grace. Any beauty you may have seen in them was a shallow reflection of the Horned God's radiance. They dabble in blasphemy, and wield magic with impunity."

"What's wrong with magic?"

"It is forbidden. Warlocks steal the power that belongs to the Horned God alone. They are thieves, nothing more. All are deserving of their fate and will be consigned to the flames for eternity."

"That seems a little harsh," Bellaydin said. "I've met many skilled in the Art. In Aderilund they are called spellweavers. Some are good, some are bad, like all people."

Morgan shook her head. "*All* warlocks are bad people."

How many do you know?"

"It is said that Mael the Apostate counted a warlock upon his companions, the wretch Ailill," Morgan spat. "It is said that this warlock betrayed him in the final battle, as is the nature of their kind."

"That's just one story. Surely there are examples of warlocks doing good."

Morgan shook her head. "This is not the place to tell such stories. And I cannot think of... No. Wait..."

"What?" asked Bellaydin.

"There is one. A story my mother told me." Morgan looked around, her eyes flitting about impatiently.

With the dagger still pointed at him, Bellaydin worried that Morgan might do something rash. He tried to stall the girl. "What is the story? Tell it to me."

Morgan looked uncertain. "There is no time."

"I'm not going anywhere," Bellaydin said, raising his hands.

She appeared to consider it. "Well, in the days before the Prophet-King Ygarak, when Karlicia was whole and undivided and our ancestors ignorant of the Horned God there was a king over our people – a High King, Taran ap Aodhan. He was wise and judicious in all things. In this, he was assisted by his closest friend and advisor, his brother, the warlock Salman."

"And what happened with these brothers?"

"They ruled together for many years until rivals to the throne had High King Taran murdered. Salman vowed vengeance, and eventually enacted a bloody revenge for his brother. But the kingdom was shattered beyond repair and Taran was the last High King to ever rule over us."

"So there are good warlocks," Bellaydin said.

"His actions led to the destruction of the realm. So you see, in the end, his influence was baleful."

Bellaydin did not continue the argument. He could see the girl was getting impatient.

"You should not have come here, Enparran," Morgan said, shaking her head. "I saved your life once, but I will not do it again. It has already cost me too much."

"Cost? What cost?"

"The Horned God was angered by what I did, and in my place, my father has received a terrible punishment. Did you see him?"

Bellaydin swallowed. He knew that there was something off with the war chief. "What happened to your father?"

"His eyes have lost their colour, they have become blank white pits. He no longer speaks nor even shows any sign of recognising me. He only speaks to my uncle."

"Cathan, the high priest?"

Morgan nodded. "But I can fix it. I can fix all of this." She touched the dagger's blade.

"Fix it? How?"

She held the dagger point towards his throat. "I will take you to him. I will deliver you to the Horned God as I should have done in the first place. It will be my recompense."

Bellaydin swallowed nervously, trying to ignore the sweat beading on his forehead. "You didn't before. Why was that?"

Morgan's hand wavered slightly, and her face seemed to soften. "I don't know. But it was a mistake. I let my feelings cloud my decisions. My uncle says that it is a woman's weakness."

Bellaydin nodded. "You felt sorry for me. That is not weak."

Morgan shook her head. "No, not just that. I –" She stopped, blushing. "It does not matter. I must make amends."

"Morgan, please," Bellaydin said, reaching out to touch her. "Don't do this."

She snapped back, brandishing the dagger. "Don't you dare touch me, infidel."

He raised his hands again. "I'm sorry."

She seemed to calm down. "Come, my father's tent is this way."

With her dagger in Bellaydin's back, Morgan guided Bellaydin to the centre of the camp. As he passed, Goriinchians looked at him with a mixture of pity and disdain. Even if they might not know of his true identity, they knew that where he was headed was a place of dread. Other soldiers had clustered around a small clearing in the middle of the camp, where a Goriinchian priest stood over three bound and kneeling prisoners. They wore tabards with the emblem of the twisted snakes of House Highcrown.

"Enparrans," Morgan said. "From the same army you came from."

Bellaydin turned his head to look, and caught a few scattered words of Goriinchian as the priest recited something over the prisoners. "What is going on there? What is the priest saying?"

Morgan didn't turn. "He is inviting them to the True Faith. They are being asked to embrace the Horned God."

"What happens if they refuse?"

One of the prisoners shouted a curse, and spat on the ground. There was a silence, followed by a sickening crunch and the man's head rolled into a ditch, a trail of blood behind it.

Morgan frowned. "As with all who refuse the Horned God, the penalty is death. I have no doubt the other two will make a different decision."

The girl's instincts were correct, as Bellaydin saw that the surviving Emparians submit to the priest. They knelt in front of him, mute, as the priest branded the symbol of the Horned God on their foreheads. Their resulting screams from the pain made Bellaydin's blood run cold. *Is this to be my fate?*

"They are converting just to save their lives," Bellaydin said. "Their faith is not there. They will flee the first opportunity they get."

"Perhaps," said Morgan. "But they belong to the Horned God now. As the Prophet-King said: *Once a slave of the Horned God, always a slave of the Horned God.*" Morgan's nonchalance made Bellaydin uneasy. "Come," she said. "We have dallied enough. This way."

A great tent stood on a hill, and though drab and brown it was well marked with the symbol of the Horned God. Two guards stationed outside eyed Bellaydin warily as he and Morgan approached. The girl spoke something to them in Goriinchian, and they parted the tent's opening and allowed them access.

Inside, the night gloom was absent, and there were several brightly burning braziers placed around the tent's edge. The interior was comfortably furnished, and dominated by a large table and a wooden throne. The Goriinchians must have wanted their war chief to be comfortable if they were willing to drag all these all the way out here.

"They are not here," Morgan said. "But the guards said they should return at any moment."

Bellaydin looked about for some way to escape. As if reading his thoughts Morgan pushed the knife against his back. "Don't even try it," she said.

She fumbled for something. "Hands behind your back." After she prodded him again with the knife, Bellaydin did as asked, and he felt her tying his hands together with rope. "There."

He turned around to look at her. "Please don't do this."

For a moment, her face softened. Bellaydin almost thought that she was about to cry, but she just frowned. "Do not look at me with those big dark eyes, Enparran. I cannot and will not be weak again."

"Morgan, Cad é seo?" said a voice. It was Cathan Culainn, Morgan's uncle. With him loomed the figure of Warchief Aonghus, who stood next to his brother, silent as a statue, his hand gripping tightly to the sword on his belt.

"Uncle, I have done as the Horned God wishes. I have brought to you the one you seek."

Cathan looked at Bellaydin, and a smile slowly grew across his lips. "Have you now?"

He turned to Aonghus. "Deartháir, suí." The warchief did as asked, striding across the room without a word and taking a seat.

"The Heir of Lydin," Cathan said. "Well, well, well. Here you are at last. We have met before, haven't we? I should have known better than to believe you to be just a simple squire. Was this his doing, a plan to keep you from me? He always believed himself to be more cunning than he was."

Bellaydin blinked. "I don't know what you mean. Who are you talking about?"

"We of the Truth Faith have many allies, even in the lands of the infidels. No matter, you will learn this in time."

"What do you want with me?"

"What do *I* want with you?" asked Cathan. "Seeing your head on a spike like any other Enparran would be enough for me, but for reasons unknown, the Horned God has marked you. You are part of his divine plan. The Prophet-King wishes for you to be delivered to the Tower of the Horned God, unharmed. Any who would do so would be rewarded greatly."

"If it's gold you want, I can get it for you," Bellaydin said, speaking quickly. "However much you want. Just let me go."

Cathan's face contorted with rage, and he slapped Bellaydin across the face. "Do you wish to insult me, Enparran? The rewards I speak of are not monetary. I am a slave of the Horned God, the one true power. The Prophet-King is the divinely appointed ruler of the world and entitled to obedience from all the faithful. With this action, I will secure my place in the life that is to come." He smiled greasily. "And yes, there will be other, more tangible rewards given to me, but to think that you can bribe one of the faithful such as myself shows that you infidels believe all are steeped in the same perversion and decadence as yourself ."

Bellaydin sought the answer to another mystery. "You destroyed the bridge, how?"

"There are no limits to the Horned God's power," Cathan said. "You should know that by now, Enparran."

"I was told that it was most likely Tarkenese alchemy. Does the Horned God work through foreign unbelievers now?"

Cathan smiled. "Infidel, the Horned God can work through any vessel he wishes. In this case, it was captured alchemists in Ygarak's employ." There was a sardonic tone to his words. "Do not worry. As they wished, we have rewarded them for their work."

"So you are not above offering coin to others," Bellaydin said.

"Your kind thinks of nothing but gold. The idolaters have been given what they deserve. They are being judged by the Horned God now."

Bellaydin had no doubt what that meant. "Your Prophet-King seems foolish to squander such an asset."

Cathan laughed. "Is that so? Do not concern yourself with it, Enparran. The faithful will destroy your heathen nation without any assistance from secret infidel weapons. You think that the pathetic strategies of your generals have caught us by surprise? We knew of your plots to encircle our army, thanks to the faithful who hid amongst you. When your armies were divided, we struck. Now only a pathetic remnant remains, a girl's soldiers, led by a drunkard."

Bellaydin's thoughts swirled. Again Cathan had seemed to imply that there was a traitor within the ranks of the Emparians, someone who had spilt the details of the duke's strategy.

Who was it? Have Tancred and the Zalltors stooped low enough as to betray their nation by treating with the Goriinchians?

Morgan spoke up. There was a quaver in her voice. "Uncle, I have done as you asked. I wish to speak to my father."

Cathan waved a disinterested hand at her. "Then speak, girl."

Morgan came up to Aonghus, who had not said a word since he sat down. The war chief merely stared ahead, blankly. "Father, I have come to beg for our forgiveness. I have done as the Horned God wanted. I have atoned."

Though he turned his head to look at her, Aonghus said nothing.

"Make him speak, uncle," Morgan said. "Call on the Horned God to restore him as he was, just like you promised."

Cathan laughed. It was a cruel, mocking sound. "Promised, girl? This was a sacred duty from the Horned God, a duty any true slave would have taken without any sort of guarantee in return."

Morgan's voice quavered. "But you said that his voice was held by the Horned God because of his failure to capture the Heir. You told me that it was the Horned God's punishment when the Enparrans killed him. You said that if I did this, he would be restored."

Cathan strolled past his niece, looking down at her over his nose. "Aonghus' death was indeed punishment for his failures, but the Horned God would never act through infidels. I was the instrument of the Horned God's will when I struck down your father, just as I was when I breathed life back into him. And let me tell you this girl, because of the sins that both you and he have committed, your father shall never speak again."

Morgan stood, eyes wide in shock. Her voice came out as scarcely more than a whisper. "You killed him? But you said that..."

"The Enparrans? I know that your faith is weak, Morgan. You have too much of your pagan mother in you. I had to motivate you."

"You killed my father?"

"His death was the Horned God's will," Cathan said.

"Liar!" Morgan screamed. She pulled out the knife.

Cathan laughed and drew his sword. "Come then, you pagan bitch, I can send you to join him if you wish." He stepped forward but then halted, thrusting his blade back in its scabbard. "Perhaps I should not bother to sully my hands. Brother, do away with the sinner."

Aonghus stood from his throne and grabbed Morgan. His teeth were bared and his eyes bloodshot with rage. He drew his sword from its scabbard; its blade glinted blue in the flickering light.

Blue. It was Kaltban that the war chief held – William's sword. Even though Bellaydin had recovered his cousin's body, his sword had been nowhere to be found. Now Bellaydin knew why. As Aonghus raised Kaltban above his head, Morgan screamed, dropping her knife to the ground.

Bellaydin took advantage of the confusion. He shuffled to one side and kicked one of the braziers, sending it tumbling to the ground. Immediately flames ran up the side of the tent. Cathan looked towards him, lunging with the sword, but Bellaydin fell backwards, knocking another of the braziers to the floor, filling the tent with smoke. Fumbling as flames shot up around him, he managed to cut his bonds on the knife, freeing his hands. Reaching out he grabbed Morgan's hand, pulling the girl with him, and they scuttled out from the burning tent.

There was pandemonium about them as soldiers and camp followers rushed about, attracted by the conflagration. He could hear the voice of Cathan Culainn rise above the din, shouting orders in Goriinchian. Others called out too, responding to the high priest's orders. Bellaydin knew it would not be long until he and Morgan were caught. They had to escape.

"We have to get out of here, quickly," Bellaydin said to her, and, ignoring the pain in his foot, he pulled her with him, stumbling through the camp.

Reasoning that assistance might be helpful, Bellaydin tried to lead Morgan back to Myfanwy. Unfortunately when they reached the cooking area, Myfanwy and her family were nowhere to be seen. Instead he almost ran into two burly Goriinchian soldiers. Their eyes widened with surprise upon seeing Bellaydin with Morgan. After a brief moment of confusion, the Goriinchians reached for their weapons. Desperate, Bellaydin lunged at a nearby table, picking up one of the pots and hurling it at the men. As his foes tried to shield themselves from the sudden assault, Bellaydin grabbed Morgan by the hand and ran in the opposite direction.

As they ran through the camp there were several more occasions when Bellaydin was sure that they would be caught, but the mayhem aided in making good their escape. Bellaydin could hear the Goriinchians behind him, calling out to their comrades with urgency. It was a great relief when Bellaydin and Morgan reached the edge of the camp, but that relief was quickly tempered by the grisly sight that awaited them.

Three tall wooden stakes had been erected on the edge of the Goriinchian camp and on each of these stakes was impaled a man. Each of the corpses hung limply, their body mangled and covered in blood, their faces contorted in soundless screams. Even with the state of the bodies, Bellaydin knew that these unfortunates were not Goriinchians. Their pale skin and distinctively shaped eyes spoke of distant lands. *Tarken.*

A memory flashed through Bellaydin's mind, a spark lit by the gory sight in front of him. He had seen another man's corpse in Aderilund so many months ago. The Eldara, what was his name? *Keras.* He remembered the twisted features of that poor wretch's face and felt his stomach convulse. Bellaydin vomited on the ground. Next to him, Morgan frowned, fresh tears coming to her eyes.

Bellaydin panted, disgust still evident in his tone. "The Tarkenese alchemists…why?"

"It is as my uncle said," Morgan said quietly. "Those who reject the Horned God are not worthy of life." Her eyes came to settle on Bellaydin. "It will be our fate, soon enough."

"Not if I can help it." Bellaydin dragged the two of them down a hill into a sheltered gully. He could hear voices, and booted footsteps through the forest as the Goriinchians searched for the fugitives. Bellaydin and Morgan took shelter in the roots of an ancient tree, waiting for the danger to past. As the flickering torchlight ebbed into the night, he turned to Morgan. "I think we lost them."

Morgan looked at Bellaydin, her face pale. "What have you done to me, Enparran?" she said quietly. "I can never return now."

Bellaydin was surprised by the girl's lack of gratitude. "What did I do? I just saved your life. Didn't you hear your uncle? He was going to have you killed, and by your own father, of all people."

Morgan fell to her knees. "It is all I deserve. I failed my father. I failed the Horned God."

"How can you say that? Don't you see what happened? Your uncle lied to you, he tricked you. Emparians didn't kill your father, your uncle did."

"He restored my father to life."

"You call that life? He doesn't speak, he stares ahead without any sort of reaction. He's lost his soul, he's little more than a puppet on your uncle's strings."

Morgan looked away, biting her lip without responding to him.

"Look at me. You know I'm speaking the truth."

"Then I am without family in this world, I am alone," Morgan said. She sat down on the grass, eyes downcast. Her chest was wracked with sobs.

Bellaydin sat down next to her and touched her reassuringly. "I know how you feel."

Between tears, Morgan scoffed. "How can you possibly know? Are you without family or loved ones?"

"Everyone I have ever loved is dead or far away from here. My sister, I will most likely never see again. My cousin died at Wishapton."

"And what of your parents?" she asked.

"Dead since I was a boy. I never got a chance to know them."

Morgan was silent for a moment, looking at him. "I am sorry to hear that. I didn't know. I lost my mother when I was a girl."

"Tell me about her." His voice was warm.

"I wouldn't know where to start."

"Just tell me what she was like."

"She was beautiful," Morgan began, wistfully.

"In that case, you take after her," Bellaydin said. He was immediately self-conscious for having said so.

"Much more than me. I have my father's nose. My mother was of the old blood, with Saldarri ties. She lived in the borderlands, where the Prophet-King's rule was less firm."

"What does that mean?"

Morgan frowned. "My uncle said she was half-pagan, and that her family were involved in deviance against the Horned God. He said they did wicked things."

"What do you remember of her?"

Morgan smiled briefly. "She used to dance."

"I thought that was frowned upon."

"It is, but it was the dancing that caught my father's eye. He saw her one day, and from that day he would never look at another woman."

There were tears in Morgan's eyes. "They loved each other, deeply. Too much, my uncle would say: such love should be kept for the Horned God alone."

Morgan's words about her mother's family reminded him of the Seeress, the old woman who Morgan had taken him to see the first time they had met, where he had experienced a startling vision of Goriinchia's past.

"The Seeress, she is your grandmother on your mother's side?"

"My mother's grandmother. She always favoured my mother, even after she married my father. I do not know why. My uncle did not approve of them being close, but my father let it be because it made my mother happy."

"He was a good man," Bellaydin said.

"Was," Morgan said. "So you do think him gone."

"Whatever has happened to your father, I don't think it was part of any divine plan."

Morgan hissed disapprovingly. "Blasphemy."

"Does it seem like something a loving god would do?"

Morgan didn't respond.

"Look, I have to get back to Goriinch Hill. Will you come with me?"

Morgan's eyes widened. "The hill? That is right in full sight of my uncle's army, why would you want to go there, Enparran?"

"My friends, the ones I came with. They are there and trapped. I know there's a way out. I need to let them know, otherwise, they will eventually die of thirst, starvation, or Goriinchian assault. We need to get back in and lead them out."

"From bad to worse," Morgan said. "But I have nowhere else to go, I suppose."

They headed off in the direction of Goriinch Hill. As they walked, Morgan looked at him out of the corner of her eye.

"I knew it wasn't you."

"What?"

"My father. I knew you would not have hurt him. Other Enparrans, yes, but not you."

"Why not?"

Morgan smiled. "I trust you."

"For someone who trusts me, you have an odd way of showing it. You handed me over to your uncle."

Morgan looked down. "Yes, I am sorry. I was desperate. I just wanted my father back. I should have known that my uncle was lying. He has never liked me. He used to call me the pagan whelp."

"Because of your mother?" Bellaydin asked. Morgan nodded.

"You're worth twenty of him."

The girl smiled. "Thank you."

Goriinch Hill was in sight, but Bellaydin and Morgan kept to the bushes nearby in an attempt to not be seen out in the open. Goriinchian scouts would be scouring the area for them, and Bellaydin didn't relish the chance of being captured again. He imagined that Cathan would brook no escapes from him this time, and both he and Morgan would pay with their lives if found. Avoiding that fate was their top priority.

Morgan looked at him. "So, how do we get to your friends, Enparran? Are we to walk in through the front door?"

"There's another entrance. A hidden way. The Goriinchians haven't

362

found it yet."

"You hope."

They came to a ravine, the very same one that Bellaydin had fallen down the previous day. He winced as the memory came back. His leg, while nowhere near as painful as it had been, still throbbed and ached with every step. A patchwork of bruises covered his thigh and calf.

Bellaydin felt his neck hairs stand up as if someone was watching him. He heard Morgan call out, and turned around just in time to see a bow pointed at him, complete with notched arrow and taut string. His heart lurched in his chest but then relaxed when he recognised the bearer of the bow.

"Talthas," Bellaydin breathed a sigh of relief. "What are you doing here?"

"Looking for you." The Eldara kept the arrow ready, looking at Morgan with suspicion. "Who is this?"

"A friend," said Bellaydin. "I'll explain later. What are you doing out here?"

Talthas, still keeping an eye on Morgan, lowered his bow. "Only Tancred returned after you two went looking for an exit," Talthas said. "He said he lost you in the tunnels and that there was no other entrance."

"There was. We found it, and he tried to get rid of me shortly afterwards by pushing me off the cliff."

"By the gods, are you alright?" Talthas asked. "Why would he want to do that?"

"Apparently for the honour of his family. If he hadn't told anyone we found the exit, he must intend for everyone to either starve within or be slaughtered by the Goriinchians. I just don't understand how that helps the Zalltors."

Talthas looked shocked and wiped his forehead with his hand. "And to think I thought spellweaver politics to be cut-throat. We need to get back. Can you walk?"

Bellaydin frowned. "That's what I've been doing until you arrived."

"Of course," said Talthas. "Quickly, this way, I found the path." The Eldara led them up a steep and rocky trail, barely wide enough for a single person to travel on. Bellaydin and Morgan, lacking the Eldara grace, struggled, but Talthas was there to support them whenever they were about to lose their step. They reached the top of the cliff just in time to see the great stone doors seal shut.

Talthas cried out in alarm. "Quickly, wedge them open with something."

But it was no use. The doors closed completely before they could do a thing to stop it. Worst of all, Bellaydin caught a glimpse of a familiar face glaring at him from behind the closing doors.

Tancred.

CHAPTER 22

The morning light shone through the cracks in the wall. Another day was dawning, another day trapped inside underground. If nothing changed it would soon become their tomb. Their supplies were running low, and though the Goriinchians had not even tried to breach the doors, it would not matter. Their enemies only had to wait it out.

Kahlaf arrived. His cold, reptilian eyes looked at Geoffrey.

"Talthas has not yet returned?" Geoffrey asked.

The Ahktarran shook his head.

"Damn," Geoffrey said, pounding his fists on the table. He looked back towards Kahlaf. "You look troubled, is there something else?"

"The Zalltor squire has also disappeared."

"Gone? Do you suppose he has gone to look for Bellaydin again? Does he feel guilty?"

Kahlaf shrugged. "I do not know. It was the other squires that noticed him missing."

Geoffrey shook his head and turned on to other matters. "What is our situation? Water?"

"A few brackish pools, quickly exhausted. They fill again at night from condensation, but the taste is awful. Still, it is enough, for now."

"And what of our food?"

"A day or so."

"Halve the rations."

"I already have," said Kahlaf.

"Then halve them again."

Kahlaf nodded.

Geoffrey sighed. "We may be just putting off the inevitable, but I still have confidence that the duke will arrive."

"If he still lives," Kahlaf said.

"Kahlaf, you and I know that even the gates of the Underworld themselves wouldn't stop Wulfric Highcrown."

Kahlaf looked like he was about to respond but then the floor shuddered beneath them. A deep rumbling sound echoed through the chamber. They heard the sound of ancient gears whirring into life and then watched with horror as the great doors in front of them started to swing open.

"The doors!" Kahlaf shouted.

Geoffrey rushed to the mechanism. He tried the lever. "It's jammed. Someone has meddled with it."

Kahlaf looked at the doors. "Clearly someone has found another method of operating them." He tried to close them, but they continued their steady opening and pushed back the Ahktarran, his clawed feet scraping the stone.

"What is going on?" Geoffrey demanded. "Men, I want those doors closed again."

Soldiers hurried towards the chamber and began to push against the opening doors with all their might. Kahlaf joined them, putting his whole seven-foot frame into the fray. Despite their efforts, they could not halt the doors, which continued their inexorable movement.

"We can't close it, Sir Geoffrey," Kahlaf said in between grunts. The doors stopped their movement, but only because they were opened fully. The Goriinchians now had a clear entrance into the chamber.

"This is not good," Geoffrey said, looking at the wide-open view to outside. "How long until the Goriinchians will notice, you think?"

"Not long, an hour at the most," Kahlaf said.

"We must prepare then. Men, I want barricades up as soon as we can. We need weapons at the ready, and whatever traps we can set up, do it. If they're going to come this way, we'll make them pay for it. Kahlaf, find the squires. Let them know what's going on. We want them to be ready."

"What of Talthas, and the two missing squires?"

"Let's hope they come back soon. And with good news. We could use it."

Soldiers went to work as ordered, and soon the chamber was a hive of activity.

"It won't be enough," the Ahktarran said, his voice stern. "The Goriinchians will slaughter us."

"I know," Geoffrey admitted. "But we have no other option. There is nowhere left to flee to."

"Well, then let us do this," Kahlaf said. "And let us make sure that they do not take our lives without a fight. I shall find the squires and inform them." He nodded to Geoffrey as he departed.

In the adjoining chamber, Kurth sat with Otto and Edgar, watching hurried soldiers rush about. "They're all certainly in a rush. What do you suppose is going on?" Kurth wondered aloud.

Kahlaf strode beside them, holding a bundle of weapons. "The situation has become more dire," the Ahktarran said brusquely. "And it seems the time has come to fight."

Edgar propped himself up against a wall. "What has Sir Drunkard done now? I should have known we'd end up trapped in a cave, our enemies at our throats."

"This is the inevitable outcome of the tragedy at the bridge," Kahlaf said. "Sir Geoffrey has done his best, but now we must face the inevitable. Death comes for us and one should not face it unprepared."

He unfurled the bundle and passed swords to each of the squires. Edgar laughed nervously. "You're not going to give Piggy a knife, are you?"

Kahlaf focused his eye on Edgar and the boy turned pale. "I am giving you one each. You will need to defend yourselves."

Otto's eyes widened as he looked over the blade. "We haven't had much practice."

"Your skill no longer matters. Each of us will be required to fight. Most of us will die. If we are to have any chance at all, we must fight together. As one. Remember, none of our lives are more precious than any others, regardless if you are third in line to the throne or the bastard child of a travelling vagabond."

"What of Tancred? Is he still missing?" Edgar asked.

"As are Bellaydin and the elf," Kurth said.

"Talthas was sent to find them, but he has still not returned. By now it may be too late. For their sakes, let us hope that they are somewhere far from here," said Kahlaf.

"Is there no escape?" Edgar asked. His voice trembled as he did.

The Ahktarran blinked. "Only in death."

***

Talthas pounded on the stone door. "Tancred! Let us in!"

Bellaydin pulled the Eldara's hand back. "It's no use. He didn't close this door by mistake. It was entirely intentional."

Talthas turned to Bellaydin. "You were right. This is, for all intents and purposes, murder. He means for us to all die."

Talthas felt across the door, scrutinising the carvings on it. "What are you looking for?" asked Bellaydin.

"There must be a way to open the door from this side," he said. After a few minutes of searching, Talthas gave up. "Mother Hydria save us," he said, "I can't find any way."

"We cannot stay here," Morgan said. "Can you hear that?"

Faintly, in the distance, was the sound of men shouting, overlayed with the drone of bagpipes.

"You're right," he said. "The Goriinchians are on the move."

"My uncle will be looking for us," Morgan said. "He won't be alone."

"We need to find shelter," Bellaydin said. "But the only place is inside the caves. Talthas, do you think we can get to the other gate?"

"There are a multitude of Goriinchian scouts there, Bellaydin," said Talthas. "It won't be easy."

"We have to," said Bellaydin. "We're the only ones who can get Geoffrey and the others out alive. We can open the other doors and lead everyone to the secret exit."

"What about Tancred?" Talthas said.

369

"We can deal with him. We'll expose him to the others."

"What about the girl?" Talthas asked. "I cannot expect that anyone there will be happy to see a Goriinchian. Odds are they'll think she's a spy."

"I can explain it to Sir Geoffrey. He will listen to me."

Talthas sighed. "Very well then." Slinging his bow over his back, Talthas took a quick look around and led them back down the ravine. "This here is the quickest route," he said, "but we must be cautious. The Goriinchians will have eyes everywhere."

Talthas' words proved prescient as shortly after, Bellaydin spied a Goriinchian scout, patrolling the perimeter around Goriinch Hill. Bellaydin pointed him out to Talthas, and within seconds the Eldara aimed his bow and loosed the arrow straight at the Goriinchian, leaving the scout to crumple to the ground wordlessly.

"You think there's any more of them about?" Bellaydin asked.

"I don't know."

Above them, grey clouds were beginning to gather. The skies let loose an ominous crackle of thunder. "A storm is coming," Talthas said. "If any of us still need the incentive to get moving." He stopped, wheeled about, and let off another arrow. There was a yell, and another scout fell from the cliffs, followed by some more shouts. The Goriinchians were almost upon them.

"Go, go," hissed Talthas, ushering the others past him. Bellaydin ran as quickly as his injured leg could manage, his hand gripping Morgan's tightly. His feet caught on a tree root as he ran, and he tumbled to the ground. Luckily, Morgan was there to help him, offering her hand. For a brief moment, their eyes met and Bellaydin found himself caught in them, like a fly in amber. Talthas' voice brought him back to reality.

"Come on, no time for contemplation, we're almost there."

When they reached the gates Bellaydin noticed, much to his surprise, that they were wide open.

"Be cautious," Talthas whispered. "It may be a Goriinchian trap."

Carefully he crept forward, motioning for Bellaydin and Morgan to remain close behind. It was dark inside the chamber, and someone had hastily constructed barricades. As Bellaydin came closer, he heard sudden shouts and Sir Geoffrey, Kahlaf, and other soldiers leapt from behind their shelters, swords drawn.

The surviving soldiers were so on edge that they shouted and immediately charged at the newcomers. Bellaydin was too surprised to act. Luckily Talthas quickly called out a greeting. "Sir Geoffrey!"

The sound of his name caused Sir Geoffrey and his companions to halt their charge. "Talthas! It's you... and Bela. Thank the gods," the knight exhaled in relief. "Where have you been?"

"Here and there, Sir Geoffrey," Talthas said. "We come with good and bad news."

"I don't know if I like the sound of that," Geoffrey said. He stiffened when he noticed Morgan. "Are you getting in the habit of bringing the enemy to us, Talthas?"

"This is Morgan," Bellaydin said. "I can vouch for her. She helped me save William."

Geoffrey's face softened at the mention of William's name. "I will take your word for it," he said. "Now, what's this news?"

"The good news is that we have found another way out of here," said Talthas. "One that doesn't lead us straight into a Goriinchian army."

Geoffrey let out deep breath. "Thank the gods. What is the bad news?"

"There is a traitor in our midst," said Talthas. "Squire Tancred."

"Him?" Geoffrey went pale. "Why would he betray us?"

"It's a Zalltor ploy," Bellaydin said. "He used Sir Dallen to kill the Duke of Emperor's Palace and I believe he wants us all to die. We found the other exit and he tried to kill me so I couldn't tell you."

"Why?" Geoffrey repeated.

"He wants the Duke of Oldharbour to fall from the queen's favour." All eyes turned to Kahlaf, who continued. "Do you notice how he is conveniently missing now that the Goriinchians are upon us? If he returns the sole survivor of what he hopes will be a massacre, the Duke of Oldharbour will be humiliated."

"While the Duke of Georgeton is put in charge of the armies." Geoffrey's voice dripped with both realisation and resignation. "The doors... he must have somehow opened them." His hand reached for the liquor flask on his belt, but then slackened.

Bellaydin sighed. "We found a control room for the doors at the other end. My guess is that he sabotaged them here so he can control them unopposed over there. He'll wait until you're all dead and then escape."

"You almost have to admire the deviousness of it all," Geoffrey chuckled half-heartedly. He closed his eyes for a moment before righting himself up. He clapped his hands, his eyes steely with determination. "Right! Talthas, take Bela to the other squires. I want you to get them out of here before the battle begins."

"What about you?" Talthas asked.

"Kahlaf and I will be here with any other volunteers. We'll hold them off for as long as we can."

Kahlaf nodded respectfully. "Sir Geoffrey, I am impressed. Most men in your position would have tried to flee to save their own lives."

Geoffrey shrugged and smiled. "What can I say, I feel a sudden bout of courage coming on." He had a quick drink, then handed his liquor flask to Bellaydin. "Take it. You'll need this more than I do."

Bellaydin accepted the gift and fastened the flask to his belt.

"Bellaydin, Morgan, come with me," Talthas said.

Bellaydin entered the adjoining chamber with Talthas and Morgan, where the other squires were shocked to see him.

"Bellaydin, you're alive," Kurth said. "Where have you been?"

"You wouldn't believe me if I told you," Bellaydin said. He looked at Edgar. "How's he doing?"

"He's fine," Otto said, "But he'll be limping for a while."

Edgar pulled himself up to look at Bellaydin in the face, "So, where have you been, Ap'Lydin? Out enjoying the scenery?" Edgar noticed Morgan. "By the looks of it, that's not all you've been enjoying."

Bellaydin ignored him. "This is Morgan," he said, placing a hand on the girl's arm. "Morgan, this is Squire Kurth, Squire Otto and Squire Edgar."

Morgan looked confused. "Why do all of them have the same name?"

Edgar gave a snide laugh. "It's not a name, you barbarian. It's a title. You know, like simpleton."

Morgan barely showed any expression when she replied, "You remind me of my uncle."

Edgar scoffed, having no idea that he had just been insulted.

"Morgan cannot return to her people," Bellaydin said. "And she saved my life more than once. I couldn't leave her there to die."

Otto nodded, smiling at Morgan. Kurth shook his head with some affection. "You always were too noble for your own good, Ap'Lydin."

"So, Ap'Lydin," said Edgar, "I take it you found this exit? Did you decide to take the scenic route after that?"

"Actually," said Bellaydin, "Tancred betrayed me and left me to die."

"What?" Kurth and Otto exclaimed in unison.

Edgar nearly exploded in rage. "You bloody liar, Ap'Lydin. Tancred is from one of the greatest and wealthiest families in the realm. He'd never do that."

Bellaydin related to the rest everything he had been through since he left with Tancred. He also recounted the discussion he had with Geoffrey and Kahlaf about Tancred's possible motives. Otto put a hand to his mouth, while Kurth listened wide-eyed.

Edgar was unconvinced. "Ridiculous, I don't believe a word of it. And neither does anyone else."

Kurth and Otto stared at Edgar. Their expressions said otherwise, and that was not lost on Edgar who seemed more furious by the minute. "You jealous idiots." He pointed at Kurth. "Your father is a faded drunk and lecher, and yours, Piggy, has his nose so far up the Duke of Georgeton's backside that you'd need a surgeon to separate them."

Bellaydin stood his ground. "Say what you will Edgar, I know what happened. I was there."

Edgar looked like he was about to respond, but Talthas quickly broke in. "We all leaving need to leave now, Sir Geoffrey's orders."

Edgar eased himself up, and limped to Bellaydin. "You'd best stop tapping into your friend Geoffrey's keg, Ap'Lydin." Turning to Talthas, Edgar asked. "Where do we go then?"

"Through the tunnels," Talthas said. "The exit is on the other side, near an ancient control chamber."

"We're all ready when you are," Kurth said.

"Good," said Talthas, "take the torch." He handed an unlit torch to Kurth who struck flint against steel to ignite the torch; they were ready to set off.

The journey was slow but steady. Only half the group – Morgan, Edgar and Otto – were unfamiliar with the route, but by sticking close to the others, they made it through in a fairly orderly fashion. For her part, Morgan clung to Bellaydin, who felt oddly comforted by having the girl so close. She was warm and smelled of the earth and tartan cloth.

They continued down the labyrinth of corridors, the torch casting shadows on the walls as they passed. For a moment Bellaydin thought he heard muffled voices, but the sounds ended as quickly as they had began. After a few more turns they reached the chamber with the crystal shards; this was where Bellaydin and Kurth had been separated from each other the day earlier. As they entered, Kurth warned, "Don't touch anything. And if you do, make sure you head for the right door."

"What's that sound?" said Otto.

"I hear it too," said Bellaydin. "Shouting, from back in the main chamber."

Talthas stopped to listen. "The Goriinchians have arrived. The battle has begun. We must move quickly."

"What about Geoffrey and Kahlaf?" Bellaydin asked.

"Let us hope that they survive until help arrives."

They continued gloomily, with Bellaydin trying to put out the desperate shrieks and noise of the battle taking place behind them. Talthas guarded the rear, his bow drawn and ready. Bellaydin knew they must keep moving, or Geoffrey and Kahlaf's sacrifice would be for nought. The squires jostled against each other, flinching at every shadow and half-heard sound they encountered.

In the torchlight Bellaydin could see the chalk marks that he had left on his previous journey through these tunnels. Even with this guide, however, they moved agonisingly slowly through the twisting corridors. He heard cries from behind him. *Geoffrey*. It was followed by a guttural roar. *Kahlaf*.

He had to resist the urge to turn around, to run back to his friends who were fighting for their lives. He knew that if he survived, it would be solely due to the battle behind him. He had to respect their sacrifice.

"I see light," said Kurth. "Is this it?"

They had reached the arch that marked the entrance to the Magister's Chambers. Bellaydin nodded to the others and stepped into the room, but there was someone was already there.

"Tancred," Bellaydin said.

Tancred, hunched over the table in the centre of the room, looked up at the newcomers, evident shock on his face. He slammed a palm down on the table, opening the rear doors, and made for outside as quickly as he could.

"Don't let him get away," Talthas said. As Bellaydin gave chase, Talthas nocked an arrow in his bow.

An incensed Edgar jumped in front of him and tried to wrest the bow from the Eldara's gasp. "What are you doing, you mad elf? You can't murder him because of some lies."

Talthas tried to bat Edgar aside. "Move, he's getting away."

"No!"

Talthas's fist slammed into Edgar, sending him sprawling to the floor, but by then, Tancred had escaped.

"You hit me," Edgar said, his eyes bulging.

"You were in the way."

"We can still catch him, can't we?" Otto asked.

"I intend to," said Talthas. "Come on."

Outside it was pouring down rain, and a flash of lightning illuminated the dark sky. The group had only just stepped out when they found themselves face to face with a wall of steel. Heavily armed Goriinchians surrounded them, spears at the ready. Tancred stood nearby, a superior smile on his face. Talthas raised his bow, but the group was surrounded by a dozen Saldarri bowmen who stood ready to loose an arrow at a moment's notice. Grimly, the Eldara lowered his bow.

"It looks like our secret exit has become decidedly less secret," said Kurth.

"Believe us now, Edgar?" said Bellaydin.

From the assembled Goriinchians came a familiar voice. "Heir of Lydin," Cathan said, stepping forward, "I could have told you that escape was futile. I will present you to the Prophet-King, intact or not." Cathan was wearing full religious regalia, including armour and a fearsome ceremonial horned helmet. He saw Morgan and frowned. "I see the whore is with you as well. She will be punished, as the Horned God wills."

Morgan's eyes flashed with rage at Cathan, which only further amused him,

"Tancred, what is this?" Edgar said. His voice sounded softer and more vulnerable than Bellaydin had ever heard it.

The squire from Georgeton looked upon Edgar with contempt in his eyes. "I will tell them to make your death quick, Edgar. You have earned that."

Cathan chuckled. "Are you giving orders to us, Enparran? We are the chosen slaves of the Horned God. What are you, boy?"

Tancred spoke up. "Do you forget, Goriinchian? I am the boy who is going to pay you a great deal of coin, just as you asked."

Cathan smiled and turned to one of the soldiers nearby, and laughed.

"That's right," Tancred said to the others, "if nothing else these barbarians understand gold. Now, down the path to the ridge below. It is not safe near the cliff, as Bellaydin well knows."

The Goriinchians moved forward as one, pushing Bellaydin and the others down the path, spears at their back. They were force-marched for a few minutes, until the Goriinchian high priest called a halt. Cathan looked towards his brother Aonghus, who loomed beside him, his face impassive and Kaltban tightly in his grip. "It is time then, brother, do it."

Tancred nodded. "When they are all dead, the gold is yours. I promise."

Cathan turned to him. "Boy, I am the Horned God's slave. What need I of infidel gold?" He turned to Aonghus. "Kill him first."

"What?" said Tancred. His eyes went wide and he stepped back. Two Goriinchians grabbed him by his arms. "Let me go, I've promised you gold - all the gold you could ever want!"

Cathan laughed. "Who said it was your gold we wanted?"

Tancred struggled in vain. "No-I mean – no – stop!"

Aonghus swung the sword. Bellaydin averted his eyes. When he opened them, Tancred's head was rolling past his feet.

"Rewarded as a traitor deserves," Cathan said. "Now, Aonghus, the others."

Just as Cathan gave the order, they all heard the long bellow of a signal horn.

"It's Emparian," said Otto to his companions.

"The Duke of Oldharbour's forces," said Kurth. "About time."

Cathan looked alarmed. "Enparran reinforcements, but how?" As the high priest stammered, the Goriinchian soldiers around him looked uneasy. They began to mutter amongst themselves. Cathan turned around to reprimand them, only for the muttering to turn into shouts. Some of the soldiers began to back down, and flee down the hill. Aonghus stood by, his sword still stained with Tancred's blood. The Goriinchian war chief did not move, only continued to stare at Bellaydin and the others.

With a roar, two horseman burst from the forest below, galloping up the ridge, swords held aloft. Shouting in Emparian, they engaged the distracted Goriinchians, their blades making quick work of two before the others regrouped. One of Cathan's soldiers thrust forward with his spear, catching one of the horses in its side while another Goriinchian was trampled underfoot by the other horseman.

"Now is our chance, squires," said Talthas. "Flee, I will cover your escape."

Talthas let off half a dozen arrows in quick succession. One hit Cathan in the shoulder, causing the high priest to double over in pain. The others went straight into Aonghus. The war chief did not even blink, showing no pain even after he was stuck full of arrows. He raised his sword and hurled himself at the Eldara.

Bellaydin did not wait to see what might happen. Instead, he and Morgan ran down the hill with the other squires. In the dark and claustrophobic forest, they were quickly separated, and the heavy rain had turned the ground to mud. At moments, he almost found himself letting go of Morgan's hand as they ran, but he managed to hold on tight. Behind him, he heard shouts in Goriinchian and Cathan's voice coming in over the din.

"They are chasing us, Enparran," Morgan warned. "It is not your friends they want."

"I know," Bellaydin said. He looked about, breathing in short ragged gasps. "I hear water, where are we?"

"Not far from the edge of the cliff here, the river runs below," Morgan said. "It is a long drop. We need to be careful."

A Goriinchian warrior burst through the trees, charging towards him, but the man was already bleeding from arrow wounds and Bellaydin could dodge his blows before the man collapsed on the ground, his blood pooling about him.

"Take his weapon, and whatever else you can use," Morgan said. "We need it more than he does."

Knowing it was no time to be squeamish Bellaydin searched the corpse for anything he could use, but found nothing but a few personal effects. Bellaydin took the man's sword and left the rest.

"Listen," Morgan said, gripping Bellaydin's hand.

"What?" Bellaydin asked. He wheeled about, listening for whatever he could. Despite the heavy rain he could hear breathing nearby.

"Talthas is that you?" he called out. Silence.

"Kurth? Otto? Edgar?" There was still no response.

Bellaydin started to sweat. He heard squelching and turned around. "Show yourself."

The trees parted as Aonghus Culainn stepped forward, wheezing heavily. The war chief was a horrific sight. Countless arrows were stuck in his body and his eyes were blank white, but still, he lived. Bellaydin looked on with horror. *What sorcery was this that Cathan had wrought, to turn his brother into this?*

Morgan's eyes were red and rimmed with tears. "Father, please..."

Aonghus' eyes narrowed, and his face contorted into a snarl. He swung towards them, all savage fury and bloodthirsty rage. Bellaydin interposed himself between Morgan and her father, and he swung up his own blade, clashing with Kaltban. As the two weapons clashed flakes of blue frost spun from Kaltban.

"Morgan," Bellaydin panted, "go, save yourself."

Aonghus growled, kicking Bellaydin in the chest, and then picking him up by the collar of his tunic. The Goriinchian's strength was unnatural as he lifted Bellaydin with ease, bringing him high enough so that his white eyes were looking into Bellaydin's own. Bellaydin could feel the war chief's breath on his face; There was no warmth in it. As Bellaydin struggled in Aonghus' grip he heard the words.

"Help me." It was barely more than a whisper and Aonghus' lips hardly moved. Bellaydin felt sure he had imagined it in a delirium, but then he was quickly disproven.

"HELP ME," Aonghus roared through clenched teeth. His face seemed to plead with Bellaydin.

Before Bellaydin could react the war chief's expression changed, and with a howl he tossed Bellaydin aside, turning around to face Morgan. As Bellaydin tumbled, bruised and sore into the bushes, Aonghus strode towards his daughter, a vicious look in his eyes. Morgan stumbled backwards, drawing her knife from her belt. She held it in front of her face, trying to ward off her father but the blade looked tiny and insignificant compared to the glittering Kaltban. He lunged for Morgan, who stabbed him with the knife. Although she pierced the flesh of his arms over and over, Aonghus did not even flinch. He grabbed Morgan by her throat and lifted her off the ground. Her knife clattered to the ground, tumbling out of reach.

Bellaydin looked around him, and seeing nothing better he grabbed a rock, and hurled it at Aonghus' head. The war chief shook it off, so Bellaydin threw more, one after the other until the Goriinchian turned from Morgan, and looked back in Bellaydin's direction. He dropped Morgan to the ground, and then, swinging Kaltban for emphasis, stormed back towards Bellaydin.

"Enparran, no," Morgan screamed.

"It's alright, Morgan," Bellaydin said, standing up. "I have it worked out. He has to leave me alive."

Bellaydin's last word trailed off as the pommel of Kaltban connected with Bellaydin's stomach, knocking the wind from him. As Bellaydin staggered about stunned, the war chief swung again, and sliced through Bellaydin's tunic, exposing the mail below. The Eldara-made steel held, sending blue sparks flying in an arc above Aonghus' head. Bellaydin returned the favour, thrusting his sword forward into Aonghus' side, but it did little to slow him, and the war chief once again threw Bellaydin aside, this time leaving him perilously close to tumbling from the cliff. Bellaydin grabbed on to a rock to steady himself, as Aonghus once again lurched towards Morgan with murderous attempt. The girl backed away, her cheeks stained with tears.

"Father, please...Father, no..." Morgan pleaded with Aonghus in between sobs and gasps. Bellaydin looked up at Aonghus and thought he could see tears in the war chief's eyes as well.

Resolve gripped Bellaydin and he rose to his feet, sword in hand. "Aonghus! I am the Heir of Lydin. Face me!"

That seemed to stop the war chief in his tracks. Aonghus swung around, Kaltban carving a blue arc through the air as he threw himself into battle with the young squire. Bellaydin blocked the blow, and Aonghus drew back and swung a second time. Again and again, their swords clashed, with Aonghus pushing Bellaydin backwards with every thrust. One swing hit Bellaydin particularly savagely on the thigh, staggering him backwards. It was sheer luck that kept the blow from sending him sprawling into the mud. A final swing sent him teetering on the edge of the cliff. He had run out of space to retreat.

Aonghus raised the blade threateningly and seemed about to bring it down.. Bellaydin flinched and faced away, but when no blow came, he looked at his assailant. From the back of Aonghus' neck protruded Morgan's blade. The girl herself stood behind her father, breathing heavily.

Morgan's latest blow, like those before, had no more than a momentary effect on Aonghus, but a moment was all Bellaydin needed. He twisted his body around, away from the cliff, and then swung upwards with his own sword, slicing through the war chief's wrist, and sending his sword arm, Kaltban and all, tumbling down the cliff to the river below.

The war chief let out a piteous howl and dropped to his knees. Bellaydin thrust forward with his blade, pushing it through the war chief's chest. Aonghus collapsed to the ground. As he did, a tiny bronze sphere dropped from his mouth, disappearing into the undergrowth. As it did, the white dissolved from his eyes, and for the first time in a long time, Aonghus looked at the world with his own face.

"Morgan..." Aonghus rasped through cracked lips. Blood trickled from his mouth.

"Father," Morgan cried in despair. She ran towards him, kneeling close.

His voice was soft. Scarcely more than a whisper. "Morgan...I...I'm sorry." His eyelids closed and his head went slack.

Morgan burst into tears and threw herself on her father's corpse. Bellaydin dragged himself up. Every part of him was aching, and he was covered in a multitude of cuts and grazes.

"Morgan, I'm...I'm sorry. I had no choice."

The girl wiped a tear away and nodded. "I know. I know you didn't. At least now he is at peace."

Bellaydin knelt next to her. "Is there anything I can do?"

She sniffed and looked at him. Her bright blue eyes were wet with tears. "Yes. Hold me Bellaydin, would you?"

He did.

CHAPTER 23

The rain eased.

Bellaydin and Morgan held each other tightly, the warmth of their bodies shielding each other from the biting wind. For some time they remained on edge, expecting Goriinchian soldiers to find them, but the sounds of men's voices in the distance faded away. A tranquil peace descended on the glade. It seemed that the rest of Cathan's soldiers had gone elsewhere.

Once they were sure that they were safe, they turned to the matter of what to do with the remains of Aonghus Culainn, Morgan's father. The Goriinchians did not burn their dead as did the Emparians, rather they preferred to entomb them in the ground. Bellaydin briefly wondered if he should suggest something but before he could, Morgan began to collect stones and place them over her father's corpse. Bellaydin followed her lead without prompting, and together they constructed a simple cairn.

Bellaydin broke the silence. "Do you want to say something? Ask for the Horned God's blessing?"

"That is usually our way," Morgan said. "But I don't know, somehow invoking the Horned God's name... it just feels wrong."

"Say something else then," Bellaydin said.

Morgan looked up at him. "What?"

Bellaydin shrugged. "He's your father. Say something from your heart. Use your own words, not those belonging to any god."

Morgan said a few sentences in Goriinchians over her father's remains, holding tightly on to Bellaydin's hand as she did. Afterwards, Bellaydin attempted to sit down.

"Ah," he said, grunting.

"Are you alright?"

"I don't know," he said, reaching his hand just below his tunic. When he withdrew his hand it was covered with blood. "I must be more badly wounded than I thought."

Morgan looked at him with concern. "Show me," she said.

"It's my thigh, I think," Bellaydin said.

Morgan gave him a look. "Show me."

Blushing, Bellaydin removed his leggings, showing Morgan his thigh. She looked over the wound carefully. "It will need to be stitched."

She reached into her pouch, pulling out a needle and some thread. She pointed to the liquor. "I will need that. We must clean the needle first." She dipped it in the liquor, keeping it there for a while, before bringing it forth. Then she took the task, carefully sewing up his wound.

Bellaydin looked straight at Morgan. "Did you expect this was how our day would end?"

She smiled at him, letting out a small chuckle.

Bellaydin raised an eyebrow. "What's so funny?"

"I didn't think I would be touching your bare flesh, Bellaydin."

Bellaydin blushed, and Morgan flashed him a quick smile. He winced as Morgan pulled the thread through the wound. He noticed Morgan glance at him.

"I'm fine," he said. "Don't worry."

Morgan smiled. "There, done." She bit off the end of the thread, as she did so she noticed him staring at her.

"What?" she asked.

"It's just I noticed you've stopped calling me Enparran and started calling me by my name."

She avoided his gaze. "I haven't noticed," she said.

He thought for a moment. "What are you going to do when we leave here? You can't go back to your uncle."

"He will damn me as a traitor and an apostate. He will blame my father's death on me. I don't think I could ever go back."

"Where would you go then?"

She thought for a moment. "I can go to my grandmother's. She will protect me. I am the last of her kin. My uncle would not dare interfere, not even the Prophet-King himself would."

"There are other alternatives," Bellaydin said. His voice was tentative.

"Such as?"

"You could come with me."

Morgan chuckled. "Where to? The land of the Enparrans?"

"Yes, Emparia," Bellaydin said. "What's so funny about that?"

"I hardly think the Enparrans would welcome me."

"I would vouch for you," Bellaydin said. "And there are many who would believe me. My cousin is the Countess of Genio. I am friends with the Dukes of Oldharbour and Alariat. I would make sure that it was a safe place for you. No one would hurt you ever again."

"And what then," Morgan said. "Would I become your lady?"

Bellaydin flushed. "If you'd like."

She smiled faintly. "There are worse things I suppose."

"I wouldn't force you to do anything you didn't want. You've had enough of that."

"You are sweet to me. I never thought that I would say that to an infidel."

"We aren't all irredeemably evil," he teased her gently. Just he said that he felt dizzy, and his vision swam.

"Are you alright?" Morgan asked.

He clutched his head, "I feel a bit faint."

Morgan frowned. "You have lost quite a bit of blood. Lie your head down here." She sat down next to him and carefully laid him down in the grass, propping his head up on her lap.

"Don't try to take advantage of me in this weakened state now," Bellaydin chuckled weakly.

"I won't if you stop trying to tempt me with your heathen ways," Morgan said, her voice wafting into a whisper to Bellaydin.

Soon Bellaydin felt his eyes close and he drifted into a dreamless sleep.

***

He awoke abruptly to the sound of shouts.

"There he is, I see him," came a voice.

Bellaydin opened his eyes. He was alone in the clearing. Morgan was gone. There was nothing but the faint smell of tartan cloth. The cairn for her father was the only other evidence that she had ever been there.

The voices came closer, and soon others were upon him.

"Bellaydin," said Kurth, pushing his way through the leaves. "Thank the gods."

"Kurth." Bellaydin was relieved to see the squire. He noticed the two figures emerging behind Kurth. "Otto, Edgar, how did you find me?"

"It wasn't easy," said Kurth. "We've been looking for hours. We were all separated."

Edgar spotted the cairn, "What is that?"

"It's...uh...it's the remains of the war chief, Aonghus Culainn."

"You killed the war chief?" Kurth raised his voice in excitement.

"I had some help," Bellaydin looked around. *Where is she?*

"The Goriinchian girl?" Edgar said. "Where did she go?"

"I don't know," he said.

"We have to go," said Otto. "Talthas is in danger."

Bellaydin stood up. "Talthas? What's happened?"

"Come quickly," said Otto. "And see for yourself."

Bellaydin briefly considered staying put in the hope Morgan would return, but the other squire had started to leave and Otto's tone had sounded urgent. The thought of Talthas in peril pushed him forward.

The other squires led Bellaydin to a nearby glade where on a makeshift stretcher, was Talthas. Blood covered his face, and there were multiple wounds on his body. The rise and fall of his chest indicated he was still alive, but with the extent of his injuries, it was hard to tell if he would be for much longer.

"He endured this so that we could escape," Bellaydin said. "We can't let him die."

Edgar sighed. "What do you expect Ap'Lydin? Those in the caves have already been slaughtered, and we will surely be next, especially if the Goriinchians discover that you've murdered their war chief."

"I think they're gone," said Bellaydin. "For the moment at least. But I don't know why."

"We did hear horns earlier," said Kurth. "There must be Emparians nearby. Reinforcements, surely."

Edgar scoffed. "Just as likely more Goriinchians."

"No, they announce themselves with bagpipes," Bellaydin said. "You hear them from miles away."

"What do we do then?" said Kurth, looking at Talthas. "Should we move him?"

Otto stood up. "No. Some of you will have to go fetch help. He's stable at the moment, but I wouldn't want to try to make him walk."

Kurth nodded. "Let's go, Ap'Lydin."

"You must be joking," Edgar exclaimed. "I'm not staying here with Piggy."

"Yes you are," said Kurth, as he prepared to leave.

"I'll be damned if I – "

"Listen here, you shit. You're staying because you're an ass. I don't like you and you're of no use to us at all. I'm not making *you* stay with Piggy. I'm making *Piggy* stay with you because I wouldn't trust you to watch over a dead mouse, let alone Talthas. You'd best shut up, stay put and do as he says."

Kurth turned to nod at Otto, who was trying not to smile. Edgar's eyes bulged but he didn't say anything.

"We'll be back once we find help," Bellaydin said to Otto.

Neither of the squires looked back at Edgar as they left him behind, but Bellaydin could not help giving Kurth a pat on the back.

They walked for about fifteen minutes, and once they were about a half mile or so from the glade, the ground below them began to incline. Another half a mile after that they arrived at Goriinch Hill. Bellaydin saw corpse after corpse, mostly Goriinchians but also a few Emparians wearing the livery of the House of Ap'Lydin. *They must have escaped the caves.* Bellaydin's thoughts moved to his friends. *Are Kahlaf and Geoffrey alive, or did they fight to the death?* His stomach twisted with anxiety.

They emerged back on top of the hill. The door to the caves was there, still open, but it was quiet. Bellaydin hesitated for a second, then took a step forward.

"Do we go in?"

Kurth grabbed his arm. "You don't know what might be waiting inside."

Bellaydin pulled Kurth's hand off. "Talthas need help. Do you have a better idea?"

Kurth was about to respond when he caught sight of something. "Yes, in fact, I do. Look over there." Kurth pointed towards the horizon. A large mass of soldiers was marching in formation no more than a mile away at most. They carried banners depicting the twisted serpent of House Highcrown.

"The army of Oldharbour," Bellaydin said. "The duke has finally arrived."

Kurth squinted. "And it looks like the Goriinchians don't quite know what's about to hit them."

The bulk of the Goriinchian army was still camped within walking distance from the caves. Only the vanguard had been sent in for the assault. It seemed the Culainns had been holding troops in reserve.

Kurth seemed to read Bellaydin's mind. "I think the Goriinchians intended to flush out Geoffrey's forces and then use their rested troops to run them down in a rout."

"You think so?"

"Well, what I think now is that they've lost their chance. Pity...for them." He sat down on the edge of the cliff.

"Shall we watch?"

Smiling, Bellaydin sat down beside him. He uncorked Geoffrey's flask and passed it to Kurth.

"Here, have some."

Kurth raised the bottle in a toast. "To our continuing good health. We live to fight another day."

Bellaydin nodded. As he did, his mind drifted to Morgan. *Was she safe with her grandmother, the Seeress? Why didn't she stay with him?* Bellaydin hoped she was safe, even if it meant she had abandoned him. He was sure she must have had good reason. His heart ached as he thought of her. Twice she had saved his own life, at great risk to her own. She had lost her father, then her home. *All because of me.*

As they passed the bottle between each other the battle unfolded below. It was short, messy and above all, brutal. The Goriinchians had not expected a new army to appear on their flank and the Emparians caught them by surprise. While the Goriinchian archers struggled to come into formation, the Emparian crossbowmen unleashed a hail of bolts. The Goriinchian lines broke, and soon things descended into mayhem. The Goriinchians attempted to flee; at the same time, their compatriots poured out of the caves, alerted to the battle outside. The Emparian cavalry ran down the unruly mass of people without effort and in a matter of hours it was all over. The Goriinchian lines broke again and they fled into the setting sun.

"It looks to be finished," Bellaydin said, draining the last of the bottle. In the approaching twilight he could see the faint outlines of the four moons. "Let's go down and get help for Talthas."

By the time they had descended from the hill the Emparian army had moved in its attempt to pursue the Goriinchians. However, the enemy lines had disintegrated to such an extent that it was impossible to round up all the Goriinchians at once. Most escaped in any direction they could, while a few stalwart ones stood their ground and fought the Emparians to the death.

As the standards of House Highcrown came into view, a bulky knight with a shaved head and hazel eyes noticed Bellaydin and Kurth's arrival. He held out his sword warily.

"Halt, who goes there?"

Bellaydin and Kurth raised their arms as quickly as they could. "Squire Bellaydin Ap'Lydin and Squire Kurth Bauer."

The knight looked from one squire to the other. A flicker of scepticism seemed to register in his face, but then, he relaxed, lowering his sword. "Two of the missing squires, eh? You are supposed to be dead."

Kurth smiled. "I hope we haven't disappointed anyone."

"Hardly. I'm Sir Hal Borrowdale. His Grace will be pleased to see you."

"We are anxious to meet him, but first we need your help. Two of our fellow squires are protecting another of our comrades. He is gravely wounded and needs urgent attention."

"I'll see what can be done," said Sir Hal. He motioned to some of his soldiers, who nodded in assent. "They will go fetch the healers. One of you will need to accompany them, show them where your comrades are."

"I'll go," Kurth said.

Bellaydin knew that while Kurth was concerned for Talthas' health, the gesture hadn't been completely altruistic. The Duke of Oldharbour was known for his caustic ways, and Kurth may have wanted to avoid meeting him in person. Indeed, the squire seemed to be positively relieved as he went with the other soldiers to seek the healer, leaving Bellaydin alone with the rather gruff Sir Hal.

"Come then, Squire," the knight said.

"What of the Goriinchians?"

Sir Hal looked scornful. "Let them run. My men will take care of them."

The knight took Bellaydin into the ranks of the army, past the foot soldiers and archers emblazoned with the symbol of House Highcrown to the very centre of the force where the duke and his bodyguard were.

"Ap'Lydin," Wulfric acknowledged Bellaydin. The duke was dressed the same as he had been when they had first left Emperor's Palace, if a little dirtier. He did not seem to be shocked by Bellaydin's appearance, which rather puzzled Bellaydin.

"You aren't surprised I survived?"

The duke shifted in the saddle of his horse. "Nothing surprises me these days," he said. "What of the other squires?"

"One of us didn't make it, Your Grace. Tancred."

"The Zalltor squire," Wulfric said. He ran his tongue over his teeth. "That may prove to make things difficult. His grandfather will demand someone takes responsibility for it."

"His grandfather may have other matters on his mind," Bellaydin said. "Tancred betrayed us, and other members of his family may have helped him plan it."

Wulfric looked sceptical. "Unexpected. That complicates matters. I will need to speak to Sir Geoffrey to hear more. Does he live? And what of Kahlaf?"

"Last time I saw them they were expecting to have a last stand in the caves under Goriinch Hill," Bellaydin said.

"The caves, you say?"

"Yes, there's a series of-"

"I know all about that, squire, thank you. I just wonder what possessed them to take cover there."

"It was a trap, Your Grace," Bellaydin said. "The battlefield, the Goriinchian army, the bridge; it was all planned by the Zalltors."

"That much seems plain to all of us now, thank you squire," Wulfric said. "But we must complete what we have started. The brothers Culainn will be taken into custody. We can cripple the Goriinchian war effort, and force Ygarak to become personally involved."

"The war chief is dead, Your Grace," Bellaydin said.

Wulfric narrowed his eyes. "Oh, is he? And how do you come to know this?"

"I-"

"Killed himself yourself, did you?" Wulfric smirked. "If you have, you will have done us all a great favour. Now all that remains is to capture his brother, Ygarak's chief lickspittle."

"He was near Goriinch Hill when I last saw him."

"He would be fleeing south again by now. Sir Hal, take a few of your comrades. Ride to the south and intercept the high priest. He will be brought back to Emperor's Palace in chains. See it done."

"Yes, Your Grace," said Sir Hal. He signalled to some other knights, and they rode off without delay.

Wulfric pulled on his reins. "Now, let us see if Sir Geoffrey and Kahlaf live, or if this is a mission to retrieve corpses. Climb on."

Bellaydin pulled himself onto the back of the duke's horse. Once Bellaydin was secure behind him the duke pushed his horse forward across the battlefield towards Goriinch Hill. The Goriinchians who had surrounded it had mostly melted away, but a few stragglers remain. One of them challenged the duke, but after Wulfric dispatched the Goriinchian with a single swipe of his sword, the other Goriinchians gave Bellaydin and the duke wide berth. As they arrived at the main entrance to the Goriinch Hill caves, the duke dismounted, helping Bellaydin to the ground.

"Steel yourself, squire," Wulfric said. "You need to be prepared for whatever might face us in there."

Bodies were everywhere – both Goriinchian and Emparian. Trails of blood and gore weaved through the heavy doors, open at their hinges, into the cavern. As Bellaydin entered the cave he couldn't see a thing, but his eyes slowly adjusted to the gloom. Inside, between debris and scorched earth, was a sight of even more carnage, with bodies stacked sometimes three or four high. The stench of blood and sweat permeated the air. Bellaydin found it difficult to believe that anyone could still live in a place that smelled so much like death. Yet he thought he heard movement. Judging by his expression, so did the duke.

Wulfric stepped forward warily. "Are there any survivors? Identify yourselves."

In the darkness, Bellaydin heard hushed muttering, shortly before a small group of soldiers emerged from behind the rubble, their weapons at the ready.

"Easy, boys," said a familiar voice. "Your Grace, I see you've finally decided to join us. I was beginning to worry that you'd miss out on all the fun.

"Sir Geoffrey Keslin," Wulfric said. "I see despite all the setbacks, you have managed to survive. Well done." Uncharacteristically, Wulfric's praise seemed genuine.

"Master," said Kahlaf, dragging himself from the ground and kneeling before the duke.

"Rise, Kahlaf," Wulfric said, "you have acquitted yourself well. There is no need for apologies. You have held off the entire Goriinchian force long enough for my own to arrive. The day is won."

Geoffrey looked about. "Yes, but at great cost."

Wulfric eyed the knight coldly. "There are always casualties in war, Sir Geoffrey, and in many cases, the survivors envy the dead."

Sir Geoffrey rubbed his arm. "Oh trust me, that isn't the case here."

Sir Wulfric. "You may feel differently. There have been more losses. Your father, for one."

"My father is dead?" His voice was quieter than Bellaydin had ever heard it.

Wulfric nodded. "We united with the remnants of his forces before we arrived here. He was ambushed by Goriinchian warriors near the border. His men said he died as he wished, sword in his hand, cutting down the enemy."

"Yes," Geoffrey said with a tone of wistfulness. "That sounds about right."

"You are now Baron Drakeford, Sir Geoffrey," Wulfric's tone turned cold. "Think on your responsibilities."

As Wulfric and Kahlaf went off to speak privately, Bellaydin approached Geoffrey. "I'm sorry for your loss, Geoffrey. It must be difficult, especially after what you've been through."

"You'd be surprised, Bela," the knight said. "I haven't seen my father for ten years, not since my mother died. He's little more than a stranger to me. Still it seems strange to finally hear that he's gone. Even stranger to think that I'm now head of my House." He gave Bellaydin a smile. "We're both orphans now. How about that?

Wulfric returned, Kahlaf at his side. The duke looked Geoffrey up and down, a smile on his face. He gave him a brief nod, and then motioned to the corpses nearby. "Let us do our due by the dead."

Bellaydin lent a hand as Wulfric, Geoffrey, Kahlaf and the surviving soldiers collected the bodies of the dead. They stacked them in two piles, one Emparian and the other Goriinchians, and once the task was done Bellaydin was passed a blazing torch.

"Bela, it is time," Sir Geoffrey said.

Bellaydin brought the torch close to the pile and set each alight in turn. As he watched the piles of corpses erupt into flames a thought flashed through his head – the Goriinchians did not like cremation. He thought better about bringing it up. After such a brutal battle it was unlikely anyone cared what funeral methods their enemies preferred.

"I have made camp nearby, Sir Geoffrey," Wulfric said. "I believe there has been enough exertion for the day. We will rest overnight and then return to the north, now that the Goriinchians have been dealt with here."

"What of the commanders?" Geoffrey asked. "The brothers Culainn."

Wulfric glanced towards Bellaydin. "I have been reliably informed that Warchief Aonghus Culainn is dead and his cowardly brother, High Priest Cathan, has fled the battlefield. Sir Hal and a detachment of his most trusted men are in pursuit of the priest. They will catch him and return him to Oldharbour, most likely before we ourselves arrive there."

Geoffrey stroked his beard. "I didn't see them in the battle. Odd..."

"Why is that odd?" Bellaydin asked.

"Well, it's almost as if they had somewhere more important to be."

Geoffrey chuckled. "I don't know, I'm probably seeing mysteries where there aren't any. Doesn't pay to overanalyse things, especially when it comes to Goriinchians."

"Wise words, Sir Geoffrey," Wulfric said. "Come, we have dallied long enough here."

With the surviving men of Geoffrey's force following them and the duke leading away, the small group filed out of the caves, and back into the valley below, on their way to the army camp.

***

Some distance away Kurth led the healer towards the wounded Talthas. As he approached, however, he could tell something was not right. A Goriinchian soldier, obviously cut off from the main group, was battling with Edgar. Though the de Morcor squire was skilled, his injury and general state were taking their toll, and the Goriinchian battered the boy into submission, knocking him to the ground.

"Stay here," said Kurth to the healer, before drawing his sword to jump into the fray. The Goriinchian noticed him immediately and forced him back with a savage berserker rage.

Edgar stood up, and charged, sword in hand, back into the melee. The Goriinchian kicked Kurth in the chest, sending him sprawling to the ground and turned to challenge Edgar again. Three quick fists to the face felled the de Morcor squire and the Goriinchian raised his blade for the killing blow.

Out from seemingly nowhere, Otto barrelled into the Goriinchian, knocking him to the ground. Gripping his blade tightly, Otto stabbed it into the Goriinchian's chest repeatedly. As the dead man's blood pooled on the ground, Otto collapsed to the ground panting.

"Otto," Kurth said. "That was...outstanding."

The Mainstream squire nodded, exhausted.

"What happened?" Edgar said, raising his head from the ground. He was still groggy from the blows to the head.

"Otto here just saved your life."

Edgar looked at Otto, mouth open, and then mumbled something.

Kurt cupped a hand to his ear. "What's that Edgar? I don't think anyone heard you." Kurth looked at him expectantly and a tiny shy smile spread across Edgar's face.

"Thank you, Otto."

Otto looked at Edgar with a sense of wonderment. "You're...welcome."

Kurth chuckled and gave Otto an affectionate pat on the back. "Well Otto, you earned his respect. And to think, all you had to do was save his life."

The healers unpacked their kit, and went to work bandaging Talthas and treating his wounds as best they could. "We need to move him back to the camp if so he can be treated properly."

One of the healers unfurled the stretcher and placed Talthas on to it carefully. The three squires helped lift the stretcher up above their shoulders. Kurth held up the front of the stretcher with one of the soldiers while Edgar and Otto shared the responsibility of the back. With Kurth leading the way they moved up the hill and through the forest making their way back to the Emparian army camp.

***

"Bellaydin!" Otto called out.

Bellaydin turned to the direction of the voice. He saw Kurth, Edgar and Otto coming towards him, carrying a stretcher with the injured Talthas.

"Oh no, Talthas, what happened?" said Geoffrey, coming up next to them.

Talthas stirred. "Sir Geoffrey," he said weakly, "I assume we won?"

Geoffrey smiled. "Yes Talthas, yes we did."

The Eldara smiled faintly. "I am glad of it."

As the soldiers took Talthas away to the surgeon's tent to receive more treatment, Geoffrey faced the squires. Kurth was the first to speak. "Quite the first battle, wasn't it?"

Geoffrey smiled. "Enough of the glory of war for you?"

"It didn't really feel glorious," Otto said. "All that death..."

Geoffrey smiled gently. "Squire, that's the truth of it, I'm afraid. They're never as glorious or noble as the stories make out. It's mostly a lot of brutal, desperate squabbling in the mud."

"There's courage to be had," Kurth said.

"That is true," said Geoffrey. "There is courage, and sacrifice, and loss. But there's more. Whether of despair or relief, there are always tears and the realisation that you have survived." He placed a comforting hand on the shoulder of each boy in turn.

Edgar hadn't said anything. Geoffrey came up to him. "I know it is hard for you, Edgar, to accept Tancred's betrayal —"

"He didn't betray us," Edgar said. He stared straight ahead, his eyes unblinking. There was defiance in his face. "He couldn't. You don't understand."

"Maybe we don't. What I do understand is your grief, and what it feels like to lose a friend." Geoffrey's eyes were red with tears. Bellaydin knew he was thinking of William.

"They live on, in here," he said, touching his chest. "While we remember, they will never truly die."

"Tancred was my friend," Edgar said, his voice breaking. "And I say he

401

died a hero."

Bellaydin felt he should say something, but the words died on his lips. *What could I even say?* Edgar wouldn't listen to anyone. Grief was twisting his mind. He would believe what he wanted to believe.

"You all must be tired and hungry," Geoffrey said. "Go get yourselves something to eat and then get some sleep. We'll be leaving in the morning."

As the squires moved off to take a well-earned rest, Geoffrey grabbed Bellaydin by his arm. "Just a moment, Bela. Where did she go?" Geoffrey said quietly.

"Where did *who* go?" Bellaydin said, feigning ignorance.

"You know who I mean, Bela."

Bellaydin looked away. "I don't know. She left me. There was no explanation."

"The ways of women are mysterious, Bellaydin."

Bellaydin looked straight at Geoffrey. "If you find her, please don't hurt her. She's innocent in all of this."

"I don't think you need to worry. I haven't heard anything that would lead me to believe anyone has found her. I think she's far away from here now, with any luck. Besides, it's her uncle we're interested in. She wouldn't be travelling with him, would she?"

Bellaydin shook his head. "Unlikely."

"Then I think she's safe."

"Will I see her again, you think?"

Geoffrey placed an arm on the young man's shoulder. "You will, if the gods are kind."

"Thank you, Geoffrey," Bellaydin said.

The Slaves of the Horned God

As Geoffrey left him to his thoughts, Bellaydin looked out into the forest. Morgan was somewhere out there. He wished he knew why she had left. What were her reasons? Why couldn't she tell him? He made a silent prayer to whatever gods were listening to watch over the girl, and see her safely to her grandmother.

It was the least he could do.

CHAPTER 24

This time there were no rose petals.

Emperor's Palace looked colder and greyer than Bellaydin remembered, and the morose skies reflected the mood of the weary soldiers who marched through the city gates. Wulfric rode at the army's head, with Sir Geoffrey next to him. Bellaydin and the other squires were some distance to the back, escorted by Kahlaf. The Ahktarran was in front, with Bellaydin, Kurth, Edgar and Otto riding in a single line behind him.

"There it is boys," said Kurth. "A hot bath, good food, and a soft, warm bed. Then we get to go home."

To Bellaydin's left, Otto smiled and nodded, while Edgar said nothing. Instead, the squire continued to stare straight ahead, in a world of his own. Edgar had hardly said two words since they left Goriinch Hill. The events there had obviously rattled him; Tancred's betrayal and death most of all.

"Where are you going to Bellaydin?" asked Otto. "Back to Genio, I suppose?"

"What?" Bellaydin responded. He hadn't really been paying attention.

"Genio, that is the seat of House Ap'Lydin, isn't it?"

"Yes, but I don't know if I'm going there." Bellaydin hadn't been to Genio since he was five years old, and going there now held little attraction. *What would I even do there?*

Otto pursed his lips. "Well, where are you headed then?"

Bellaydin realised he hadn't the faintest idea. He couldn't return to Aderilund, he most likely wouldn't be staying in the capital, only Wishapton seemed to hold any familiarity. But was that where he truly belonged? Maybe he didn't belong anywhere.

"I don't know," he said. His answer sounded feeble, but he continued, his face feeling hot as he spoke. "I guess I'll have to wait and see what happens."

Before long Castle Emparia loomed before them, and they split off from the bulk of the army, travelling only with the duke, Sir Geoffrey, Kahlaf and a few solders from the duke's personal guard. The steward, Martin FitzGarns, greeted them at the gate.

"Your Grace," Martin said, as servants came to take care of the mounts. "I am glad that you have returned. We have all heard the news. Congratulations on your victory."

Wulfric looked disgruntled as he took off his riding cloak. "It would be charitable to call what happened at Goriinch Hill a victory, Martin. We lost half of our army and only carried the day due to the weakness of the Goriinchian battle leadership."

"Nevertheless, Your Grace," Martin persisted, "you have done the best you could with the situation you were faced with."

The duke gave a brief smile. "Indeed. Is the Privy Council assembled?"

"Indeed they are, Your Grace," Martin said. "They are waiting for you in the meeting chambers."

As Wulfric and Kahlaf departed, Martin turned to the others, "Welcome back, Sir Geoffrey. I see a few new scars on that face of yours."

"I've certainly looked prettier," Geoffrey said. "But I'm still alive, that's what counts."

"No doubt, Sir Geoffrey," said Martin. "You and the squires must be hungry after your long trip. Food will be prepared in the great hall forthwith."

The prospect of food made Bellaydin perk up, and he, Geoffrey and the other squires quickly navigated the corridors of Castle Emparia, closely following Martin until they reached the great hall.

Bellaydin could smell the food before they entered, thanks to the rich aromas that were wafting into the corridor. When he finally laid eyes on what had been prepared for them, he found his mouth watering with anticipation. Roast venison, pork and fowl vied for table space with an array of pastries, cheeses and nuts along with an assortment of apples and pears.

"Where is everyone else?" asked Geoffrey.

"The queen and nobles have already eaten, along with their attendants, and now the Privy Council is meeting. It will just be yourself and the squires," said Martin.

"I think that means you're in charge," Bellaydin said to Geoffrey.

"Eat, drink," said Martin. "You squires should enjoy your last day in the capital. I will come for you once dinner is over."

Martin departed and Sir Geoffrey and the squires looked at the food eagerly.

"I don't know where to start," Sir Geoffrey said. He spied a bottle of wine. "Well, this is as good a place as any." He poured a goblet for himself and the four squires. "Well, here's to not dying."

Bellaydin and the other squires laughed. "I'll drink to that," said Kurth.

"I think I will eat elsewhere," said Edgar. He grabbed some food and disappeared out the doorway.

Otto started to pick through the food gingerly. "You think he's still upset about the betrayal?"

"They were very close," Kurth said. "Tancred was his only friend here."

Bellaydin knew that what had happened with Tancred had affected Edgar, but not in the way that the others imagined. "You're all wrong,"

"What?" asked Kurth, putting down the ladle of gravy. "How so? You don't think it's about Tancred?"

"It is about Tancred, but he's not upset about the betrayal. He's upset because he still doesn't think Tancred was a traitor."

Kurth looked sceptical. "How could one delude himself in such a way?"

Geoffrey smiled. "For a friend, easily."

"Do you think anything will happen from it?" Kurth asked. "I mean, someone has to take responsibility for his treachery ."

"But Tancred's dead," Otto said.

"But it couldn't have been just Tancred," Bellaydin said. "I'm sure other members of his family were involved."

Geoffrey looked worried, "Do you mean his grandfather, the duke?"

Bellaydin sighed. "I'm not sure, to be honest. Only... he's just a squire. At the very least, someone like his father or his uncles would have to had to make that deal with Goriinchians. Right?"

"That's a dangerous line of thinking, Bellaydin," said Geoffrey, frowning. "The Zalltors are powerful. They will protect their own. You'd have to take it to the Privy Council and the queen herself."

"We are all witnesses. We saw what happened," said Otto.

"I don't know what I saw," Geoffrey admitted. When he saw Bellaydin's face, he quickly added, "You know I would back you any day of the week, Bela. I'll always believe you. But if it's just the word of one knight and three squires..." His voice trailed off and he looked grim.

"You're not thinking we just try to pretend nothing like that happened?" Bellaydin demanded.

"No," said Geoffrey, "all I'm saying is tread carefully. This is the royal court. You'd find it easier navigating a pit of vipers."

"I think I need a drink," Kurth said. He called out to the kitchens. Within a few moments, a familiar serving girl had emerged with jugs of wine and ale.

"Now there's a sight for sore eyes," Rhiannon said, her hand on her hips.

Kurth grinned as his lover came towards him and ran her hand over his back. She whispered something in his ear and the squire looked scandalised. "Later," he said to her in a hush.

Rhiannon winked at Bellaydin. "You are still skinny."

"Soldiers don't exactly eat well," Bellaydin said.

"No drinking either, I'd hazard a guess?"

"Not really," said Bellaydin.

"In that case," she said, pouring him another, "best make up for lost time."

They continued to eat and drink into the night, spending hours talking and laughing together. After the stress of the recent days, it was good to feel safe amongst friends. Talking about the shared experiences helped them all gain a sense of much needed catharsis.

It was late when Bellaydin finally climbed the stairs to his quarters and collapsed onto his bed, falling into a deep sleep within minutes. For the first time in a long while, he dreamed. Figures from his past and present appeared, blurring into one another within an instant. He was with his sister Polnygar standing in front of an ancient ruin. A ruin that seemed oddly familiar to him, though he knew he had never seen it in his waking moments. From this tower's gates poured thousands of soldiers, but not soldiers of flesh and blood, instead men of burnished bronze, their metal skin gleaming in the morning sun. He knew he had seen them before. He had dreamed of them once before, with the Seeress, but he had also seen them, in the caves under Goriinch Hill. They came towards him and Polnygar, and though they fought tenaciously, they were soon overwhelmed. He saw his sister panicked, disappearing under the crush of metal bodies and then...

He woke up.

It was morning. He arose from his bed, shaking the last tendrils of the dream from his mind. Whatever it meant was not apparent to him at this moment. After washing his face he decided not to preoccupy himself with the thought at this time.

His morning was spent unproductively. The lessons he had taken upon his first stay in the capital were now completed and there was little for him to do. He hoped to visit Maria, but the countess was in Genio and was not expected to return to the capital for many months. Sir Geoffrey seemed preoccupied with the carriage of whatever duties the countess had delegated to him in her stead, and so was unable to spend time with Bellaydin. It was only when a page arrived, bearing a message from Wulfric Highcrown that his day started to take on some semblance of meaning.

"The Duke of Oldharbour wishes you to meet him in his chambers," the boy said. "It is urgent and you are required as soon as you are able."

Bellaydin was worried. He wondered what could be so important. When he arrived at the duke's chambers, he was surprised to find Geoffrey emerging from within the rooms, a distracted look on his face.

"Geoffrey," Bellaydin said, "is something wrong?"

"No, I've just been talking to the duke."

"What about?"

"I-" His eyes darted about. "I think I'll let him explain it. I'm sorry Bela, I have to go."

Bellaydin, confused, watched as Geoffrey walked away in a hurry. He was still wondering why as he was led inside and told to wait.

He was not there for long. From one of the rooms emerged Wulfric. The duke had changed from the armour he had worn upon his arrival in Emperor's Palace and was now clothed in the fine garb coloured purple and green, the colours of House Highcrown. Kahlaf towered behind him, as still as a statue, giving Bellaydin only the briefest of glances.

"Ah, yes, Bellaydin," Wulfric said. "Please take a seat. There are some things we need to discuss."

There was a decanter of wine and two goblets on a table next to the two chairs. A servant looked towards Bellaydin, who nodded and filled both goblets.

"A fine Eldara vintage from Aderilund," the duke said. "I am sure you will appreciate it."

Once the servant had made himself scarce, the duke began to talk. His face was serious and drawn. "Bellaydin. What do you know about a Ducal Council?"

Bellaydin shook his head. "Is this like the Privy Council?"

Wulfric leant back in his chairs. "In composition, yes, but not by function. The Privy Council advises the monarch in matters of state. A Ducal Council dispenses the queen's justice. Three dukes act in the stead of the queen in deciding over judicial matters."

"I see. Why are you telling me this?"

"Oswin Zalltor has called a Ducal Council to adjudicate in the matter of his grandson's death. He wishes to know the truth of what happened to Tancred."

Bellaydin tried to avoid Wulfric's penetrating gaze. "I see."

Wulfric swirled the wine in his goblet. "And what is it that happened to Tancred, Bellaydin?"

Bellaydin sipped his wine. "The Goriinchians killed him, just as I said. But only after he had already betrayed us to them."

"Ah," said Wulfric, pursing his lips, "so it is as Sir Geoffrey said. Who else knows of this?"

"The other squires, Kurth, Otto and Edgar, and Kahlaf."

The Ahktarran seemed to bristle at the mention of his name but said nothing.

Wulfric narrowed his eyes. "And you would be willing to testify as to what you saw in front of a Ducal Council?"

"I'd tell them everything I saw," Bellaydin said. "The truth."

Wulfric leant back and clicked his tongue with disapproval. "The truth," he said, "is not always the wisest path."

"What do you mean?"

Wulfric took a quaff of wine. "I want you to explain how Tancred was killed by Goriinchians. And no more."

Bellaydin was flabbergasted. "No more? But he betrayed us."

"Did he now? What evidence is there of that?"

"I saw it."

Wulfric placed his goblet back on the table. "So you say, who else can back up your tale of betrayal?"

"The other squires, and Sir Geoffrey."

"Ah yes, three boys and a knight known for being into his cups whenever the opportunity presents itself. Do you think a Ducal Council, especially one led by Oswin Zalltor, is going to believe that?"

Bellaydin froze. Oswin would be on the council – Tancred's own grandfather. He hadn't thought of that.

"I also hear rumours that not all the squires are in agreement on what happened."

Bellaydin knew what Wulfric was referring to before the duke even revealed it.

"It seems that Squire Edgar de Morcor has claimed that Tancred died trying to defend the other squires from the Goriinchians. Furthermore, he claims it was Tancred who killed the Warchief Aonghus Culainn."

Bellaydin tried another tack. "The other dukes on the council will believe me. Yourself and Haakon. He for one has always treated me with kindness. He would not side against me."

"Edgar is Haakon's own blood," Wulfric said. "What makes you sure he won't see the necessity of backing his own House?"

"He does not favour Edgar, though."

"The Duke of Alariat has grand plans, Bellaydin. Plans that could do without Zalltor complications. He longs for a marriage between his House and yours, and has for many decades. He will not let you turn this into a House feud, you can be sure of that."

"There's that knight, Sir Dallen Withers," Bellaydin said. "He must know the truth. He can be questioned, surely. He won't want to take the fall now that Tancred's dead."

"I wouldn't be so sure of that, Bellaydin," said Wulfric. "Leaving that aside, I have heard that Sir Dallen is no longer incarcerated."

"What?"

"The man has vanished. Apparently he was in his cell one night, and by the next morning, he was gone. The Duke of Georgeton was most vexed."

"I'm sure he was," said Bellaydin. "Very convenient for him."

"Perhaps," said Wulfric. "All the same, Sir Dallen will not suffice as evidence of your claims."

Bellaydin felt frustrated. "Well, you know the truth, won't that be enough?"

Wulfric frowned. "These are trying times, and divisions have weakened our war effort. It has become apparent to me that we need a rallying point. A martyr. Tancred can fulfil that role."

"You can't be serious," Bellaydin said, shaking his head.

"A grandfather's grief over his grandson's death might prove just the thing to bringing the Zalltors onside and end the squabbling in the Privy Council. What sense is there to destroy everything by antagonising them?"

"It's the truth," Bellaydin said. "That's what happened."

"The lie saves us all, Bellaydin."

Bellaydin regained his composure. "What stops me from telling the truth?"

"You are free to say what you will. But I would consider the consequences of such an action. The Zalltors are powerful, and well resourced. They have a wide reach."

"I don't care what they say about me."

"The consequences are not on you alone. There are others who the Zalltors might punish for slights that you commit. There is another of your blood in this kingdom, Bellaydin, and she is vulnerable."

Maria. Bellaydin closed his eyes. He hadn't dreamed there could be danger to her.

"Maria inherited her father's title, Bellaydin, but you must help her keep it. How long would she last if the Zalltors truly wanted her gone?"

Bellaydin shook her head. "They wouldn't harm her, surely not. She's family. The Duke of Georgeton is her grandfather."

"Do you think that no noble has ever hurt their own kin before?"

"Not like this," Bellaydin said. "Surely not."

"Perhaps you are correct, Bellaydin." Wulfric shrugged. "But is it really a risk you are willing to take?"

Bellaydin did not answer.

"I see that understanding dawns on you, at last, Bellaydin," Wulfric said. "See that you do what we discussed, and think of what's best for all concerned. Oh, and Bellaydin? Best you not speak of such matters to anyone else, particularly not to any of the other squires or the kitchen staff. Gossip travels quickly, you know."

Bellaydin's mind was a mess as he walked back from Wulfric's chambers to his own. The old duke's words had been persuasive. He spied Geoffrey just ahead. The knight noticed Bellaydin's attention and tried to turn away.

"The duke spoke to you?" Geoffrey asked, looking at the wall. He seemed reluctant to look at the younger man. Bellaydin wondered if Geoffrey was ashamed of something.

"Yes, he did," Bellaydin said.

"And I take it he explained things to you?" Geoffrey said. He still refused to meet Bellaydin's gaze.

"If you mean he asked me to lie, then yes. He wants me to lie and say Tancred died a martyr's death."

Geoffrey shook his head. "The only thing that boy was martyred for was his own family's greed and lust for power. But you know that this is how things must be. And not for our sakes, but for that of someone we both hold dear."

"Maria," Bellaydin said.

"Yes," said Geoffrey. "Tell a lie, and she is safe. Tell the truth, and the Zalltors come for her. Not much of a choice."

"And the others," asked Bellaydin. "Edgar won't implicate Tancred, but Otto and Kurth might."

"You will have to convince them not to," said Geoffrey. "They are your friends, they will listen to you. Especially if you make it convincing."

Bellaydin frowned. "A veritable web of lies. To save the life of a girl."

"No," Geoffrey said, "not just a girl. William's girl."

***

The next day Bellaydin stood in the Great Hall, before the Ducal Council. On a dais in front of him, Wulfric Highcrown, Haakon de Morcor and Oswin Zalltor were presiding.

"Bellaydin Ap'Lydin," the Duke of Oldharbour said. "You have been summoned to this Ducal Council to give testimony regarding the death of Squire Tancred Zalltor. You will confine your questions to the event at hand and answer all questions posed to you honestly and without prevarication."

"The council has heard testimony from others about the details of the campaign at Goriinch Hill. Sir Geoffrey Keslin has explained to us the circumstances in which his force became trapped under the battlefield," said the Duke of Georgeton. "And that he sent three squires to ascertain an escape route: yourself, Kurth Bauer and Tancred Zalltor. To your best recollection, are these details correct?"

"It is, Your Grace," said Bellaydin. He felt like he had a lump in his throat the size of a pigeon's egg.

"And would you tell the council what happened next?" Haakon asked.

Bellaydin swallowed. "Tancred and I were separated from Kurth, but we eventually made our way to the Magister's Chambers."

Haakon continued. "And this Magister's Chambers, that had the master controls for the gates, did it not?"

"That is correct. Tancred and I got the gate open and we found our way outside. I lost my footing while looking over the cliff face. And then Tancred…"

Wulfric directed a narrow-eyed stare towards Bellaydin, as if daring him to continue. Images swirled about in Bellaydin's head – memories of Tancred bending down to mock him, of Tancred stepping on his fingers, and then pushing him off the cliff to presumed death below. He swallowed hard, finding the will to continue. *Maria*, he thought. *I am doing this for Maria and for William.*

Bellaydin licked his lips nervously. "Tancred tried to save me. He reached for my hand, but it slipped out of reach. I fell."

Oswin Zalltor stroked his beard with thought. *And pride*, Bellaydin surmised. "But you survived, obviously."

Wulfric interjected. "The details of Squire Bellaydin's survival and trials at the Goriinchian camp are not relevant to this inquest. If the council is willing, I would ask Squire Bellaydin to continue his testimony from the moment he returned to Goriinch Hill."

"Yes, Your Grace," Bellaydin said. He tried to put into words the next part. "The Goriinchians were readying their assault. Before the attack, Sir Geoffrey ordered Kahlaf to take us squires to safety through the tunnel –"

Oswin looked confused, "Who is this Kahlaf you speak of?"

Wulfric informed Oswin of Kahlaf's identity before Bellaydin was allowed to continue.

"We were ambushed by Goriinchians, including the brothers Culainn," Bellaydin said. "Tancred tried to fight to defend us, but he was killed."

Wulfric raised his head, "By Aonghus Culainn, is that correct?"

"Yes, Your Grace," said Bellaydin. His cheeks were bright red and he was sweating. He wondered if anyone had noticed, especially with all eyes in the room on him.

Haakon read from a piece of parchment in front of him. "The council has heard tell that you avenged Tancred's death, by defeating the warchief in personal combat. Is this true?"

"Yes, Your Grace," Bellaydin said.

"A most remarkable feat," said Oswin. "And I thank you for giving my grandson justice."

"Of course, Your Grace," Bellaydin mumbled, his face hot.

"That appears to be enough testimony," said Wulfric. "Thank you, Squire Bellaydin."

***

Much later Bellaydin was sitting alone when two visitors came for him. It was Haakon, and with him, the duke had brought Bellaydin's cousin, Countess Maria who enveloped him in a tight hug.

Bellaydin smiled widely, squeezing his cousin back. "It's good to see you, Maria," he said. "How have things been?"

"I missed you and Geoffrey. "

"We both missed you too," Bellaydin said.

"I'm glad you both came back unscathed," she said. She looked visibly concerned as she added, "I was worried something terrible was going to happen to you. I can't lose anyone else."

Bellaydin touched her arm tenderly. "I'm not going anywhere. What brings you both to see me?"

Maria turned to Haakon who smiled at Bellaydin. "Well first, let me offer my congratulations to you, Bellaydin. Slaying the war chief Aonghus was no mean feat."

"Thank you, Your Grace," said Bellaydin. "But it was mostly luck."

"What battle isn't?" Haakon said, his eyes twinkling. "Welcome back to the capital."

"Thank you, Your Grace," said Bellaydin. "I didn't feel at home the first time I was here, but after Goriinchia, I've grown a bit more fond of anywhere my life isn't in imminent danger."

"Well, you shouldn't get too comfortable, Bellaydin, not if your cousin has her way. Shall we tell him, your lady?"

Maria grinned. "Bela, I want you to be my castellan for Wishapton."

"Castellan?"

"A castellan holds a castle in stead for their noble lord. Maria wishes for you to govern Wishapton as her vassal."

Bellaydin was floored. "But I'm just a squire."

"You may be now, but it won't be long until you are knighted, especially when news spreads of your feats in Goriinchia. This is an important step, Bellaydin. You are beginning to catch the attention of the great and mighty."

"Please, Uncle Bela?" Maria pleaded. "It would mean a lot to me. It was where we first met, after all. It's a special place."

"Not only that," said Haakon, looking at Bellaydin, "but your father held the title of castellan too, in vassalage to William and William's father

Caradoc."

"It would be good to keep it in the family," Maria said. "I don't have anyone else I can trust."

Haakon looked at Bellaydin expectantly. "Are you in agreement with this, Bellaydin?"

Bellaydin nodded. "You can trust me. I will do my father proud."

Maria squealed with delight and gave him another hug.

"I knew we could count on you," said Haakon. "Maria, might I have a word with your cousin alone?"

"You men and your secret business," she teased.

As she departed, Haakon looked at her with a tender approval. "She is growing wiser and stronger with every day. She has the makings of a great countess. And once we have found her a suitable marriage William's line will be assured."

Bellaydin felt a slight twinge. He still wasn't comfortable with Maria's future being planned like that, not without her consent, even if there was little he could say or do about it.

Haakon looked at Bellaydin with concern. "How are you feeling, my boy? You have had a most trying experience."

"I'm fine, mostly," Bellaydin said. "I think I just need to rest."

"Then I shall not keep you any longer, Bellaydin. Do not concern yourself with what tomorrow holds. For now, just rest assured that your future is in good hands. We will be watching and looking out for you."

Bellaydin looked askance at Haakon. "'We, Your Grace?"

The duke chuckled. "Merely a turn of phrase, Bela. Get some rest. Your future awaits."

EPILOGUE

Summer, Year 235 of the Third Epoch

Cathan chafed against his bonds.

He knew he should've known better than to flee when he first heard the horsemen behind him, but instinct had taken over. The knight leading the horsemen, this "Sir Hal", had taken great pleasure in incapacitating and humiliating him during the capture. Now here Cathan was, bound in iron, and set to be dragged off to the infidel capital.

"You are making a mistake, Enparran," Cathan said to the knight. "The faithful will find me. The Horned God will guide them."

The horsemen laughed amongst themselves. Sir Hal struck Cathan. "Quiet, Goriinchian dog," the knight snarled. "We have a long journey ahead of us, and I don't have the patience for your blathering."

Another knight accompanied Sir Hal – a Sir Antony Bluetowers, if Cathan remembered correctly. *This one is forgettable*, Cathan thought, *with the typical fair hair and decadent features of an Enparran.*

"Feel free to strike him if he speaks again, Sir Antony," said Sir Hal.

"With pleasure sir," Sir Antony said.

Sir Antony looked at Cathan, and the high priest tried to avoid his gaze. "What's the matter priest? Afraid to look us in the eyes? What is your Horned God good for if he can't save your wretched life? Where is he now?"

Almost as if on cue there was a reverberating thud in the distance, like the rolling of thunder – but no storm was brewing.

"Did you hear that?" Sir Antony said. The other knights looked about, puzzled.

One of the horses reared. "There, I heard it again," Sir Antony said. The rumbling echoed again. It was louder this time, as if the sound was coming closer.

"What was that?" said Sir Hal, after nearly being thrown from his mount. The other animals showed similar signs of anxiety. At the same time, the ground below them seemed to shudder, as if it might tear apart at any moment.

Sir Hal turned around. "Earthquake?"

Sir Antony looked about and went pale. "Gods in heaven."

Turning around to where the other knight's finger was pointed, Sir Hal's mouth opened wide in shock. Arrayed on the horizon was a regiment of metal men, their burnished bronze skin glittering in the afternoon sun. Their heavy feet shook the ground as they came inexorably closer.

"Swords ready," called out Sir Hal. His horse reared up to full height, throwing him from the saddle. The metal men picked up their pace, and were almost upon them. It was too late to run. Cathan plunged to the ground, hearing screams and the ringing of clashing swords around him. Sir Antony was flung backwards, landing next to Cathan. The man's face was a brutalised mess of blood. Cathan heard Sir Hal cry for help, followed by that plea ending in an agonised gurgle. Then, just as quickly as the attack had begun, there was silence.

Cathan stood, opening his eyes. All around him was death, the mutilated bodies of knights and soldiers. No survivors, none at all.

Except for Cathan. The metal men stood in a circle around him, their weapons held ready and their blank eyes staring at him. "What are you...what do you want?"

The metal men said nothing, but a few of them moved, parting way to open a gap in the circle. Then one by one the others dropped to one knee. Through the gap stepped a newcomer, clad in ornate armour, a tartan cloak and wearing a great horned helm.

Cathan immediately prostrated himself to the ground. "Your Holiness," he said, "You have saved me from the infidels."

Ygarak stepped towards Cathan, looking down upon the priest crouching in the dirt. His voice rumbled as deep as the ocean. "Indeed I have, Cathan, but this should not have been necessary. I warned you of this. So did others who serve me."

Cathan stood, stuttering. "Your Holiness, I merely wished to serve you. I thought that if I were to deliver you the Heir of Lydin then perhaps –"

Ygarak clenched a fist. Immediately Cathan felt his breath constrict and his heart thump wildly in his chest. A firebolt of pain shot through his body and he crumpled onto the ground.

"Your Eminence," Cathan gasped, writhing in agony. "I only wished to regain your favour –"

Ygarak waved a hand, and the pain ceased. "Your rivalries are of no interest to me, High Priest, and you are no war chief. You must do as you are commanded."

Cathan bowed his head. "Of course, Your Holiness." He hesitated and spoke again, "What of the war? The infidels are relentless, and we have few soldiers left, Your Eminence."

"I no longer need war chiefs, nor soldiers of flesh and blood," Ygarak said. "As you can plainly see."

Cathan nodded. "I see, Your Eminence. But I don't understand how."

"In time you will, but for now you need only know that this is the future. Soon Karlicia will be whole again, and the Horned God will rule over all."

Cathan stood, trembling. "I am your man, Great King. Command me."

"You are to return to the Tower of the Horned God. A new ally will be arriving soon, and you are to make him feel welcome."

Cathan's mouth went dry. "Who is this ally? The duke?"

"No," Ygarak said. "For the moment I still require him to live amongst the Enparrans as one of them. No, this is another. One who has proven himself to be one of the Horned God's most valued slaves."

Jealousy grew in Cathan's heart. "And what has he done to earn this title?"

"Something that you never could," said Ygarak. "He will deliver the Tears of the Divine to the Horned God, as the prophecy demands."

"The prophecy still requires the Heir of Lydin." Cathan's tone was biting.

"And the duke shall deliver that when the time is right," Ygarak rumbled. "For you Cathan, the war is over. You have no more role to play."

Cathan was lost for words. "Your Holiness, I can still be useful. Just let me-"

Ygarak held up a hand to interrupt him. "Enough, Cathan. You have your orders. You shall fulfil them."

Two of the automata grabbed Cathan's arms roughly, their cold metallic hands clutching him like a vice.

"What is this?" Cathan said, panicked.

"My new soldiers will see you home," said Ygarak. "It is time to prepare for our friend's arrival. It is time to welcome Ivellios."

APPENDIX

CHARACTERS

In order of appearance

Bellaydin Ap'Lydin: human squire, cousin to the late William, Earl of Genio.

Carfel: Steward of Castle Wishapton

Maria Ap'Lydin: Countess of Genio

Haakon de Morcor: Duke of Alariat, cousin to Queen Amaryllis

Wulfric Highcrown: Duke of Oldharbour

Sir Geoffrey Keslin: sworn sword to the Countess of Genio

Talthas li'Lyros: Eldara ranger, nephew to Neriaos

Kahlaf el'Lahn: Ahktarran bondsman of the Duke of Oldharbour

Edmund Tallcastle: Duke of Emperor's Palace

Amaryllis de Morcor: Queen of Emparia

Martin: Steward of Castle Emparia

Aidan Hennessy

Edgar de Morcor: Squire at Castle Emparia, third in line to the throne

Anson Mainstream: Earl of Warding

Otto Mainstream: Squire at Castle Emparia

Tancred Zalltor: Squire at Castle Emparia

Oswin Zalltor: Duke of Georgeton

Alfred Bauer: Earl of Tyronsville

Kurth Bauer: Squire at Castle Emparia

Rowena: Cook at Castle Emparia

Rhiannon: Serving girl at Castle Emparia

Father Athelstan: Chaplain at Castle Emparia

Sir Bors Thornton: sworn sword to the Earl of Warding

Don Jalagado: Sword master at Castle Emparia

Eloise de Dilmun: Dowager Queen of Emparia, mother to Queen Amaryllis.

Sir Dallen Withers: Sworn sword to the Duke of Georgeton

Edith Foxfield: Teacher of etiquette at Castle Emparia

Ferdy: Horse master at Castle Emparia

Brother Alcuin: Teacher of history at Castle Emparia

Polnygar Ap'Lydin: Half-sister of Bellaydin Ap'Lydin

Augustin Bauer: Brother to the Earl of Tyronsville, former Royal Ambassador

Aelzandar: Archmage, Royal Wizard of Macrodonia, and Lord of the Nine Orders

Hebu: Royal Scribe of Macrodonia

The Slaves of the Horned God

Samir bin Adil: Qardleean merchant

Celine de Lerid: Captain of the Leridian Chevaliers.

Caerunos li'Karn-Raka: Son of King Talan and Queen Talina, Royal Prince of Liderial. Heir to the Aspen Throne.

Millandriel li'Karn-Raka: Daughter of King Talan and Queen Talina, Royal Princess of Liderial.

Shapur: Ahktarran bodyguard

Sharbhaz: Ahktarran bodyguard

Baruch ben Omri: Nemoi Vizier of Qar Arrid

Omar al'Dazhi: Emir of Qar Arrid

Huramosh: Librarian of Qar Arrid

Um Badr: Qardleean noblewoman

Madame Noor: fortune-teller and seer

Archbishop Garamond: Leader of the Emparian branch of the Church of Ralom

Sir Poul de Barry: Sworn sword to the Duke of Alariat

Sir Euan de Dilmun: Sworn sword to the Earl of Warding

Edmund Zalltor: Eldest son of the Duke of Georgeton

Reynald Zalltor: Second son of the Duke of Georgeton

Sir Emeric Lathin: sworn sword to the Countess of Genio

Sir Fulk Corivus: sworn sword to the Countess of Genio

Myfanwy Ap'Morten: Goriinchian refugee

Ciarán Ap'Morten: Goriinchian refugee

Siobhan Ap'Morten: Goriinchian refugee

Aidan Hennessy

Cathan Culainn: High Priest of the Horned God

Aonghus Culainn: Goriinchian warchief

Morgan Culainn: Daughter of Aonghus Culainn

Sir Hal Borrowdale: Sworn sword to the Duke of Oldharbour

Sir Antony Bluetowers: Sworn sword to the Duke of Oldharbour

Ygarak: Prophet-King of Goriinchia

NATION STATES AND REGIONS

Aderilund: Southern Land. Part of the Aspen Kingdom – the realm of the Eldara.

Caruillin: Vast empire dominating the north of Carurlonia. Major provinces include Skurj, Lerid, the Heartlands and the Vallistian Marches.

Emparia: Northern Kingdom populated by Emparians. It borders Goriinchia, with whom it has a long history of conflict.

Goriinchia: Southern neighbour of Emparia, inhabited by the Goriinchians and the Saldarri. Ruled by the religion of the Horned God.

Infinite Caliphate: A religious empire ruled by the followers of the Infinite Faith. Qarld is the most powerful province, and the Sultan of Qarld serves as Caliph of the empire.

Lerid: Large province to the south of Skurj. Ruled by the Grand Duke of Lerid.

Macrodonia: Hot, desert kingdom to the north of Aderilund. Ruled by a King known as "Pharaoh", and home to Macrodonians and Nemoi.

Mokeria: City-state to the south of Aderilund.

Qarld: Exotic sultanate to the north-west of Macrodonia and largest province of the Infinite Caliphate. Known for its desert mystics and proud

Bedouin tribes. Home to Qardleeans, Nemoi and Ahktarra.

Shadrish Archipelago: Island chain off the western coast of Carurlonia and a province of the Infinite Caliphate.

Skurj: Frigid land in the extreme north. Borders Alfheim. Home to the Knights of the Crux Caruillin.

Tarken: The so-called "Hermit Kingdom", reclusive and secretive realm ruled by "Dragonborn" Emperors.

Thulia: Legendary frozen land somewhere north across the sea from Skurj, believed to be the origin of the Thulian race.

Vallistian Marches: Southern lands of the Empire of Caruillin that share a border with the Infinite Caliphate.

Settlements

Aderial: Capital of Aderilund.

Alariat: City in Emparia. Seat of the Duke of Alariat and the Archbishop of Alariat

Drakeford: Small town near the border of Emparia and Goriinchia, seat of Sir Edric Keslin, Baron Drakeford.

Emperor's Palace: Capital of Emparia. Seat of the monarch and of the Duke of Emperor's Palace.

Genio: City of Emparia. Seat of the Earl of Genio.

Georgeton: City in Emparia. Seat of the Duke of Georgeton.

Gorin: Capital of Goriinchia.

Oldharbour: Large port city in Emparia. Seat of the Duke of Oldharbour.

Harralin: Major settlement in Skurj.

Korfar: Goriinchian settlement near the Emparian border.

Liderial: Ancient city of the Eldara. Situated just north of Skurj. Seat of the elven monarchs and capital of the Aspen Kingdom.

Oldharbour: City of Emparia, seat of the Duke of Oldharbour.

Qar Arrid: City of Qarld, home to the Great Library

Qar Dal: Former capital of the Caliphate, site of the defeat of the archmage Ralur almost two and a half centuries ago.

Qar Udel: Prominent city of Qarld, and seat of the Sultan.

Ralom: The Holy City. Centre of the Triune faith of the Church of Ralom.

Tower of the Magi: Ancient ruin in Goriinchia. Sacred temple to the Horned God.

Tyronsville: Emparian city. Seat of the Earl of Tyronsville

Wishapton: Emparian town. Close to the Goriinchian border and southern-most city of the Earldom of Genio.

Warding: Emparian city. Seat of the Earl of Warding

NATIONALITIES AND ETHNICITIES

Ahktarra: Lizardmen from the land of Qarld.

Caruillani: Humans from Caruillin

Emparians: Humans from Emparia.

Goriinchians: Humans from Goriinchia.

Eldara: People of the Aspen Kingdom. Known to outsiders as "Elves" or "Fey".

Leridians: Humans from Lerid.

Macrodonians: Humans from Macrodonia

The Slaves of the Horned God

Nemoi: A diminutive people from the land of Macrodonia.

Qardleeans: Humans from the land of Qarld.

Saldarri: A Goriinchian tribe of mixed human and Eldara blood. Expert trackers and archers.

Sarrisite: Follower of the Infinite Faith. Named for the Prophet Sarrius, founder of the Infinite Faith.

Soldara: Ancient ancestors of the Spellweaver caste. Believed extinct.

Selvara: Nomadic cousins of the Eldara. Named for Selvaros, who rejected the founding of Liderial by Lideros.

Skurjans: Humans of Skurj.

Shadrish: A dark skinned sea-faring folk from the Shadrish Archipelago, western province of the Infinite Caliphate.

Tarkenese: Humans from Tarken.

Thulians: One of the three ancestor races of humanity, believed to be the common ancestors of Skurjans, Emparians, Goriinchians and Caruillani, among others.

MAGIC

Art, The: The term for magic, most commonly used by humans and the Eldara.

Automaton: Animated metal construct in the shape of a human. Created by the Soldara through unknown techniques.

Draconic: The script used for recording knowledge of the Art. Purported to be the language of dragons.

Far-speaking: The ability used by practitioners of the Art to speak to others over long distances.

Kaltban: Magical sword recovered by Sir William Ap'Lydin during the siege of Ralom. Lost by his grandson, Earl William, after being captured by the Goriinchians at Wishapton

Lich: A practitioner of the Art who has succumbed to magic addiction and become a creature sustained only by the power of the Art.

Moon-seer: An individual who can use the Art to perceive the future or grant visions.

Sablium: Black, oily mineral, believed to be crystalline form of Nether. Renowned for its ability to resist the Art.

Sakkaru: The so-called "Flame of Justice", the sword of the archmage Cassian, now wielded by his apprentice Aelzandar.

Sending: Visual message sent via the Art from one mind to another. Similar to Far-speaking, but less precise and commonly manifests as vivid dreams.

Spellweaver: An Eldara Mage.

Skymetal: Extremely rare substance, used in the manufacture of weapons enchanted by the Art, such as *Kaltban* and *Sakkaru*. Believed to be a crystalline form of Ether

Tears of the Divine, The: An ancient magical artefact. Broken into four pieces and scattered around the known world.

Tome of Divine Metaphysics, The: A theoretical work by the archmage Ralur, written after he captured the Tower of Magi in Goriinchia. It is believed to contain Ralur's discoveries into the methods by which a mortal might attain divine power.

RELIGION

Bahamut: Messenger of the Infinite Faith, considered to have passed the words of the Infinite to the Prophet Sarrius.

The Slaves of the Horned God

Celestial Architects, The: Religion of the Nemoi, centred on the book *Nemoinomicon*, and without priests or places of worship.

Divine Martyr, The: Also known as Kytilas. God of chivalry, self-sacrifice and valour. Worshipped by the Church of Ralom, centred in Ralom.

Heir of Lydin, The: Prophesised messiah figure in Goriinchian mythology.

Horned God, The: The deity of the staunchly monotheistic Goriinchians. Followed outside of Goriinchia in secretive, subversive cults.

Hydria: Mother Goddess of the Eldara.

Infinite Faith, The: State religion of the Infinite Caliphate, based on the teachings of the prophet Sarrius

Realms of Righteousness, The: The heavenly realm believed to exist by followers of the Church of Ralom.

Sarrius: Founding prophet of the Infinite Faith.

Silver Lady, The: Also known as the Queen of Light and Life. The wife of the Sun King and mother to the Divine Martyr. Goddess of childbirth, women and the home. Worshipped by both the Church of Ralom.

Sun King, The: God of the Sun, Light and Nobility. Worshipped by the Church of Ralom, centred in Ralom.

Transcendent Faith, The: Religion of the Eldara, centred of the worship of Hydria, "The Great Mother", and her children – the so-called "Firstborn of Hydria".

Triune, The: Worshipped by the Church of Ralom, the Triune is the collective name for the Sun King, the Silver Lady and the Divine Martyr.

Underworld, The: The hellish netherworld believed to exist by followers of the Church of Ralom and the Infinite Faith.

435

CULTURE AND HISTORY

Alarion I: First king of the unified Emparian nation.

Alusine the Last: Final king of the Ran-Tyron dynasty. Died at the Battle of Goriinch Hill

Ancient Ones, The: Founding heroes of Macrodonian civilisation, revered by later generations as divine figures. One of them, Aldion the High, is counted as first of the archmages.

Black Talons, The: Rebel group during the occupation of Macrodonia by the Caliphate. Later resurrect as a secret police by Pharaoh Jagontay II.

Cassian: Archmage and vanquisher of the Night Dragons. Aelzandar's master.

Eldaric: Name given to the script and spoken language of the Eldara.

Emparian Civil War: The three decade conflict between House Tyron and House Morcor over who was the rightful monarchs of Emparian. It began with the death of Alusine the Last at Goriinch Hill.

Fostering: A tradition whereby young members of noble houses are raised in the households of other families to forge bonds of friendship and amity.

Great Fostering, The: A form of fostering specific to the royal court.

Knights of the Crux Caruillin, The: Chivalric Order headquartered in Skurj and dedicated to the Divine Martyr. Led by Grand Master Agmar Keller.

Mal-halyth: Eldara pejorative to describe a human or one of human heritage.

Night Dragon, The: Legendary creature that terrorised Macrodonia. Defeated by Cassian and Aelzandar

Tragedy of Belial'ad-Dīn, The: A folk tale from Qarld that describes the tragic and sad life of a man born the son of a demon and a human woman.

Tyron: The "Last Davorean", founder of one of the proto-Emparian kingdoms. Ancestor to Alarion I.

Zohra: Legendary beauty of the Infinite Caliphate.

ABOUT THE AUTHOR

Aidan Hennessy lives in Canberra, Australia, with his wife, two children and two ginger cats. He will not be spared when the revolution comes.

theaplydinchronicles.wordpress.com

www.ingramcontent.com/pod-product-compliance
Lightning Source LLC
Chambersburg PA
CBHW050914030726
47503CB00007BB/2293